Paul Finch is a former cop and journalist, now turned full-time writer. He cut his literary teeth penning episodes of the British TV crime drama, *The Bill*, and has written extensively in the field of children's animation. However, he is probably best known for his work in thrillers, crime and horror. His first three novels in the DS Heckenburg series all attained official 'best seller' status.

Paul lives in Lancashire, UK, with his wife Cathy and his children, Eleanor and Harry. His website can be found at www.paulfinchauthor.com, his blog at www.paulfinch-writer.blogspot.co.uk, and he can be followed on Twitter as @paulfinchauthor.

By the same author:

Stalkers
Sacrifice
The Killing Club
The Chase: an ebook short story
Dead Man Walking
A Wanted Man: an ebook short story

Want more? Read the rest of

The Burning Man

when it hits the shelves in November 2015.

a priority than evading them. Shawna lay limp. Heck tore open her jacket and gasped with relief when he saw the slug flattened on her Kevlar vest – it hadn't penetrated. However, her pretty face was a mass of bloodied pulp, her splayed hair glutinous with gore. He probed for the carotid artery. Her throat was also slick with blood, but at last he found a pulse.

An engine now growled to life somewhere inside. Fresh sweat pinpricked Heck's brow.

As he leapt to his feet, a pair of double-doors some twenty yards to the left of the van exploded outward in a shower of splinters and rusted hinges, and a powerful SUV came barrelling through. Heck backed away from Shawna's body to try and get a clear shot at it. But Sagan was already firing through the open passenger window, wildly, blindly. Heck let off one round before diving for cover, aiming at the SUV's front tyre but missing by centimetres. In the process he caught a fleeting glimpse of the vehicle's make and model. A Jeep Cherokee, dark in colour with bull bars across the front, but with its headlights switched off it was impossible to make out the registration number. It was towing a gleaming white caravan, which tilted onto one wheel as the car swerved away across the wasteland, finally righting itself again as it accelerated into the darkness. Heck gave chase for several yards. He even got off one final shot, hitting the caravan's rear door, which judging by the lack of visible damage, was armoured. And then the target was gone, vanishing around the corner of a warehouse, the roar of its engine diminishing.

He got urgently onto the radio, relaying as much info as he could while scrambling back to Shawna. As before, she lay worryingly still, and now the blood had congealed in her hair. When he felt her carotid a second time, there was no pulse.

PAUL FINCH

Hunted

A V O N

AVON

A division of HarperCollins*Publishers*
1 London Bridge Street
London SE1 9GF

www.harpercollins.co.uk

A Paperback Original 2015
1

Copyright © Paul Finch 2015

Paul Finch asserts the moral right to
be identified as the author of this work

A catalogue record for this book is
available from the British Library

ISBN 978-0-00-749233-6

Set in Sabon LT Std by Palimpsest Book Production Limited,
Falkirk, Stirlingshire

Printed and bound in Great Britain by
Clays Ltd, St Ives plc

MIX
Paper from
responsible sources
FSC **FSC C007454**
www.fsc.org

For my lovely wife, Catherine, whose selfless and unswerving support has been the bedrock on which I've built my career.

Chapter 1

Dazzer and Deggsy didn't give a shit about anyone. At least, that was the sort of thing they said if they were bragging to mates at parties, or if the coppers caught them and tried to lay a guilt trip on them.

They did what they did. They didn't go out looking to hurt anyone, but if people got in the way, tough fucking shit. They pinched motors and had a laugh in 'em. That was their thing. And they were gonna keep doing it, because it was the best laugh ever. No one was gonna stop them, and if some geezer ever got pissed off because he'd just seen his pride and joy totalled, so what? Dazzer and Deggsy didn't give a shit.

Tonight was a particularly good night for it.

All right, it wasn't perishing cold, which was a shame. Incredible though it seemed to Dazzer and Deggsy, some numbskulls actually came outside, saw a bit of ice and snow and left their motors running for five minutes with the key in the ignition while they went back indoors for a cuppa; all you had to do was jump in the saddle and ride away, whooping. But if nothing else, it was dank and misty, and with it being the tail end of January, it got dark early – so there weren't too many people around to interfere.

1

Not that folk tended to interfere with Dazzer and Deggsy.

The former was tall for his age; just under six foot, with a broad build and a neatly layered patch of straw-blond hair in the middle of his scalp, the rest of which was shaved to the bristles. If it hadn't been for the acne covering his brutish features, you'd have thought him eighteen, nineteen, maybe twenty – instead of sixteen, which was his true age, though of course even a sixteen-year-old might clobber you these days if you had the nerve to look at him the wrong way. The second member of the tag team, Deggsy, though he wasn't by any means the lesser in terms of villainy, looked more his age. He was shorter and thinner, weasel-faced and the proud owner of an unimpressively wispy moustache. His oily black thatch was usually covered by a grimy old baseball cap, the frontal logo of which had been erased long ago and replaced with letters written in Day-Glo orange highlighter, which read: *Fuck off*.

There was barely thirty years of experience between them, yet they both affected the arrogant swagger and truculent sneer of guys who believed they knew what was what, and were absolutely confident they were owed whatever they took.

It was around nine o'clock that night when they spied their first and most obvious target: a Volkswagen estate hatchback. A-reg and in poor shape generally: grubby, rusted around the arches, occasional dents in the bodywork; but it ticked all the boxes.

Posh motors were almost impossible to steal these days. All that top-of-the-range stuff was the sole province of professional crims who would make a fortune from ringing it and selling it on. No, if you were simply looking for a fun time, you had to settle for this lower quality merchandise – but that could also be an advantage, because when you went and smacked a bit of rubbish around on the streets, the coppers would tow it away afterwards but would rarely investigate. In addition, this one's location was good. The old Volkswagen estate was sitting right in the middle of a CCTV black spot that Dazzer and Deggsy had made it their business to know about.

They watched it from a corner, eyes peeled for any sign of movement, but the dim sodium glow of a lone streetlamp illuminated only a rolling beer can and a few scraps of wastepaper flapping in the half-hearted breeze.

Still, they waited. They'd been successful several times on this patch – it was a one-lane access way running between the back doors of a row of old shops and a high brick wall, ending at three concrete bollards. No one was ever around here at night; there were no tenants in the flats above the shops, and even without the January miasma this was a dark, dingy place – but such apparent ease of opportunity only made Dazzer and Deggsy more suspicious than usual. The very fact that motors had been lifted from around here before made the presence of this one seem curious. Did people never learn? Maybe they didn't. Though maybe there were other factors as well. The row of shops was a bit of an eyesore. Only one or two were occupied during the day, most of the others were To Let, and a couple were even boarded up as if they'd just been abandoned. God bless the Recession.

The lads ventured forth, walking boldly but stealthily, alert to the slightest unnatural sound – but no one called out, no one stepped from a darkened doorway.

The Volkswagen was locked of course, but Deggsy had his screwdriver with him, and in less than five seconds they'd forced the driver's door open. No alarm sounded, which was just what they'd expected given the ramshackle state of the thing; another advantage of pillaging the less well-off. With rasping titters, they jumped inside, to find that the steering column had been attacked in the past – it was held together

3

by wads of silvery duct tape. A few slashes of Dazzer's Stanley knife and they were through it. Even in the pitch darkness, their gloved but nimble fingers found the necessary wiring, and the contact was made.

The car rumbled to life. Laughing loudly, they hit the gas.

It was Dazzer's turn to drive today, and Deggsy's to ride, though it didn't make much difference – they were both as crazy as each other when they got behind the wheel. They blistered recklessly along, swerving around bends with tyres screeching, racing through red lights and stop signs. There was no initial response from the other road-using public. Opposing traffic was scant. They pulled a handbrake turn, pivoting sideways through what would ordinarily be a busy junction, the stink of burnt rubber engulfing them, hitting the gas again as they tore out of town along the A246. They had over half a tank of petrol and a very straight road in front of them. Maybe they'd make it all the way to Guildford, where they could pinch another motor to come home in. For the moment though, it was just fun fun fun. They'd probably veer off en route, and cause chaos on a few housing estates they knew, flaying the paint from any expensive jobs that unwise owners had left in plain view.

Some roadworks surged into sight just ahead. Dazzer howled as he gunned the Volkswagen through them, cones catapulting every which way – one struck the bay window of a roadside house, smashing it clean through. They mowed down a 'keep left' sign, taking out a set of temporary lights, which hit the deck with a detonation of sparks.

The blacktop continued to roll out ahead; they were doing eighty, ninety, almost a hundred, and were briefly mesmerised by their own fearlessness, their attention completely focused down the borehole of their headlights. When you were in that frame of mind there were almost no limits. It would have taken something quite startling to distract them from

4

their death-defying reverie – and that came approximately seven minutes into this, their last ever journey in a stolen vehicle.

They were now out of the town and into the countryside, at which point they clipped a kerbstone at eighty-five. That in itself wasn't a problem, but Deggsy, who'd just filched his mobile from his jacket pocket to film this latest escapade, was jolted so hard that he dropped it into the footwell.

'Fuck!' he squawked, scrabbling around for it. At first he couldn't seem to locate it – there was quite a bit of junk down there – so he ripped his glove off with his teeth and went groping bare-handed. This time he found the mobile, but when he pulled his hand back he saw that he'd found something else as well.

It was clamped to his exposed wrist. Initially he thought he must have brushed his arm against an old pair of boots, which had smeared him with oil or paint. But no, now he could feel the weight of it and the multiple pinprick sensation where it had apparently gripped him. He still didn't realise what the thing actually was, not even when he held it close to his face – but then Deggsy had only ever seen scorpions on the telly, so perhaps this was unsurprising. Mind you, even on the telly he'd never seen a scorpion with as pale and shiny a shell as this one had – it glinted like polished leather in the flickering streetlights. It was at least eight inches from nose to tail, that tail now curled to strike, and had a pair of pincers the size of crab claws that were extended upwards in the classic defensive pattern.

It couldn't be real, he told himself distantly.

Was it a toy? It had to be a toy.

But then it stung him.

At first it shocked rather than hurt; as though a red-hot drawing pin had been driven full-length into his flesh, and into the bone underneath. But that minor pain quickly expanded, filling his suddenly frozen arm with a white fire, which in itself intensified – until Deggsy was screaming hysterically. By the time he'd knocked the eight-legged horror back into the footwell, he was writhing and thrashing in his seat, frothing at the mouth as he struggled to release his suddenly restrictive belt. At first, Dazzer thought his mate was play-acting, though he shouted warnings when Deggsy's convulsions threatened to interfere with his driving.

And then something alighted on Dazzer's shoulder.

Despite the wild swerving of the car, it had descended slowly, patiently – on a single silken thread – and when he turned his head to look at it, it tensed, clamping him like a hand. In the flickering hallucinogenic light, he caught brief glimpses of vivid, tiger-stripe colours and clustered demonic eyes peering at him from point-blank range.

The bite it planted on his neck was like a punch from a fist.

Dazzer's foot jammed the accelerator to the floor as his entire body went into spasms. The actual wound quickly turned numb, but searing pain shot through the rest of him in repeated lightning strokes.

Neither lad noticed as the car mounted an embankment, engine yowling, smoke and tattered grass pouring from its tyres. It smashed through the wooden palings at the top, and then crashed down through shrubs and undergrowth, turning over and over in the process, and landing upside down in a deep-cut country lane.

For quite a few seconds there was almost no sound: the odd groan of twisted metal, steam hissing in spirals from numerous rents in mangled bodywork.

The two concussed shapes inside, while still breathing, were barely alive in any conventional sense: torn, bloodied and battered, locked in contorted paralysis. They were still aware of their surroundings, but unable to resist as various miniature forms, having ridden out the collision in niches and crevices, now re-emerged to scurry over their warm, tortured flesh. Deggsy's jaw was fixed rigid; he could voice no complaint – neither as a mumble nor a scream – when the pale-shelled scorpion reacquainted itself with him, creeping slowly up his body on its jointed stick-legs and finally settling on his face, where, with great deliberation it seemed, it snared his nose and his left ear in its pincers, arched its tail again – and embedded its stinger deep into his goggling eyeball.

Chapter 2

Heck raced out of the kebab shop with a half-eaten doner in one hand and a carton of Coke in the other. There was a blaring of horns as Dave Jowitt swung his distinctive maroon Astra out of the far carriageway, pulled a U-turn right through the middle of the bustling evening traffic, and ground to a halt at the kerb. Heck crammed another handful of lamb and bread into his mouth, took a last slurp of Coke, and tossed his rubbish into a nearby bin before leaping into the Astra's front passenger seat.

'Grinton putting an arrest team together?' he asked.

'As we speak,' Jowitt said, shoving a load of documentation into Heck's grasp and hitting the gas. More horns tooted despite the spinning blue beacon on the Astra's roof. 'We're hooking up with them at St Ann's Central.'

Heck nodded, leafing through the official Nottinghamshire Police paperwork. The text he'd just received from Jowitt had consisted of thirteen words, but they'd been the most important thirteen words anyone had communicated to him for quite some time:

Hucknall murder a fit for Lady Killer
Chief suspect – Jimmy Hood
Whereabouts KNOWN

Heck, or Detective Sergeant Mark Heckenburg, as was his official title in the National Crime Group, felt a tremor of excitement as he flipped the light on and perused the documents. Even now, after seventeen years of investigations, it seemed incredible that a case that had defied all analysis, dragging on doggedly through eight months of mind-numbing frustration, could suddenly have blown itself wide open.

'Who's Jimmy Hood?' he asked.

'A nightmare on two legs,' Jowitt replied.

Heck had only known Jowitt for the duration of this enquiry, but they'd made a good connection on first meeting and had maintained it ever since. A local lad by birth, Dave Jowitt was a slick, clean-cut, improbably handsome black guy. At thirty, he was a tad young for DI, but what he might have lacked in experience he more than made up for with his quick wit and sharp eye. After the stress of the last few months of intense investigation, even Jowitt had started to fray around the edges, but tonight he was back on form, collar unbuttoned and tie loose, careering through the chaotic traffic with skill and speed.

'He lived in Hucknall when he was a kid,' Jowitt added. 'But he spent a lot of his time back then locked up.'

'Not just then either,' Heck said. 'According to this, he's only been out of Roundhall for the last six months.'

'Yeah, and what does that tell us?'

Heck didn't need to reply. Roundhall was a low-security prison in the West Midlands. According to these antecedents, Jimmy Hood, now aged in his mid-thirties, had served a year and a half there before being released on licence. However, he'd originally been held at Durham after drawing fourteen years for burglary and rape. As if the details of his original crimes weren't enough of a match for the case they were currently working, his most recent period spent outside prison put him neatly in the frame for the activities of the so-called 'Lady Killer'.

'He's a bruiser now and he was a bruiser then,' Jowitt said. 'Six foot three by the time he was seventeen, and burly with it. Scared the crap out of everyone who knew him. Got arrested once for chucking a kitten into a cement mixer. In another incident, he led some other juveniles in an attack on a building site after the builders had given them grief for pinching tools – both builders got bricked unconscious. One needed his face reconstructing. Hood got sent down for that one.'

Heck noted from the paperwork that Hood, of whom the mugshot portrayed shaggy black hair fringing a broad, bearded face with a badly broken nose – a disturbingly similar visage to the e-fit they'd released a few days ago – had led this particular street gang, which had involved itself in serious crime in Hucknall, from the age of twelve. However, he'd only commenced sexually offending, usually during the course of burglary, when he was in his late teens.

'So he comes out of jail and immediately picks up where he left off?' Heck said.

'Except that this time he murders them,' Jowitt replied.

Heck didn't find that much of a leap. Certain types of violent offender had no intention of rehabilitating. They were so set on their life's work that they regarded prison time – even a prolonged stretch – as a hazard of their chosen vocation. He'd known plenty who'd gone away for a lengthy sentence, and had used it to get fit, mug up on all the latest criminal techniques, and gradually accumulate a head of steam that would erupt with devastating force once they were released.

He could easily imagine this scenario applying to Jimmy Hood and, what was more, the evidence seemed to indicate it. All four of the recent murder victims had been elderly women living alone. Most of Hood's victims when he was a teenager had been elderly women. The cause of death in all the recent cases had been physical battery with a blunt instrument, after rape. As a youth, Hood had bludgeoned his victims after indecently assaulting them.

'Funny his name wasn't flagged up when he first ditched his probation officer,' Heck said.

Jowitt shrugged as he drove. 'Easy to be wise after the event, pal.'

'Suppose so.' Heck recalled numerous occasions in his career when it would have paid to have a crystal ball.

On this occasion, they'd caught their break courtesy of a sharp-eyed civvie.

The four home-invasion murders they were officially investigating were congregated in the St Ann's district, east of Nottingham city centre, and an impoverished, densely populated area, which already suffered more than its fair share of crime. The only description they'd had was that of a hulking, bearded man wearing a ragged duffel coat over shabby sports gear, which suggested that he wasn't able to bathe or change his clothes very often and so was perhaps sleeping rough. However, only yesterday there had been a fifth murder in Hucknall, just north of the city, the details of which closely matched those in St Ann's. There'd been no description of the perpetrator on this occasion, though earlier today a long-term Hucknall resident – who remembered Jimmy Hood well, along with his crimes – reported seeing him eating chips near the bus station there, not long after the event. He'd been wearing a duffel coat over an old tracksuit, and though he didn't have a beard, fresh razor cuts suggested that he had recently shaved one off.

'And he's been lying low at this Alan Devlin's pad?' Heck asked.

'Part of the time maybe,' Jowitt said. 'What do you think?'

'Well . . . I wouldn't have called it "whereabouts known". But it's a bloody good start.'

Alan Devlin, who had a long record of criminal activity as a juvenile, when he'd been part of Hood's gang, now lived in a council flat in St Ann's. These days he was Hood's only known associate in central Nottingham, and the proximity of his home address to the recent murders was too big a coincidence to ignore.

'What do we know about Devlin?' Heck said. 'I mean above and beyond what the paperwork says.'

'Not a player anymore, apparently. His son Wayne's a bit dodgy.'

'Dodgy how?'

'General purpose lowlife. Fighting at football matches, D and D, robbery.'

'Robbery?'

'Took some other kid's bike off him after giving him a kicking. That was a few years ago.'

'Sounds like the apple didn't fall far from the tree.'

As part of the National Crime Group, specifically the Serial Crimes Unit, Mark Heckenburg had a remit to work on murder cases across all the police areas of England and Wales. He and the other detectives in SCU (as it was abbreviated) tended to have a consultative investigating role with regard to the pursuit of repeat violent offenders, and would bring specialist knowledge and training to regional forces grappling with large or complex cases. They were usually allocated to said forces in groups of four or five, sometimes more. On this occasion, however, as the Nottinghamshire Police already had access to experienced personnel from the East Midlands

Special Operations Unit, Heck had been assigned here on his own.

SCU's presence wasn't always welcomed by the regional forces they were assisting, some viewing the attachment of outsiders as a slight on their own abilities – though in certain cases, such as this one, SCU's advice had been actively sought. Detective Superintendent Gemma Piper, head of SCU, had been personally contacted by Taskforce SIO Detective Chief Superintendent Matt Grinton, who was a keen student of those state-of-the-art investigations she and her team had run in previous years. He hadn't specifically asked for Heck, but Gemma Piper, having only recently reincorporated Heck into the unit after he'd spent a brief period attached to Cumbria Crime Command, had felt it would be a good way to ease him back in – Nottinghamshire were only looking for one extra body, someone who would bring expertise and experience but who would also be part of the team, rather than a bunch of Scotland Yard men to take over the whole show.

SIO Grinton was a big man with silver hair, a distinguished young/old face, and a penchant for sharp-cut suits, though his most distinctive feature was the patch he wore over his left eye socket, having lost the eye to flying glass during a drive-by shooting fifteen years earlier. He was now holding court under the hard halogen glow of the car park lights at the rear of St Ann's Central. Uniforms clad in full anti-riot gear and detectives with stab vests under their jackets and coats stood around him in attentive groups.

'So that's the state of play,' Grinton said. 'We're moving on this quickly rather than waiting till the crack of dawn tomorrow, firstly because the obbo at Devlin's address tells us he's currently home, secondly because if Jimmy Hood is our man there's been a shorter cooling-off period between each attack, which means that he's going crazier by the

13

minute. For all we know, he could have done two or three more by tomorrow morning. We've got to catch him tonight, and Alan Devlin is the best lead we've had thus far. Just remember . . . for all that he's a hoodlum from way back, Devlin is a witness, not a suspect. We're more likely to get his help if we go in as friends.'

There were nods of understanding. Mouths were set firm as it dawned on the Taskforce members just how high the stakes now were. Every man and woman present knew their job, but it was vital that no one made an error.

'One thing, sir, if you don't mind,' Heck spoke up. 'I strongly recommend that we take anything Alan Devlin tells us with a pinch of salt.'

'Any particular reason?' Grinton asked.

Heck waved Devlin's sheet. 'He hasn't been convicted of any crime since he was a juvenile, but he wasn't shy about getting his hands dirty back in the day – he was Jimmy Hood's right-hand man when they were terrorising housing estates around Hucknall. Now his son Wayne is halfway to repeating that pattern here in St Ann's. Try as I may, I can't view Alan Devlin as an upstanding citizen.'

'You think he'd cover for a killer?' Jowitt said doubtfully.

Heck shrugged. 'I don't know, sir. Assuming Hood is the killer – and from what we know, I think he probably is – I find it odd that Devlin, who knows him better than anyone, hasn't already come to the same conclusion and got in touch with us voluntarily.'

'Maybe he's scared?' someone suggested.

Heck tried not to look as sceptical about that as he felt. 'Hood's a thug, but he's in breach of licence conditions that strictly prohibit him from returning to Nottingham. That means he's keeping his head down and moving from place to place. He's only got one change of clothes, he's on his own, he's cold, damp, and dining on scraps in bus stations.

Does he really pose much of a threat to a bloke like Devlin, who's got form for violence himself, has a grown-up hooligan for a son and, though he's not officially a player anymore, is probably well respected on his home patch and can call a few faces if he needs help?'

The team pondered, taking this on board.

'We'll see what happens,' Grinton said, zipping his anorak. 'If Devlin plays it dumb, we'll let him know that Hood's mugshot is appearing on the ten o'clock news tonight, and all it's going to take is a couple of local residents to recognise him as someone they've seen hanging around Devlin's address. The Lady Killer is going down for the rest of this century, ladies and gents. Devlin may still have a rep to think of, but he won't want a piece of that action. Odds are he'll start talking.'

They drove to the address in question in five unmarked vehicles; one of them Heck's maroon Peugeot 308, and one a plain-clothes APC. They did it discreetly and without fanfare. St Ann's wasn't an out-of-control neighbourhood, but it wasn't the sort of place where excessive police activity would go unnoticed, and mobs could form quickly if word got out that 'one of the boys' was in trouble. In physical terms, it was a rabbit warren of crumbling council blocks, networked with dingy footways, which at night were a mugger's paradise. To heighten its atmosphere of menace, a winter gloom had descended, filling the narrow passages with cloying vapour.

Arriving at 41 Lakeside View, they found a boxy, redbrick structure, accessible by a short cement ramp with a rusty wrought-iron railing, and a single corridor running through from one side to the other, to which various apartment doors – 41a, 41b, 41c and 41d – connected.

Heck, Grinton and Jowitt regarded it from a short distance

15

away. Only the arched entry was visible in the evening murk, illuminated at its apex by a single dull lamp; the rest of the building was a gaunt outline. A clutch of detectives and armour-clad uniforms were waiting a few yards behind them, while the troop carrier with its complement of reinforcements was about fifty yards further back, parked in the nearest cul-de-sac. Everyone observed a strict silence.

Grinton finally turned round, keeping his voice low. 'Okay . . . listen up. Roberts, Atherton . . . you're staying with us. The rest of you . . . round the other side. Any ground-floor windows, any fire doors, block 'em off. Grab anyone who tries to come out.'

There were nods of understanding as the group, minus two uniforms, shuffled away into the mist. Grinton checked his watch to give them five minutes to get in place, then glanced at Heck and Jowitt and nodded. They detached themselves from the alley mouth, ascended the ramp, and entered the brick passage, which was poorly lit by two faltering bulbs and defaced end to end with obscene, spray-painted slogans. The same graffiti covered three of its four doors. The only one that hadn't been vandalised was 41c – the home of Alan Devlin.

There was no bell, so Grinton rapped on the door with his fist. Several seconds passed before there was a fumbling on the other side. The door opened as far as its short safety chain would allow. The face beyond was aged in its mid-thirties, but pudgy and pockmarked, one eyebrow bisected by an old scar. It unmistakably belonged to one-time hardman Alan Devlin, though these days he was squat and pot-bellied, with a shaved head. He'd answered the door in a grubby T-shirt and purple Y-fronts, but even through the narrow gap they spotted neck-chains and cheap, tacky rings on nicotine-yellow fingers. He didn't look hostile so much as puzzled, probably because the first thing he saw was Grinton's eye patch. He put on a pair of thick-lensed, steel-rimmed glasses, so that he could scrutinise it less myopically.

'Alan Devlin?' the chief superintendent asked.

'Who the fuck are you?'

Grinton introduced himself, displaying his warrant card. 'This is Detective Inspector Jowitt and this is Detective Sergeant Heckenburg.'

'Suppose I'm honoured,' Devlin grunted, looking anything but.

'Can we come in?' Grinton said.

'What's it about?'

'You don't know?' Jowitt asked him.

Devlin threw him an ironic glance. 'Yeah . . . I just wondered if *you* did.'

Heck observed the householder with interest. Though clearly irritated that his evening had been disturbed, his relaxed body language suggested that he wasn't overly concerned. Either Devlin had nothing to hide or he was a competent performer. The latter was easily possible, as he'd had plenty of opportunity to hone such a talent while still a youth.

'Jimmy Hood,' Grinton explained. 'That name ring a bell?'

Devlin continued to regard them indifferently, but for several seconds longer than was perhaps normal. Then he removed the safety chain and opened the door.

Heck glanced at the two uniforms behind them. 'Wait out here, eh? No sense crowding him in his own pad.' They nodded and remained in the outer passage, while the three detectives entered a dimly lit hall strewn with litter and cluttered with piles of musty, unwashed clothes. An internal door stood open on a lamp-lit room from which the sound of a television emanated. There was a strong, noxious odour of chips and ketchup.

Devlin faced them square-on, adjusting his bottle-lens specs. 'Suppose you want to know where he is?'

'Not only that,' Grinton said, 'we want to know where he's been.'

There was a sudden thunder of feet from overhead – the sound of someone running. Heck tensed by instinct. He spun to face the foot of a dark stairwell – just as a figure exploded down it. But it wasn't the brutish giant, Jimmy Hood; it was a kid – seventeen at the most with a mop of mouse-brown hair and a thin moustache. He was only clad in shorts, which revealed a lean, muscular torso sporting several lurid tattoos – and he was carrying a baseball bat.

'What the fucking hell?' He advanced fiercely, closing down the officers' space.

'Easy, lad,' Devlin said, smiling. 'Just a few questions, and they'll be gone.'

'What fucking questions?'

Jowitt pointed a finger. 'Put the bat down, sonny.'

'You gonna make me?' The youth's expression was taut, his gaze intense.

'You want to make this worse for your old fella than it already is?' Grinton asked calmly.

There was a short, breathless silence. The youth glanced from one to the other, determinedly unimpressed by the phalanx of officialdom, though clearly unused to folk not running when he came at them tooled up. 'There's more of these twats outside, Dad. Sneaking around, thinking no one can see 'em.'

His father snorted. 'All this cos Jimbo breached his parole?'

'It's a bit more serious than that, Mr Devlin,' Jowitt said. 'So serious that I really don't think you want to be obstructing us like this.'

'I'm not obstructing you . . . I've just invited you in.'

Which was quite a smart move, Heck realised.

'We'll see.' Grinton walked towards the living room. 'Let's talk.'

Devlin gave a sneering grin and followed. Jowitt went too. Heck turned to Wayne Devlin. 'Your dad wants to make it look like he's cooperating, son. Wafting that offensive weapon around isn't going to help him.'

Scowling, though now looking a little helpless – as if having other men in here chucking their weight about was such a challenge to his masculinity that he knew no adequate way to respond – the lad finally slung the baseball bat against the stair-post, which it struck with a deafening *thwack!*, before shouldering past Heck into the living room. When Heck got in there, it was no less a bombsite than the hall: magazines were scattered – one lay open on a gynaecological centre-spread; empty beer cans and dirty crockery cluttered the tabletops; overflowing ashtrays teetered on the mantel. The stench of ketchup was enriched by the lingering aroma of stale cigarettes.

'Let's cut to the chase,' Grinton said. 'Is Hood staying here now?'

'No,' Devlin replied, still cool.

He's very relaxed about this, Heck thought. *Unnaturally so.*

'So if I come back here with a search warrant and go through this place with a fine-tooth comb, Mr Devlin, I definitely won't find him?' Grinton said.

Devlin shrugged. 'If you thought you had grounds you'd already have a warrant. But it doesn't matter. You've got my permission to search anyway.'

'In which case I'm guessing there's no need, but we might as well look.' Grinton nodded to Heck, who went back outside and brought the two uniforms in. Their heavy boots thudded on the stair treads as they lumbered to the upper floor.

'How often has Jimmy Hood stayed here?' Jowitt asked. 'I mean recently?'

Devlin shrugged. 'On and off. Crashed on the couch.'

'And you didn't report it?'

'He's an old mate trying to get back on his feet. I'm not dobbing him in for that.'

'When did he last stay?' Heck asked.

'Few days ago.'

'What was he wearing?'

'What he always wears . . . trackie bottoms, sweat-top, duffel coat. Poor bastard's living out of a placky bag.'

The detectives avoided exchanging glances. They'd agreed beforehand that there'd be no disclosure of their real purpose here until Grinton deemed it necessary; if Devlin had known what was happening and had still harboured his old pal, that made him an accessory to these murders – and it would help them build a case against him if he revealed knowledge without being prompted.

'When do you expect him back?' Heck asked.

Devlin looked amused by the inanity of such a question (*again false*, Heck sensed). 'How do I know? I'm not his fucking keeper. He knows he can come here anytime, but he never wants to outstay his welcome.'

'Has he got a phone, so you can contact him?' Jowitt wondered.

'He hasn't got anything.'

'Does he ever come here late at night?' Grinton said. 'As in . . . unusually late.'

'What sort of bullshit questions are these?' Wayne Devlin demanded, increasingly agitated by the sounds of violent activity upstairs.

Grinton eyed him. 'The sort that need straight answers, son . . . else you and your dad are going to find yourselves deeper in it than whale shit.' He glanced back at Devlin. 'So . . . any late-night calls?'

'Sometimes,' Devlin admitted.

'When?'

20

'I don't keep a fucking diary.'

'Did he ever look flustered?' Jowitt asked.

'When didn't he? He's on the lam.'

'How about bloodstained?' Grinton said.

At first Devlin seemed puzzled, but now, slowly – very slowly – his face lengthened. 'You're not . . . you're not talking about this Lady Killer business?'

'You've got to be fucking kidding!' Wayne Devlin blurted, looking stunned.

'Interesting thought, Wayne?' Heck said to him. 'Is that *your* bat out there – or Jimmy Hood's?'

The lad's mouth dropped open. Suddenly he was less the teen tough-guy and more an alarmed kid. 'It's . . . it's mine, but that doesn't mean . . .'

'So if we confiscate it for forensic examination and find blood, it's *you* we need to come for, not Jimmy?'

'That won't work, copper,' the older Devlin said, though for the first time there was colour in his cheek – it perhaps hadn't occurred to him that his son might end up carrying the can for something. 'You're not scaring us.'

Despite that, the younger Devlin *did* look scared. 'You won't find any blood on it. It's been under my bed for months. Jimbo never touched it. Dad, tell 'em what they want to fucking know.'

'Like I said, Jimbo's only been here a couple of times,' Devlin drawled. (*Still playing it calm*, Heck thought.) 'Never settles down for long.'

'And it didn't enter your head that he might be involved in these murders?' Grinton said.

'Or are you just in denial?' Jowitt asked.

'He was a good mate . . .'

'So you *are* in denial? Can't see the judge being impressed by that.'

'It may have occurred to me once or twice,' Devlin retorted. 'But you don't want to believe it of a mate . . .'

'Even though he's done it before?' Grinton said.

'Nothing this bad.'

'Bad enough.'

'You should get over to his auntie's!' Wayne Devlin interjected.

That comment stopped them dead. They gazed at him curiously; he gazed back, flat-eyed, cheeks flaming.

'What are you talking about?' Heck asked.

'He was always ranting about his Auntie Mavis . . .'

'*Wayne!*' the older Devlin snapped.

'If Jimbo's up to something dodgy, Dad, we don't want any part in it.'

These two are good, Heck thought. *These two are really good.*

'Something you want to tell us, Mr Devlin?' Grinton asked.

Devlin averted his eyes to the floor, teeth bared. He yanked his glasses off and rubbed them vigorously on his stained vest – as though torn with indecision, as though angry at having been put in this position, but not necessarily angry at the police.

'Wayne may be right,' he finally said. 'Perhaps you should get over there. Her name's Mavis Cutler. Before you ask, I don't know much else. She's not his real auntie. Some old bitch who fostered Jimbo when he was a kid. Seventy-odd now, at least. I don't know what went on – he never said, but I think she gave him a dog's life.'

So Hood was attacking his wicked auntie every time he attacked one of these other women, Heck reasoned, remembering his basic forensic psychology. *It's a plausible explanation. Although a tad too plausible, of course.*

'And why do we need to get over there quick?' Jowitt wondered.

Devlin hung his head properly, his shoulders sagging as if he was suddenly glad to get a weight off them. 'When . . . when Jimbo first showed up a few months ago, he said he was back in Nottingham to see her. And when he said "see her", I didn't get the feeling it was for a family reunion if you know what I mean.'

'So why's it taken him this long?' Jowitt asked.

'He couldn't find her at first. I think he may have gone up to Hucknall yesterday, looking. That's where they lived when he was a kid.'

Cleverer and cleverer, Heck thought. *Devlin's using real events to make it believable.*

'Someone up there probably told him,' Devlin added.

'Told him what?'

'That she lives in Matlock now. I don't know where exactly.'

Matlock in Derbyshire. Twenty-five miles away.

'How do you know all this?' Grinton sounded suspicious.

Devlin shrugged. 'He rang me today – from a payphone. Said he was leaving town tonight, and that I probably wouldn't be seeing him again.'

'And you still didn't inform us?' Jowitt's voice was thick with disgust.

'I'm informing you now, aren't I?'

'It might be too late, you stupid moron!' Jowitt dashed out into the hall, calling the two uniforms from upstairs.

'Look, he never specifically said he was going to do that old bird,' Devlin protested to Grinton. 'He might not even be going to Matlock. He might be fleeing the fucking country for all I know! This is just guesswork!'

And you can't be prosecuted for guessing, Heck thought. *You're a cute one.*

'Don't do anything stupid, Mr Devlin,' Grinton said, indicating to Heck that it was time to leave. 'Like warning Jimmy we're coming. Any phone we find on Hood with calls traceable back to you are all we'll need to nick you as an accomplice.'

23

Out in the entry passage, Jowitt was already shouting into his radio. 'I don't care how indisposed they are – get them to check the voters' rolls and phone directories. Find every woman in Matlock called Mavis bloody Cutler . . . over and out!' He turned to Grinton and Heck. 'We should lock that bastard Devlin up.'

Grinton shook his head, ignoring the door to 41c as it slammed closed behind them. 'He might end up witnessing for us. Let's not chuck away what little leverage we've currently got.'

'What if he absconds?'

'We'll sit someone on him.'

'Excuse me, sir,' Heck said. 'But I won't be coming over to Matlock with you.'

Grinton looked surprised. 'All this groundwork and you don't want to be in on the pinch?'

Heck shrugged. 'I'll be honest, sir: good show Devlin put on in there, but I don't think Hood has any intention of going to Derbyshire. I reckon we're being sent on a wild goose chase.'

Jowitt looked puzzled. 'Why would Devlin do that?'

'It's a hunch, sir, but it's got legs. Despite the serious crimes Jimmy Hood was last convicted for, Alan Devlin let him sleep on his couch. Not once, but several times. This guy is not too picky to associate with sex offenders.'

'Come on, Heck,' Jowitt said. 'Devlin's in enough hot water as it is – he's not going to aid and abet a multiple killer as well.'

'He's in lukewarm water, sir. Apart from assisting an offender, what else has he admitted to? Even if it turns out he's sending us the wrong way, he's covered. It's all "I'm not sure about this, I'm only guessing that" – there aren't even grounds to charge him with obstructing an enquiry.'

'We can't *not* act on what he's told us,' Grinton argued.

'I agree, sir. But while you're off to Matlock, I'm going to chase a few leads of my own. If that's okay?'

'No problem . . . just make sure you log them all.'

While Grinton arranged for a couple of his plain-clothes officers to maintain covert obs on Lakeside View, the rest of them returned to their vehicles and mounted up for a rapid ride over to the next county. Jowitt was back on the blower again, putting Derbyshire Comms in the picture as he jumped into his car. Heck remained on the pavement while he too made a quick call – in his case it was to the DIU at St Ann's Central. As intelligence offices went, this one was pretty efficient.

'Heck?' came the hearty voice of PC Marge Propper, a chunky uniformed lass whose fast, accurate research capabilities had already proved invaluable to the Lady Killer Taskforce.

'Marge – am I right in thinking that, apart from Alan Devlin, Jimmy Hood has no other known associates in the inner Nottingham area?'

'Correct.'

'Okay . . . I want to try something different. Can you contact Roundhall Prison in Coventry? Find out who's been visiting Hood this last year and a half. Any regular names that haven't already cropped up in this enquiry, I'd like to know about them.'

'Wilco, Heck – might take a few minutes to get a response at this hour.'

'No worries. Call me back when you can.'

He paused before climbing into his Peugeot. The other mobile units had driven away, leaving a dull, dead silence in their wake. The surrounding buildings were little more than blurred, angular outlines, broken by the odd faint square of window-light, most of which leached into the gloom without making any impression. The passage leading towards Lakeside View was a black rectangle, which bade no one re-enter it.

Heck climbed into his car and switched the engine on.

It was impossible to say whether or not they were on the right track, but it *felt* right. He still didn't trust Alan Devlin, but the guy's partial admissions had revealed that Jimmy Hood had been in this district as well as Hucknall – which put Hood close to all the identified murder scenes and in roughly the right timeframe. Of course, with the knowledge of hindsight, it was all so predictable and sordid. As Heck drove out of the cul-de-sac it struck him that this decayed environment, with its broken glass and graffiti-covered maze of soulless brick alleys, seemed painfully familiar. So many of his cases had brought him to blighted places like this.

His phone rang and he slammed it to his ear. 'Yeah, Heckenburg!'

'We could have something here, Heck,' Marge Propper said. 'In his last year at Roundhall, Jimmy Hood was visited nine times by a certain Sian Collier.'

'That name doesn't ring a bell.'

'No; she hasn't been on our radar up to now, though she's got minor form for possession and shoplifting. She's white, thirty-two years old and a local by birth. Her last conviction was over five years ago, so she may have cleaned up her act.'

'Apart from the bit where she gets mixed up with sex killers?'

'Yeah . . .'

Heck fiddled with his sat nav. 'Where does she live?'

'Mountjoy Height, number eighteen – that's in Bulwell.'

'I know it.'

'Heck, if you're going over there, you might want to speak to Division first. It's a lively place.'

'Thanks for the warning, Marge. But I'm only spying out the land. Anyway, I've got my radio.'

The murkiness of the winter night was now to Heck's advantage – mainly because it meant the roads were empty of traffic, but also because, once he arrived in Bulwell, he was able to cruise its foggy, run-down streets without attracting attention.

When he finally located Mountjoy Height, it was a row of pebble-dashed two-storey maisonettes on raised ground overlooking yet another labyrinthine housing estate. First, he made a drive-by at the front, seeing patches of muddy grass serving as communal front gardens, with wheelie bins dotted across them and rubbish strewn haphazardly. There were only a couple of other vehicles present, but lights were on in most of the maisonette windows. After that, he explored at the rear, working his way down into a lower, winding alley, which ran past several garages. Some of these stood open, some closed. The garage to number eighteen didn't have a door attached, but was of particular interest because a large, good-looking motorcycle was parked inside it.

Heck glided to a halt and turned his engine off.

He climbed out, listening carefully; somewhere close by voices bickered. They were muffled and indistinct, but it sounded like a couple of adults; he wasn't initially sure where it was coming from – possibly number eighteen itself, which towered behind the garage in the gloom and was accessible by a narrow flight of steps.

He assessed the motorbike through the entrance, and despite the darkness was able to identify it as a new model Suzuki GSX; an expensive make for this neck of the woods.

'DS Heckenburg to Charlie Six,' he said into his radio. 'PNC check, please?'

'*DS Heckenburg?*' came the crackly response.

'Anything on a black Suzuki GSX motorcycle, index Juliet-Zulu-seven-three-Bravo-Foxtrot-Alpha, over?'

'Stand by.'

Heck moved to the side of the garage and glanced up the steps. The monolithic structure overhead was wreathed in vapour, but lights still burned inside it and the argument raged on; in fact it sounded as if it had intensified. Glass shattered, which wasn't necessarily a bad thing – it might grant him the right to force entry.

'*DS Heckenburg from PNC?*'

'Go ahead.'

'*Black Suzuki GSX motorcycle, index Juliet-Zulu-seven-three-Bravo-Foxtrot-Alpha, reported stolen from Hucknall late last night, over.*'

'Received, thanks for that. What were the circumstances of the theft, over?'

'*Fairly serious, Sarge. It's being treated as robbery. A motorcycle courier got a bottle broken over his head outside a newsagent, and then had his helmet stolen as well as his ride. He's currently in IC. No description of the offender as yet.*'

Heck pondered. This sounded more like Jimmy Hood by the minute. On the basis that he was now looking to make an arrest for a serious offence, Heck had the power to enter the garage – which he duly did, finding masses of junk littered in its oily shadows: boxes crammed with bric-a-brac; broken, dirty household appliances; even a pile of chains, several of which were wrapped round an upright steel girder supporting the garage roof.

'*DS Heckenburg . . . are you saying you've found this vehicle, over?*'

'That's affirmative,' Heck replied, pulling his gloves on as he mooched around. 'In an open garage at the rear of eighteen, Mountjoy Height, Bulwell. The suspect, who I believe to be inside the address, is Jimmy Hood. White male, early thirties, six foot three inches and built like a brick shithouse. Hood, who has form for extreme violence, is also a suspect in the Lady Killer murders. So I need backup ASAP. Silent approach, over.'

'*Received Sarge . . . support units en route. ETA five.*'

Heck shoved his radio back into his jacket and worked his way through the garage to a rear door, which swung open at his touch. He followed a paved side path along the base of a steep, muddy slope, eventually joining with the flight of steps leading up to the maisonette. When he ascended, he did so warily. Realistically, all he needed to do now was wait until the cavalry arrived – but then something else happened.

And it was a game-changer.

The shouting and screaming indoors had risen to a crescendo. Household items exploded as they were flung around. This was just about tolerable, given that it probably wasn't an uncommon occurrence in this neighbourhood. Heck reasoned that he could still wait it out – until he got close to the rear of the building, and heard a baby crying.

Not just crying.

Howling.

Hysterical with pain or fear.

'DS Heckenburg to Charlie Six, urgent message!' He dashed up the remaining steps, and took an entry leading to the front of the maisonette. 'Please expedite that support – I can hear violence inside the property and a child in distress, over!'

He halted under the stoop. Light shafted through the frosted panel in the front door, yet little was visible on the other side – except for brief flurries of indistinct movement. Angry shouts still echoed from within.

Heck zipped his jacket and knocked loudly. 'Police officer! Can you open up please?'

There was instantaneous silence – apart from the baby, whose sobbing had diminished to a low, feeble keening.

Heck knocked again. 'This is the police – I need you to open up!' He glimpsed further hurried motion behind the distorted glass.

When he next struck the door, he led with his shoulder.

It required three heavy buffets to crash the woodwork inwards, splinters flying, bolts and hinges catapulting loose. As the door fell in front of him Heck saw a narrow, wreckage-strewn corridor leading into a small kitchen, where a tall male in a duffel coat was in the process of exiting the property via a back door. Heck charged down the corridor. As he did, a woman emerged from a side room, bruised and tear-stained, hair disorderly, mascara streaking her cheeks. She wore a ragged orange dressing gown and clutched a baby to her breast, its face a livid, blotchy red.

'What do you want?' she screeched, blocking Heck's passage. 'You can't barge in here!'

Heck stepped around her. 'Out the way please, miss!'

'But he's not done nothing!' She grabbed Heck's collar, her sharp fingernails raking the skin on his neck. '*Can't you bastards stop harassing him!*'

Heck had to pull hard to extricate himself. 'Hasn't he just beaten you up?'

'That's cos I didn't want him to leave . . .'

'He's a bloody nutter, love!'

'It's nothing . . . I don't mind it.'

'Others do!' Heck yanked himself free – to renewed wailing from the woman and child – and continued into the kitchen and out through the back door, emerging onto a toy-strewn patio just as a burly outline loped down the steps towards the garage, only a few yards in front of him. The guy had something in his hand, which Heck at first took for a bag; then he realised that it was a motorbike helmet. 'Jimmy Hood!' he shouted, scrambling down the steps in pursuit. 'Police officer – stay where you are!'

Hood's response was to leap the remaining three or four steps, pulling the helmet on and battering his way through the garage's rear door. Heck jumped the last steps as well, sliding and tumbling on the earthen slope, but reaching the garage doorway only seconds behind his quarry. He shouldered it open to find Hood seated on the Suzuki, kicking it to life. Its glaring headlight sprang across the alley. The roars of its engine filled the gutted structure.

'Don't be a bloody fool!' Heck bellowed.

Hood glanced round – just long enough to flip Heck the finger and hit the gas, the Suzuki bucking forward, almost pulling a wheelie it accelerated with such speed.

But the fugitive only made it ten yards, at which point, with a terrific BANG, the bike's rear wheel was jerked back beneath him. He somersaulted over the handlebars, slamming upside down against another garage door before flopping onto the cobblestones, where he lay twisted and groaning. The bike came to rest a few yards away, chugging loudly, smoke pouring from its shattered exhaust.

'Bit remiss of you, Jimmy,' Heck said, emerging into the alley, toeing at the length of chain still pulled taut between the buckled rear wheel and the upright girder inside the garage. 'Not checking that something hadn't got mysteriously wrapped round your rear axle.'

Flickering blue lights appeared as local patrol cars turned into view at either end of the alley, slowly wending their way forward. Hood managed to roll over onto his back, but could do nothing except lie there, glaring with glassy, soulless eyes through the aperture where his visor had been smashed away.

Heck dug handcuffs from his back pocket and suspended them in full view. 'Either way, pal, you don't have to say anything. But it may harm your defence . . .'

Chapter 3

It took a near-death experience to make Harold Lansing realise that he needed to start enjoying life more. Of course, those who didn't know him would have been startled to learn that he wasn't leading a very full and pleasurable existence in the first place.

A 45-year-old multi-millionaire bachelor, he was exceptionally handsome – sun-bronzed, with a shock of crisp, grey hair – always fashionably dressed even in casuals, and the owner of two nifty motors, a Bentley Continental V8 and a Hyundai Veloster sport, so it seemed highly unlikely that he wasn't already one of the most contented men in Britain. He also owned three sumptuous properties: a villa on the Côte d'Azur, where he spent the odd three-day break, a flash apartment in Swiss Cottage, purpose-bought as a crashpad from which to take in the London scene, and his 'rural retreat', as he referred to it, though it was actually his regular residence: a palatial, eight-bedroom former farmhouse in the Surrey countryside called Rosewood Grange. With 300 acres of verdant gardens attached, a private tennis court and croquet lawn, its own indoor swimming pool and the near-obligatory complement of priceless artworks and antiques, you'd have expected Rosewood Grange to be the jewel in a party king's crown, the epicentre of a lavish, playboy lifestyle, where all the best people, including the most glamorous and connected women, came every weekend to get off their face.

Except that it didn't serve that purpose, and it never really had.

Looks could be deceptive.

Aside from the occasional round of golf and a few restful hours spent angling on the River Mole, Lansing dedicated more energy towards supporting charitable causes than he did his own leisure. In addition, he was a workaholic. He ran several computer companies from his private office in Reigate, and had made the bulk of his money selling software products in the United States and the Far East. He also owned a chain of country inns and hotels aimed at a wealthy clientele. What was more, he liked to stay hands-on with all these interests – not because he didn't trust his carefully appointed underlings, but more because he couldn't conceive of a lifestyle spent, to use one of his own phrases, twiddling his thumbs all day.

However, now maybe – just maybe – thanks to a recent accident and a subsequent two-week sojourn in hospital, several days of which he'd spent hooked to a bank of 'vital signs' monitors in Intensive Care, he was beginning to readdress things.

As he threw his briefcase into the back of his Bentley that beautiful July morning, he paused briefly to admire the lush, sun-dappled greenery enclosing his home, and to breathe the seductive scents of the English woodland: rosebud, honeysuckle, fresh mint. Quite an improvement on the starch, bleach, and liberally applied antiseptics of the hospital.

Good Lord, it was great to be alive. But how much of a life was he actually living?

Okay, he'd made a kind of resolution while he was in

hospital to take more holidays, to travel more regularly and extensively, maybe even to hook up with Monica again. And yet here he was, the first morning of his officially being 'fit for work', and he was already heading for the office at seven sharp. It was as though nothing had happened to disrupt his regular-as-clockwork routine. But it wasn't like it would be difficult to make changes to this; Lansing was the boss after all – the only pressure he ever felt was the pressure he applied to himself. But he would still only get home after eight p.m., and as usual would dine alone on whatever collation Mrs Beetham, his housekeeper, had set out for him – except that no, Mrs Beetham was currently on holiday with Mr Beetham, Lansing's gardener, so he would actually dine alone on whatever morsel of fast food, most likely a greasy fish and chip supper, he remembered to pick up on the way. His main viewing that night would be the business news, and his bedtime reading the financial press. This was his normal weekday schedule – and he was used to it and satisfied with it. But it was hardly a life in the true sense of the word.

A solitary individual with few real interests outside work, golf and fishing, Lansing had no yearning to 'go out and do stuff' as Monica had once tried to persuade him – not long before they broke up, in fact – but the incident on the river had made him realise that unforeseen disaster could be lurking around any corner, and that there were probably quite a few things he had yet to experience that would undoubtedly enrich his time on Earth. The mere memory of the roiling green water thundering in his ears as he was swept over the weir – the weight of it bearing down on top of him, pummelling his body, slamming him again and again on the slimy brickwork at the bottom of the plunge-pool, pinning him deep in that airless, icy void – was enough to set him quaking. How easy to recall the horrific realisation that *this was it*; that without expectation, anticipation, or even a hint of warning, it was all suddenly, irreversibly over. Everything. The whole show. There would be no goodbyes, no sorting out of affairs, no time to fix the things that needed fixing. This was simply it. His allotted time had run out. Gone. Zip.

Almost in reflex, Lansing stripped off his blue silk tie.

It wasn't necessarily a rebellion against the regimented world in which he'd so long been immersed. It didn't mean that he was suddenly casting his sights further afield – looking out for a good time when he'd normally be assessing the markets. But it was a start, he supposed. Monica would certainly be surprised. He'd try and Skype with her later on, and gauge her reaction – and not just to the missing tie, perhaps to an on-the-hoof dinner invitation for whenever she was next in the UK.

Lansing tossed the tie into the back seat of his Bentley as he climbed behind the wheel. With a few deft strokes, he brought the magnificent machine's six-litre twin-turbocharged engine purring to life. The dulcet strains of Vivaldi filled its leather interior. He eased it down his white gravel drive, increasingly enthused by his new outlook on life, by his determination to have some fun for a change. At the end of the day, why not? The nearby woods were thick with summer leaf, filled with birdcalls. The sun speared through the overhead canopy. When he looked beyond his desk, this world – which had so very nearly been snatched away from him – really was a glorious and invigorating place.

A short distance from the house, he slowed as he approached the drive entrance. The road beyond was only a B road, but it ran in a more or less direct line between Crawley and Dorking, and passed for long, straight stretches through gentle forest and farmland. As such, it was popular with boy racers, even at this early hour – idiots who'd left it too late to set out for work; idiots who were in danger of missing their flights from Gatwick; idiots who were trying to get home before the day began, so they could try to convince their wives or girlfriends that they hadn't stayed out all night. But even without such a crowd of jackanapeses on the road, the point where Lansing's drive connected with it was a bad one; right on a blind bend. To compensate, he'd had a large convex mirror fixed on the twisted oak trunk opposite, giving him excellent vantage in both directions for a considerable distance, and right now the way was clear.

As the 'Spring' harpsichord kicked in, he thumbed the volume control on the steering column. Lansing loved classical music, but he particularly loved the pastoral pieces, especially while driving through lush countryside on summer mornings. He checked the mirror opposite one final time – the road was still empty in both directions – and casually cruised out between the tall redbrick obelisks that served as his gateposts.

The sound of his collision with the Porsche Carrera was like a volcanic eruption.

When the sports car struck his front nearside it was doing over seventy miles an hour, and it catapulted over the top of him, flipping end over end through the air, turning into a fireball when it hit the road again some forty yards further on, from which point it continued to crash and roll, setting alight every bush and thicket along the verge, before wrapping itself round a hornbeam, which was almost uprooted by the impact.

In comparison to that, Lansing didn't come off half badly.

His own vehicle, which was also dragged out and flung on its roof along the scorched tarmac, was of course reduced to mangled scrap, but though he was slammed brutally against his belt and airbag, and his legs twisted torturously as the Bentley's entire chassis was buckled out of shape, he survived.

For what seemed like ages afterwards, he hung upside

36

down, dazed to a near-stupor. The only thought that worked its way through his head was: *The mirror . . . the road was clear, I saw it*. He cursed himself as a damn fool for having played the music in his car at such volume that he'd failed to hear the howl of the approaching engine. *But that shouldn't have mattered, because the road was clear. I saw it with my own eyes.*

And then another thought occurred to him: about the smell that was rapidly filling his nostrils, and the warm fluid running down his face – which he'd at first assumed was blood. He touched his wet cheek with his fingertips. When he brought them away again, they were shiny and slippery.

Dear God!

The petrol tank had ruptured. Its contents were already seeping in rivulets through the shattered vehicle's interior. And outside on the road of course, though Lansing's vision was fogged by pain and shock, pools of flame were burning, some of them in perilous proximity.

Though nauseated and shivering, head banging with concussion, he fought wildly with his seatbelt clip. When it finally came loose, he still didn't drop, but was held fast by the legs, the agony of which infused his entire lower body.

'Bloody broken legs,' he burbled through a mouth seething with saliva.

He could still get out. He *had* to.

So he wriggled and he writhed, and he grunted aloud, biting down on shrieks of pain as he finally shifted his contorted lower limbs sufficiently to fall like a stone, landing heavily on his shoulders and upper back, but still managing to lurch around and worm his way out through his side window. Even as he slid onto the glass-strewn tarmac, there was movement in the corner of his eye. He spied glistening fuel winding treacherously away towards the burning vegetation on the verge.

Crawling on his elbows, teeth gritted on blinding pain, Lansing dragged himself further and further away. When the car blew behind him, it didn't go with a *BANG* as much as a *WUMP*. He imagined fire ballooning above it in a miniature atom cloud, engulfing the branches overhead. Searing heat washed over him. But heat didn't hurt you, flame did. And flame didn't follow.

Realising he was safe, Lansing slumped face down on his folded arms, tears squeezing from eyes already reddened by smoke and fumes. Somewhere nearby he heard the approach of another car, but this one was slowing down. Tyres crunched on a road surface littered with wreckage; an engine groaned to a halt; a handbrake was applied; doors opened; what sounded like two pairs of booted feet clumped on the tarmac. Though it took him a stupefying effort, Lansing rolled over onto his back.

At first, he couldn't quite make out what he was seeing. When its fuel tank had exploded, the twisted, blazing hulk of his Bentley had righted itself with the force, landing on its wheels again. But more important than this, a heavy vehicle of some sort – green in colour, like a jeep or Land Rover – had parked about ten yards behind it, and two men had climbed out, both dressed in what looked like grey overalls. Instead of coming over to check if Lansing was okay, the first of these two men, the taller one, was standing with hands in pockets, surveying the burning wreck. The other had walked round to the far side of it and, through the flickering orange haze, seemed to be attempting to remove the mirror from the tree trunk.

'H-hey!' Lansing stammered. 'Hey . . . I'm over here . . .'

The one with his hands in his pockets casually looked round. Despite the momentous events of that morning, despite the delayed shock that was running through Lansing's broken body like an icy drug, he was so startled by the face he now beheld, and so horrified at the same time, that he cried out incoherently.

The shorter chap meanwhile was still fiddling with the mirror – not trying to remove it, as Lansing had first thought, but trying to remove something that had been laid over it. Or at least, laid over its glass. Was that a picture? A large, circular picture fitted inside the mirror's frame?

Good God . . .

With slow, purposeful steps, the tall one with the face that Lansing couldn't believe walked across the road towards him.

'You surely are the luckiest bastard alive, Mr Lansing.' His voice was muffled, though the words were perfectly clear. 'But sadly no one's luck lasts forever.'

'I'm . . . I'm hurt,' Lansing stuttered.

'I can see that.'

'Please . . . get me an ambulance.'

Now the other one came across the road; the one carrying the circular picture he'd torn away from the mirror. His face too brought an astonished croak from Lansing's throat, but no more so than the picture did – it was a still photograph of this very road, albeit empty, free of oncoming traffic.

'Look,' he burbled, 'this isn't a game. I'm badly hurt.'

'Not badly enough, I'm afraid,' the taller of the two men said. 'But don't worry – we can take care of that for you.'

They picked him up, one at either end.

Lansing fought back. Of course he fought back; he knew they weren't trying to help him. But despite his struggles, they carried him around his vehicle like a sack of meal. At this point he bit one of them; the shorter one, whose latex-covered hand had taken a tight grip on his sweaty, petrol-soaked shirt. He sank his teeth deep, almost through to the knuckle. The assailant yelped and tried to yank his hand free, but

Lansing – a dog with a bone, because he knew his life depended on it – wouldn't let go.

They remained calm, even as they rained blows on his face to try and loosen his clenched teeth. Each impact resounded through Lansing's skull. His nose went first; then his cheekbones and eye sockets; finally his jaw.

Though his vision was filmed by a sticky crimson caul, he was still aware they were carrying him. The heat of his vehicle washed over him as they halted in front of it.

'Pleeeaaath,' he mumbled through his shredded lips. 'Pleeeaaathe . . . no . . .'

'Think of this as a favour, Mr Lansing,' the taller one said. 'You've always been a handsome fella. Would you really want to carry on looking the way you do now? Anyway, hypothetical question. A-one, a-two, a-three . . .'

As they swung him between them his burbled pleas became gurgled wails, which rose to a peak of intensity when they released him and he bounced across the blistered bonnet and clean through the jagged maw of the windscreen into the white-hot furnace beyond.

Even then, it wasn't over.

Lansing's clothes burned away in blackened tatters, along with his skin and the thick fatty tissue beneath. Yet he still found sufficient strength to scramble out through an aperture where the driver's door had once been – to amazed but amused chuckles.

'This bloke, I'm telling you,' the taller one said, as they again hefted Lansing by his wrists and ankles, unconcerned at the flambéd flesh coming away in their grasp in slimy layers. As before, they transported his twitching form to the front of the vehicle and launched him across its bonnet, back through its flame-filled windscreen.

Chapter 4

At Nottingham Crown Court, the presiding judge, Mr Percival Shears, thought long and hard before passing sentence.

'James Hood,' he finally said, 'you have been found guilty of murdering five elderly women in this city. Women of good repute, who were never known to have hurt or offended against any person. Not only that, you murdered them in the most heinous circumstances, forcing entry to their homes and subjecting them to sustained and hideous abuse before ending their lives . . . and for no apparent purpose other than to gratify your perverted lusts. So grotesque are the details of these crimes that, were this another time and another place, and were it within my power, I would have no hesitation whatsoever in sending you to the gallows.'

There was an amazed hissing and cursing from one end of the public gallery, where a small clutch of Hood's supporters had installed themselves. For his own part, the prisoner – still a hulking brute, though for once looking presentable in a suit and tie, with his beard trimmed and black hair cut very short – was motionless in the dock, staring directly ahead, making eye contact with nobody.

'Of course,' the judge added, 'thanks to the efforts of men

41

and women vastly more civilised than you, such a course is no longer open to us. Instead, it falls upon me to impose the mandatory life sentence. But in my judgement, to meet the seriousness of this case, I recommend that you never be eligible for parole. Yours is to be a whole-life term. After such dreadful deeds, it is perfectly fitting that you spend the rest of your days under lock and key.'

There was tearful applause from the other end of the gallery, where the relatives of the victims were gathered. Down below, Detective Chief Superintendent Grinton turned to the bench behind and shook hands with DI Jowitt and Heck.

'Job done,' he said.

Heck watched as Hood was taken from the dock, glancing neither right nor left as he was escorted down the stairs to the holding cells. This was the last time he would ever be seen in public, but his body language registered no emotion. Like so many of these guys, he'd always probably suspected this was the destiny awaiting him.

Outside in the lobby, the detectives and the prosecution team were mobbed by jostling reporters, flashbulbs glaring, voices shouting excited questions.

'The full-life tariff is exactly what Jimmy Hood deserves,' Grinton told a local news anchorwoman. 'I can't say it makes me happy to see anyone receive that ultimate sanction, but this is the future he chose for himself. In any case, it won't bring back Amelia Taft, Donna Broughton, Joan Waddington, Dora Kent or Mandy Burke. Their families are also serving a full-life sentence, and even this result today, satisfying though it is for those involved in the investigation, will be no consolation to them.'

'Detective Sergeant Heckenburg,' Heck was asked, 'as the arresting officer in this case, given that five women still died before you brought Jimmy Hood to justice, do you really feel a celebration is justified?'

'I don't think anyone's celebrating, are they?' Heck replied. 'Like Chief Superintendent Grinton said, several lives have been lost. Another life is totally wasted. The whole thing's a tragedy.'

'How do you respond to accusations that it was a lucky arrest?'

'We got one lucky break for sure, and for that we ought to thank a vigilant member of the public. But you have to be on the right track to take advantage of stuff like that. The case still had to be made, and there was a lot of legwork involved. Everyone did their bit.'

'No one did their bloody bit!' came a harsh Nottinghamshire voice. 'That's the trouble!'

An alley cleared through the throng as Alan and Wayne Devlin, and a handful of similarly shady-looking characters, having descended the stair from the public gallery, now forced their way across the lobby.

'I hope you're proud, Heckenburg!' Devlin shouted, spittle flying from his lips. He and his minions were dressed in suits – Devlin was in his steel-rimmed specs again – yet they made no less menacing a picture. All the hallmarks were there: the tattoos, the facial scars, the cheap jewellery. The one or two women they had with them were blowzy types: overly made-up, chewing gum. 'You bastards betrayed Jimbo right from the start!'

'Who are you saying betrayed him, sir?' a reporter asked.

'This lot . . . the authorities.' Devlin waved a general hand at the detectives. 'Jimbo never stood a chance. As a kid it was obvious he was off his trolley, but the system kept letting him down. He was in and out of mental wards. Even though he kept telling people he was sick, that he was gonna do someone, they kept letting him go. If he'd been taken care of properly, none of this would have happened. Them poor women would be alive.'

43

Conscious that cameras and microphones were still on him, Heck merely shrugged. 'I'm not qualified to comment on any offender's mental health. All I do is catch them.'

'He's bloody lucky you *only* caught him,' Devlin retorted. 'He could have died coming off that bike.'

'Accidents happen,' Heck said, sidling towards the entrance doors.

'You lying shit!' Devlin and his cohort lurched forward en masse, and suddenly there was pushing and shoving, uniformed officers having to insert themselves into the crowd, hustling the opposing groups apart.

'And the worst accident of Jimmy Hood's life was meeting *you*!' Heck snarled, briefly losing it, pointing at Devlin's face. There was further hustling back and forth. 'You and your mates encouraged him plenty!'

'Yeah, blame us – the only ones who cared about him! You lying pig!'

'You should be up for perverting the course of justice,' Heck replied.

'You should be up for attempted murder.'

'If we'd been able to trace that phone call . . .'

'What phone call? Eh? What fucking phone call?'

Heck clamped his mouth shut, though the heat had risen in his cheeks until it was boiling. DI Jowitt's touch on his shoulder prevented him saying something he might totally regret. As Hood's legal team ushered Devlin and his pals away the bespectacled oaf grinned at Heck in stupid but triumphant fashion, as if merely goading the police was some kind of victory – which it was, of course, for those of a certain mentality.

Heck fought his way into the gents, where he had to throw water on his face to calm down. He didn't, as a rule, let himself get worked up by the crimes he investigated, no matter how brutal or revolting – but this particular case had been a little more stressful than usual, mainly because of its resemblance to a dreadful ordeal that had destroyed his family life when he was still very young. It wasn't something he talked about much these days, and in truth it had all happened an awful long time ago, but some wounds, it seemed, could never heal; they merely festered.

The face that stared back at him from the mirror looked a little more lived-in than maybe it should for a man in his late thirties: it was scarred, nicked, but not unfanciable or so he'd once been told, 'in a rugged, rugby player sort of way'. At least there was still no grey in his mop of dark hair, though that was probably a miracle in itself.

Heck straightened his collar, tightened his tie, and slipped out of the gents, leaving the chaotic court lobby via a side entrance, from where he rounded the corner into the car park – stopping short at the sight of Detective Superintendent Gemma Piper leaning against his Peugeot. Her own aquamarine Mercedes E-class was parked alongside it.

She folded her arms as he warily approached. 'By "that phone call", I take it you meant the one that warned Hood the Taskforce were onto him?'

'Erm, yeah,' he replied. 'Sian Collier received it about twenty minutes before I got there. Hood panicked big time, which is why he was legging it when I arrived.'

She chewed her lip as she pondered this. Gemma Piper was Heck's senior supervisor at the Serial Crimes Unit, and just about the most handsome policewoman he'd ever met – her intense blue eyes, strong, even features and famously unmanageable mop of ash-blonde hair (currently worn up, which matched her smart grey trouser suit no end) – gave her 'pin-up' appeal, although she was notoriously tough and determined. Her fierce nature meant that she was known throughout Scotland Yard as 'the Lioness'. And when she roared, window blinds shuddered in every department.

At present, however, even Gemma Piper seemed a little unsure how to play it where Heck was concerned. His ex-girlfriend from many years earlier, when they'd both been divisional detective constables, she and he had spent much of their careers alongside each other, but had often disagreed over procedure. As recently as last autumn, a colossal falling-out between them had resulted in Heck leaving SCU altogether and spending a short time at a remote posting up in the Lake District. He'd only returned to SCU at the end of last year at Gemma's urging, after a case they'd ended up working together in the Lakes had come to a successful conclusion. But even now, after they'd been back on the same team for several months, both of them were still wondering if their relationship would ever be the same again.

'Remind me why you couldn't trace that call back to Devlin?' she said.

He shrugged. 'It was made on a throwaway phone. And before you ask, ma'am, we searched his pad high and low after, with a warrant . . . we found nothing.'

'Well . . . some you win, some you lose.' Which was an uncharacteristically mild response given Gemma's normal perfectionist nature.

'Were you in the court lobby?' he asked. 'Only, I didn't see you.'

'Listened on the car radio. Live news feed.'

'Ah . . .' He gave a wry smile. Heck knew Gemma's moods better than anyone, and he knew she wouldn't be impressed that his brief explosion had been broadcast to the nation. Having seen SCU's work in the past badly hampered by press intrusion, she was now ultra-sensitive about the way her team was portrayed in public; she much preferred her officers to remain cool and tightlipped under pressure. However, she still seemed to be giving him leeway, consciously trying to avoid a row.

'It won't do us any harm,' he added. 'Hood's barrister has already announced that they're examining grounds for an appeal. I'd say there were considerably less after Devlin's little outburst in there. Indirectly or not, he basically confirmed that Hood is guilty as charged.'

'One of the braindead, eh?'

'One of the many.'

Heck ran the events in the lobby through his mind, and was surprised to feel dispirited by them rather than aggravated. Even after years of murder investigations, it still astonished him that so many folk would aggressively rally around killers, rapists, and other dangerous offenders, attempting to defend the indefensible simply because the accused was 'their mate', at the same time fully convinced that they themselves held no responsibility for the development of such monsters. It wasn't even as if they could all use pig-ignorance as an excuse. Alan Devlin was no dullard, for one; he'd engineered an opportunity for Hood to escape the police and at the same time had skilfully manoeuvred himself into a position where he could be accused of nothing.

'Not to worry,' Gemma said. 'You got the main result. We can't really ask for more than that.'

Heck eyed her curiously. 'You've come all the way from London just to tell me that?'

'No, I've come to buy you lunch.'

'Come again?'

She took the car keys from her jacket pocket. 'To congratulate you. You've put in a lot of hours on this job, and it's paid off.'

'No disrespect, ma'am, but I always put in a lot of hours.'

'Heck . . . I'm offering you lunch, not a knighthood. Plus I want a little chat. So get in your car and follow me. I've already reserved us a table, but they're not going to hold it indefinitely.'

Chapter 5

'Matt Grinton was on the phone last night,' Gemma said over her Caesar salad. 'Whatever today's outcome was going to be, you still got his vote. He praised, and I quote, "your work ethic, your attention to detail, your willingness to think outside the box, your all-round professionalism and, above all, the trust you place in your instincts".'

Heck paused over his chicken pie and chips. Around them, the lunchtime clientele in the country inn murmured as they ate and drank. Summer sunshine poured through the tall glazed panels of the conservatory annexe in which they were seated. He took a sip of Diet Coke. 'My instinct that Alan Devlin was lying to us was a fifty-fifty gamble. It could easily have gone the other way.'

'But it didn't. And that's the trick. If Hood had left Nottingham, Christ knows where he'd have washed up. We'd have had another spate of old lady murders in some other part of the country, which would have meant starting the whole thing from scratch.'

'We'll have to start another one from scratch again at some point, ma'am. There always seems to be someone out there with an irresistible urge to kill and kill.'

Gemma watched him eat. She'd suspected all the way through that Heck had willingly taken the Nottingham assignment because of events involving his deceased brother many, many years ago. Tom Heckenburg had been wrongly convicted of robbing and brutalising a number of OAPs while Heck was still a schoolboy. Though Tom was later exonerated, this only came after he'd committed suicide in prison. Not only had the nightmare experience driven Heck to join the police – 'clearly the bastards needed someone to show them how the job *should* be done,' as he'd once told her while drunk, a policy he'd followed to the letter ever since – but it had given him a particular bee in his bonnet about hoodlums who targeted the elderly and frail. Not that he ever lost control while investigating these kinds of crimes. Oh, Heck was a wild card; he was fully capable of 'going off on one' as they said in his native Lancashire, but in Gemma's opinion this gave him an edge that many of her other detectives lacked. He was also meticulous and thorough, but more important than any of that, he got results.

'The bigger picture,' she said, 'is that things have recently gone SCU's way. This last one's a bit of a cherry on the cake. At least two television companies, one of them American, have enquired about putting us on film in a warts and all documentary. Joe Wullerton's said no.'

'Good,' Heck replied.

'For the time being.'

'Ah . . .'

'No one's sharpening their knives for us at present, Heck, but we never know when funds will get tight again. Under those circs, a bit of positive free publicity would do us no harm.'

'And what if there are too many warts?'

'There wouldn't be. I'd keep *your* antics well away from the cameras.'

He half smiled as he finished off his meal.

'I say that because I don't want to give the impression that you're some kind of man of the moment,' she added.

'Perish the thought, ma'am.'

'Hell of a job on the Lady Killer, but that's the total of it . . . work is work. There's no reward coming; except this lunch.' Fleetingly, she looked embarrassed. 'My little thank-you. Just so you don't feel completely under-appreciated.'

He pushed his empty dish and cutlery aside. 'Sooner have a bit of nice grub than an empty promotion, ma'am.'

'Most coppers wouldn't consider any kind of promotion "empty",' she said. 'You're saying you still wouldn't accept one even if it was available?'

He shrugged. 'You know I wouldn't know what to do with an office of my own. And that I'd get bored sitting behind a desk all day, even a posh one. That said, the pay rise wouldn't go amiss.'

'We're all frozen in time on that score, Heck – which you know perfectly well.'

'In which case the free lunch will have to suffice.'

'It was the least I could do,' she said. 'Especially as I need a favour.'

He feigned shock. 'Ulterior motives, ma'am?'

'Just something I'd like your opinion on.'

'As I'm not laughing all the way to the bank this afternoon, I suppose I'll just have to sit here and listen.'

'It's an accident investigation.'

Heck raised an eyebrow. 'Not usually our department.'

'I'm not totally sure about that.' Gemma dabbed her lips with a napkin. 'But essentially you're right. In this first instance, we're just giving it the once-over. You know my mother's a member of a golf club down in Surrey?'

Heck's smile turned crooked. 'So we're actually doing a favour for your mum?'

Gemma reddened slightly. 'It's not just that. There may be something in this for us. If there is, you'll be the man to find it . . . won't you? That's Mum's opinion, I should add.'

Heck smiled all the more. Gemma's mother, Mel Piper, was a strikingly attractive and very personable lady in her late fifties; an older version of her daughter, minus the adversarial edge. She'd taken it hard when Heck and Gemma had split up while still in their mid-twenties. 'She asked for me specifically?' he said.

'You know she likes you a lot. I can't think why.'

'Okay, go on: this golf club?'

'It's just outside Reigate. Pretty exclusive, to be honest. Mum's only a member through her role as chair of the local WI. It seems that one of the other members, some bloke called Harold Lansing, wealthy local businessman, has died in a road accident right outside his own house.'

'Did your mum know him well?' Heck asked.

'Reasonably well, but not to the point where she's grieving. The puzzle is the manner of his death. Some spoiled brat in a Porsche – kid called Dean Torbert, nineteen but with half a dozen traffic violations to his name already – ran into Lansing while he was pulling out onto the main road. Before you ask, Torbert was killed too. It was a nasty smash, very high speed. The first weird thing is that Lansing, or so my mother says, was a careful driver. He'd even fitted a safety mirror onto the tree trunk opposite his drive entrance so that he could check it was clear before pulling out. Apparently it gave good vantage in both directions. Well over a hundred yards.'

'Perhaps it was suicide?'

'If so, he didn't leave a note. Plus no one who knew him felt he had any personal issues of that magnitude.'

'What have Surrey Traffic said?'

'Fatal RTA. No witnesses, no evidence to suggest third

51

party involvement. No sus circs. Coroner ruled death by misadventure.'

'Okay . . .' Heck considered this. 'So what's the second weird thing?'

'This is the one that really got me thinking. A couple of weeks earlier, Lansing closely survived another accident.'

'Maybe he was a worse driver than people realised?'

'This one wasn't on the road. Seems that Lansing was a keen angler. It was a Saturday afternoon and he was fishing at his favourite spot on the River Mole when a radio-controlled model plane from the nearby flying club swooped on him.'

Heck frowned. 'Actually *swooped* on him?'

'Well . . .' Gemma became thoughtful. 'It's difficult to say. Apparently it came down from a significant height, and it was big, not some toy – and it got close enough to knock him into the river and send him over the weir.'

'Bloody hell . . .'

'Only the vigilance of another angler saved his life. Local plod investigated the incident, but the plane was never recovered – presumably that went over the weir too and got washed away. To date, no member of the flying club will admit either responsibility or having seen anything, even though all were out in force that day in the next field.'

'Could be a coincidence.'

She arched an eyebrow. 'Really?'

'Well, real-life coincidences are few and far between, I suppose. Certainly when they're that extreme.'

'My thoughts too,' she said.

'Did the local lads do a thorough job?'

'We don't know yet.'

'What made your mum so suspicious? I mean there must be more than that.'

'Nothing solid. It was a gut feeling, apparently.' Gemma made a vague gesture. 'Sometimes she's a bit oversensitive to this sort of thing. All those years married to a copper, I suppose. She reckons Harold Lansing was strangely . . . well, to use her words, "carefree and innocent for a guy with so much dosh". He didn't have a driver, for example, or any professional security. Used to go fishing on his own, lived out in the sticks on his own – all that stuff. Sort of unintentionally made himself a target.'

'But he wasn't robbed?'

'Not as far as we're aware.'

Heck gave it some thought. 'It's a mystery for sure.'

'Which is why I'd like you to pop down there and check it out. Just cast your eye over it. See if anything strikes you as odd.'

'Okay.' He nodded as a waitress handed them two dessert menus. 'Thanks for lunch anyway.'

'Like I say, it's the least I can do,' Gemma said. 'Is Grinton having a party to celebrate the Hood conviction?'

'There'll be a few drinks. Low-key. I've told him I'll give it a miss.'

'Any particular reason?'

'Yeah.' Deciding against a slice of delicious-sounding banoffee pie, he closed the menu and laid it on the table. 'I need to catch up on some sleep.'

'Well, you shouldn't find the Surrey job too stressful. This time there'll be no ticking clock.'

'Let's hope not.'

'No . . . seriously.' She signalled to the waitress for the bill. 'Seems like a straight-up case. Someone had it in for Harold Lansing.'

'We *think* . . .'

She eyed him guardedly. 'Those instincts of yours again?'

'And yours, ma'am. I know you of old – whatever favour your mum asked, you wouldn't be sending me down to Surrey if something about it didn't make you twitchy.'

Chapter 6

If there was one county where Heck's investigations hadn't taken him before, it was Surrey. Violent crime wasn't, and never had been, an exclusively urban problem, but if there were any common denominators they tended to be deprivation and despair, and though Surrey wasn't free of these, it had deservedly earned its reputation as the English county that had 'made it'.

Though it boasted a green, leafy landscape with much agriculture, it was still densely populated; the lion's share of this concentrated in suburban villages and affluent commuter towns servicing London. It had naturally beautiful rural features such as the North Downs, Greensand Ridge and the Devil's Punch Bowl, but it was also home to numerous multinationals – Esso, Toyota, Nikon and Philips – and had the highest GDP per capita of any county in the UK. Heck was sure he'd once heard it said that Surrey claimed to have more millionaires than anywhere else in the whole of Great Britain.

But even by those standards, the district he followed the map to was a verdant haven, unbroken vistas of meadow and common alternating with beech groves and scenic tracts of rolling, flower-filled woodland. The occasional houses were rambling, timber-framed affairs – Tudor or Jacobean in style – usually located amid lush, landscaped parks. The house he was actually looking for, Rosewood Grange, stood alone in woodland but was a touch more modern – Georgian apparently, which only made it 300 years old – but he couldn't see much of it when he arrived as it stood back from the road, only its upper portions, its curly gables and even rows of tall, redbrick chimneys, showing above the yew hedge and thick shrubbery standing in front of it.

According to the thirty-page accident report, there was one entrance/exit to Rosewood Grange, a single driveway, which emerged about fifty yards further on between two tall brick gateposts. Though there was no actual gate, this gateway was located at a gentle but awkward crook in the road, which would have made it quite dangerous for anyone leaving the property by car, as they'd be blinded to oncoming traffic from either direction. That said, the circular convex mirror, which Heck saw fitted on a tree trunk opposite, about seven feet up from the ground, should have been more than adequate to show whether or not the way was clear. He parked on the verge, climbed out, and took in the air. It was another warm day, billows of fleecy cloud static in a pebble-blue sky. In either direction, the sun-dappled road dwindled off beneath natural arches formed by interwoven branches. Birds twittered and insects hummed, but aside from that there was peace and quiet. He had the immediate, strong impression that traffic around here was scarce.

Despite all this, it wasn't difficult to see where the collision had occurred, or just how catastrophic it had been.

Some ten yards along the road from the drive entrance there were swathes of torn and blackened vegetation on the opposing verge. Even now, over two weeks later, chips of paint and glass, and slivers of twisted metal, were visible along the roadside. Thirty yards beyond that, several feet past the kerb, a partially uprooted hornbeam sagged backwards into the meadow behind. Its trunk was badly charred but also extensively gashed, as though by a colossal impact. This, it seemed, was where the flying Porsche had come to rest. Heck pivoted around, surveying as much of the scene as he could. The Traffic unit who'd investigated this RTA would have done a thorough job – of that there was no question. Except that, as far as they were concerned what had happened here was an accident, not a homicide. In addition, whatever they'd discovered, whoever they'd eventually deemed to be at fault, there was no one left alive to prosecute – so how much care and attention would they *really* have exercised?

Heck glanced at his watch. It was just past noon, and his appointment with DCI Will Royton at Reigate Hall Police Station wasn't due until two – which perhaps gave him enough time to make a few quick enquiries of his own.

It was a dry day with no rain forecast, and Heck was only wearing casuals – jeans, a T-shirt and training shoes. But just to be on the safe side, in case someone came along and felt like asking questions, he donned a yellow/green high visibility doublet with the word POLICE stencilled on the back before trudging between the gateposts and up the drive. He'd been informed that there was no point calling at the house as there'd be nobody there. Apparently Lansing had lived alone; he'd employed the Beethams, an elderly couple, as housekeeper and gardener, who – very conveniently, perhaps too conveniently – had been away together on holiday on the day of his accident, and both of whom were now presumably looking for jobs elsewhere. But it couldn't do any harm to check.

He walked along the front of the house, which was very well concealed from the road by the near-impenetrable hedge, the net effect of which was to create a real air of privacy. It had five large downstairs windows, suggesting a spacious interior, though all their curtains had been drawn, which was perhaps understandable with the lord of the manor recently deceased. The front door was a huge slab of varnished oak studded with brass nail-heads, and was firmly closed. To one side of it a slate plaque bore the legend *Rosewood Grange*, and underneath that there was a brass button. Heck pushed it, the bell sounding deep inside the house; a dull, reverberating jangle, as though great pieces of hollow metal were knocking together – but it brought no response.

Eventually he continued along the front of the building and around to one side, where the drive became a parking space large enough to accommodate as many as four or five vehicles. From here, a paved path led him onto a lawn the size of a junior football pitch and dotted with white wrought-iron garden furniture. On the right of that, a newly built annexe was attached to the rear of the house, with a row of circular portals instead of full-sized windows. When Heck glanced through one of these, he saw an indoor swimming pool, a blue rubber sheet resting on its undisturbed surface. The rest of the pool area – the tiled walkways around it, the frescoes of dolphins and mermaids on the walls, the additional pieces of furniture – lay in silent dimness.

Heck turned to check out the rest of the rear garden, which was even more expansive than he'd expected. Beyond the lawn lay flowerbeds and topiary, through the midst of which a central walk led away beneath a trellis roof woven with leafy vines, presumably to connect with other lawns, maybe with one of those ornamental lakes or fish ponds. Overall, it was a majestic scene; the evergreens handsomely pruned, the blooms in full summer profusion. Yet the stillness that pervaded this place, and the quiet – it was almost as if the birds themselves were observing a reverential silence – gave it a melancholic air. It could be quite a while before anyone else enjoyed the late Mr Lansing's garden, and who knew what condition it would be in by then.

From somewhere nearby came an echoing *clank*.

Another sound followed on its heels: a splintering crack, like timber breaking.

Heck glanced around, expecting to see someone working – the gardener perhaps, putting in one last shift before sloping off to his new life. There was no one in sight, but now Heck spied the entrance to another wooded walk. This one was in the far corner of the garden, behind a wicker gate, which for some reason hung open. Thinking this off-kilter with the overwhelming neatness of everything else on show here, Heck strode over to it. When he reached the gate he peered along a grassy, rutted side path, which meandered through a clutch of shadowy thickets. Curious about the sound he'd just heard, he stepped through. It was amazing how, once he was amid the foliage on the other side, the sunlight was blotted out and yet the air remained warm, turning muggy. Insects droned; spiders' webs dangled between the intertwining branches. About thirty yards ahead stood a small wooden structure, like a shed. The door to this also hung partly open.

Heck walked towards it, feeling, for no good reason he could explain, increasingly wary. The small structure was ancient, lopsided with dilapidation. Its door jamb was visibly broken – all that remained of its latch were a few rusty scraps hanging from loose screws. But it might have been broken for years; such damage didn't necessarily need to be recent. He glanced inside, seeing nothing more than an old workbench and a few garden tools. A personal planner of some sort hung dog-eared on one of the walls. Alongside it there was a single window, its pane so thick with grime that scarcely any light passed in through it.

Heck stepped back and closed the door. Beyond the shed

lay more open space, though no grass grew here thanks to the high branches interlacing overhead. Instead, it was beaten earth covered with pine needles. On its right sat a massive compost heap. So far so normal, he supposed, except that a few yards further on there was a second shed; larger than the first and in better condition. But this hung open too.

When Heck advanced now, he did so quickly. Even from a distance it was clear that this door had also been forced, but in this case the padlock hanging from its twisted hinge looked shiny and new. Wondering if he was about to make his first arrest in Surrey (criminal damage to a garden shed, of all things), he yanked the door open. Again, there was nobody in there, and nothing of apparent value: a few more tools, an oil can, a coil of hosepipe, a few tubs of weedkiller.

A second passed before he stepped back, closing the door, glancing around.

Deep clumps of rhododendrons ringed this area, further tracts of shady woodland lying beyond them. He listened, ears attempting to attune to the breathy rural stillness. When you were isolated on foreign soil it was all too easy to imagine you were being watched, so even though this was exactly how Heck now felt, he paid it no heed. The outline of the house was vaguely visible through the foliage. It was no more than a couple of hundred yards away, and yet suddenly that seemed quite a distance. He turned again, scanning the crooked avenues between the trees. He wasn't a woodsman. If there was someone else here, he wouldn't necessarily know about it. But the chances were there was no one. This was the countryside. Odd noises were commonplace.

A fierce *clatter* split the silence, like something fragile impacting on stone.

Heck spun, gazing deeper into the encircling undergrowth – and spying something he found a little reassuring. The upper section of another manmade structure stood beyond the rhododendrons; by the looks of it, a greenhouse. Was it possible the gardener was here after all?

He pushed further into the underbrush, catching his arms and hands on thorns, but coming out alongside the greenhouse, which he now saw was extensive, maybe forty yards in length, but in a poor state of repair; its windows were cracked and grubby, the basic ironwork from which it was constructed rotted and furred with moss. However, it was still in use. When he entered, he gazed down a central concrete aisle, to either side of which thick jungles of luxuriant plants grew from trays of black soil mounted on waist-high metal shelving. Down at the far end, transverse to the central aisle, stood another rack of steel shelving, this one taller than those on either side, rising to about head height and crammed with garden breakables; plant pots and the like, even a few figurines like gnomes and elves.

There was no one down there that Heck could see. He strolled forward – only to forcibly stop himself after several yards. Okay, he'd heard something. But did it really matter? Someone was working nearby. That was all it was. In any case, time was short; he'd come here to assess the accident scene, not flog his way through the surrounding woods, freezing like a scared rabbit at the slightest irregularity. Whether he liked it or not, it was time to return to the crash site. But as he swung round to head back, a flicker of movement caught his eye.

He glanced sharply to the far end of the aisle.

And saw it again.

It was one of the figurines on the upper shelf; definitely a gnome or elf, one of those trashy little objects which, in truth, he'd never have expected to find on a stylish estate like this – and it had just moved.

Of its own accord.

Heck stared in astonishment, trying to laugh it off as a bizarre optical illusion. But now it moved again – just slightly, the merest quiver. Again of its own accord.

Slowly, disbelievingly, he walked down towards it. 'You're losing it, pal,' he said to himself. 'You've got to be . . .'

The figurine quivered again, more violently, bringing Heck to a dead halt.

A few moments passed as man and manikin stared at each other, Heck's neck hairs prickling. This time the thing remained stationary, even when he advanced again and came up close to it. It was exactly what he'd thought it was: a garden gnome, complete with beard, pointed nose, pointed ears, and pointed hat. It was about a foot and a half in height, and its once-garish colours had mostly weathered away. And yet it was hideous – so much so that he grimaced as he lifted it down from the shelf.

Where each of its eyes had once been, a black X had been etched, first gouged with a blade, and then filled in with black pen. Its mouth was a thin red line, with red trickles added to either side to create a vampire effect. Either the original paint job had run, or someone else had been handy with a different-coloured pen. For all his revulsion, Heck turned it several times in his hands, but could find nothing out of the ordinary. It was no more than a lump of sculpted, slightly mouldy plaster. He placed it back on the shelf and stepped back. Bewildered.

And then the disfigured gnome leaped at him.

Literally launched itself from its perch, and descended to the concrete floor. Its head broke off with the impact, rolling towards Heck's feet, where it came to a rest, gazing up at him with those unblinking, crossed-out eyes.

Heck was at first too stunned to react. He gazed back down at it, then at the rack – just as another object, a plant pot, also made a suicidal leap, exploding into a thousand fragments. A second pot followed from the other end of the shelf, and then another. Heck backed away involuntarily, hair prickling again, the sweat chilling on his neck and chest. A fifth object hurtled down; another gnome – this one landed upright and didn't shatter, but stood rocking back and forth as if the moment it regained its balance it would come toddling towards him. A sixth object went, and a seventh – more plant pots, all exploding on impact. Heck's hair was now standing on end, but then he spotted the culprit – the sleek brown form and whipping tail of a rat as it scuttled back and forth in the recess at the rear.

Heck sagged with absurd relief; he had to lean forward to get his breath.

When he looked again, the rat had fully emerged. It bounded to the floor and bolted away beneath the shelving on the left.

'You get a move on, lad,' Heck said under his breath, thanking God that none of the local officers he was shortly to be 'advising' had been around to witness that little pantomime. 'There's no wasting time in your game . . .'

He walked back along the aisle to the greenhouse entrance, heading through the rhododendrons, bypassing the compost heap and the two wooden sheds, and lurching down the path between the thickets. Even on reaching the front of the house, it was several seconds before he felt his heart rate begin to slow. He took a couple of deep breaths in order to regain full composure. He hadn't discovered the source of the metallic clattering, of course, but again – did that really matter? It wasn't like he didn't have any *real* work to do.

He walked on down the drive and returned to the road, where he dug a fresh pair of latex gloves from the pockets of his doublet and snapped them into place. A fingertip search was just the thing to concentrate his mind.

Inch by painful inch, sometimes on his knees, he worked his way along the verge on the side where the undergrowth had been torched, initially focusing on the glistening debris that had been swept into the gutter by passing vehicles but then scanning further afield as well. There was nothing instantly noticeable, which wasn't entirely surprising as he didn't really know what he was searching for, and was still a little distracted – he couldn't help but keep throwing glances over his shoulder at the silent, locked-up house. He still felt as if he hadn't been quite alone over there, but about ten minutes into his search something else caught his attention, something a lot more tangible: a tiny white object gleaming amid the charcoaled roughage.

He poked at it with a pair of tweezers, attempting to tease it into view.

It was a tooth – and by the looks of it human, a molar in fact. What was more it had recently been removed from its owner's jaw, because though several of its roots had been snapped, a couple had been wrenched out in full, and tiny threads of reddish-brown tissue were still attached. He fed it into a small sterile evidence sack, which he then sealed. When he held it up to the sunlight, the tooth's underside was crusted reddish-brown. More blood – which was explainable, because this was an adult-sized molar, and adult molars didn't come out easily.

Heck pocketed it, marked the spot of its discovery with an evidence flag, and continued his search, but nothing else of consequence emerged in the next hour, at the end of which he took some pegs and fluorescent tape from the boot of his car and cordoned off several areas. It irked him that this crime scene – and he already had a strong feeling that this was what the accident site was – had not been preserved for more detailed forensic examination. Of course that could still be arranged, though it might already be too late.

*   *   *

Reigate Hall was an unusually attractive building for a police station, built from eroded Georgian brick with a lopsided roof of crabby, moss-covered slates. It looked more like a moot hall or village almshouse than a focal point of modern day law enforcement, and faced onto a pleasant open green, at one end of which stood an old parish church, and at the other a timbered, ivy-clad pub called the Ploughman's Rest, which was where Heck's room had been booked. The green was surrounded on its other sides by whitewashed terraced cottages, craft shops, and village stores.

Detective Chief Inspector Will Royton appeared to suit this benign environment perfectly. He was a tall, well-built man in his late forties, with a bald pate and salt-and-pepper tufts behind his ears. He had an amiable air and a friendly face, and he greeted Heck in his office with a smile and a firm handshake.

'You found us all right?' he said, wasting no time in heading off down the adjacent corridor.

Heck followed. 'No problem, sir.'

'Only I'm a bit puzzled . . .' Royton glanced back as he walked. 'I mean about why the Serial Crimes Unit wants to look at the Lansing incident. Wouldn't have thought it'd be your cup of tea at all?'

Heck shrugged. 'There may be nothing in it for us, sir, but, I don't know, something about it caught my guv'nor's attention. I won't be in your way for long.'

At the end of the passage, a pair of glazed double doors gave through into the main CID office. Here, Royton paused to think. 'You mean caught her attention on the basis that it may actually have been a double homicide?'

'Too early to say, sir.'

'On the basis that it may be part of a *series* of homicides?'

'That would really be running before the horse to market.'

'Nevertheless . . . you wouldn't be here if that wasn't a possibility.'

'It's a very remote possibility.'

'A possibility is a possibility, Sergeant. For what it's worth, if something that serious is occurring on our patch, I'm glad you're on board. We can always use someone with expertise.'

They pushed through into the detectives' office, or DO as it was usually known, a modern, spacious area lined with desks, chairs, and computer terminals, but only occupied by one or two individuals at present, all of whom were beavering away at their desks. Royton led Heck to its farthest corner, where a large window half-covered by Venetian blinds gave out onto the village green. In front of this, two desks directly faced each other. A young woman was seated at the one on the right, tapping at a keyboard. She didn't look up as they approached.

'But I have to tell you,' Royton added, 'you're not the only one who found this event suspicious. DS Heckenburg, meet DC Gail Honeyford.'

The woman glanced round. She was even younger than Heck had first thought; in her mid-twenties at most, her lithe, youthful form accentuated by a tight blue skirt and blue silk blouse and scarf, her brunette tresses tied in a single ponytail. A pair of fashionable shades were perched above her fringe.

'Erm . . . hello,' Heck said, mildly confused.

'That's your desk.' Royton indicated the empty workstation. 'You've got a telephone line, computer link, everything you need. I thought this would be an appropriate place to put you, as you two will be working together.'

'Sir?'

'Gail's already on the Lansing case,' Royton explained.

Heck tried not to look as perplexed by that as he felt.

'Divisional CID here at Reigate Hall thought it a curious

incident too,' DC Honeyford said. 'Before Scotland Yard did, in fact.'

'Okay . . .'

'Something wrong?' Royton asked him.

'No sir, it's fine,' Heck said. 'Only no one told me.'

'Perhaps you should have asked?' DC Honeyford said. 'Just a thought.'

This is going to be great, Heck told himself.

'As long as we have an interest in this too, it seemed an obvious thing to put you two together,' Royton added. 'Create a two-man taskforce. You wouldn't want to do it *all* on your own, would you?'

'Well . . . as I say, sir, I'm only really here to see if this case fulfils the criteria for an SCU enquiry.'

'So you're not actually here to investigate the crash,' DC Honeyford said. It was an observation rather than a question.

'I was under the impression that had already been done.'

'Oh, this is superb.' She sat back as if her worst suspicions were confirmed. 'You're gonna be a load of help.'

'I'll do my best.' Heck fished the evidence sack from his pocket and tossed it onto her desk. 'Perhaps, while I'm getting my stuff from the car, you can log this in for DNA analysis?'

She peered down at it with distaste. 'That's a tooth.'

'Yep. Found it at the crash site.'

She glanced up. 'What were you doing there?'

'Nothing too strenuous.' Heck backed towards the door. 'Just my job.'

Chapter 7

It soon became evident to Heck that, while there were no obvious serial elements attached to the two attempts on Harold Lansing's life (if that was what they were), there was something vaguely weird about both. The fatal crash could conceivably have been an accident, though it was difficult to see how a man like Lansing, who had suffered no previous mishap on the roads and had no driving convictions, could have pulled out at such a dangerous spot without consulting the safety mirror first.

The previous incident was even more puzzling.

Lansing had owned a small fishing beat on a quiet stretch of the River Mole between Brockham and Sidlow; the rather unfortunately named Deadman's Reach. He was in the habit of spending several hours here each weekend, coarse fishing for barbel, bream, and chub. Not a particularly dangerous pastime, one might have thought, except that on the afternoon of Saturday 21 June a large(ish) model aeroplane, which Lansing only caught a fleeting glimpse of but later described as 'World War One style, and bluey-yellow', nosedived him from a considerable height. Lansing, who at the time was in his usual spot, standing with rod in hand on a small stone quay on the west bank, tried to dodge away, lost his footing, and fell into the river, which was running swift and deep. Some eighty yards further down, he was swept over a weir. Had it not been for another angler, who spotted him struggling under the surface and by pure good fortune happened to be a strong swimmer, Lansing would have died there and then.

But a model plane as a murder weapon?

Heck had never heard of such a thing.

Apparently a local flying club, the Doversgreen Aviators, had been using a meadow just behind Deadman's Reach at the time. All the club members who'd been present that day had been interviewed since, and all had insisted that the stringent safety regulations built into their sport had been strictly observed. None would admit to having lost control of their model aircraft, or even to having owned any model matching the description given. Lansing, though he'd half drowned and had been kept in hospital for quite a few days afterwards, had later told the police that he'd thought the plane, which had struck his arm as he'd tried to evade it, leaving a massive bruise, had then gone spinning out of control and landed in the water alongside him. The riverbank had later been searched but no such model was recovered.

Like the incident at Rosewood Grange, this whole thing read like an ultra-freakish accident, but two such events in two weeks – happening to the same person?

Heck pondered these unsatisfying facts later that afternoon as he parked his Peugeot in a car park to the rear of the Ploughman's Rest, booked himself in, and took a single heavy travel bag up to the room he'd been allocated, which was small, cosy, and neatly furnished, its lattice-paned, ivy-fringed window overlooking the green.

When he came back downstairs, he spotted Gail Honeyford in the snug. A smart suit jacket was draped over the back of her chair and a glass of what looked like iced lemonade sat on the table alongside her, but again she was tapping away on her laptop. He hadn't seen much of her after they'd been introduced that afternoon. Vacating the office for the pub was not unusual in CID circles when there was someone new in the team who needed 'breaking in', but it wasn't often the case that you fled to the pub to try and get some work done. Had she felt she was more likely to make progress with whatever she was doing if she didn't have to keep updating the new guy?

Heck wandered towards her, hands tucked into his jeans pockets. She watched him from the corner of her eye, but her facial language remained neutral.

'Mind if I join you?' he asked.

'Suppose it's a free country.'

'Was when I last checked.' She glanced at him fleetingly, unamused by the quip. He pulled up a chair. 'That was supposed to be a joke, by the way.'

'Hilarious.' She got on with her work.

'We've really started on the wrong foot, haven't we? Can I get you a drink maybe?'

'No thanks.'

'DC Honeyford . . . you ever heard the phrase "work with me"? I'm trying to be friendly here.'

'Yeah, I appreciate that, and look . . .' She sat back, her expression softening – which suited her. On closer inspection, she was peaches-and-cream pretty with fetching hazel eyes. 'I'm sorry if I've come over a little brusque. But you aren't going to be around here very long, so I don't see the point in us developing a relationship. Professional or otherwise.'

'Correct me if I'm wrong, but aren't we supposed to be forming a taskforce?'

'That was the boss's idea, not mine. I've already got this case covered.'

'Okay, fine. In the meantime, you sure you don't want that drink?'

'I'm sure. Thanks.'

Heck strolled to the bar, where the landlord, a jovial, beefy-cheeked local man with a frenzy of ginger hair was happy to serve him a pint of Best. When Heck sat down again, DC Honeyford clucked with barely disguised annoyance.

'Problem with the laptop?' he asked.

'No.'

'Good; perhaps we can get on then. What's the hypothesis?'

She glanced up. 'Pardon?'

'You've obviously done a lot of work on this, and I respect that massively. So what's your main theory?'

'If you must know, this is a murder – and it's almost certainly connected to Lansing's business affairs.'

'You're sure Lansing was the target, and not Dean Torbert?'

She glanced at him again, as if he was some kind of buffoon. 'If it wasn't Lansing, that model aeroplane attack was a hell of a coincidence.'

'Coincidences sometimes happen.'

'Torbert was a first-year university student. He hadn't lived long enough to upset anyone that badly.'

'How do we know he wasn't the one with the grudge? Perhaps it was Torbert who tried to run Lansing off the road, and it all went horribly wrong.'

'I've looked into that. They didn't even know each other, let alone have a grudge.'

'What's the background on Torbert?'

She shrugged. 'Spoilt little rich kid, boy racer . . . take your pick.'

'How did he come to own a Porsche?'

'Mummy and Daddy are both wealthy, and separated. Sounds like he bounced between them like a shuttlecock. They rivalled each other buying him expensive presents.'

'A Porsche?'

'Look – this is Surrey, stockbroker country.'

'Where did Torbert actually live?'

DC Honeyford sighed, not remotely afraid to show how frustrated the persistent questions were making her. 'With his mother. In a millionaire pad in Guildford.'

'I'm not a native, but that's nowhere near Reigate, is it?'

'It's not too far away, but I agree; it seems odd Torbert was over in that neck of the woods at such an early hour. No one knows what he was doing there. But it's no crime to drive around the county, is it? I mean, he may have had a girl this way – or even a boy. Who knows?'

Heck mulled this over. If Dean Torbert had simply been another bored youth who got his kicks tearing up and down the country lanes in his latest souped-up toy, it reinforced the impression that his involvement in this incident was no more than a bit of tragic misfortune. In fact, it would have been odd from Torbert's perspective if some kind of accident hadn't occurred. As a uniformed bobby up in Manchester, where, as a rule, idle young men did not get high-powered cars for Christmas, Heck had still watched on numerous occasions as their mutilated corpses were cut from heaps of twisted wreckage after a night spent blistering the blacktop.

'Torbert was just in the wrong place at the wrong time,' DC Honeyford added, clearly hoping to bring the conversation to an end.

'But overall, you still think this was murder?'

'Of course it was. But whoever did it lured Lansing out into the oncoming traffic to try and make it *look* like an accident. Any speeding road user would have done the job. Look, DS Heckenburg . . .' She seemed genuinely exasperated by his sudden appearance in her life, and had to take a second to compose herself. 'This thing *must* be connected to Lansing's professional life. He ran a chain of multi-million-pound companies. He's worth a fortune, but his finances are a tangled web. I've been trying to penetrate them for the last three days.'

'Who would stand to gain most from his death?' Heck asked.

'Why are you even interested? I thought you were only here to see if this was part of a series?'

Heck shrugged. 'If you can prove to me that it isn't, I'll happily go home. Then I won't have to stand here looking over your shoulder.'

'You won't be looking over my shoulder anyway!' she replied, her cheeks colouring. 'I can assure you of that!'

'Ahhh, so that's it. You're worried I'm going to steal your thunder.'

'No, of course I'm—' She paused, regarding him for a long time. Then, with slow, careful deliberation, she closed her laptop. 'Yes, if you want the truth. That's exactly what it is. Listen, DS Heckenburg . . .'

'Call me "Heck". All my friends do.'

'DS Heckenburg. I made CID in three years by showing nous and initiative. That's what I do. That's my thing. If I get a sniff of something, I chase it down. I work hard. I don't give up on it. The fact is, I wasn't at all happy when I heard the coroner's verdict on the Lansing case. But no one would listen to me. In fact, they said I was barmy.'

'That's because the gaffers don't like unsolved murders. Doesn't look good on the crime stats.'

She waved a hand, uninterested in his opinion. 'Will Royton only okayed me to look at this again because he's a decent bloke.'

'Not because he trusts your judgement?'

'Er . . . maybe a bit of that, but I had to badger him for two or three days before he was persuaded. Course, the truth is he's not even persuaded now. That's why I think

72

he's happy to see *you* here. He hopes you'll swan in, some big shot from the Smoke, and wrap this whole thing up in a single day. Then I can get back to my routine duties and there'll be no more discussion. Well sorry, but that isn't going to happen.'

Heck sipped at his pint. 'Sounds to me like you *want* Harold Lansing to have been murdered?'

'I didn't mean it like that.'

'Neither did I. I mean you want your instinct to have been proved right.'

'And that's somehow incorrect of me?'

'Not at all. Look.' Heck put his drink down. 'I'm here for a similar reason. Another officer looked at this case and felt the same way as you. You've been very honest, Gail, so I'll be honest too – I can call you "Gail"? Feels less formal than DC Honeyford.'

'Whatever.'

'I'm only actually in Surrey as a favour to my guv'nor, who's doing a favour for someone else. As soon as it becomes evident there's nothing in this case for SCU, I'll head home. I promise you. You'll have a clear run at it without any interference from the Yard. But for the moment it can only help if we work on this together. You've already gone out on a limb. I appreciate you're an independent-minded detective, but you must have felt pretty alone on this so far.'

She watched him warily. 'Just so long as you know I'm not your gofer.'

'Course not.'

'I know you work for a specialist outfit and all that, but I'm good at my job too.'

'I totally believe that.'

'I'm not going to be bossed around or made to feel like an office junior.'

Heck displayed empty palms. 'Not my style at all.'

'Someone else surrendering to your charms, Gail?' came a gruff but amused voice.

A man had approached them, unnoticed. He was tall, with a big, angular frame, clad in a rumpled brown suit and an open-necked green shirt. He had longish, sandy hair, pale blue eyes, and gruesomely pockmarked cheeks – as if he'd ploughed his fingernails through rampant acne while still a juvenile. He'd wandered over uninvited and now stood so close that Heck could smell his rank combination of cigarette smoke and cologne.

'What do you want, Ron?' Gail asked in a patient tone.

'Me?' He feigned hurt. 'Nothing . . . just a quick pleasantry.'

'That'd be a first.'

He chortled. 'Still wasting your time chasing ghosts at Rosewood Grange?'

Gail flicked her gaze to Heck. 'This is DS Pavey. Street Thefts.'

Heck glanced up at him. 'How are you?' he said, nodding.

'And who's this?' Pavey asked her, not bothering to respond to or even acknowledge Heck's question.

'This is DS Heckenburg. Serial Crimes, New Scotland Yard.'

Pavey gave a low whistle, and finally deigned to look round at Heck. 'Am I supposed to be impressed?'

'Up to you, I guess,' Heck replied.

Pavey turned back to Gail; evidently that question had been addressed to her too. 'You two working on something?'

'What's it to you, Ron?' she wondered.

Pavey smiled to himself before sauntering away to the bar. 'Don't do anything I wouldn't do, DS Heckenburg.'

'Dare I ask?' Heck said, watching him rejoin a group of several other suited men, presumably fellow detectives gathering for an end-of-shift drink.

Gail sipped her lemonade, though she'd flushed a noticeable shade of pink. The ice maiden wasn't perhaps as cool as she'd have him believe. 'Do you really need to?' she said.

'Idiot from the past, eh?'

'Not long enough in the past. Don't worry about it. He's gone.'

But several times over the next fifteen minutes, Heck caught DS Pavey stealing irritable peeks in their direction. From the expression on his ugly, notched face, it didn't look as if he'd gone very far.

Chapter 8

'So who arranged Lansing's funeral?' Heck asked.

'His former girlfriend,' Gail replied as she gunned her canary-yellow Fiat Punto along the twisting Surrey lanes. 'Monica Chatreaux.'

Heck glanced up from the paperwork littered across his lap. 'As in Monica Chatreaux the supermodel?'

'Correct.'

Heck mused on this. He was seated in the front passenger seat. Beyond the windows, woods and farmland skimmed past in sunny shimmers of green and gold.

'And was she *really* his former girlfriend . . . or just his friend?'

'Girlfriend apparently.'

'So he wasn't gay?'

Gail shook her head. 'I considered that possibility – bloke of his age living alone, but apparently not.'

Heck glanced again through the documentation. 'Death occurred on 6 July, funeral held on 16 July. Not a lot of time between the two.'

'Week and a half is about normal where I come from.'

'When there are sus circs?'

'Once the coroner had delivered his verdict, it was a bit difficult hanging on to the body.'

'So was Lansing cremated or buried?'

'Buried. Banstead Municipal Cemetery.'

'Good.'

She fired a glance at him. 'Good?'

'Yeah . . . if we need to dig him up again, we can.'

Gail shook her head at the mere thought, and returned her attention to the road, though at this early hour on a Saturday morning it was unlikely they'd meet much other traffic. In truth, Heck wasn't keen on the idea of exhumation either. He'd been present at several in his time, and it never failed to knock him sick. Lord alone knew what condition Lansing's body would be in by now. It was bad enough in the photos taken on first arrival at the mortuary. He flipped through them again, one after another.

The poor guy had effectively been chargrilled. All five layers of his epidermis had vanished. In its place lay a coating of crispy fat and melted muscle tissue. Here and there, nubs of bone gleamed amid the glutinous, oil-yellow pulp. Worst of all was Lansing's face. No distinctive features had remained. Most of the flesh was gone; the grey orbs of his eyes had sunk into their sockets like ruptured grapes; the bones themselves sagged inward, fragmented, reduced to a jigsaw puzzle.

'Died as a result of fourth-degree burns,' Heck noted, scanning the details of the postmortem. 'Yet it's interesting that his corpse displayed other significant traumas too.'

'Yeah, but all consistent with him having experienced a high-speed impact.'

'Was he wearing his seatbelt?'

'Difficult to say. The interior of the car was reduced to ashes. We think the airbag deployed.'

'And yet he still suffered extensive facial injuries?'

'I wondered about that too,' Gail said. 'Especially as it wasn't a head-on collision.'

'What's even odder is that this is a guy with no prior driving convictions and no previous insurance claims. He's as conscientious as they come, and yet we're expected to believe that he pulled out onto a main road without checking it was clear.'

She glanced at him again. 'When you say "we're expected to believe", what other choice do we have? That's evidently what he did?'

'And no drugs or alcohol in his system either,' Heck mused. 'I see he lost several teeth in the accident.'

'Most were discovered in his stomach.'

'Most but not all.'

'I've put a request through to have that one you found on the roadside fast-tracked. Don't see how it could have ended up out there when he was still in the car.'

'Neither do I.' Heck looked up as they entered the outskirts of Horsham. 'Course, it's not necessarily Lansing's tooth.'

'Don't fret, once we find the motive we'll find the method.' Gail spoke with an air of confidence. 'And that won't be difficult. Lansing was filthy rich. What better reason to knock someone off?'

'It depends. I asked you yesterday who his main beneficiaries are. We got distracted before you could answer.'

'His will was straightforward enough,' she replied. 'Written some time ago, with no suggestion that it's been altered since. He has no dependants, no relatives. Quite a bit of his estate was to be divided up between the various charities he supported. They're all squeaky clean, I've checked them. Monica Chatreaux's in for a cut. She gets Rosewood Grange . . .'

Heck assessed a shot of the 38-year-old supermodel which had once adorned the cover of *Vogue*: doe eyes and Cupid lips set beneath a glorious mop of tawny tresses.

'Interviewed her yet?' he asked.

'Not yet. Bear in mind she's a wealthy woman in her own right. She could probably have given Lansing a run for his money.'

'Just because you've already got a lot, that doesn't mean you don't want more.'

'Plus she's been out of the country for the last three months, doing fashion shoots in the States. She only came back for Lansing's funeral, and now she's gone over there again.'

'She could have hired someone to do the dirty deed.'

'I don't know . . .' Gail looked unconvinced. 'She and Lansing hadn't been an item for quite some time when it happened. They stopped dating about eleven months ago. Broke it off by mutual consent. No acrimony, no spat. Think she's dated someone else since.'

'How did she behave at the funeral?'

'With dignity. No histrionics.'

'But there *were* tears?'

'Yep.'

'You were there, you saw that?'

Gail nodded, but looked distracted as she negotiated the narrow streets around the pedestrianised square called the Carfax, in the centre of Horsham's shopping district.

'You don't fancy her for this, do you?' Heck said.

'She's a suspect; she *has* to be. But something in my gut tells me this is more to do with Lansing's finances.'

Heck glanced at another photo. This one had been lifted from a company website and portrayed a heavy-set man, thinning on top but nevertheless handsome and rather decorous. Rich white curls grew down both of his cheeks; he wore a navy-blue blazer over a white silk shirt and blue-striped tie. His name was Tim Baker, and he was the same age as Lansing – forty-five, which would be about right as they'd been chums since they'd schooled together at Eton.

But whereas Gail had her doubts about the involvement of Monica Chatreaux, Heck had similar doubts about the involvement of Tim Baker.

Baker was a 'sleeping partner' in many of Lansing's enterprises, owning 40 per cent of the shares to Lansing's 60, but he'd not been involved in their day-to-day operation because, as an investment banker, he had his own professional affairs to conduct. Given that Lansing's shares would now go to those recipients stipulated in his will, it would make the running of said companies a complex, time-consuming process. Hardly something Baker would have sought. It might even mean that several of those companies might now go under, so Baker stood to lose out even more.

Heck couldn't help but voice these doubts. 'Unless there's something we don't know, Tim Baker has everything to lose by Harold Lansing's death, and nothing to gain.'

'I'm sure there's quite a lot we don't know,' Gail replied.

They met Tim Baker in the hedged rear garden of his large Victorian townhouse in the suburb of Southwater. The lawn was expansive and bordered by deep beds of flowers. The banker, who looked older and more tired than in the photograph they'd seen online, was wearing slacks and a polo shirt, and hosted them at a small wrought-iron table set out in the middle of the grass.

Gail sat facing him, while Baker's rotund wife, a pleasant woman called Milly, provided them with beakers and a pitcher of orange squash filled with ice cubes and slices of real fruit. Heck preferred to stand, but accepted a beaker of juice.

Baker shook his head solemnly. 'Harold . . . well, he just wasn't into anything strange.'

'You seem very sure of that, Mr Baker,' Gail said.

'I ought to be. Every idea he ever had, he bounced off me first.'

'*Every* idea?'

Baker gave this some thought. 'Obviously I can't say every *single* idea; but, well, Harold was a straight bat. All his career – and I was there for most of it – there was never a hint of impropriety or shady dealing.'

'I understand he had various offshore bank accounts,' Gail said.

'My dear, that's not unusual. It's just to take advantage of different tax regimes. There's nothing illegal about it if it's all declared. I'm sure if you consult your financial intelligence people, you'll find there's never been anything in Harold's business past to arouse suspicion.'

'What were you doing on the morning of 6 July, Mr Baker?' Heck asked him.

'Ahhh . . . I might have thought I'd be a suspect.'

'I'm sorry we have to ask this.'

'No it's all right. I completely understand.' Baker fingered his brow. 'I was on holiday with Milly. We were on a month-long cruise, the Caribbean and American East Coast. We had no idea Harold had even had his first accident, let alone the second one. Only got back a couple of days before he was due to be buried. I must say . . .' He eyed them warily. 'I'm rather surprised by these enquiries. I mean with Harold in his grave. Everyone was under the impression it was all just ghastly misfortune.'

'We're not ruling out anything at this stage,' Gail said.

'But you suspect foul play?'

'We just don't know,' Heck replied.

Baker blew out a sigh. 'Well you obviously have to cover every possibility. It's unbelievable, to be honest. Harold was a genuine good egg. If you look at some of the things he did in his spare time . . . he was a governor of the local grammar school, he sat on several church committees, put money into numerous charities. Why on earth would anyone want to hurt him, let alone kill him?'

'Could it be a disgruntled ex-employee?' Heck wondered.

'Harold was always popular with his staff. He was a good leader, a firm decision-maker. He respected them as individuals, he was concerned for their welfare, he took responsibility during a crisis.'

'Because you see, Mr Baker,' Heck watched him carefully, 'it's occurred to me that if someone was trying to get even with Mr Lansing for some past grievance – maybe an imagined grievance – they might want to get even with *you* as well.'

'Oh, Sergeant . . .' Baker sighed again, as if this was a minor concern. 'No face or name springs to mind in that regard, not even from the mists of time.'

If nothing else, Heck thought, *this guy is not frightened. He's telling me what he believes to be the truth.*

Baker shook his head. 'I can't think of a single person who Harold and I might have upset so much that he would resort to vengeance on this scale.'

'Lansing's too good to be true, isn't he?' Gail said as they drove back towards Reigate.

Heck glanced round at her. 'How do you mean?'

'All that "holy Joe" stuff,' she said cynically. 'I don't know why they don't just give him a sainthood.'

'There are good people in the world you know.'

'You really believe that?' She chuckled. 'After some of the cases the Serial Crimes Unit's investigated? I've looked you up, in case you were wondering. The Nice Guys Club, the Desecrator killings . . . that business up in the Lake District? And you still have idealistic notions about human nature?'

Heck didn't reply. Fleetingly he was lost in thought.

'This is a different ballgame, of course,' she added. 'These white-collar criminals – they're not drooling nutters running around with meat cleavers. They're clever. They can squirrel all sorts of important stuff away where it won't be found. I can see you have doubts about that, Heck, and you must do whatever you feel is necessary; but I intend to go through Lansing's business transactions with a magnifying-glass. Let's see who gets to the bottom of it first, eh?'

That final comment caught his attention. 'You mean like we're in a contest together?'

'Well, not exactly a contest . . .'

'I should hope not. We're on the job, in case you'd forgotten. Not playing stupid bloody games!'

'All right, take it easy!'

'You know . . .' Heck forcibly moderated his tone, not wanting to pull rank so quickly when he'd promised that he wouldn't. 'Gail, if you want to follow that line, be my guest. But good luck to you. I've no experience investigating white-collar crime, if that's what you want to call it, and I've been a detective fifteen years. To start with, you'll have to liaise with FIU, the Serious Fraud Office, probably the City of London Police – and on the basis of what? Unfounded conjecture. On top of that, you're going to attract a lot of publicity you don't want.'

'Like I care about bad publicity.'

'Think about this, Gail. Harold Lansing is the victim, possibly of a catastrophic accident, but more likely of a skil-fully stage-managed murder. Either way, it resulted in him being burned alive. And you're trying to uncover evidence of criminality in *his* past.'

'It's only a means to an end.'

'You'd better hope there is an end. Because you blacken the name of a pillar of the community like Harold Lansing, someone with high-powered friends all over the county, and it's not inconceivable that your career, which I have a feeling you are very concerned about, might suddenly hit the buffers.'

Gail drove for several minutes without speaking. 'Okay. So what's *your* theory?'

'I don't have one yet. But I think we need to go back to the beginning.'

'What do you mean?'

'Back to where it all kicked off. Let's try to understand exactly what's happened.'

Chapter 9

The River Mole was one of the most scenic waterways in southern England, snaking eighty miles from its headwaters near Gatwick Airport in West Sussex across the rolling Surrey Weald to its confluence with the River Thames close to Hampton Court. It boasted an abundant diversity of wildlife, from water voles, herons and kingfishers on its banks to all types of game fish – eels, brown trout, lamprey and pike – in its cool green depths.

There were several rapids along the Mole, but Deadman's Reach, which Heck and Gail finally located after leaving the Punto in a National Trust car park and walking several hundred yards along a well-trodden towpath, was located in a broad, shallow valley through which the river meandered at a sedate pace, though Heck felt this was probably deceptive. He'd researched the Mole the previous night, and had learned that its flow rate was highly responsive to rainfall. Though this past June and July had largely been warm and dry, there'd been heavy rain in April and May, which might suggest why Harold Lansing had so easily been swept away.

The Reach itself was a jutting promontory of aged brickwork, a quayside in the past, though with hunks of rusted

85

metal where mooring ropes had once been tied and tufts of weed growing around its footings there was no sign it was used for that purpose now. Some eighty yards to the north-west, the river plunged over the lip of a weir into a flat rocky basin before curving away through lower lying water meadows.

Heck halted and glanced around, wafting at midges. Both to east and west, the gentle slopes of the valley were thinly wooded. Immediately beyond the footpath, thick stands of gorse ascended to the skyline. He weaved his way up through these, Gail following, until they reached a stile, beyond which lay level pasture land. This was most likely the spot where the Doversgreen Aviators flew their model planes, though there was nobody here at present.

Heck shielded his eyes against the sun. Several hundred yards to the west, occasional vehicles flashed by along a main road. A similar distance to the north-east, more sporadic traffic passed over a bridge with iron latticework sides which crossed the river, running west to east. Satisfied, he turned back to the stile and, rather to Gail's irritation, commenced a slow, cautious descent back to the riverbank. It wasn't easy for either of them, he in his suit and lace-up leather shoes, she in her skirt.

At the bottom, Heck leafed through their sheaf of paper-work. 'This guy who saved Lansing after he fell in . . . Gary Edwards. Where was he exactly?'

'That headland.' Gail pointed past the weir to a bend in the river about fifty yards short of the iron bridge.

'But he didn't actually see Lansing fall into the river?'

'No. Nor the plane as it made contact. Apparently Lansing screamed for help as he was going over the weir. That's when Edwards noticed he was in trouble. He told me he'd seen the model planes buzzing around overhead, but hadn't thought much about them. He said they're here every other weekend, usually too high up to pose any kind of problem for walkers or anglers.'

Heck read through Gary Edwards's statement. Edwards was young, only twenty-five, but fit; apparently he played football for a local amateur club. 'How high is too high?'

'About sixty to seventy feet.'

'And what do we know about Edwards?'

'He's clean. Well, he's not in the system.'

Heck thought about this. 'That meadow where they fly these planes is . . . what would you say, fifty, sixty yards in that direction?' She nodded. He mused again. 'Only a stone's throw. Wouldn't be difficult for the odd one or two planes to stray over this way.'

'Gary Edwards said he's seen that occasionally, but he's never seen any of them come down to ground level. I think there are rules governing that.'

Heck nodded. 'There are. It's a code of conduct laid down in the Air Navigation Order. The main elements of it, for our purposes, stipulate that the fly zone must be unobstructed, the model craft must at all times be a safe distance from persons, vessels, vehicles and structures, and – this is the really important bit – must never leave the sight of the operator at any time.'

'I see . . .'

'I saw that online, just in case you were thinking I'm a bottomless pit of knowledge.'

She shrugged. 'The main thing is I've already taken statements from the Doversgreen Aviators.'

'Yeah, I've read them. They're not having it, are they?'

'Not a single one will admit responsibility.'

'Surely that doesn't surprise you?' Heck walked back along the towpath. 'Even if it was an honest accident, it could lead to prosecution by the Civil Aviation Authority.'

'Okay, so where are we going now?'

'For a pint.'

'Come again?'

'You know a pub called the Ring O'Bells?'

'Sure. It's next to the local parish church.'

'Good – that's where they're meeting us.'

'Who is?'

'The Doversgreen Aviators.' Heck checked his watch. 'In approximately twenty-five minutes.'

'And when did you arrange that?'

'I rang their club chairman last night. Wasn't difficult, his details are on the website. I said I wanted them at their usual watering hole at two this afternoon. It's Saturday, so there shouldn't be a problem.'

'And he agreed, did he?' She sounded amused. 'Just like that?'

'Yep.'

'Or so he said.'

'I told him I didn't need every member there; just the eighteen who were present at the meeting on 21 June.'

'Some chance.'

'Chance won't come into it.' Heck diverted from the path up a gravel track to the car park. 'I told their chairman the alternative was that we visit them all at home, with search warrants and a view to seizing their model aircraft for forensic examination. I made sure he understood that anyone whose craft shows signs of recent damage, or recent immersion in water, or maybe has threads of unexplained fabric connected to it, no matter how microscopic, may have to answer questions under caution.'

They'd now reached Gail's Punto. She regarded him over its roof as she unlocked the driver's door. 'Bit heavy-handed, don't you think?'

'What was that phrase you used – means to an end?'

*   *   *

The vault of the Ring O'Bells was a small side chamber into which only a corner of the bar protruded. Its low, smoke-browned ceiling was supported by heavy oak beams. Its handsome original features served to create the aura of a confined space, as did the double doors to the beer garden when they were closed – as they were now.

The eighteen members of the Doversgreen Aviators were crammed in like so many sardines, sitting along the benches, standing in corners, clustered around the brass-topped tables. They were exclusively male, but every group was represented, from teenagers to the husky middle-aged. Most looked like countrymen – weather-beaten faces, wild hair, patched woollen jumpers, but there were also shirts and dicky bows on view, even the occasional walking stick.

Not one of them had ordered a drink. Instead they sat or stood perfectly still, regarding Heck in silence as he leaned against the bar. He'd already checked, and found that none of the nervous faces in front of him had a criminal record. That was perhaps to be expected, as he didn't actually believe that any of these weekend recreationists would be a regular offender.

'Okay . . .' He cleared his throat.

They listened with rapt attention.

He glanced at Gail, who was standing in front of the double doors, equally fascinated to know what was coming next.

'I'm Detective Sergeant Heckenburg from the Serial Crimes Unit. You already know Detective Constable Honeyford, as you've all given statements to her in the recent past. Statements in which you acquit yourselves and your fellow club members of any wrongdoing. Which is unfortunate, because I have to tell you that I'm not at all satisfied by that . . . not least because this sad affair is looking like it may turn into a murder enquiry. I don't mean it possibly will, I mean it *probably* will.'

He scanned them with his best 'interview room' intensity. There were more than a few facial tics. Several brows had moistened with sweat.

'Excuse me,' one of them said. It was the club chairman. His name was Rex Murgatroyd; he was a tall, elegant sixty-year-old, wearing a tweed suit. 'I understood that Mr Lansing died in a car crash?'

'You've been following the case,' Heck said. 'Excellent – that'll save us a few explanations.'

'But how is that anything to do with us?'

'It's quite simple, Mr Murgatroyd. I'd like to dismiss you all from this enquiry. But before I can do that, I need to know the exact truth about what happened at Deadman's Reach on 21 June. How is it that Harold Lansing was knocked into the river by a model aircraft?'

There was a discomforted shuffling of feet.

'I've already explained to you gentlemen that the stakes have been raised significantly since you were last interviewed. If anyone has something to tell me, now would be the time. Perhaps you lost control of your model? Perhaps it wasn't adequately fuelled? If anything like that happened, I need to know right now. So stick your hand up.'

Their hands stayed resolutely down. They fixed him with bright, unblinking stares.

Heck folded his arms. 'I can assure you that we are not going to let this drop. So the next thing I'll do, if I'm forced to, is look through the statements that you men gave to DC Honeyford. I'll be taking very careful note of who said what, so when I find the person responsible for the incident at Deadman's Reach, I may also be charging him with perverting the course of justice. And that could mean prison.'

The Aviators exchanged haggard glances.

'Up to you, fellas. Come clean now. Tell me what happened, and that mendacious statement can be filed in the dustbin.'

He was pleased to see a number of downcast eyes, various bottoms squirming on seats. One more layer of menace should do it.

'And if there's anyone here who may be trying to protect a friend – say, for example, you happen to know that one of your fellow Aviators owns a model plane matching the one involved in this incident, and now all of a sudden there's no sign of it, and you've decided not to say anything – well, let me tell you what such misguided loyalty is going to cost you: *all* your other friends.' Heck's taut gaze roved from one to the next. 'If I walk away from this pub without an adequate answer, I'll be getting straight in touch with the Civil Aviation Authority, not to mention the British Model Flying Association, expressing grave doubts about your group's suitability to function. I'll make sure they know exactly what happened down at Deadman's Reach, and exactly how uncooperative you were with the resulting investigation.'

'But please,' Rex Murgatroyd said. 'We can't cooperate if we don't know anything.'

'You think the CAA will buy that?' Heck said. 'You think they'll believe it was someone else's plane that knocked Harold Lansing into the River Mole? Will they write it off as mere coincidence that you guys were right on the spot where it happened?'

'Sergeant Heckenburg . . . please,' Murgatroyd insisted. 'None of us is responsible for this incident. I would know, I'm sure.'

'I'd like to believe that, Mr Murgatroyd, but how do you expect me to?' And yet, in truth, Heck *was* starting to believe it. The silence greeting him was not the stubborn bull-headedness of seasoned suspects. By their body language alone, these men weren't being furtive – they were disconcerted, alarmed, frightened.

Gail seemed to sense this too. 'Look, guys,' she said,

'Harold Lansing did not die as a result of what happened at Deadman's Reach. At the end of the day, an accident is an accident. There'll be no far-reaching consequences for his being knocked into the river. But we need to establish what happened.'

Still there was no reply.

'Did any of you film the meeting on 21 June?' Heck asked.

Murgatroyd shrugged. 'Not officially.'

'Unofficially?'

Hesitantly, one of the men, the youngest there – a scruffy youth of no more than eighteen – put a hand up. At the same time, he placed a mobile phone on the nearest table. 'I . . . I don't know how much you'll be able to see,' he said in a reedy voice. 'It was just a fun day, you know. I shot a few minutes' worth. That's all.'

'And you are?' Heck said.

'Ed Pritchard.'

'Want to show it to us, Ed?' Gail said.

The youth did as they asked, and they had to squint to watch a series of confusing, apparently meaningless events unfold on a small, badly pixellated screen. The image cavorted back and forth, whipping from face to face, down to scuffed boots on green grass, and back up to clear blue sky, where a clutch of minuscule, insect-like objects wove in and out of each other. There was distorted shouting and laughter, and a very distant drone of tiny engines. Occasionally, when the camera's eye returned to the level, men were visible – some of them identifiable among those gathered in the pub – standing in groups, eyes shielded against the sun as they operated their controls.

In total, it lasted no more than four and a half minutes. After they'd watched it through a second time, Heck knuckled at his chin. 'Ed, can you email this video to me?'

'Erm . . . yeah.' The youth looked surprised as he took

the ID card Heck was offering, which held all the necessary contact details. 'But it doesn't show anything, does it?'

'Why don't you let us decide? If you can send it now, that'd be great.'

Five minutes later, with the Doversgreen Aviators – many of them in a mild daze that they'd actually been released – trooping stiffly out of the pub, Heck and Gail had settled at a quiet table in the fireplace nook where, thanks to the pub's free wi-fi, they were able to access Heck's emails on his laptop. They ran through the flying club footage again, now as a blown-up image. One minute in, Heck advised Gail to take note of the vehicles, which the camera occasionally glimpsed parked in a row on one side of the meadow.

'And what's that supposed to signify?' she asked.

'Just wait . . .' Another minute in, he hit pause and thumbed at a different part of the image. It was distant and blurred, and had only been captured fleetingly, though on this larger screen it was more evident what they were looking at: another vehicle, but this one parked alone on the iron bridge over the river.

Gail said nothing while Heck advanced the MPEG slowly.

The vehicle on the bridge, though no details of its actual make or model were distinguishable, looked like a four-by-four of some sort and was metallic green in colour; it was visible on each occasion the camera flirted by, in exactly the same position.

'That motor was there at least as long as Ed Pritchard was filming,' Heck said.

'There could be any reason for that.'

'One of which might be so that a non-club member could fly his own model plane.'

'And hope it wouldn't get noticed because of all the others, you mean?'

Heck nodded.

Gail mused. 'And then use it to strike at Harold Lansing, assuming we would blame the resulting death or injury on the incompetence of the Doversgreen Aviators?'

'Which is exactly what happened, isn't it?'

She sipped her lemonade. 'Interesting thought, but pure guesswork.'

Heck pondered. 'I can't see any other obvious reason why anyone would park on that bridge, can you?'

'Unless they wanted to watch the model aircraft?'

'It's quite a distance away.'

She twisted her lips as she gave it further thought. From the corner of his eye, Heck caught the last of the Aviators drifting towards the pub exit. 'Excuse me,' he called. 'Mr Murgatroyd?'

The club chairman ventured over. He still looked a little nervous.

'I notice from this video that you chaps usually park on the meadow where you fly your planes?' Heck said.

'We have full permission, I assure you.'

'I don't doubt it. But do any of you ever park on the surrounding lanes?'

Murgatroyd looked puzzled. 'Not to my knowledge. What would be the point? There's ample room on the meadow.'

'And do any of your members drive a metallic green four-by-four?'

'No such vehicle springs to mind. I can certainly find out and let you know.'

'If you would that'd be excellent . . . again ASAP, yeah?'

Murgatroyd nodded and shuffled away.

Gail regarded the image on the screen, still undecided about what she was seeing. 'Heck . . . you don't think this a tiny bit fanciful?'

'Only one way to know for sure.'

They found their way to the bridge some fifteen minutes

later, and were able to park the Punto on the same side of it where they'd seen the four-by-four. The road crossing over the bridge was easily wide enough to permit this – occasional passing vehicles were unimpeded, though the pavements to either side were very narrow. Heck climbed onto the latticed barrier, and found that he could see along the river valley for several miles. It made a peaceful scene, the curved waterway gliding lazily between fertile terraces, only broken by the brief foamy obstacle of the weir. Deadman's Reach was easily identifiable – Harold Lansing must have made a solitary but distinct figure standing down there alone.

'Perfect vantage point from which to fly a model plane,' Heck said. 'He could even sit in his car and do it, so there'd be even less chance he'd be spotted.'

Gail was still pondering this when her mobile rang. 'Yeah, DC Honeyford?' She moved away from the barrier.

Heck peered again along the valley. If his thesis was correct, someone had gone to an awful lot of trouble, and it had very nearly worked. Harold Lansing's death would almost certainly have been written off as a fatal accident, with the Aviators carrying the can – the only problem was that Harold Lansing hadn't died. Not on that first occasion.

'That was the lab,' Gail said, coming back round the car. He climbed down from the lattice. 'And?'

'That tooth you found on the roadside belonged to Harold Lansing.'

'Thought it probably did.'

'There's something else.' She chewed her lip. 'A trace of foreign DNA, in other words someone else's blood, is embedded in the tooth cavity.'

Heck felt a stirring among his neck hairs. 'So he was punched in the mouth?'

'Or he bit someone.' She pocketed her phone and glanced again towards Deadman's Reach. 'The problem is, the foreign

DNA is unknown to us. They've run it, and there are no comparisons anywhere on the database. So it doesn't really confirm much.'

'Well . . . it confirms Harold Lansing was murdered. You must admit, that's a step forward.'

Chapter 10

'He must have been outside the car at some point, otherwise his errant tooth couldn't have ended up in the roadside undergrowth,' Heck said.

Gail pondered this as they walked the stretch of lane outside Rosewood Grange. It was now two days since Heck had arrived in Surrey and though she had taken the Sunday off, he apparently hadn't because it was only Monday morning and already, at his request, extensive crime-scene tape and forensic shelters had been deployed along several sections of the verge, and a single uniformed bobby was on guard; he currently stood by the left gatepost, lunchbox in hand, chomping his way through a pile of cheese sandwiches. Despite this, both Heck and Gail knew that no specialist analysis of the scene would be authorised unless they came up with something fairly conclusive; in fact, unless they found something soon, they'd lose the site security as well.

'I don't know,' she replied. 'Hot summer day . . . his tooth got knocked out on impact, went flying through an open window.'

'That's a stretch.'

'You're saying you think he survived the impact and got out?'

'And had an altercation with someone.'

'The other driver maybe?'

'Nah. Dean Torbert was killed instantly in the crash. Or so his postmortem said.'

'A passenger?'

'Could be. But according to the accident investigation team, there was no sign of a passenger in either of the two vehicles.'

'And yet, somehow or other, Lansing finished up back inside his burning vehicle?'

Heck nodded. 'A third party is the only explanation.'

She pursed her lips. 'I must admit, someone else leaving a speck of blood in Lansing's mouth is pretty undeniable.'

'I hoped Will Royton might have given us a couple of extra bodies.'

She considered. 'Will's onside, but even he has to balance the books. He probably hasn't got that many bodies to spare. He was playing devil's advocate when I spoke to him this morning. Even suggested Lansing might have been having sex with someone before he set out. Bit a tongue, bit a lip – it happens, doesn't it?'

'Monica Chatreaux wasn't even in the country at the time.'

'Perhaps it was someone else? His housekeeper? That happens too.'

Heck glanced sidelong at her. 'His housekeeper is married. Plus she's sixty-eight.'

'You never know.'

'That's pushing it. Anyway, she was away. And if you want my opinion, that in itself is a contrivance. What're the chances that if this was a genuine accident, it occurred in a week when both the gardener and the housekeeper were absent; in other words when there was nobody else here to witness the event?'

'Agreed.'

Heck gazed at the tree trunk directly across from the drive entrance, and the mirror positioned on it. 'But how do you engineer an accident like this? How do you ensure someone will drive out into the path of a speeding vehicle?'

Gail shrugged. 'You can't. But if you knew the driver was going to pull out at a certain time, I suppose it's not inconceivable you could arrange for someone to be driving past at that particular moment. And by all accounts, Lansing was regular as clockwork. His housekeeper said he left the house on the dot of seven every morning. It was near enough a compulsion.'

Heck wasn't convinced. 'Presumably not such a compulsion that he'd pull out in front of oncoming traffic . . . which his safety mirror would clearly have revealed to him?'

'Perhaps he just didn't check it that morning?'

'And as the mastermind behind the plan, how do you ensure *that* happens?'

She shrugged again, before turning to the PC on guard duty. He'd been under orders to take note of any passing vehicles whose drivers or passengers showed interest in the house or the tents along the roadside, and now dug out his pocket-book to share the number plates with her. Meanwhile Heck approached the mirror and stared into its convex glass. At first he thought it was his imagination that the reflection it cast was blurred around the edges, but then he looked a little closer and noticed paper-thin smears of a semi-transparent, paste-like substance. When he tapped it with the tip of a pen, he saw that it had hardened into a resin.

'Glue?' he muttered.

An idea was slowly forming. Had the mirror been covered by something, deliberately obscured? But if so, why had Lansing pulled out when he wasn't sure the road was clear? Behind him, Heck could hear Gail chatting with the uniform.

He tapped at the resinous substance again. Definitely hardened glue. He was about to call Gail over, when something else – or rather some*one* – caught his eye.

A previously unnoticed figure stood alongside another tree trunk several dozen yards back from the road, on the other side of a low, barbed-wire fence. It was difficult to say how long he'd been there; it was equally difficult to say how Heck had managed to miss him before. He was a huge guy, at least six foot four and heavily overweight. He wore khaki trousers and a khaki combat jacket, the latter of which bulged over his waistband. His pink, porcine face was fringed with red-gold sideburns and a straggling, red-gold beard. Similarly coloured, straw-like hair poked out from under a battered green bush hat.

The figure turned and walked quickly away.

'Hello?' Heck called after him. 'Hey, mate!'

The guy began to run, weaving through the trees towards open ground.

'*Hey!*' Heck shouted, dashing to the barbed wire.

'What's up?' came Gail's voice from behind. He turned fleetingly, spotting her crossing the road.

'Not sure . . .' Heck didn't fancy a foot-race over open countryside. But the burly figure was already diminishing from view. Pretty soon he'd be out of the coppice and onto the open ground. 'Someone's interested in our crime scene but doesn't want to talk to us. Get that foot soldier to put something over the mirror. And tell him not to put his fingers on it. Meantime, you take the car and see if you can head this bugger off.'

'How am I supposed to know where he's running to?' she called as Heck lurched over the fence.

'You've more chance of guessing correctly than me.' Heck broke into a run, immediately stumbling on loose soil and slimy roots.

The khaki-clad shape had now emerged into the open, and was sprinting downhill into a shallow valley. His garb might suggest that he was an outdoorsman but, as Heck had already seen, he was in poor condition. He surely couldn't keep that pace up for long. Not that Heck was sure *he* could either. Swearing, he yanked at the tie-knot constricting his throat.

'Hey!' he shouted again, emerging from the trees. Somewhere behind, he heard the Punto's engine rumble to life. He snatched the radio from his pocket as he tottered down an increasingly difficult gradient. He and Gail had each other's mobile numbers, but had also secured a private radio channel by which to converse on talk-through.

'Heck to Honeyford,' he shouted.

'*Go ahead,*' came her reply, the Punto engine revving – it sounded as if she was pulling a rapid three-point turn.

'Any idea what's on the other side of this valley, over?'

'*Probably another one. It's all farmland around here . . .*'

Heck descended to the valley bottom, where, from a distance, it had appeared to level out again, though now that he was actually here it comprised rough, undulating pasture, which was just as difficult to run across in shoes. Again he half stumbled, his smooth soles sliding on the sun-dried grass. Fifty yards ahead, a ribbon of brown, fast-flowing water was visible beyond a belt of hawthorn breaks. The khaki-clad figure threaded his way through towards this and vanished from sight.

'Heck to Honeyford – there's a river down here!'

'*Yeah, that's the Fosswick,*' she replied. '*It's a small tributary of the Mole. That may be where he comes unstuck. The only way he can get across is if he heads north towards the Charlwood Bridge. See if you can shepherd him in that direction, over.*'

'Wilco,' Heck panted. He shouted out again as he approached the hawthorns. 'Look, mate . . . I only want to talk to you! I'm a police officer!'

101

From what he could see, the hawthorns were ranked at least five deep, but the path his quarry had taken, though rutted and well used, did not cut through them cleanly. As Heck followed it, it weaved between shadowy dells and dense stands of thorn. Overhead, branches and leafage interwove to create a ceiling. He slowed to a cautious walk, breathing hard, sweat soaking his shirt under his armpits. He could hear the muffled burble of the river, which from the glinting flickers of sunlight lay only a few yards ahead.

'Look!' he called out again. 'You're not in any trouble.'

Twigs rustled behind him.

He spun round.

Several leafy boughs were quivering on the left of the path. He approached, one arm outstretched to push the foliage aside. Only for it to explode right in his face – and for three frightened woodpigeons to scutter away through the canopy.

Involuntarily, Heck jumped backwards – at which point he spotted something else.

A small sack-like net, with a drawstring at its opening, hung from one of the lower branches. Possibly it had been yanked from his quarry's pocket as he'd blundered through here, catching himself on the undergrowth. Below it, a sharp, heavy-bladed knife stood at a slant, its tip buried in the earth. Heck assessed both items quickly before plodding on towards the river, and emerging onto its bank. The Fosswick was indeed nothing more than a tributary, only about twenty yards across but flowing fast and deep; apart from its immediate muddy shallows he couldn't see the bottom. It dwindled away for several hundred yards to left and right before curving out of sight. No one was visible in either direction, or on the opposite shore, though on that side the undergrowth came right up to the water so it was difficult to be sure. On this side, the river was edged by a broad path, where the grass had been churned by the passage of hooves, suggesting it was also used as a bridleway.

Remembering what Gail had said about the Charlwood Bridge, he turned in the direction he thought was north. Radio static crackled in his pocket.

'*Where are you?*' Gail asked.

'On the bank of the Fosswick.'

'*I'm at the bridge, and there's no sign of you.*'

'I think I've lost him. Just keep watching the river. I'm heading that way in a sec.' Heck doubled back a couple of yards, pulled on a disposable glove and picked up the knife by the tip of its hilt. He slipped it into an evidence sack and wrapped it in a handkerchief before inserting it into his pocket.

'*What did he run for?*'

'Damn good question.'

Heck shoved the radio back into his pocket, and tramped on, now following the course of the river – at which point, his target stepped out onto the path some twenty yards in front. Heck froze in mid-stride. In the same instant, the target realised he had company, and glanced left. His mouth dropped open in a perfect O. Then he turned and clumped away. Heck gave chase again, but now from a lot closer. He could hear the grunting and puffing of his quarry, though the guy was really going for it – he did *not* want to be caught, and as he sensed Heck gaining on him he increased his pace and lengthened his stride. They rounded a bend in the river, and Heck saw a sheer stone-built wall looming ahead, rising maybe forty feet. The river vanished underneath it through a black, semi-circular tunnel mouth. The diminutive form of Gail peered down from the high parapet.

At the same time the slopes to either side of the river steepened, the hawthorns giving way to thickly clustered birch and alder. One after another, sub-paths diverged from the river's edge, winding upwards among the trees. But the fugitive, who had probably reasoned that he couldn't attempt an uphill dash with Heck so close, ploughed resolutely on, and now that they were only thirty yards from the tunnel mouth Heck saw why: a remnant of the riverbank continued through it – a narrow strip of pebbles and sandy sediment, just sufficient for a man to sidle his way along.

As the fugitive ducked beneath the rugged arch and disappeared from view, Heck indicated to Gail to try and get down the other side. She too vanished from sight. Heck also ducked beneath the arch, and found himself negotiating a shifting shelf of river rubble. Icy wavelets lapped over his shoes. The curved roof of dripping, mould-encrusted rock bent him leftwards, threatening to unbalance him as he advanced. But the sight of the fugitive, an ungainly form silhouetted on the blot of light about forty yards ahead, gave him new energy.

'Pack it up, man!' Heck shouted, his voice echoing over the hiss of the water. 'Come on, this is ridiculous!' Then he slipped – only slightly, a cobblestone tilting under his tread – and his left ankle turned, white fire streaking up his leg.

'Damn!' Heck shouted hoarsely. 'Goddamn it!'

Ahead, his prey glanced round once before exiting the tunnel.

Heck stumbled after him, but when he emerged into daylight it was on open grassland, which slanted up to his right. The hefty form of the fugitive was already halfway to the top, ascending at a virtual crawl but perhaps having taken heart from Heck's injury.

'Damn bloody fool!' Heck spat as he followed.

His ankle ached abominably, and within ten minutes of commencing the climb he was limping, his body angled forward, mouth agape as he struggled to suck in sufficient oxygen to keep his muscles pumping. At the crest of the slope there was a slatted wooden fence with a steel farm gate in the middle. Heck was about thirty yards short of this when the fugitive reached it and, with much wheezing, clambered over the top. Heck swore again, volubly. When he reached the gate himself, it was only about eight feet high, but it might as well have been eighteen. He hauled his weary, sweating body over the top, landing heavily on the other side, which sent a fresh spasm of pain through his ankle. From here, a stony track led over rough pasture – but there was no sign of the fugitive. Heck prowled forward, confused, until a dozen yards later, when he noticed a derelict, weatherboarded structure on his left. It was a barn, nestling amid a clutch of trees.

Heck veered towards it, by logic as much as instinct. He himself was exhausted after traversing such rough ground, so how did his overweight quarry feel? He surely couldn't keep going at this rate, not without inducing a coronary.

The barn's main door stood wide open, but Heck hesitated before entering. When no sound reached his ears, he ventured forward – to be assailed by a pungent mix of farm odours: oil, straw, rancid, age-old manure. Sunlight shafting through the decayed planking revealed most of the empty interior. He saw a beaten earth floor, fragments of rusting machinery, empty seed bags, veils of cobweb . . . and unless he was mistaken, plumes of dust, which had recently been kicked up.

Heck glanced overhead to where a dark, heavy beam ran crosswise, linking two separate haylofts. On top of the right one a stack of old bales, five large cubes of matted, rotted vegetation, teetered on the very edge. It might have been an optical illusion caused by the dimness, but even as Heck gazed up he fancied eddies of fresh dust were trickling down – and that the bales were moving slightly.

He tried to leap sideways, but his sprained ankle sent

105

another white-hot lance up his shinbone. He twisted and fell full-length, but still had the wherewithal to roll away as, one after another, the massive hundredweights of mulch impacted on the floor behind him, exploding apart.

As debris showered over him, Heck glimpsed a burly shape descending a vertical ladder in the far corner. But only as he got to his feet did it register that his assailant was wielding a pitchfork. The fugitive had lost his bush hat, revealing longish red-gold locks, stringy with sweat, and, somewhat incongruously, a bald cranium. But there was nothing comical about the way he stalked forward, his two-pronged weapon levelled on Heck's belly.

'Look, pal,' Heck said, backing away. 'Whatever you've done, I'm sure you realise this is only going to make it a hell of a lot worse.'

The giant's mottled face broke into a desperate grin as they circled each other. His eyes – one blue and one green – were bright but glassy, like mismatched buttons; his unruly beard had filled with spittle. 'You ain't sending me to court, copper.'

'And this is how you hope to achieve that?'

'I'm not going back to prison. Not for nobody . . .'

The pitchfork was old and corroded, but its twin points still looked sharp enough to rip through flesh and the soft organs beneath.

'All I want to do is ask you some questions,' Heck said.

'*I ain't going!*' The fugitive drove the pitchfork at Heck's midriff.

Not as agile on a single leg, Heck only just managed to evade it. Before he could counterstrike, his opponent had retracted the weapon and pivoted to face him again.

'Are you mad, or what?' Heck gasped. 'I've told you . . .'

The fugitive lunged a second time. For a big man, he was quick. Heck pirouetted out of the way again, though it felt as though a horse had kicked him in the ankle. He tried not to cringe too obviously.

'Let's just be reasonable, eh?'

'*Fuck you, copper!*'

With the third lunge, the right prong hooked the material of Heck's jacket, yanking it hard, tearing it. Heck ducked and turned, pulling himself free of the garment. The fugitive only realised the business end of his weapon was cushioned with fabric when it was too late. He grabbed at the jacket to try and rip it away, but a flying left from Heck smacked him on the cheekbone, and a flying right smashed into the middle of his nose, spattering blood in a wide arc. The fugitive tottered backwards but, to Heck's amazement, kept his feet and this time attacked with the fork's haft, swinging it down and around like a quarterstaff, cracking it first on the side of Heck's left knee and then up into his ribs. Both impacts were sickening, but with the second Heck slammed his left arm down and trapped the pole against his body, before slicing in a right-hand uppercut, which clunked the fugitive hard under his jaw.

This time the big guy released his weapon and reeled away, turning his back. Heck tried to jump on him, and caught an elbow in the solar plexus. He sank to his knees, winded, while the fugitive lumbered away through a narrow side door. Unable to believe he was still chasing this sagging human behemoth, Heck lugged himself to his feet. Outside, a narrow path beat its way through forty yards of wiry grass towards another farm gate, on the other side of which a road passed. The fugitive was already halfway there, but he was walking rather than running.

'You stupid bastard!' Heck panted.

The fugitive glanced back, one hand clutched to his nose, which was streaming gore. As such, he wasn't watching where he was going, and tripped, falling forward. He covered the final few yards to the gate on his hands and knees, gasping loudly, not initially noticing as a canary-yellow Punto pulled up on the other side. He glanced back again as he used the rungs of the gate to haul himself to his feet – and was astonished when a pair of handcuffs were snapped into place, one bracelet round his fat wrist and one round the gate's topmost bar.

'Well, well,' Gail said, shaking her head. 'Been poaching again, have we, Vinnie?'

'Ohhh, Miss Honeyford, come on!' the big guy protested, yanking on the cuffs, but quickly seeing it was futile. 'I've just had me lights punched out – for nothing!'

'I can see that, Vinnie, but I'm sure it wasn't for nothing.'

'Poaching?' Heck said, hobbling up, clutching his bruised ribs. All of a sudden the small net and the dropped knife made sense, and it was more than a little disappointing. 'Don't tell me you know this clown?'

Gail half smiled. 'DS Heckenburg, meet Vinnie Budd. Bit of a celebrity round these parts. Likes his wildlife of course, but he likes his booze too. There isn't a pub he hasn't got pissed in; there isn't a police cell where he hasn't spent the night. Vinnie . . . meet DS Heckenburg, another living legend.'

'You wouldn't be living if you'd come after me a few years ago, mate,' Budd said under his breath, though he'd now slouched against the gate, shoulders heaving. 'I'd have had you back in the day, no problem.'

'You almost had me as it was, you stupid great lummox.'

'Gonna take another shot at me, are you? Now I'm cuffed and can't fight back.'

'I've got a better idea.' Heck leaned into him. 'Why don't I get that pitchfork and shove it up your arse – like you tried to do to me?'

'Tut, tut, Vinnie,' Gail said. 'Don't tell me we're going to add attempting to murder a police officer to your list of achievements?'

A groan tore itself from Budd's palpitating chest. 'Look, please . . .' He shook his head. 'I can't go back to prison, I just can't.'

'Why not? You've been there often enough before.'

'Small stuff. You know it's always small stuff, Miss Honeyford.'

'It all adds up, Vinnie.'

'Last time I was up . . . few rabbits, couple of snipe. That's all it was. Beak slapped me wrist, but said he was sick and fed-up seeing my great ugly face. Those were his exact words, the cheeky bastard – "my great ugly face". Said if he saw me again I'd go down for a proper stretch.'

'It won't be a magistrate this time,' Heck said. 'You know why? They can't give sentences long enough.'

'Come on, Miss Honeyford!' Budd protested again. 'I'm a poacher, I've never denied it. I didn't know who this bloke was . . .'

'I clearly identified myself,' Heck countered. 'Several times.'

'You going to take *his* word for it?' Budd asked her.

She chuckled. 'You think I'm going to take *yours*?'

'All right, look, I admit it,' Budd said. 'I knew he was a copper. Last time I was up at the Grange, I saw him – he had one of them jackets with "Police" on it.'

'That was you, was it?' Heck said, pleased that at least one mystery was solved.

'I was only poking around.'

'Looking for something to pinch, you mean.'

Budd almost seemed affronted by that. 'Just noseying! Seeing what was in the sheds!' He turned to Gail. 'Thing is . . . I went at him with a pitchfork, yeah. But I didn't want to get arrested, see, so I panicked. I wasn't actually trying to kill him.'

109

'Save it for the interview,' she said.

Budd looked genuinely distraught as she unfastened the cuff binding him to the gate. His cheeks had reddened until they were almost purple, but his shoulders slumped as Heck twisted his arms behind his back, locking them together – there was no strength left in him to fight. 'Listen,' he said, as Heck marched him through the gate, pushing him chest first against the Punto while he searched his capacious pockets. 'I know . . .' Budd was still so exhausted by the chase that he struggled to get the words out. 'I know something that may interest you.'

'That opportunity's gone,' Heck replied.

'It's about Mr Lansing.'

Heck glanced up at him, and then at Gail.

'Go on,' she said.

'You . . . you obviously want to know what happened to him. I mean, that's what you were doing at his house, yeah?'

'Never mind us,' Heck said. 'What do *you* know about Harold Lansing?'

Budd shrugged. 'Local bigwig. Decent bloke actually. Spoke to him in the pub a couple of times.'

'Did you witness his accident?' Gail asked.

'No.'

'Nothing else to talk about, is there?' Heck said.

'But I saw what happened after.'

Again, the two cops glanced at each other. Budd had watched them studying the crime scene – it wouldn't have been difficult for him to deduce that they thought the tragic event suspicious. They had to be careful how they played this.

'Tell us exactly what you mean by that,' Gail said.

'I wasn't there at the time; I admit it. But I saw something weird later that day. I think it may have had something to do with it.'

110

'Okay, we're all ears.'

Budd eyed them warily. 'You're not going to dump that heavy shit on me – that attempted murder stuff?'

'Depends what you've got for us,' she replied.

He shook his head. 'No way. I can't make a deal without some kind of guarantee.'

Heck opened the Punto's rear door. 'The only guarantee I've got for you, Vinnie, is that there are no rabbits or snipe where you'll be spending the next twenty years.'

'Come on, Miss Honeyford . . . look, I can't go back inside. *They bully me!*'

Even Heck was thrown by that. He gazed up at the man-mountain in disbelief.

'I know it's stupid, bloke of my size.' Budd's cheeks burned again, but this time with shame. 'But they pick on me because they think I'm someone – and I'm not a young bloke anymore. I can't take it, I'm telling you. It's a fucking nightmare.'

'Tell us what you saw, Vinnie,' Gail said. 'If it's any good I just *might* be able to persuade DS Heckenburg to drop the charges.'

'It happened on 6 July, right? When Mr Lansing got killed?'

'That's right,' she said.

'It was about . . . I don't know, eight-ish in the morning. I was up in Gatcombe Wood. You know that place?'

'Tell me.'

'It's off the main road, about six miles north of Rosewood Grange. I'd been out all night and was checking my traps when I sees this vehicle park at the end of a track. When I say track, I mean like a muddy hollow. There's no road surface or anything. The only folk who go down there normally are shaggers.'

'What kind of vehicle?' Heck asked.

'Didn't see the number plate, but it was a Land Rover.'

This time Heck and Gail tried *not* to glance at each other, though the same thought occurred to both of them – about the four-by-four on the bridge over the Mole.

'What colour?' Gail said.

'Green or grey, not sure which. Kept my head down, you see . . . waiting till they'd gone.'

'And?'

'Well, two blokes got out in gloves and overalls.'

'What made you think this had something to do with Lansing's death?' Heck asked.

'Seemed a bit out of place.'

'Nothing you've told us is out of place so far, Vinnie,' Gail replied. 'Could have been a pair of forestry workers, farm labourers . . .'

'For half a sec I thought they might be legit too,' he said. 'They had some roadworks gear in the back of the car. You know, cones, barriers, "Road Closed" signs and stuff.'

'And what decided you they *weren't* legit?' Heck asked.

'The masks.'

'Masks?'

'Yeah.' Budd nodded. 'This was the really weird thing. This was the bit that put the shits up me. They both had masks on. And they were laughing and high-fiving each other. Like they had something to celebrate.'

'Did they take these masks off?' Gail asked.

'Maybe . . . they were stripping their overalls off. Had jeans and T-shirts underneath. But I didn't hang around to see. I told you, it freaked me out . . . I skedaddled.'

'Specifically *what* freaked you out?' Heck asked.

'Them bloody masks. I wasn't close, I didn't get a really good gander, but I recognised them all right. It was Laurel and Hardy.'

'Excuse me?' Gail said.

'I'm telling you.' Budd shook his big, shaggy head, perplexed. 'One was Stan Laurel, the other was Oliver Hardy.'

Chapter 11

'Look, I want to help,' Vincent Budd said for the eighth or ninth time, 'I'm just not sure whether the Land Rover was green or grey.'

At the other side of the interview-room table, Heck tried to contain his frustration. 'Try and think, eh? It could make all the difference.'

'They're similar colours early in the morning. Especially under the trees.'

'You know, Vinnie, you're here to assist with our enquiries, but there's nothing to stop me arresting you right now and dragging your arse down the corridor to Custody.'

The poacher's saggy, jowly face had a greyish tinge, and was bathed in sweat even now, a good two hours after the chase had finished. If possible, it paled even more. 'Don't even joke about that – not after I came here willingly.'

'I'm not joking,' Heck said. 'Me and you exchanged punches. I ought to lock you up just to cover my back. I'm taking a big risk not doing. And now you're bloody stonewalling me.'

'I'm not stonewalling you. Look, I'm doing my best, I promise . . .' Budd's words tailed off as he involuntarily shuddered and mopped more sweat from his brow.

'You all right?' Heck asked. 'You want me to take you to hospital?'

The poacher waved it away. 'I'm fine, fine. Just bloody knackered. Don't tell me you're not.'

The door swung open and Gail entered, carrying a tray of drinks and a computer printout. She shoved the latter at Heck. 'Here's a list of all the Land Rovers stolen in England and Wales in the last two months. None of them are green or grey.'

Heck snorted, as if he'd expected nothing else.

Gail placed two steaming mugs down, one for each of them. The third she kept for herself. Heck scanned quickly through the printout. There were only six items on the list in total; of those, two had been recovered before Harold Lansing's accident on the Mole, and none had been stolen anywhere south of Birmingham. It didn't help much, but no less than Budd's inability to determine the colour of the vehicle he'd spotted in Gatcombe Wood, as that meant they wouldn't be able to tie it in with the vehicle on the bridge overlooking the river.

'SOCO gone up there to make a tyre cast for us?' he asked.

'They've said they'll go but they reckon it's a fool's errand. God knows how many courting couples have been parked up there since.' She switched her attention to Budd. 'Were you actually there, Vinnie, or weren't you? It isn't difficult to distinguish green from grey.'

'It is if it's early in the morning,' he replied. 'If you ever went out at that time, you'd see what the light's like.'

'You cheeky sod. I must have worked nights and earlies a thousand times, if I've worked them once.'

'Well you know what I'm talking about.'

'This is futile!' Heck slammed the printout down on top of the incomplete witness statement.

'Listen . . .' Budd shrugged. 'I can *say* it was green. Or grey. If that's what you want.'

'What are you talking about?'

'Well.' Budd shrugged again. 'You've already let me off this one. So perhaps if another occasion were to arise in the future . . .'

Gail glared at him. 'Are you trying to play us, Vinnie? Is that what all this is about?'

'No, no, it's just, well, you scratch my back and I'll scratch—'

'No one is scratching anyone's backs,' Heck interrupted. 'We don't tell lies in court.'

Budd looked baffled. 'Since when?'

'And we certainly don't rely on members of the public telling lies for us,' Gail added.

'All we want from you is the truth.' Heck pushed Budd's mug across the table. 'So take five minutes and drink your tea, and try and remember what you saw.'

The two detectives stepped out into the corridor, leaving Budd perplexed and alone.

'How's the ankle?' Gail asked.

Heck grunted. 'Stiff, but the pain's easing.'

'Well, whatever happens next, we'll need more than Vinnie Budd's word. He's a poacher and a petty thief, but he's mainly known round here for being a wino and a gobshite. Give him a couple of beers and he'll tell you anything. Any decent defence would rip us a new one if he was *all* we had.'

Heck sipped tiredly at his tea.

'What are you thinking?' she asked.

'I'm thinking that roadworks gear in the back of the Land Rover was most likely used to temporarily close the road, if they needed to. You know, make sure they had time to pull this thing off without other road users interfering.'

She mused, indicating that she supposed this was possible.

'I'm also thinking Laurel and Hardy,' Heck said. 'I mean – how weird is that?'

'I don't know . . . you commit a crime, you wear a mask. I don't suppose it's incumbent on you to find one that makes you look like a criminal.'

'A toy plane. Laurel and Hardy masks. Seems to be a kind of joke shop vibe here.'

'Joke shop?'

'What kind of goofballs are we dealing with?'

'You're not saying you think killing Lansing was just a bit of fun?'

'I don't know.'

'Let's be sensible, Heck. Whatever Vinnie Budd saw in that wood may or may not be related to this case, but it doesn't change the fact that whoever's responsible for Harold Lansing's death will be found somewhere among his personal contacts.'

'The *fact*?'

'Heck, we need to stop chasing around the countryside after idiots like Budd, and get into the guts of Lansing's affairs. In fact . . .' She checked her watch. 'I'm expecting a callback from FIU any time now. Can you finish getting Budd's statement?'

'Sure, go on.'

Heck watched as she walked away along the passage to the CID office. If he was brutally honest with himself, he suspected that Gail was probably right. Lansing, for all his reputation as a good egg, had been a self-made multi-millionaire with his fingers in a number of different pies. It was impossible to imagine there weren't at least a few naughty secrets somewhere in his background. He'd also reached a stage of life where he'd moved widely in well-heeled circles. Thanks to his ex-girlfriend, he'd even mixed with the fashion and showbiz crowd. He'd likely known and interacted with a significant number of individuals who, for all their wealth, lived outside the norms and conventions of Middle England. But then again . . . when Heck considered the nature of the two accidents, doubts gnawed at him. The aeroplane incident in particular had been like something from a silent comedy. His thoughts wandered back to a major case of the recent past, when he'd been confronted by the 'Desecrator' murders. On that occasion, the victims had been abducted and tortured to death on specific feast days – Good Friday, St George's Day and so forth – in a perverse fashion designed to mock the legitimate festivities normally associated with those events. But if the purpose of those crimes had been to offer insult to the communities that normally celebrated such events, the purpose of the toy aeroplane attack was, seemingly, to snigger.

To chuckle.

To have a giggle.

Heck considered the second, fatal accident. That was less of a clever joke. At least on the surface. Anyone could veil a mirror to prevent someone spotting a reflection, but if that was the case why had Lansing persisted in pulling out onto such a dangerous road? And how, if someone had simply obscured the mirror, was there any guarantee it would have led to Lansing's death? The more Heck pondered it, the more that too felt like a joke or dare – as if the perpetrator had said: 'Let's see if we can make it work. This'll be a hoot.'

Heck knew from bitter experience that some small minds were all too easily amused. Several times he'd investigated so-called 'thrill killings', where the victim was unknown to the perp, and there was no sexual or financial motive – it was one of the most incomprehensible types of crime, committed purely because the gruesome act itself, and the complexity and challenge of arranging and carrying it out, was a source of excitement in its own right.

He went back into the interview room, where Budd sat with hands clasped on the table in front of him.

'Well?' Heck asked.

'Sorry.' Budd regarded him worriedly, as if such a failure might merit a punitive response. 'You want the truth. I can't be any more truthful than green *or* grey.'

Heck stared at him long and hard, before resuming his chair and picking up his pen. 'At the end of the day, honesty's always the best policy.'

When the witness statement was finished and signed, for what it was worth, and the burly poacher was trudging off home with a stern warning ringing in his ears, Heck strolled back through the station to the CID office. En route he passed a window looking out on the personnel car park, where two figures caught his eye. One of them was Gail. She stood stiffly with arms folded; a tense, irritated posture. Towering over her was the tall, angular shape of DS Ron Pavey. The big guy was talking *at* her rather than to her; keeping it quiet, but, from the speed of his delivery, laying down the law.

When Gail finally came back indoors, she looked surprised and perhaps a little vexed to see Heck already at his desk, flipping through paperwork.

'Thought you were waiting for FIU to call you back?' he said.

She shrugged. 'No rush. No one at Bramshill is ever going to get off his arse to do anything quickly for the likes of us.' She sat, shifting documents to check her answering machine, but its steady green light indicated that no messages had been stored. She puffed out her cheeks before booting up her PC – and catching sight of Heck slouched back in his chair, hands in pockets, watching her.

She raised a querying eyebrow.

'There's a problem with your theory that Lansing may have been hit by a pro,' he said.

'I didn't say I thought he'd been hit by a pro.'

'Okay . . . hit by a business rival, a jealous ex-lover or someone.'

She regarded him coldly; the more amenable personality that had emerged during the last day or so had evaporated. She gestured, implying he should explain.

'There isn't much traffic passes Rosewood Grange,' he said. 'If you were the one trying to kill Lansing, how would you make sure he drove out in front of a speeding car? Would you really just be prepared to cover the safety mirror and hope for the best?'

She pondered this, tapping her desk with a pen.

'The way I see it,' he added, 'if they really wanted to get rid of him – if the whole object of the exercise was to eliminate Harold Lansing – surely they'd opt for a method with a more certain outcome?'

'But if the greater priority was making it look like an accident?'

'How much of a priority can that be? You want him dead. You don't want him injured, or shaken up, or worse still, driving off to work without a worry in the world because no dickhead in a sports car happened to come along at the right time.'

'Suppose they locked him in the car, waited till the right moment, and pushed it out?'

'The accident report said the car was being driven at the time of impact. The key was still in the ignition.'

'Okay, but there are several improbables where *your* theory's concerned.'

'Such as?'

'You're suggesting someone did this for a lark,' she said. 'That they covered his mirror, hoping he'd drive out in front of a car – any passing car – and they got lucky. But how does that fit in with the toy aeroplane? They missed him the first time, so they clearly tried again. However you try and package it, Heck, your crazy jokers aren't just picking people at random. They clearly had it in for Harold Lansing.'

'That's a good point.'

'Thank you.'

Not that Heck felt much better having acknowledged this. Mainly because there seemed to be even less logic to it. They had two guys who dressed like Laurel and Hardy to carry out a joke-type murder. And yet because they'd missed him the first time, they went back for a second bite. Perhaps they'd have gone back for a third if the road accident thing hadn't worked – either because the desire to kill Lansing was of overriding importance to them (even though that didn't seem to fit in with the 'comedic' style of the attack) or maybe, simply, because they didn't like to be thwarted; because they'd derived so much pleasure and satisfaction from the planning and execution of such an atrocity that failure to complete it was never going to be an option. Then again, maybe it was both – and how far beyond the bounds of normality would *that* put them?

'Gail?' A woman wearing a trouser suit had appeared at their desk; she was fortyish, tall and raw-boned, her fluffy mat of mouse-brown hair held in place by several messily arranged clips. 'A DS Hart rang you from the Financial Intelligence Unit.'

'Bloody great!' Gail exclaimed. 'So I've missed him?'

The woman handed her a note. 'Here's his direct line if you want to call him back. He's in till five.'

Gail took it. 'Thanks Sally.'

'DS Hart?' Heck mused as the woman walked away. 'Never met him.'

'Are you going to hang around there all day?' Gail asked tersely.

'Aren't we supposed to be working together?'

'If you've got a lead on these practical jokers, why don't you go and follow it?' She grabbed her landline and tapped in the number. 'I mean, no offence, but I never really knew why we needed Scotland Yard's help in the first place. And as I see it, there's even less reason for you to be here now. This is not part of a series, it's not a terrorist plot, we're not dealing with some maniac rapist or kidnapper. It's a straight-up murder-one, and I'm all over it – oh yeah, DS Hart?' Her tone promptly thawed. 'DC Honeyford here, at Reigate Hall Police Station.' She sat forward, grabbed a pen and smiled – an attractive smile, Heck thought enviously, not yet having been treated to one himself. 'Yeah, fine, how are you?'

Heck glanced at his watch, and seeing that it was almost one o'clock decided to head upstairs to the canteen for a bite of lunch. On the way he passed the tall woman referred to as Sally, who was leafing through the contents of a filing cabinet. She offered her hand. 'Hi – Sally Bullock.'

'Oh, hi.' He shook hands. 'DS Heckenburg.'

'I know.'

'DC . . .?'

'No.' She chuckled. 'Strictly a civvie, Sarge. CID admin, but anything I can help you with, just give me a shout.'

'Thanks.' Heck felt immediately warm towards her. Aside from Will Royton, who'd been polite enough about Heck's presence here, the rest of the staff at Reigate Hall had been studiedly indifferent to him – except for Gail Honeyford of course, who still seemed to be shifting between relaxed toler-ance and surly hostility.

'So, how's it going?' she asked.

'Well . . .' He glanced back to the corner where Gail was chatting animatedly on the phone. 'I thought we were starting to get somewhere. Suddenly I'm not so sure.'

Sally Bullock smiled. 'Don't take it to heart. You've caught her during a bad week . . . maybe a bad month, maybe even a bad year.'

'Sorry, I don't get you?'

Sally indicated the swing doors at the entrance to the office, and led him through them into the adjoining corridor. 'Gail's a great young detective,' she said confidentially. 'She's sharp and she works hard, but she's going through a bad patch. Her recent ex is a guy called Ron Pavey.'

'Yeah, I've met him.'

'If you've met him, you won't need me to tell you what an arse he is. "Control freak" doesn't cover it. He has this idea that he helped Gail with her career – and who knows, maybe he did; she was in uniform when they were first going out together. But they've been history for six months now, and he still behaves as if she owes him. They're forever having spats.'

'Well, that's a sad story,' Heck replied, wondering why he was being told all this, and deducing that Sally Bullock was a friend of Gail's and had taken it on herself to unofficially apologise. 'But we're investigating a murder here, and it would be a pity if she was to let personal issues interfere with that.'

Sally shook her head adamantly. 'She won't, don't worry. Look, I've known Gail since she was a young PC. She's dead keen on this job, and ambitious to go places. She'll get her priorities right, trust me.'

'Good to know.' Heck moved to the foot of the stairs. 'The sooner the better, mind you.'

Sally nodded again. Heck smiled and headed upstairs. As he did, his mobile bleeped in his pocket. He put it to his ear. 'DS Heckenburg?'

'Heck, it's me.' It was Gemma Piper.

'Ma'am?'

'Where we up to?'

'Well . . . I'm pretty sure Lansing's death's a homicide.'
He reached the top of the stairs and paused. 'That said, I'm
not one hundred per cent there's anything it for us, and
neither are Reigate CID.'

'They're on board?'

'Sort of. They've already got someone investigating it as
a murder.'

'Oh?' Gemma sounded nonplussed. 'I didn't know that.'

'I'm guessing that as soon as you expressed interest, they
got interested too.'

'So are you saying you want to come home?'

He hesitated. 'Not yet . . . if you leave me with it a couple
more days I'll have a better idea.'

'What's your gut feeling?'

He walked through the station rec room, where various
uniforms lounged about, shooting pool or munching sandwiches while watching television. The canteen doors were
located on the far side.

'For the first time in a while, I don't have one,' he said.

'That bothers me, Heck.'

'Bothers me too. I can't say this one falls within our normal
remit, ma'am. But there's nothing routine about it, I can tell
you that much.' He entered the canteen, at which point
further words briefly failed him.

'You still there?' Gemma asked.

'Yeah – erm, can I call you back.'

'No problem. Just keep me informed, yeah?'

'Yeah, sure,' Heck said, still distracted by the sight of the
newspaper cuttings plastered all over the canteen noticeboard.

Arresting officer abuses family and friends

Beneath that headline was a grainy image depicting Heck
and Alan Devlin head-to-head in the lobby at Nottingham

Crown Court. Various officials were holding the two men apart, and Heck was in the midst of shouting and pointing an accusatory finger.

Heck didn't need to scan through the text underneath to know that it would give a one-sided account of the confrontation. Several times now, Devlin had given press interviews to the effect that Heck had blamed Jimmy Hood's loved ones for his Nottingham crime spree rather than the mental health authorities who had ignored his deteriorating condition for so many years.

Cops tried to kill my mate

This was the header on an even larger clipping, and it featured two further photographs, the first portraying Heck – again as he left the court, his face written with an angry snarl – the second portraying Devlin, posing some time later and looking suitably mournful; with his thick-lensed glasses, he'd even managed to adopt a bookish air.

Heck had seen this particular item on its day of publication. It elaborated on Devlin's accusation that Heck had contrived a motorcycle accident to capture Jimmy Hood, even though at the time Hood was deemed to be innocent. Again, Devlin went on at boring length about society being to blame for Hood's crimes. Heck felt much about the article now as he'd felt then – that there were two sides to every story, but that it still set his blood boiling when certain sections of the press so quickly changed allegiances just to secure a headline. Not that it served any purpose getting angry now.

He glanced around. There were several other people in the canteen: a few more off-duty uniforms grouped around tables, eating their lunch; a couple of traffic wardens doing the same; even one or two plain clothes. No one would look at him. The same applied to the two ladies behind the serving hatch. One was engrossed in mopping down the aluminium counter while the other had her back turned as she made slow, careful adjustments to a chalkboard menu. In the far corner of the room, DS Ron Pavey sat alone, cupping a mug of coffee. He gazed at nothing, a vague smile playing around his thick, smug lips.

Heck smiled too and strode to the hatch, where he placed an order and made idle pleasantries with the two ladies. There were occasions when he hated this job and some of the people in it almost as much as the scum they pursued. But there was a time and place for showing that. And this wasn't one of them.

Chapter 12

Sally Bullock looked puzzled. 'Any strange or bizarre accidental deaths?'

Heck stood in the entrance to her small, cramped office. 'Force-wide if possible.'

'Force-wide?' She sounded dropped-on.

'Going back twelve months.'

'Oh my goodness.' She sat back from her computer. The CID Admin office was an annexe to the main CID office, but it only had a small window overlooking the local green, and this was half concealed by potted plants. The room was lined floor to ceiling by shelves loaded with binders and folders, all bulging with paperwork. One window panel was open, but it was a warm day outside, so this didn't afford much relief from the close, stuffy atmosphere.

Sally gave it some thought. 'Well, unless there are suspicious circumstances, they won't be logged on our database. But I can cross-ref with the Coroner's Office files, and see what they've got.'

'That'd be good,' Heck said gratefully.

'We're not just talking RTAs?'

'No. Anything . . . so long as it's weird.'

'Perhaps you can define "weird"?'

Heck realised that he couldn't, under which circumstance he was asking far too much of the admin officer. It was self-evident that she was trying to be helpful, but she also looked bewildered. This really was 'wing and prayer' stuff. Going through a list of fatal accidents in as highly populated a police force area as Surrey would likely take hours, but add to that the problem of not knowing exactly what you were looking for; well, it was plain selfishness to ask someone else to do it for him.

'Perhaps it's better if I just set my laptop up in here, and do it myself, eh?'

She smiled, relieved. 'Might be easier.'

Heck took up residence at a small side table, on a bum-numbingly uncomfortable stool, and once he'd linked through successfully and had refined his search to 'Accidents' spent the next two and a half hours perusing the Surrey Coroner's Officer's files, assessing a wide variety of unfortunate deaths. The vast majority were connectable only by the tragedy of their circumstances, and in many cases by their sheer banality. The ordinariness of the events surrounding incidents that had proved so devastating to families and loved ones was depressing: a middle-aged man who fell off the roof of his house while trying to adjust his television aerial; a fairground attendant who attempted to make repairs to a generator in pouring rain; a secretary in an office car park, smoking at the same time as emptying a container of petrol into her Ford Fiesta's fuel tank; children cycling through traffic inter-sections without looking; children playing unsupervised close to deep water; an old couple who went to bed one night without realising they had a gas leak; a young couple who went to bed without remembering to blow out their Christmas candles . . .

For all that, however, there were three that *did* catch

Heck's eye – mainly because, like the two attempts on Harold Lansing's life, there was something unlikely, not to say sinister, about them. Heck wasn't the only person to feel this, because when he mentioned them to Sally she remembered two of them straight away, pointing out that on both occasions the coroner had not been convinced of their accidental status and had returned open verdicts. In both those cases crime reports had been filed, and one had eventually led to a man being imprisoned.

'The victim in that case was a guy called Freddie Upton,' Heck said, reading from his laptop screen. 'A sales rep from Wales. He died last September near Dorking, when he was impaled through the back after the lorry behind him braked hard and its cargo of loose scaffolding catapulted forward. The lorry driver claimed he had to brake because an unknown cyclist deliberately swerved in front of him.'

'That was a shocker,' Sally said as she printed off the relevant documentation. 'The lorry driver got two years for causing death by dangerous driving.' She consulted the paper as it scrolled from the printer. 'His name was Gordon Meredith. Says here that he couldn't explain how his load had become unsafe, but insisted that it was secured properly when he set out that morning.'

'And the mystery cyclist was never traced,' Heck added.

'That's correct. Meredith was never able to produce any witness who even remembered seeing a cyclist there.'

Heck read on. 'I see Meredith is now in Wayland . . .'

'Category C. Shouldn't get into too much trouble there. Ruined his reputation, of course. I mean, if it wasn't his fault, he's paid a terrible price.'

'Not as terrible as Freddie Upton.'

Sally handed him the second printout. This one dated to the previous January and concerned a Leatherhead pet shop owner named Larry Briggs, who had initially been arrested on suspicion of murder, though after some investigation was released without charge. In his case, two local thieves – their names Richard Dasby and Darrel Degton – were bitten to death by poisonous spiders after they stole Briggs's car. Briggs was first arrested as it was suspected that he might have deliberately left several dangerous specimens from his private collection – all of whose highly toxic venom was found riddling the two corpses – in unsecured containers inside the vehicle in an effort to ambush thieves, though Briggs maintained throughout that he had lost this valuable stock during a burglary at his shop several months earlier.

'Briggs was held in custody for two days because it was felt he had motive,' Sally remarked. 'Apparently thieves had been terrorising that neighbourhood for months. As I say, his own premises had been burgled, and he'd had his car pinched before.'

'Perfect fall guy,' Heck said. 'I see Briggs still lost his dangerous animals' licence.'

'Well . . . there were doubts about him even after he was released without charge. People wondered if it had been an accident because his stock was inadequately stored. You know, he'd been transporting the creatures somewhere and they'd escaped.' She handed him the third printout. This was a single sheet, which she'd run off direct from the Coroner's Officer's record. 'Can't help you with this one, I'm afraid. First time *I've* seen it; which is no surprise if there was no criminal investigation.'

Heck reread the document, hair prickling as he pondered its sheer implausibility.

A farmer named Mervin Thornton, who owned extensive land near Woldingham, North Surrey, had failed to come in for his tea one evening. His son searched for him, and when he found his dead body almost had a heart attack at the condition it was in. It seemed that Mervin Thornton had been attempting to reinflate one of the tyres on his tractor. The police were duly called, but by the state and position of Thornton's body they concluded that he'd slipped in fresh-churned mud and had fallen heavily on the gas cylinder, tearing the air hose loose and at the same time penetrating his abdomen with its steel nozzle. Compressed gas had thus flowed into his body, swelling it grotesquely and crushing his internal organs. Thornton's failure to extricate himself from the nozzle was never fully explained, though an assumption was made that he'd knocked himself senseless when he'd fallen over. Heck couldn't help wondering about that. How senseless did you have to be not to respond when a stream of inrushing gas was pumping you up like a football?

Though perhaps the bigger question – if all this stuff actually *was* connected to Harold Lansing – was just how warped did you have to be to perpetrate it?

Heck had encountered all kinds of creepy killers in his time, but as a rule the creepiest were those who prized the chase more than the catch. These were the slow hunters, the patient planners, the ones who set themselves complex tasks and gradually brought them to completion, revelling in their own genius as they did. Unless he was way off in his assessment, this was very possibly what they had here – though in some ways it could be even worse. The pet shop thing, not to mention the hideousness of the actual attacks – death by inflation, by slow burning, by poisonous spider – all that was bad enough, but apparently *other* buttons were being pushed as well. Finding pleasure in horrific suffering? Finding comedy value in it? There was abnormal, and then there was super-abnormal.

Of course, it all boiled down to the same thing in the end.

'Enjoy your sadistic gratification while you can, boys,' Heck said to himself. 'Time's almost up.'

* * *

When Heck returned to the CID office later, Gail was no longer there.

By the tidied state of her desk, she'd set off for home. However, glancing through the window outside the office, he spotted her crossing the car park with a lidded travel mug in one hand and her briefcase in the other. She threw the case into the back seat of her Punto, pulled down her shades, and climbed in. The car growled to life, but she was only halfway to the exit when Heck stumbled into her path, waving his documentation.

She slowed to a halt and powered her window down.

'Can I have a few secs?' he asked.

'If you must.'

'Can I get in?'

'I thought you only wanted a few secs?'

'Gail – you ever heard the phrase never focus solely on one hypothesis?'

'All right . . .'

'Constantly re-evaluate theories, always keep an open mind . . .'

'Okay! I hear you.' She hit the locking mechanism. 'Hop in.'

Heck rounded the car and clambered into the front passenger seat, thrusting his paperwork at her. 'What do you think of this lot?'

She lifted her sunglasses and leafed patiently through it all, finally separating the impalement and the poisonous spider incidents from the gas cylinder tragedy. 'These two I've heard about. This other one is new to me. So?'

'You don't think there's anything odd about them? Something a bit, I don't know, contrived?'

'Contrived?'

'Come on, Gail . . . if these are genuine accidents, they're once-in-a-lifetime events. Yet you've got three of them, all in the same force area, all within a few months of each other. And then you've got Lansing as well.'

She gave him a long, disbelieving stare. 'Heck . . . I know you have to justify your existence somehow. But this is far-fetched even by those standards. Are you seriously telling me you've been through all the accident records in the county – that you've literally been scraping the barrel to try and find something, *anything*, to reinforce this notion of yours that what we've actually got here is a pair of psycho pranksters?'

'Psycho pranksters?' He pursed his lips. 'Apt description. I like it.'

'Well I don't.' She slapped the paperwork back into his lap. 'Can we just try and be professional. I hear you when you remind me that it's poor policy to throw all your eggs in one basket, but might I remind you that it's equally poor policy to bend the evidence to fit the facts? Though frankly I'm being generous in referring to that lot as evidence. We haven't got anything circumstantial, let alone something approaching a smoking gun. There are no obvious links between any of those victims.'

'We haven't established that yet,' he said.

'Two scrotey car thieves from Leatherhead, a sales rep from North Wales – two hundred miles apart? Harold Lansing – a self-made Surrey millionaire?'

'Like I said, it's just a hypothesis . . . which is all *you've* got. Unless you've uncovered something solid this afternoon that you haven't bothered sharing with me?'

Gail looked flustered at that. 'Look, if your job is to *imagine* these sorts of things, fine, you're earning your money. But mine's to try and figure out what actually happened. Now presumably there's an evening meal waiting for you somewhere. Why don't you go and find it?'

'What about Mervin Thornton, this farmer from Woldingham? What do we know about him?'

132

'*We*, as in Surrey CID, don't know anything, because according to that Coroner's Office report – the one you've got in your hot little hand – he died through misadventure. There was no crime and no criminal investigation.'

Heck eyed the report again, wondering if maybe in this case he was taking things a bit too far. Had this material landed on his desk back at SCU, he'd probably have dismissed it out of hand. *There's no obvious, identifiable link – and lack of evidence is not evidence in itself. Next case.* So why was he taking a different tack now? His gut told him there were too many coincidences here, but was there something else too? Gemma had sent him down to Surrey almost casually, not expecting he'd uncover much. She'd also said he wasn't underappreciated, that his talents weren't taken for granted . . . at least not by her. In the light of his recent disputes with her, perhaps this was a chance to prove how ill-advised taking him for granted could be.

'Listen Heck,' Gail said, making an effort to sound conciliatory. She took her shades off and placed them on the dashboard. 'I know you're here to do a job – but it seems to me that you've already done it.' She indicated his paperwork. 'Leave those with me. I promise I'll cast my eye over them, but I honestly think that it's a waste of both our time.'

Before he could reply, a set of large, hairy knuckles beat a tattoo on her driver's window. They jerked round, shocked, neither having noticed Ron Pavey come red-faced across the car park.

Gail powered her window down again. 'What do you want, Ron?'

He leaned in. 'What do you think you're doing?'

'I'm sorry?'

Pavey pointed at Heck. 'Why is *he* in *this car* with *you*?'

Again, to Heck's fascination, the tough police girl seemed to melt away.

'I don't think that's any of your business,' she said, looking to her front.

'I'm making it my bloody business. The working day ends at five-thirty, my love. It's now ten to six, so that means you go home to *your* gaff, and he goes home, preferably permanently, to whatever shithole he calls *his* gaff. Do you understand me?'

'Ron, what do you not understand about this being over?'

'Nothing's over! And don't give me that liberated woman crap! You're where you are, Gail, because I put you there. That means you owe me . . . and in the light of that, the very least you can do is stop shaking your ambitious little arse at every big city wannabe who comes along with a line of fucking dogshit—'

Heck leaned across, grabbed Pavey's slime-green tie and powered the window up, trapping it firmly.

'Heck!' Gail protested. 'What do you think—'

But Heck was already out of the car, Gail's mug of coffee in hand.

Pavey was at first too startled to respond, but now began wrestling with his tie. Finding it jammed fast, he tried to open the driver's door but, by instinct, Gail locked it.

'You little shit!' he snarled, eyeing Heck as he circled the vehicle towards him. 'You think you're fucking clever? I'll show you clever . . .' He worked frantically at his knot, but that wasn't easy, bent forward as though waiting to take it up the backside.

'Congratulations Ron,' Heck said.

'Gail, open this window – *open this fucking window now*!'

'In two days you've achieved what it takes some villains ten years or more: you've pissed me off.'

'You'll be fucking sorry for this.'

'So let me lay it on the line.' Heck halted close by. 'DC Honeyford and I are investigating a murder, which is proving unexpectedly time-consuming. So we're getting increasingly frustrated by your constant interference.'

'You know fuck all about what's going on here!' Pavey snapped. 'Me and her have a history . . .'

'On which subject, your newspaper gag gave everyone a bit of a giggle. So thanks for that.' Heck flipped the lid from the beaker. 'Allow me to return the compliment.' He tossed its contents onto Pavey's groin, saturating his crotch and both his inside legs.

'Ahhh – you shit! You fucker!'

The big sergeant finally got himself free and swung round, drawing himself to full height. His sand-coloured hair hung in damp, sweat-sodden strands. The eyes burned in his florid, pitted face. But Heck had learned from long experience that you didn't flinch from someone threatening violence. Most lowlifes who did it were bluffing. This lowlife, apparently, was no exception.

Pavey held his ground, eyes fixed on Heck's stony half-smile, but *not* advancing. His big, gnarly hands clenched and unclenched by his sides, but neither balled into a full-blown fist.

'No,' Heck said slowly, 'something told me you weren't so dumb as to make a complete spectacle of yourself twice in one day.'

Pavey worked his thick lips together, but finally he too smiled. 'Clever . . . trying to goad me into giving you a pasting when there's cameras around and people at windows. But there'll be time, don't you worry. Then there'll just be you and me.'

'How about an hour from now?' Heck asked. 'We've both finished work. I'm sure we can find somewhere quiet.'

That was something else Heck had learned. Not only do you not back down, you push on hard and confident; once you've got them on the back foot, you advance; force them into open retreat.

Pavey's eyes widened. 'You're a real piece of work, aren't you?'

'Don't let that put you off. If tonight's no good, I'll be around a few days yet. You'll get your chance.'

'I bloody will.' Slowly, reluctantly, Pavey backed away. 'I absolutely will.'

He was too angry to realise how ridiculous he looked, a guy who no doubt valued his rep – his cool, his street cred – now with a huge, wet stain down the front of his trousers. He turned and walked stiffly towards the personnel door, just as two young female PCs came out of it.

'Too bad you couldn't find a toilet, Ron,' Heck called after him.

Pavey could only stand there helpless as the two women walked away, tittering. He threw a final bellicose glance in Heck's direction and crashed into the building, slamming the door closed behind him.

Heck turned to find that Gail had got out of the car and now regarded him with an odd combination of outrage and reproach. 'You know,' she said, voice quavering, 'I left school ten years ago.'

'What?'

'I don't want macho boneheads flexing their muscles over me, okay?'

'Are you serious?'

She stabbed a finger at him. 'DS Heckenburg, I'll say this once and once only. Despite having you round my neck like a millstone, I'm halfway to cracking this case. So why don't you just back off once and for all? Bury yourself in a few more accident reports, maybe. That ought to keep you busy. But please, please, please – from this moment on, stay out of my way.' She turned to get back into her car.

'Hey, this isn't just about *you*, DC Honeyford!'

She glanced back, startled, but now it was Heck's turn to point the finger.

'I don't care if you're content to be a rubbing rag for some alpha male prat like Ron Pavey. I genuinely don't. But as soon as it starts hampering my investigation, it becomes a problem!'

'*Your* investigation?'

'I don't know exactly what your issue is with that guy, but you clearly can't deal with it, so I had to.'

She rapidly turned pink. 'Excuse me?'

'If he sticks his nose anywhere near me again while I'm trying to work, or anytime in fact, he'll get it flattened. And you can tell him that when you next apologise to him for living.'

'Oh, you've got me wrong.'

'That makes two of us.' Heck was aware that he was going too far, but suddenly this persistent dismissal of his thoughts and ideas – from someone who, with the length of time she currently had in, would be regarded as the tea-girl back at SCU – was more than he could take. 'If you think I've come all the way down here to occupy a ringside seat while you and your ex-squeeze have an ongoing domestic, you've got *me* very wrong.' He waved his handful of crime reports. 'Now if you're not interested in this stuff, fine – but if that *is* the case, then *you* stay out of *my* way.'

Chapter 13

The Leatherhead pet shop owner, Larry Briggs, had a small unit in a row of old, run-down shops quite close to the town centre. It was mid-evening when Heck got there, and those few shops that weren't *To Let* were already closed – except one. A light burned on the other side of its window, which was now obscured by sheets of crinkly newspaper. The hoarding over the top had seen better days; it was lopsided and painted with flaky lettering, which read:

Pets 4U

Heck tried the front door, but it was locked. He wandered round to the rear, noting from his documentation that it had been at the back where, one night last October, a burglar had forced entry through an upper window. Apparently the car in which the two car thieves had died the following January, a battered old Volkswagen estate, had also been stolen from the back. When he got there, Heck immediately saw why. The rear access road was a blind spot. There was little lighting and no sign of CCTV – most likely the retailers here, those few that were left, had been unable to afford proper surveillance. It was also a cul-de-sac; there was only one way in and one way out, which made it less enticing to vehicle thieves, but if the vehicle in question had been pointed in the right direction that was less of a problem.

As Heck strolled along the street, he read back through the notes. Apparently Larry Briggs had been the owner of two vehicles – his own private car, which he used to get to and from home, and the Volkswagen estate, which was strictly for business. Given the regular vehicle thefts in this district, it seemed odd that he'd been happy to leave the Volkswagen overnight, but he'd explained this by pointing out that, as a single man, he had no means of taking both cars home when the working day was over.

The back of the shop came into sight. Its rear door was recessed between two buttress walls, both about six foot five high and covered with moss. The one on the left had given access to an upper window, which the burglar last October had entered by removing the entire pane with something like a handyman's knife. Even though the premises had an alarm fitted, which was subsequently activated, this hadn't stopped the intruder pressing on with his task, which was curious – the only thieves who tended to gamble that the police wouldn't respond quickly were those who were after something valuable or something specific.

At present, the shop's rear door was open and a small hired van was parked outside. As Heck watched, a man came out of the building carrying a sealed cardboard box. He was a big, rugged chap in his late forties, with horn-rimmed glasses, a shock of mouse-brown hair, and a heavy beer gut pushing against his sweat-stained T-shirt. Sweat also gleamed on his forehead and in the pelt of hair covering his forearms.

He unceremoniously dumped the box into the back of the van, and turned to face Heck, beating sawdust from his hands. His expression was not welcoming.

'Larry Briggs?' Heck asked.

'And who are you?'

Heck flashed his warrant card. 'Detective Sergeant Heckenburg.'

'Oh yeah . . . come to lock me up again?'

'No reason why I should, is there?'

The big man gave a wry grin. 'Not unless it's a crime to defend your property against light-fingered little bastards. They'd strip the bloody country if we gave them half a chance.'

'Sorry, I don't understand.'

'Why does that not surprise me?' Briggs turned and headed back inside the shop.

Heck followed him, finding that its downstairs consisted of a single open space, which, though it was still scattered with sawdust and bore that musty odour of animals, was now empty except for a small stack of cartons and boxes, all packed and sealed. One or two posters still adorned the walls, advertising dog food brands or deals for pet insurance; what looked like a budgerigar cage sat alone in a corner, its door hanging from broken hinges.

'Thieves, Sergeant,' Briggs said, picking up more boxes, one under each brawny arm. 'I'm talking about thieves. In the normal world they'd be your bread and butter, but not around here apparently, where they're free to roam the streets at will.'

Heck followed him outside again. 'Well there are two thieves who haven't roamed any streets around here since last January, aren't there?'

Briggs smiled as he loaded his packages into the van. 'And there was me, thinking you'd come to update me on the crimes *I've been* the victim of. You know, the burglary last year, the three occasions when my car was stolen – including the last one, when those two little fuckers died.'

140

'You don't sound very sorry about that, Mr Briggs.'

'I do my best, but somehow I can't find the tears.'

Briggs went back into the shop for yet more items. Heck waited, again assessing the rear of the premises. The alarm notwithstanding, it looked pretty vulnerable – almost the only one in the row that was occupied, the loading area at the back concealed from passing traffic. Heck had pulled the crime report and associated paperwork on the burglary last October, and quickly read through it again. It was no surprise that it hadn't been actioned very far. There'd been no witnesses, no local informants had offered leads. SOCO had turned up hundreds of dabs, but those upstairs in the shop matched the elimination prints taken from Larry Briggs himself, while those downstairs were rendered useless as the general public had had regular access to it. As was par for the course, suspects arrested for other burglaries since had been spoken to about it, but though most had been willing to admit other crimes so long as they were taken into consideration, none had coughed to the pet shop job.

Briggs reappeared with more boxes, which he shoved unceremoniously into the back of the van.

'You going somewhere?' Heck asked.

'I've closed the business, if you must know,' Briggs replied. 'I've had enough and I'm moving on. Early retirement beckons, worse luck.'

'Let me guess, you can't compete with those big warehouse stores that are opening in out-of-town retail parks all over the country?'

'Well . . . the annihilation of the town centres isn't doing the likes of me any good. But the main thing is that since that incident last January, I've become a pariah in this neighbourhood.'

'Yeah?'

'Everyone's on my side – slap me on the back when they

meet me in the street. Buy me a pint in the pub. But they won't come to the shop anymore. Those little bastards Dasby and Degton have got mates, you see. I've had paint on my windows, shit through my letterbox. I've had notes threatening to burn me out. Even customers who've come to the shop have been followed home, had their cars tagged, their own windows messed up.'

'Why didn't you report any of this?'

Briggs snorted. 'I did, but just because your lot didn't charge me with murder, that doesn't mean they don't suspect me of it. They're not interested. Anyway, can I help you with something, or are you just here to pass the time of day?'

'It's actually to do with the burglary you had here on 15 October last year.'

Briggs looked surprised. 'Yeah?'

'The livestock you reported missing: a Brazilian wandering spider, a "brown widow" spider, an African sand spider, an Australian funnel-web and a Deathstalker scorpion from the Middle East.'

'That's correct. Cost me an arm and a bloody leg to assemble that collection.'

'It's an exotic list. Some of the top predators in the animal kingdom, or so I'm informed. Any particular reason behind it?'

'I've always had stuff like that – before I was disqualified from holding a licence of course. Attracts the punters, doesn't it? But none of them were ever for sale. All the animals were kept in adequate and secure facilities, properly fed, watered . . . all the requirements were satisfied.'

'Between you and me, Mr Briggs, I'm surprised there wasn't more of an uproar when these specimens got lifted; given how dangerous they are.'

Briggs shrugged. 'I suspect that the officer who came to the scene didn't really believe me. Thought I was spinning a line for the insurance. The other thing is, it's not easy keeping animals like these. All of them were from the tropics or sub-tropics, and needed specialist care. The probability of some scrounging, jobless, pillhead bastards having the know-how is fucking laughable, if you'll pardon my French. They wouldn't have lasted long, poor little mites – I'm referring to the arachnids in case you were wondering.'

'I wasn't,' Heck said. 'But it does beg the question how they turned up in your car four months later.'

Briggs slammed the van's rear door. 'You know, I seem to remember going through all this sometime in the recent past. When would it be . . . oh yeah, when I was under arrest on suspicion of murder.'

'Seeing as you're a recognised expert handler, you can surely see why no one believed it was an accident, that they'd just escaped from their containers in the back of your car?'

'I told you, I didn't even have possession of them at the time. They got stolen the previous October. I would never have left them in my car, especially not overnight.'

'So someone broke into your car the following January and planted them there?'

'Obviously.'

'It's not inconceivable, though, Mr Briggs, that you staged the earlier burglary, reported the specimens stolen, and then planted them at a later date to try and get even with the kids who've been making your life hell.'

'Good luck proving that.' Briggs walked back into his shop. 'The last lot didn't have any.'

Heck considered this. The more he thought about it, the more difficult it was to imagine that opportunist thieves – the sort who were only after money so they could buy stuff to shove up their noses or down their necks – were responsible for this. As Briggs said, the specimens would have needed ultra-careful handling. That in itself would have required significant pre-planning. According to the crime report, other items had been taken as well: a small portable television kept upstairs and a laptop that Briggs had inadvertently left overnight, and even though the till was empty that too had been broken into – typical targets for opportunists, yet that could have been to provide cover for the real object of the exercise: the theft of the spiders. There'd certainly been no other signs of a routine break-in: for example, no random damage to indicate the raiders had searched for other valuables. At the same time, though, there'd been footprints on the mossy upper surface of one of the supporting walls out back; they'd been featureless, as if whoever had left them had first covered the soles of his shoes with cloth; a rare precaution for the average scrote to take.

Heck wandered back inside. Briggs had grabbed a broom and was now in the midst of a rather desultory and perhaps pointless sweep-up.

'Okay, Mr Briggs,' Heck said. 'So if someone else planted those animals in the Volkswagen, do you have any ideas who?'

'Forgive me if I haven't got time to do your job as well as mine.'

'You haven't got any enemies – I mean apart from the local nightlife? No business rivals, no one you owe money to, no one who owes money to you?'

Briggs laid his broom aside. 'I'm a small businessman – a tiny fucking businessman, if I'm honest. How is any of that stuff going to come into my life?' He wiped sweat from his brow as he walked back outside.

Another indiscriminate target, Heck thought as he stood alone in the gutted shop. *A guy who hadn't really offended anyone – he just happened to be convenient*. He skimmed again through the documentation. According to the accident report, none of the arachnids responsible had been recovered from the wreckage last January. In fact they'd only been identified as the culprits from the toxicology reports on the corpses. Experts from Chessington Zoo had said that all were likely to have gone to ground in the surrounding hedgerows, but had also concluded that none of them would have lasted long in the British winter, and thus wouldn't pose any further threat, which – from the state of the bodies depicted on the accident scene glossies – was quite a blessing.

Outside, Briggs was busy rearranging the boxes in the rear of his van. It seemed like another pointless task, and perhaps was an unconscious means of delaying his departure from this place, which presumably had been the centre of his life for so long.

'You say pillheads wouldn't have a clue how to look after these specimens,' Heck said. 'How about everyday folk? Could a reasonably educated person keep a Deathstalker scorpion alive for four months?'

'Well . . .' Briggs gave it brief thought. 'Someone like you could probably get the information off the internet – if you were prepared to put in the research.'

'So if someone really, really wanted to keep the animals alive, they wouldn't need any formal training?'

'Probably not.'

Heck pondered this. Gail had used an interesting phrase: 'psycho pranksters'. This would have been one hell of a prank: complex to prepare, risky to execute, and still with an uncertain outcome – at least, there'd be uncertainty about who the victims would be. And good Lord – he flicked again through the images of the crash site: the faces of Richard 'Dazzer' Dasby and Darrel 'Deggsy' Degton – necrotic blue, bloated like rotten fruit, their straining, jaundiced eyes popping (one had erupted from its socket and lay swollen like a crimson duck egg on the puffy cheek). Their jaws had sprung open so violently that they'd unhinged; their hands had twisted into blackened, rheumatic knots . . . anyone chuckling about this was either very bad or very mad.

Or maybe a bit of both.

Chapter 14

Gus Donaldson wondered if he was getting too old for this kind of thing. He'd been in security for the last fifteen years, and before that had been a copper for twenty, so he wasn't unused to spending lonesome night shifts, but these days, thanks partly to his age – he was only a year off sixty-six – he found it increasingly difficult to stay awake. He stood up, yawning, and for the second time that night crossed the cabin to the tea-making table, where he brewed himself a coffee and, taking a half-pint bottle from the pocket of the high visibility coat hanging over the back of his chair, liberally dosed it with Napoleon brandy.

He shouldn't be drinking on the job of course, but at three in the morning no one else would be out here to stop him. And increasingly he felt it was the only way he could get through these long, tedious hours. The spicy cuppa hit just the right spot, but pretty soon torpor was stealing over Gus again, especially once he'd settled back into his chair. He tried hard to focus on the bank of monitors in front of him, the scene constantly switching from the Equestrian Centre to the main office, the workshops to the boating lake, and so on, though within a few minutes this itself became mesmerising, almost hypnotic. Abruptly deciding he needed some fresh air, he shook himself and stood up. Almost robotically, he pulled on his coat, slotted his torch into his belt, opened the front door, and stepped outside.

The security cabin, which was located on the east side of the Showground, wasn't really a cabin as such – it was a flat-roofed prefabricated structure, which had originally been brought here on a trailer. It consisted of only two rooms if you counted its small toilet. Outside, a velvet summer night lay over the Showground, the air scented with grass and young wheat, warmth still rising from the sun-baked fields encircling it, courtesy of the recent heatwave. This was a bit more like it; peaceful yet at the same time invigorating.

There was scarcely a sound, only the slightest breath of wind ruffling the flags atop the two rows of poles that formed an honour guard inside the east gate. Aside from the lamp in the cabin, the only other light came from a distantly setting moon and of course the myriad stars spangling the purple/black sky, which, as so often at the height of summer, appeared to fade the further east one looked until eventually blending with a faint, salmon-pink horizon.

Gus's car was parked round the back, but a couple of times now his supervisors had sternly advised him that foot patrols were a preferred option on the Showground itself, as that way he could *hear* if something was going on. That wasn't a bad shout, if he was honest, despite the arthritic twinge he was currently feeling in his left knee. For one thing, having just downed his second pick-me-up of the shift, it wouldn't do if the police turned up for some reason and caught him behind the wheel. For another, foot patrols were a good way to pass the time. The Southern Counties Showground covered several square miles in total, and Gus had already worked out that if he made two full circuits at a slow, easy pace, and then patrolled the central area too, dividing it up into quadrants, which he could explore one at a time in similar leisurely fashion, it could eat up an entire three hours – not to be sniffed at when he still had four hours to kill.

At first everything was fine. He perambulated along the central drag towards the Showground's western edge; the only sounds the thud of his rubber-soled boots, or the occasional distant call of a nightjar. As the air was clear and dry, his vision seemed to adjust more speedily than usual. There wasn't even any need to switch his torch on. Soon he was strolling down a long avenue between ranks of newly manufactured farming machines: harvesters and hay balers, the moon and stars glinting off their smooth chrome finishes. When he thought he spied a flicker of movement on the road ahead, he wrote it off as an optical illusion created by these shadowy, sleeping giants and their reflective surfaces. Nevertheless, he now felt better taking the torch from his belt, even though he still didn't turn it on – it was large and heavy, and he'd always thought it would make a good substitute for the truncheon he'd used to carry on the beat.

He covered another hundred yards, seeing nothing else, and reached a small crossroads. He halted, glancing right to the main offices and left towards the Learning Centre. Once again, there was a faint flutter of movement down there – about sixty yards distant, as if some fast-moving form had flitted across the road.

Gus held his ground for several long moments, and then felt cautiously for the radio at his belt – only to discover that it wasn't there. Frustrated, he recollected placing it on the desk alongside the CCTV monitors several hours ago. When he felt instead for the mobile phone in his pocket, that was absent too. Gus remembered leaving that near the kettle back at the commencement of his shift, after using it to call Marsha and wish her goodnight. He swore quietly to himself as he proceeded down the left-hand lane. It could still have been a trick of the light that he'd seen, but he knew he couldn't afford to make assumptions. More neatly arrayed farm machinery passed him on either side: threshers, crop sprayers – heavy complex forms in the darkness, all silent and still.

Eventually he reached the Hatchlands Pavilion: a palatial tent-like structure that would serve as one of the Trade Fair's official exhibition halls. He halted again, listening – aside from the canvas of the pavilion flapping in the breeze, there was still no sound. Glancing in through its wide-open door, he saw the vague shapes of empty tables and stands. They wouldn't be empty for much longer of course. The exhibitors would be arriving first thing to set up. Gus stepped inside the roomy interior. Even at night, with no sun to beat through the thick canvas, it felt significantly warmer in there than it did outside – it was stuffier too: mingled odours of must and trampled grass. By this time tomorrow, it would also smell of manure. He smiled to himself. Even though the stables and animal pens, and the Pirbright Hall, where most of the livestock shows were held, were a good twenty minutes' walk away, it would still smell of manure. Somehow or other, agricultural trade fairs always ended up stinking of poo.

A shadow rippled along the rear wall of the tent.

Gus blinked and it had gone.

Just as quickly as he'd jumped, he relaxed again.

The canvas awnings rustled and ruffled in the breeze. That was all he'd seen – a loose billow of material. But still he didn't switch his torch on, even though he now clutched it in a hand that was moist with sweat. He glanced more closely at the far wall – and was shaken to see that his 'loose billow of material' had halted midway and resolved itself into the silhouette of someone standing very still on the other side, as though peering through the canvas at him.

Gus again tried to tell himself that it was an optical illusion, but his blood was tingling and his mouth had gone dry. He assured himself that it would still serve no purpose to switch his torch on – its bright beam would not illuminate whatever was standing on the other side of the pavilion wall. Not that he really needed to, because the more his eyes attuned, the more he was able to visualise that motionless figure: a broad, strong torso, two arms, two legs, a head. The real reason of course, and now he couldn't help but admit this, was that if he turned his light on he would reveal his own presence here, assuming it hadn't already been detected – and what would be the purpose of that? Suddenly, Gus Donaldson felt his age. He was sixty-five years old, overweight and had a bad knee, and he hadn't tried to run anywhere in as long he could remember, much less attempt to apprehend someone.

The figure remained motionless. It knew that he was here – he could sense it.

Gus cursed himself again for not having brought his radio or phone.

Then it ran. As simply as that, the tall, stationary form turned and bolted away into invisibility.

Still Gus held his ground, though his courage was ebbing back, even more so as he heard thumping footfalls recede into the night – so the intruder really *was* running away. Well, perhaps it was understandable. Whoever it was, they'd halted out there to listen because they thought they'd heard someone inside the pavilion. On realising it was a night watchman, they'd fled.

'Okay . . . okay,' Gus said, treading back outside. He'd have a quick, cursory look around, to see if there was any sign of them. And then he'd scoot back to the cabin, where he'd give serious thought to reporting the incident. Slowly, he circled the flimsy structure, the torch gripped tightly in his shaking fist.

Alongside the Hatchlands, another portable cabin had been set up, this one a public lavatory. Gus sidled down the narrow passage between the two, having to step over pegs and guy ropes, tufts of elephant grass reaching as high as his knees. If he was honest, he hoped the intruder just kept on running – all the way until he'd vacated the Showground. Gus was definitely too old for this. His memories of distant days in uniform – *real* uniform – came back to him. When he was a strapping young beat bobby he'd never known the meaning of fear; there was almost no one he couldn't handle, and even on the rare occasion when there had been, he'd had the biggest support network any man could want at the other end of a radio. Failing that, what was the worst that could have happened? He'd get battered, but be able to spend a few days off work on full pay, with no one able to criticise him. Things were so different now.

He emerged from the side passage. Open grass lay in front, and a few yards beyond that a dark row of brand new tractors, all glinting in the starlight.

Gus stumbled to another halt. It wouldn't be difficult for someone to hide around here, to climb onto the back of one of the tractors, or conceal themselves underneath. How easily they'd be able to jump out on him.

And yet that was nonsense, surely? Why would they do that? Why would they even be here? They could hardly steal anything. Yet he'd seen someone, hadn't he? Whoever it was, they'd been here for *some* reason. Perhaps they just wanted to cause damage? Perhaps they sought to play some juvenile game of cat and mouse? Either way, Gus decided that he'd done enough. He would head back to the cabin (keeping a constant watch over his shoulder as he did), and from there he'd call the police. Brandy-coffee be damned. But just as he was turning, he was stopped by something else – a dazzling light show in the sky to the south-west.

Gus peered at it in a near-daze, thinking at first that he was seeing a UFO, but, when he squinted, realising his mistake.

Someone had raised the Trade Fair's official blimp.

That fifty-metres-by-thirty neoprene dirigible, covered with stroboscopic lighting designed to create a series of colossal brand names and advertising slogans, now hovered above the Showground at a height of forty or fifty feet. This was considerably less than the two hundred feet at which the blimp would fly once the expo team launched it in the morning to signify that the Fair was open, but even so it shouldn't have been launched at all just yet.

It struck Gus that the blimp probably hadn't been secured properly after testing during the previous day, or maybe its launch mechanism had developed a fault? At first warily, but with increasing speed, he made his way over there, threading between rows of silent machines. As he did, the blimp's lights went out – all at once, as if a switch had been thrown, though the blimp itself remained where it was, now in silhouette, framed on the waning moon.

Gus halted again – in a narrow passage between two combine harvesters.

What was going on? Was it something to do with the intruder?

It suddenly seemed highly probable that it was.

He stared ahead, still unwilling to switch on his torch and attract attention, but now feeling very strongly that he owed it to himself, if not to his employers, to at least sneak over there and see what was happening. There was just sufficient moonlight to reveal the narrow alley running on between the machines. So he proceeded, until at last he came to the edge of the caravan park – a vast plain of tarmac, largely empty though, in the very centre of which was the flatbed lorry from which the blimp flew.

Gus squinted in the dimness, half-expecting to see diminutive figures dancing around it; a party of hoodie hooligans rejoicing like some bunch of urban baboons. But though he stared long and hard, he saw no one and nothing. The idea rekindled in his mind that some kind of technical fault might be the cause, and that the intruder he'd seen had left the area. Cautiously, Gus ventured into the open. There was no mistake – the lorry, which was about fifty yards away, looked completely unattended, the blimp swaying high above it on its tensioned cable. His confidence grew as he strode forward. True, it seemed odd that the lights had gone off apparently of their own accord, but they must have come on of their own accord as well – he certainly hadn't spotted them earlier, so maybe the whole system was misfiring.

He finally felt brave enough to switch his torch on, its powerful beam shooting far ahead of him. He was the security officer here, he reminded himself. He would take charge of this situation. If there was a fault with the blimp, he might even be able to fix it somehow. That would win him a few brownie points; Gus was only too aware that his bosses were developing concerns about his advancing years.

He reached the lorry, his light playing over it. The driving cab appeared to be closed and locked, as it should be. In the centre of the rear deck was the blimp's launch mechanism, which in appearance was like a large drum spooled with steel cable, a couple of crank handles fixed to it, one on either side. It could be operated either manually or automatically from a transistorised control panel, though in truth that was as much as he knew about it. A creaking of metal and groaning of ropes drew his attention to the vast inflatable overhead, and Gus was surprised to see that its four tether lines were hanging loose, one of their tail ends drifting on the tarmac only a few yards to his right. That was quite an oversight by the operators, though it might explain a few things: for instance how, even though the blimp was still anchored by its central cable, a gust of wind might have caught it and turned the launch-drum around a few times. Gus wasn't sure if this was actually possible, though he guessed it probably was if the drum hadn't been secured either. Again, his torchlight roved over the heavy vehicle. The blimp was probably safe – it was purpose-designed to fly much higher than this, and in much stronger turbulence. But it seemed wrong to ignore this situation.

He stood on his toes to peer onto the lorry's deck, and there spotted another mechanical assemblage. This one looked like a gas cylinder resting upright on a wheeled, two-handled trolley. It had various attachments: loops of rubber hosing connected to what resembled a metallic pistol with a large trigger.

Gus was baffled. Surely that couldn't be right?

Was that a cutting torch, maybe?

Though on reflection, perhaps this made sense. If there'd been a fault with the blimp's launch mechanism, maybe they'd been trying to fix it and hadn't quite finished when darkness came. But shouldn't security have been informed? And wouldn't this be a dangerous piece of kit to leave lying around?

Gus circled the vehicle, and found a narrow aluminium ladder fixed to the nearside flank. He climbed up it and approached the suspect gear, shining his light over it. He'd been correct – this was industrial cutting equipment. It should never have been left insecure like this; that was quite ridiculous. He supposed he'd better take it back to the cabin for safekeeping, but the question was how to lug it down from the lorry. He tried moving it, only to find it heavy and awkward – the cutting torch fell to the deck with a clatter. He picked it up and hooked it back on the trolley, before stepping back, hands on hips – and heard what sounded like a high-pitched titter.

Gus twirled round, blasting his beam of light across the deck.

There was nobody there with him. That much was plain. Another sound distracted him, this one from down on the car park: a light skittering, like the pitter-patter a dog makes when it trots across tarmac. Either that, or someone running on tiptoes.

Before he could react properly, that titter sounded again, this time behind him.

Gus swung back, inclining the torch beam upwards – and now thought he was seeing things, because a figure appeared to be sitting cross-legged on the roof of the lorry's driving cab. Initially, Gus felt surprise rather than alarm. He couldn't understand why he hadn't noticed the figure before. Unless it had either been crouching low or lying flat. Shakily, he shone his torch over it. This could not be the intruder from earlier; that had been a large person, tall and burly. This one was slight, even if he was clad in grey overalls, and even if he did have his gloved hands clasped across his face.

'What . . . what are you doing here?' Gus demanded.

The figure didn't move.

'Look, I know this place is tempting. Lots of ways to have fun and all that. But it's not a playground, see. There's dangerous gear. Particularly this lot . . .' Gus waved a hand behind him to indicate the cutting torch. He was attempting a placatory approach because even though the intruder's smallish stature was encouraging, these bloody kids could supposedly turn nasty. 'Look sonny, you've got to get away from here. For your own good. The police are coming . . .'

The figure dropped its hands.

Gus audibly gasped.

At worst, he'd anticipated missing teeth, sneering feral features.

One thing he'd never expected was the dim-witted smile of Stan Laurel.

With a dull *clank, clank, clank*, a second person climbed to the lorry's deck.

Gus pivoted round, and saw a taller, broader figure ascend into view. When he shone his torch on it, this one also wore grey overalls and a shiny plastic mask. Almost inevitably, that mask bore the plump, mustachioed visage of Oliver Hardy.

Gus turned to flee, though he didn't know where he could flee to, only to find that Stan Laurel had jumped silently from the cabin roof and was standing directly behind him. This close, Laurel wasn't particularly small either, and by the firm, no-nonsense way that he grabbed hold of the watchman, he was strong and athletic.

'Help – help!' Gus bawled as, together, they dragged him down onto the wooden planking, his torch rolling away across the deck, falling from the lorry and smashing on the tarmac. Grotesque grinning parodies of Laurel and Hardy – those gentle, genial comedians of an age long forgotten – peered soullessly into his eyes as they pinned him there. 'Take . . . take whatever you want,' he gasped as they searched through his clothing. 'Only I've not got nothing worth pinching, nothing.'

He heard again that eerie, ululating giggle.

Laurel had located a prize, which he held aloft in the spectral moonlight: the half-pint bottle of Napoleon brandy, still three-quarters full. Gus keened helplessly as gloved fingers were forced between his lips and teeth, levering his mouth open. He watched through tear-filmed eyes as the cap was unscrewed and the bottle upended – and hot spirit poured down his throat, wave after spiteful wave. He gulped and glugged and gargled. Laurel tittered again – a truly deranged sound – and even slapped the bottom of the bottle, as one does when attempting to loosen chunks of sludgy ketchup from a plastic dispenser.

Of course he couldn't drink it all; not even an old soak like Gus. So when his gurgling turned to choking they relented, even though there were still a couple of measures left. Hardy gripped Gus by the lapels of his jacket and yanked him upright so that his leaner partner could pour what remained in the bottle all over their victim's head. They released him and he fell back, his skull clouting the wooden planking, though he was in such a state by now that he barely felt it.

Ages seemed to pass as they let him lie there, two featureless shadows busying themselves around him, still chuckling and tittering, highly amused by their own actions. But it was only when an intense red light spurted into view that Gus groggily realised he had to take action. He shook his head to clear it; blinked to try and focus – but the alcohol was sinking through his body like a strong narcotic.

The red light intensified to a blinding white, and sparks flew from it – illuminating the head of the taller of his two attackers, who now wore a pair of black goggles over his Oliver Hardy mask.

Good Christ . . . were they doing what Gus thought they were doing?

Oh, good Christ!

The revelation galvanised him to dig his heels into the deck, bend his knees and try to raise himself on his elbows – only for a trainer-clad foot to slam down on his shoulder and knock him flat again. Laurel, who had briefly vanished, presumably having descended from the lorry, was back, now with something hanging from his hand, and tittering again, insanely. Gus couldn't be sure, but it looked as if he was holding a length of rope, almost certainly the end of a tether line.

Chapter 15

'The problem is,' Heck said, 'until you admit that your load was insecure, sloppily packed . . . whatever, there'll be no chance of parole. That means you'll serve your full sentence.'

Gordon Meredith shrugged. 'Some things are worth doing time for.'

'What about your wife and kids? Don't they want you home?'

Meredith looked startled. 'You think that's a reason to lie? To tell the world I'm a criminal no-mark when the truth is the exact opposite? If I do that, my real sentence will start when I get home. Because they'll think I'm a lesser bloke.'

Meredith was a short, pear-shaped man in his late thirties, with thinning blond hair, a pinkish complexion, and a vaguely fishy look – fat lips, a flat nose and wide watery blue eyes. When he'd first come waddling across the otherwise empty exercise yard, where they now sat facing each other over a bolted-down plastic table, he'd looked more than a little ridiculous in his baggy grey sweats.

'Fair play,' Heck said. 'If you think you can stick it.'

Meredith shrugged again. 'I can stick it. I've only got another year and a bit to go. This place isn't as bad as I thought it would be.'

This place was Wayland Prison, in Norfolk. Even under a blue sky and bright sunshine, its admin buildings and housing blocks had the usual air of no-frills functionality, while its exercise yard was enclosed by a twelve-foot wall and beyond that several extra layers of electrified fencing. But Heck had seen worse.

'Low-risk offenders, you see,' he said. 'Play your cards right, they might move you to open prison in a couple of months. You may even qualify for home leave.'

Meredith regarded him curiously. 'Are you here to offer me some kind of inducement?'

'What? No way. I'm not going to try and persuade you to change your story. You want the truth, Gordon, I'm starting to believe *your* version of events.'

The prisoner looked perplexed. 'Who did you say you were again?'

Heck flashed his warrant card. 'Heckenburg. Serial Crimes Unit.'

'Serial Crimes? Sounds a bit heavy.'

'It may be that I'm completely wasting my time here – and yours. But anything that could help us get to the actual truth has got to be worth looking at, don't you think?'

'Well, yeah, obviously.'

'Don't get your hopes up, though. Because I'm telling you, this is the long shot of all long shots.'

'Okay . . .'

'Tell me about the accident again. Exactly what happened?'

Meredith leaned forward onto his elbows. 'I was delivering scaffolding between the depot at Leatherhead and a site down in Horsham. I was on the A24. It was late morning and busy. I'm telling you . . .' and he clenched his fist on the

160

table, 'I categorically assure you that before I set out the scaffolding was secure.'

'You checked it yourself?'

'Absolutely.'

'Anybody else check it with you?'

'No; that was a mistake on reflection. But . . . I trust myself, you know.' Meredith screwed up his face as he relived the memory. 'I've been doing this for fifteen years. I'm not a novice.'

Attached to his paperwork Heck had a few glossies, all taken at the scene of the accident. He flipped through them again. They depicted a large section of road, which Traffic cops had cordoned off with cones and incident tape. A drop-sided truck was standing skew-whiff in the middle of the carriageway, numerous scaffolding poles, each one twelve to fifteen feet of gleaming, cylindrical steel, which had clearly been propped up over the driving cab, were scattered all around it or hung over the windscreen. Evidently, they had all pitched forward at the moment of the emergency stop. Some ten yards in front of the truck sat a silver Renault Megane. Two scaffolding poles had slammed into it, one from above, punching down through its roof and now standing vertical like a flagpole, the other smashing through its rear window. Only five or six feet of this second pole were exposed outside the car, but interior shots revealed the rest of it. They also portrayed a male figure in the driving seat, though now he lay slumped across the steering wheel. He wore what looked like a white shirt and black waistcoat, though both of these were drenched with blood. The scaffolding pole had pierced him through the middle of the back, a position from which it must have sheared his spine and torn clean through his cardiovascular system.

'How long did the overall journey take?' Heck asked.

'An hour to an hour and a half,' Meredith replied. 'Not what you'd call long-haul.'

'And yet you stopped en route?'

'Only for a cup of tea and a bacon sarnie. It was a driver's caff near Dorking, close to the Pixham roundabout.'

Heck continued to scan the photos. Even though the driver's head lay sideways on the wheel, a mass of longish curly hair hung down, obscuring his face. From the accompanying notes, the guy had been completely transfixed, the front of the pole embedding itself in the steering column.

'And you think that's when someone might have interfered with your load?'

'They must have done.' Meredith scratched confusedly at his balding scalp. 'Must have loosened some of the straps at least. I was in the caff about twenty minutes. More than enough time. Okay, I'll admit that when I came out again, I didn't check my load. I know I should have done. I know that was remiss of me, but you don't think someone's going to try and pinch a load of scaffolding at a truckstop in the middle of the day, do you? I mean, I've never heard of that before.'

'This whole thing's got some pretty unique aspects to it.'

'Yeah . . . trust it to happen to me, of all people.'

'And to Freddie Upton,' Heck reminded him. 'I'm sure his family would want you to remember that.'

'Yeah – point taken.' Again, Meredith grimaced. 'Poor bastard, eh? He was in the motor in front of me. A Megane. Didn't really notice him at first, but it's imprinted on my bloody brain now. Everything was fine. Traffic was too heavy for anyone to be driving dangerously. We probably got up to about fifty at times, but mostly it was between thirty and forty. And then this fucking cyclist!' Meredith shook his head. 'I don't know where he came from. I'm driving along and suddenly he's on the nearside, between me and the kerb. And absolutely tonning it, like he's trying to stay abreast of me.'

'He was overtaking you on the inside?'

'Fucking right, he was. You've seen these fucking gypsies of the road. Talk about one rule for us and none for them. Weaving between vehicles, sailing through red lights. And they're always the first to quote their fucking rights if there's an accident.'

'Can you describe the cyclist?'

Meredith slumped back on his bench. 'I only saw him properly when he got ahead of me, when I had to slow down a bit. He was on a green Boardman's racing bike, I know that much.'

'And what did he look like?'

'As I say, only saw him from behind. A lad, by the looks of him. Lean, rangy frame, fit – you know. He had all the gear on: blue vest, black shorts, blue racing helmet with silver flashes on it. I remember he had short, dark hair. It'd got so I just wanted him gone. Traffic was too heavy for me to get past him, so I just sat behind, hoping he'd veer off somewhere. But he didn't. Just stayed there, ten yards in front, going like the clappers. Then the traffic opens up a bit. And I'd said "here we go, I'm sorted". I can see this red light about a hundred yards ahead, but I thought I'll get up to that, leave this idiot behind once and for all, and clear on through as it changes. And then . . .' Beads of sweat burst on Meredith's forehead. 'Just as I hit the accelerator, he swerved right – like he was going to swing across in front of me. Deliberate, like. He must have had a fucking death wish. It's a miracle I didn't cream him . . .' He chewed his lip, his words tailing off.

'And?' Heck said.

'Well, I hit the brakes. Probably doing just over forty. The wheels locked and I went into a forward skid. Must have slid thirty yards, then bang, hit the stop. And the scaffolding just launched itself over the cab – it was like a flock of missiles all taking off at the same time. Most of them clattered down onto the road, but two smacked into the Megane. One hit the roof, the other went through the back window and straight through Freddie Upton. Jesus . . .' Meredith licked his ashen lips. 'The rest you know.'

'And what happened to the cyclist?' Heck asked.

'Well, he didn't actually swerve in front of me, or he'd have got killed too. He'd manoeuvred as if he was going to, and then he just darted back out of the way.'

'Definitely a deliberate act?' Heck said.

'Seemed like it. Anyway, I lost sight of him after that. This was quite a built-up area. There was any number of side streets and turn-offs. Once he realised what he'd done, he probably scarpered.'

Heck eyed him carefully. 'Gordon . . . the Traffic officers who investigated this incident spoke to a number of witnesses, and none reported seeing this cyclist. Not just at the time of the accident, but at any time during the ten minutes leading up to it.'

'Course they fucking wouldn't!' Meredith blurted. 'I told you, most of the time he was riding on my nearside. I was probably screening him from the other road users. Besides, they were all probably too shocked to notice. You ever witnessed a bad accident? I'm sure you have. Do you remember every single thing that happened?'

Heck could find nothing to dispute in that. 'The thing is, Gordon, I'm wondering if this whole thing might have been stage-managed.'

Meredith stared at him for several disbelieving seconds. 'What?'

'As I said, this is a long shot. So keep your feet firmly on the ground. However, I am considering – and that's the only word I can use at present, I'm *considering* the possibility that this guy on the racing bike had something to do with loosening your load at the café near Dorking.'

'Are you serious?'

'I should also tell you that I have absolutely no evidence for that whatsoever.'

'But why would he do that?'

'It beats me, I'll be honest. But this seems like a curious succession of coincidences, and that's not something I encounter very often in my job.'

'Nah.' Meredith shook his head. 'I don't want to rain on your parade, Christ knows I don't, but there's no way someone could have been targeting Freddie Upton deliberately. When those scaffolding poles flew, any number of innocent people could have been hurt or killed, but you couldn't have picked a target out specifically.'

'I don't think Freddie Upton was targeted,' Heck said. 'I think *you* were. Is there anyone who dislikes you enough to do that?'

Again, Meredith looked flabbergasted. 'To trick me into causing a fatal accident? No . . . I'm a family man. I live quietly and mind my own business.'

That was the second time Heck had heard this sentiment expressed in the last two days. How often, it seemed, the collaterals were always the least deserving of such a fate. And yet how chilling that it was ordinary, innocent folk like these, whom the perpetrators probably didn't even know and yet were happy to shatter like clay ducks.

'When you came out of the supply depot at Leatherhead, did you notice anyone hanging around who shouldn't have been?'

Meredith shrugged. 'No.'

'No one looked like they may have been following you afterwards?'

'You think someone actually followed me to that truck-stop?' If possible, Meredith's face had paled even more; folk were never happy to learn that they'd been under observation. 'It couldn't have been that cyclist. He'd never have been able to keep up. Not for that whole distance.'

'I agree,' Heck said. 'He couldn't have been working alone.'

'You mean there's more than one of them? For Christ's sake, how many people could hate me that much?'

'I don't know, Gordon, that's why I'm asking you. Did you see anyone hanging around, tailing you . . . did anything strike you as unusual that morning?'

'No – oh wait. The CCTV at the supply depot. That would have caught someone.'

'I've already rung the supply depot. Their cameras are focused on the inner yard, where all the goods are kept. I can't believe this guy would have been waiting for you *inside* the actual yard. That would have been a bit conspicuous.'

'This is incredible.' Meredith looked shell-shocked, but his tone had lightened, and why not? – against all the odds, it suddenly looked as if he might be off the hook.

'I said don't get your hopes up,' Heck reminded him, 'and I meant it. I may still be imagining all this.'

'No, no – what you're saying makes sense. It's unbeliev-able, but it actually makes sense.'

'Glad you think so. That's two of us, at least.'

When Heck left the prison it was lunchtime, and the traffic around Thetford was heavy. It would take him a good three hours to get back to Surrey as it was, so he pulled in at the first country pub he saw to get something to eat.

The Farmer's Arms seemed a reasonable bet – all white-washed stucco with a thatched roof and baskets spilling summer blooms under its mullioned windows. But he walked inside feeling tired and disheartened. His sprained ankle was aching slightly and, with his suit jacket ripped apart, he was back in casuals – jeans, a T-shirt and a light jacket – which, though they were comfortable, never gave him that official aura so beneficial when he was on duty.

It was an incredibly ugly thought that someone might have *manufactured* Gordon Meredith's accident. Perhaps it was the wholesale indiscriminate nature of the thing – anyone could have died or been horrifically injured, literally *anyone*: a woman, a child, an elderly person. At the same time, the high level of chance reinforced the notion that this really was a bizarre kind of game from which the perpetrators were deriving immense enjoyment. While anybody might have been killed, it was equally possible that nobody might have. In his mind's eye, Heck could picture his faceless adversaries eagerly awaiting the outcome of their scheme, yearning for it to pay off. And just out of interest, if it didn't, what would they do? Presumably write that job off as a misfire and move on to the next one. Perhaps that had happened a dozen times already. It didn't matter as it would never be anything more than an accident; these things happen, you know, and those involved had been very unfortunate.

The more Heck pondered this, the more disturbing it was to him how simple the overall ploy was. If you really wanted to hurt people – to maim them, to disfigure them, to kill them – what better way than to set up accidents? And what fun you could have planning it all and rehearsing. And of course, if you weren't too picky about who specifically was to suffer – if you just wanted to injure *someone* – then it didn't really matter if, on occasion, things didn't come off. It wasn't as if you weren't covered. Fatal outcome or not, there would always be stooges like Gordon Meredith to cop the blame.

The pub taproom was half full, a bunch of regulars clustered around a widescreen TV. Heck sat at the bar and, as there was no bartender in view, helped himself to a menu. Everything in there was 'guaranteed locally sourced and home-cooked', and it all looked good. Opting for a steak sandwich with salad, he replaced the menu on the counter and glanced around, puzzled as to why there was still nobody serving. He spied a buxom redhead wearing an apron, but she was standing with the punters, all of whose attention was riveted on the TV. Heck glanced at the screen, wondering what the interest was, and seeing live news footage of what looked like a massive barrage balloon drifting languidly above hills and treetops, a helicopter in close attendance.

'. . . *in what is now thought to be a disastrous and outlandish accident,*' the newscaster was in the process of saying, his voice tense.

Heck looking away, wondering at the absurdity of such comments. Disastrous? An escaped balloon?

'*The opening of the Southern Counties Agricultural Trade Fair at the Royal Surrey Showground has obviously been delayed,*' the newscaster intoned. '*Nobody can say when it will actually go ahead.*'

Surrey . . .

Belatedly, the word struck Heck.

He shifted round on his stool.

Now that he was looking closely at the screen, a diminutive shape was dangling beneath the balloon on the end of a line.

'*The problem is that we don't know whether the man suspended from the dirigible – and he appears to be suspended by his left foot, is conscious or even alive,*' came a second voice from the television, possibly a reporter at the scene. '*Medical experts tell us that if a person is inverted for long enough, some suggesting that it may be as short a time period as two or three hours, it can lead to blood clots and strokes . . .*'

The newscaster cut back in. '*And there is absolutely no way the emergency services are able to bring him down at this stage?*'

'*Well . . . as you can see, John, there is a police helicopter on the scene, and there are fire crews and ambulances in pursuit on the ground. But the dirigible isn't stationary. It's been caught in this strengthening northerly wind and is currently sailing across the Surrey countryside at a height of roughly four hundred feet, and speeds of up to thirty-five miles an hour. In that respect, it isn't far off posing a hazard to passing aircraft.*'

Heck climbed from his stool and crossed the taproom.

'*This is an extraordinary situation, James,*' the newscaster replied. '*I mean, I'm assuming there are no protocols for dealing with this?*'

'*It's never happened before as far as we're aware. Not in modern times. And to be honest, John, it's difficult to see how this can end . . .*'

The scene reverted to the newsroom, where the anchorman was seated at his desk with a suitably grim expression. The ongoing drama, now with two police helicopters circling the escaped dirigible, continued as a thumbnail in the top left-hand corner.

'*We have a development on this breaking story,*' the anchorman said. '*To recap, the escaped balloon is thought to be an advertising blimp, which was somehow released from its mooring at the Southern Counties Agricultural Trade Fair due to open today at the Royal Surrey Showground in Woking. We're now getting reports that the man caught up underneath it is one of the Showground security guards. We must state that this isn't fact. We can't confirm those details. But what we seem to be dealing with here is a truly unprecedented accident, for which there are no established procedures . . .*'

Heck retreated from the crowd of viewers, fished his mobile

from his pocket and tapped in Gail's number. She answered it quickly, but in a distracted tone.

'Tell me you're watching this,' he said.

'Yeah, we've got it on the telly in the office.'

'Is this, or isn't it, a made-to-measure addition to our series?'

'Heck . . . we don't even know what's happened yet.'

'Have we got anyone over there?'

'Where?'

'The Trade Fair at Woking. What else are we talking about?'

'Erm . . .' She was clearly preoccupied by what she was witnessing. 'There are local lads on the scene, dealing, yeah.'

'We need to find out what happened.'

'I'm sure we'll get a report in due course.'

'Look, Gail!' He hadn't intended to raise his voice, and tried to lower it again. 'This could be the first live crime scene we've had – the first one we can tackle while we're still inside the Golden Hour.'

'Heck, I know what you're doing here, and I can sympathise to a point—'

'Will you get it out of your head that I'm trying to invent something! I don't *need* extra work, Gail!'

'All you're doing is throwing a net over every unfortunate incident in the—'

'There's unfortunate and there's bloody ridiculous. This one needs looking at.'

She sighed. 'You want me to go to Woking, don't you? Where are *you?*'

'Norfolk. You tell me which of us is closer.' Before he could say more, he was distracted by gasps of horror from the locals around the television.

'*Oh my goodness!*' came the strained voice of the anchorman. '*Oh no, oh no . . .*'

Somehow or other, the news crew on the ground had managed to get closer to the errant dirigible. The figure dangling upside down underneath was much clearer; his spread-eagled posture and fluorescent green coat were clearly distinguishable. But for some reason, the blimp itself seemed to be deflating and with alarming speed – as if it had been ruptured. Even as a TV audience of millions watched aghast, the blimp nosed downward and commenced a rapidly accelerating descent. Four hundred feet, three hundred – by the time it hit two hundred it was little more than a ragged mass of swirling neoprene spinning towards Earth, its unwilling passenger arrowing ahead of it. To a chorus of horror on the television – clearly members of the public were gathered alongside the news crew – it vanished behind the roofs of a suburban housing estate. A cloud of dust and debris erupted upwards.

A dumbfounded silence followed.

'*I'm afraid we're lost for words here in the studio, ladies and gentlemen,*' the anchorman finally said. '*Obviously there was some kind of flaw in that inflatable object . . .*'

Perhaps for the first time in his career, his words trailed off mid-sentence.

Then there was a hubbub of voices in the pub taproom. At the other end of the phone Gail was breathing in short, sharp gasps.

'A flaw, my bloody arse!' Heck said. 'Listen, change of plan. Wherever that thing's landed, you've got to go *there*. I'll get back to base ASAP, but I'll probably call in at the Thornton farm near Woldingham first – it's on my way back.'

Gail replied as if she hadn't heard him. 'Maybe that blimp got caught on a power line?'

'It didn't.' His tone hardened. 'You just watched it happen, Gail. Don't slip any deeper into denial than you already are.'

'Look, there could be any reason for what's just happened.'

'Which is why you need to go and find out everything you can – so that we can either include it in our enquiries or dismiss it. Or is there something else you'd rather be doing, DC Honeyford? Perhaps talking to FIU again and hearing for the umpteenth time that they haven't got, and never have had, any Suspicious Activity Reports on Harold Lansing.'

Heck cut the call and, as he headed outside to his car, bashed in another number. The phone rang briefly, and then was answered.

'Serial Crimes Unit,' came a bass, husky voice. 'DS Fisher.'

'Eric, it's Heck.'

'Hey man, how you doing?'

'Not so good. We're up to our eyes in corpses down here.' Heck climbed into his car.

'I just saw that one on the news,' Fisher replied. 'Who'd have thought it in leafy Surrey, eh?'

'That's only one of them.'

Fisher, one of the most trustworthy intelligence men Heck knew, sounded vaguely surprised. 'There hasn't been anything else reported . . .'

'You're going to get it all, don't worry.' Heck opened his laptop, and was pleased to find that he was still within range of the pub's wi-fi. 'Chapter and verse. If you can spare me a few hours.'

'A few *hours*?'

'I need some background analysis, Eric. And whoever does it is going to have to dig very deep indeed.'

'Well . . . I've got other stuff on. But nothing that won't wait, I suppose.'

'Good man. Listen, I'm about to email you some case notes referring to a bunch of supposed accidental deaths. Use any and every database you can, pal. Cross-reference all the names that crop up – the victims, the bereaved, witnesses, suspects. All of them. See if there're any connections.'

'These are all just random incidents?'

'Allegedly.'

'So I may be completely wasting my time?'

'If you are I'll be delighted.' Heck hit the send button, switched his computer off and dragged his seatbelt into place. 'It'll mean I can come home, and leave this lot to their own devices.'

'Bunch of hicks, are they?'

'Suffice to say I'm not getting as much cooperation as I might. Not that I can really blame them. At present we haven't got squat.'

Fisher grunted. 'I'll give it my best shot.'

'Better than that, if you can. I need *something*, Eric. I'm flying totally blind down here.'

Chapter 16

Gail's initial decision was that she wouldn't go anywhere near the blimp crash site at Tilford. It was a principle more than anything else. Mark Heckenburg hadn't exactly pulled rank on her, but she hadn't appreciated his tone. Besides, in her opinion he was hypothesising to a ridiculous extent. The idea that someone was staging weird and unlikely accidents was beyond the pale. It came out of a TV thriller, not real life. She had her own more down-to-earth leads to follow, and was damned if she was putting them on hold purely to soft-soap her partner's know-it-all attitude. But as she went upstairs to the station canteen to get a ham sandwich and a cup of tea, she had to admit to being a little torn on the matter.

It would probably be remiss of her to not at least check with the officers investigating the blimp incident, to see if it matched up.

But matched up with what?

Harold Lansing had died in a road traffic accident, which was most likely – though this had yet to be proved – murder. There'd be nothing outrageously unusual in that. Vehicles had been used as murder weapons many times in the past.

Then there was the pet shop business, the details of which she'd only skimmed through, though from what she'd seen the shop owner had clearly been lax; he obviously wasn't looking after his animals properly, and two car thieves had got unlucky. The same applied to the lorry driver who'd shed his load. Most likely human error – a simple RTA. Nothing unusual, nothing . . . what was that word the news anchorman had used, 'outlandish'?

There was something undeniably macabre about these cases. And maybe it was curious that they'd all occurred in Surrey in the last few months, but coincidences did happen. Didn't they?

She was so lost in these ruminations that, even after she'd sat down at an otherwise empty table, her lunch lay untouched for several minutes. It was only when she'd taken one or two halfhearted nibbles at her sandwich that she noticed Ron Pavey and a couple of his Street Thefts cronies seated at the next table along, evidently discussing her. Pavey occasionally glanced around, that sardonic grin plastered to his ugly mug.

Gail looked away, trying to ignore him. She checked her watch. Truth was, she now felt a twinge of guilt. It wasn't advancing the investigation sitting here doing nothing, even though she was entitled to the occasional meal break. Someone pulled out a chair at the other side of the table, and placed down his own sandwich and teacup. Assuming this would be Pavey coming back for round eighty-nine or whatever it was, she prepared her most withering stare – and found herself face to face with Will Royton.

'Oh, guv . . .'

'Everything all right?' he asked, unfolding his napkin.

'Erm, yeah, course.'

He glanced up at her, detecting a tone. 'You sure?'

'Guv – DS Heckenburg?' She wasn't quite certain how to pose this question. 'Is he the real deal?'

'Why do you ask?'

'Well, we're supposed to be working on the death of Harold Lansing. Now he wants me over at Tilford.'

Royton bit into his sandwich. 'Let me guess: the crash site of that AWOL barrage balloon? Nasty business, that.'

'Well yeah, but I don't see what it's got to do with me.'

Royton shrugged. 'I'm sure he'd do it himself, but he was at Wayland Prison this morning, as I understand it, interviewing Gordon Meredith. You remember him?'

'Yeah, the lorry driver.' Gail was puzzled. 'Sorry guv, how do you know about that?'

'DS Heckenburg's kept me fully abreast of his enquiries. His updates are a bit short on detail, but at least they're regular. He's obviously working fast – I understand he's now off to some farm where a chap called Thornton tried to inflate a tractor tyre and somehow ended up inflating himself.'

'Yeah, it's somewhere near Woldingham.'

Royton eyed her as he ate. 'And you're liaising with FIU to see if Harold Lansing had any financial skeletons in his closet?'

'Erm, yeah . . .'

'How is that progressing?'

'Not well, I'm afraid. I've not exhausted every avenue, of course. Far from it. But for the moment it looks like Lansing was clean.'

Royton shrugged. 'Perhaps Mark Heckenburg's got something?'

'Most likely a vivid imagination.'

'You sure about that, Gail?'

'He's guessing, guv. It would be the most extraordinary thing on Earth if all these tragic deaths were connected.'

'More extraordinary than if they were all genuine accidents – all weird in nature, all happening in the same geographic vicinity, all within a relatively short time period?'

She regarded him with interest. 'You're not buying into this, are you?'

'Gail, let me tell you something about DS Heckenburg. He's come to us with the recommendation of Detective Superintendent Piper at the Serial Crimes Unit. Now I know it's fashionable to diss these specialist units in the big city – write them all off as elitist prats who won't get out of bed in the morning unless national survival is at stake, but that isn't what it's like. I know Gemma Piper well, and she runs a very efficient unit. SCU detectives have been at the cutting edge of some major and complex investigations, and Mark Heckenburg's been right there with them. I was warned that he thinks outside the box, though this is supposedly his strength not his weakness. I've been warned he's no stranger to controversy . . . that he's unconventional, unorthodox, but also that he makes things happen.'

'That's all fine and dandy, guv, but frankly I'm more concerned about my reputation than Mark Heckenburg's.' She made a dismissive gesture. 'Great, he's got a glowing track record. Fine, wonderful. I'm impressed. But at present he's off in some strange fantasy world, and I'm worried he's going to drag me into it.'

Royton gave this some thought. 'Gail, is it possible you shouldn't be so concerned about your reputation?'

'Guv?'

'Not to the extent that it's limiting your effectiveness on the job.'

'Guv, I didn't mean—'

'Hear me out, Gail. If nothing else, DS Heckenburg is a senior rank to you. That means he has tactical command.'

'Tactical command?'

'I told you, you're a taskforce of two, and I'm afraid – if it comes down to it – he's the boss. Now if you're unhappy about anything – his methods, his management style, anything at all – write it on paper and forward it up the chain. I assure you it won't be ignored. But for the time being, I don't think it would do any harm for you to treat his input a little more seriously.'

As Gail headed west along the A25, she hadn't felt so chastened in quite some time. Will Royton's stern words hardly qualified as a telling-off – not by police standards – but he had, to a degree, put her in her place. And that was something Gail didn't enjoy.

She'd been just under a year in CID, and three years in uniform before that. In a relatively brief time she'd logged a significant number of arrests, many of which had proceeded to full conviction, including two for murder, when as a young PC she'd found herself in the right place at just the right time. Some poor sod was hammered coming out of a kebab shop late on a Friday night. It was a case of mistaken identity, but the two hoodlums responsible had both broken bottles over his head, killing him instantly. Gail had been the first officer on the scene, those responsible were pointed out by shocked onlookers and, with the assistance of the public, she'd made the arrests. Those were the collars that had kick-started her career and, professionally at least, there'd been nothing to detract from it since. As a detective, she'd had a steady turnover of prisoners; there'd been no disciplinary procedures against her; she'd rarely even been reprimanded. In her last written assessment, she'd been described as 'a highly proficient officer with an excellent working knowledge of the job, a good temperament to go with it, and a determination to succeed'. She'd already passed her sergeant's and inspector's exams, and although the promotion call hadn't come yet, she was increasingly hopeful that it would, even if it did necessitate going back into uniform for a spell.

Everything had been going swimmingly – apart from that business with Ron Pavey. That hadn't been good if she was honest, which she rarely was on this subject, even with herself. Now she put all that down to having been very young and inexperienced, to having been blown away by Ron's superficial qualities of street smarts and knowhow. At least that was all over now. Okay, she'd stayed with him longer than she ought to have – mainly because she hadn't wanted to be seen as shallow, dropping a lover at the first sign of something better coming along, though that in itself could now be construed as naivety. The main thing was that she'd got rid of the idiot – eventually. She felt like such a fool, the way it had ended so messily. Not just because of the pain it had involved, but because it had happened in the sight of so many. Not *all* of it – thank God! But enough of it to turn her cheeks red whenever she recollected it. But one way or another, thankfully, she'd got rid of him.

And now this business with Detective Sergeant Mark 'Heck' Heckenburg.

'Heck!' she snorted as she drove. 'Great nickname.'

He'd seemed like an okay guy too, once she thought she'd got to know him. Until Ron had stuck his nose in, and Heck had been far too quick to enter into a dick-measuring contest. On top of that, he was now doing precisely what he'd promised he wouldn't: riding roughshod over her views and giving her orders. Even Will bloody Royton was in on the act.

At Guildford she took the A248 towards Shalford, still far from convinced this wasn't an utter waste of time. She steered her Punto through the steadily increasing mid-afternoon traffic, making progressively less headway until at last, while passing Godalming, she found herself shuffling along at less than walking pace – and all the time her doubts grew on her.

It was true that everything Royton had said about Heck

179

had made an impression of sorts. There was no doubt that he was a talented detective. He wouldn't have got where he was because of his disarming manner (which he didn't have anyway), or because of his looks (which he did have, if she was truthful). But why the hell did he have to turn up now, at just the wrong time? And why did his theories have to be so wildly at variance with hers? And yet here she was again, as Will Royton would say, thinking about herself rather than the enquiry. Even Heck had noticed it, accusing her of trying to turn this thing into a competition, and getting the hump as a result – with more than a little justification, she grudgingly admitted.

At Tilford, she found that she wasn't the first on the scene.

Local officers had cordoned off two or three residential streets at the north end of the small suburban community. Not only that, the Air Accidents Investigation Branch had arrived from Aldershot.

'Who did you say you were?' asked the uniformed sergeant minding the perimeter. He was a tall man with a military bearing and a clipped red/grey moustache.

Gail showed him her warrant card for the second time. 'DC Honeyford. Reigate Hall CID.'

He eyed her suspiciously. 'And what's your interest here, DC Honeyford?'

A couple of younger uniformed blokes, no doubt constables from this sergeant's relief, stood some distance away, watching but sticking close together so as to whisper amused confidences.

'There's a faint possibility, Sergeant, that this incident is connected to a series of crimes we've been working on.'

'Well I've heard nothing to that effect.'

'I'm sure you will, Sarge . . .' She took out her mobile, tapped in a number and offered it to him, 'when you speak to Detective Chief Inspector Royton. He'll probably be very interested to know why I'm being refused entry to the scene.'

'All right, you can put your phone away,' the sergeant said with a sneer. He stood to one side. 'Good God, the slightest sign that we aren't prepared to bow and scrape for them, and they're running off telling tales.'

Gail wasn't sure who 'they' referred to – CID officers or, more likely, female officers in general – but she didn't rise to the bait as she slipped her phone away and stooped under the incident tape.

'I'd have your sick bag handy, DC Honeyford,' the sergeant called after her. 'This isn't something *you'll* ever have seen before.'

The actual crash site was located at the end of a small suburban cul-de-sac called Willacombe Walk. In addition to the residents' cars, numerous other vehicles were now parked there, including four police cruisers and a fire engine. It seemed that the blimp had crash-landed just beyond two semi-detached houses. An enormous flap of tattered silver-grey material hung down over the front of the building. Pieces of white metal frame lay twisted and mangled across the joint garden area, along with numerous roof tiles, a length of PVC guttering and a fallen satellite dish.

Gail showed her warrant card again, and after being issued with a pair of rubberised shoe-covers was passed through a side gate and down an entry to the rear of the property. Again, long banner-like tatters of dirigible were festooned everywhere: hanging over the backs of the houses as well as the front, draped along the bushes and fencing, flying in strips from the high branches of a willow tree. There were several people present, all in Tyvek coveralls, all working the scene. She finally managed to speak to one of them; a thin, elderly man with lank grey hair and pinched, almost peevish features. When he introduced himself as Engineering Inspector

Gibson, he was far warmer to her than the uniformed sergeant had been, but then he was from the Department of Transport and was hardly likely to feel challenged by her presence.

'Possible criminal activity, you say?' He mused on that as he led her across the churned rear lawn, stepping over broken branches, heaped glass, and bundles of contorted steel cable. 'Well, the word from the Trade Fair at Woking is that crime is suspected.'

'How's that, sir?' she wondered.

'We think, or so your lads at the scene tell us, that this poor sod Donaldson was attempting some kind of crude sabotage.'

'I don't understand.'

'Believe it or not, it seems as if he'd stolen some oxy-fuel cutting equipment during a burglary at a body shop in Woking a few days ago. He'd already untied most of the advertising blimp's mooring ropes and was in the process of shearing through the main cable when he somehow got caught up.'

'Possibly a silly question,' Gail said, eyeing the large forensic tent covering the garden's north-east corner. 'But I assume he's dead.'

'I sincerely hope so,' Gibson said, lifting the flap and standing aside. 'This isn't very pretty.'

Gail went through, and found herself gazing into the semi-imploded shell of a greenhouse. Its interior was all but destroyed, nothing more now than a mountainous mass of glass shards mingled with black soil, shreds of tomato plants, and hunks of freshly butchered human meat. Though she'd tried to prepare herself for this, she felt the skin tighten around her mouth, her lunchtime sandwich curdling in her belly.

'Smell that?' Gibson said.

'Sorry?' Gail glanced sideways at him, hoping he wouldn't

notice how green she'd turned. Belatedly, she understood what he'd said, and sniffed at the air. Immediately, she detected a whiff of alcohol.

'Whatever he was doing, the poor fella was soused,' Gibson added.

'Why would he be attempting sabotage?' she asked.

'Can't help you there. Maybe his employers knew he was a drunk, and were in the process of disciplining him.'

'What about the blimp – I mean, why did it come down?'

Gibson rubbed at his chin. 'We're not sure. At least not yet. They're not designed to come down. They're compartmentalised, you see, internally. If one does get punctured or ripped – say if a bird hits it – it gets contained. The dirigible keeps flying. Just out of interest, when you say you're investigating criminal activity possibly connected to this . . . care to elaborate?'

Gail did, eyes fixed on the jumbled heap of glass and body parts, outlining Heck's theory, and rather to her own surprise giving it more credence than she felt it merited. Gibson listened with fascination, his tufty grey eyebrows arching.

'It's not the sort of thing you encounter every day, I'd imagine,' he finally said. 'But then neither are accidents like this. You mean someone deliberately hooked this poor chap to a tether line and let it go?'

'Possibly.' Now that Gail considered that, it was actually quite hideous. 'It's only a hypothesis.'

'There's something you ought to look at.' Gibson sidled left, still inside the tent, but moving along the outside of what remained of the greenhouse. Gail followed him, and they shuffled round to the rear. Here, the forensic tent had been extended to accommodate the garden's wooden-slatted perimeter fence. Crammed down between this and the greenhouse's shattered exterior wall were yet more human body parts. Foremost among them was a human leg, unevenly severed just below the knee, but still wearing a boot and sock. A fragment of rope was tangled around its ankle, so tightly that it had dug into the flesh, creating a webwork of severe postmortem bruising.

'This is how Donaldson was attached,' Gibson said. 'There's no actual knot, as you can see, but it's been wrapped round his lower leg several times, the cords interweaving each other. It could conceivably have been an accident – maybe he was standing in a coil of rope when the thing suddenly took off – but it's not impossible that someone did that to him deliberately.'

Gail pondered Heck's theory again, wondering exactly how feasible it was that they were hunting for some kind of insane practical joker.

'I don't suppose you can forward copies of your documentation to my office?' Gibson said.

'Yes sir, of course. Can you do the same for us?'

'When we actually produce some, yes. The whole scene's got to be minutely examined first. The family and neighbours have been moved out and I'm not sure when they'll be allowed back, to be honest. I'm not sure they'll want to come back. The two little girls who live here were the first to come outside and find the body.'

'Nice,' Gail said, distracted by the bleeping of her mobile.

She stepped outside as she took the call, thankful for an excuse to get away from the scene of carnage. It was Will Royton, wondering where she was up to. She told him what she knew, adding that AAIB were interested in Heck's theory.

'You'll have to liaise with them on this one, Gail,' he replied. 'This is totally their province.'

'Already arranged that, guv. Listen, can you get someone to have a chat with Woking CID? There was a burglary at a body shop a couple of days ago. Some cutting gear got lifted. It may be connected to this, so we could do with knowing everything they know.'

'I'll sort it,' he said. 'Do I detect from your tone that you're now a little more sympathetic to DS Heckenburg's ideas?'

'It's just . . . I don't know. There's still no evidence that this is anything more than a bizarre accident.' She noticed Gibson, now at the other side of the garden with one of his younger colleagues, waving to her. 'Gotta go, guv. I'll call you back.'

She joined Gibson by the far fence, alongside a young woman also clad in Tyvek. Gibson indicated another sheet of ragged fabric dangling down from the guttering on the house's gable wall. A series of three vaguely circular rents – all spaced neatly apart, each one several inches in diameter – were visible in the middle of it.

'Call me suspicious, DC Honeyford,' Gibson said. 'But these look like bullet holes. You asked how the dirigible came down. Now we know.'

At first Gail couldn't respond. Finally she managed to ask: 'That would work?'

'Absolutely,' Gibson said. 'A bullet would go clean through, ripping one compartment after another, eventually causing catastrophic damage. And there may have been more than three shots fired. We'll probably find more bullet holes in different sections.'

'How high was it when it started to lose altitude?'

'We estimate about four hundred feet.'

'It would need to be a rifle then.'

'I'd imagine so.' He observed her carefully. 'You seem happy all of a sudden.'

'I'm not exactly happy, sir – but there's only a finite number of rifles in Surrey.'

'Suppose you'd better get after them.'

'Don't worry,' she said. 'I aim to.'

Chapter 17

Heck headed down the M11, and took the M25 orbital east of the capital. It was late afternoon when he pulled off the motorway in the vicinity of Woldingham.

On a map it all looked straightforward enough, but he soon found himself following single-track lanes between deep, thick hedgerows. Surrey was a commuter-belt county and yet within a few minutes he felt farther off the beaten track than at any stage of the investigation so far. In every direction fields and woods rolled away over undulating downland. Signposts were few, and he had to negotiate several unmarked crossroads. His map wasn't as detailed as it might have been, though in all probability no map in existence was detailed enough for an outsider to find his way easily through a rural backwater like this. He stopped twice to ask for directions: once from two well-heeled young women passing by on horseback, and once at a village pub called the Old Stocks. Both times he was given vague directions, indicating that the Thornton farm was known in the area, which wasn't surprising as it was apparently a sizeable spread.

One bar-stooled regular in the Old Stocks even commented

on the sad incident that had occurred there. 'Poor old Mervin, eh?' he said. 'Blew himself up like a bloody great balloon, he did.'

'What was he like, Mr Thornton?' Heck asked.

The regular, one of a small group of middle-aged men, including the landlord, regarded him suspiciously. 'Newspaper fella, are you?'

'Uh-uh.' Heck showed his warrant card.

'Ahhh . . .' They didn't look any less suspicious. 'Well now, kept himself to himself. Older chap, you see. Mid-sixties, I'd say. Last of a dying breed, to be honest. What you'd call a "gentleman farmer", I suppose. Refined like. To speak to him, you'd think he was a doctor or some college chap.'

'Was he popular?'

The landlord shrugged. 'Not exactly popular, but never heard anyone say a bad thing about him.' The other men at the bar mumbled in agreement.

'Bit of a tough nut,' someone added.

'Tough nut?' Heck asked.

'Yeah . . . robust, independent like. Worked hard, did things for himself. Not an offensive bloke, though. Not some pompous lord-of-the-manor type.'

Heck considered this. 'Nasty accident, wasn't it?'

There were ironic chuckles.

'Can say that again,' the landlord replied. 'Daftest thing. Never heard anything like it.'

'No,' Heck agreed as he left the pub, adding under his breath: 'But I have.'

He soon found the property in question. Again, it was only accessible from a single-track road, this one hemmed in on either side by high, stone-built walls buried under luxuriant ivy, with dense stands of trees beyond them. The first entrance was closed. Heck had half turned into it when he found his path blocked by a chain, suspended in the

187

middle of which was a plank bearing the crudely painted warning:

Bridge unsafe. Please use other entrance.

He pulled back out onto the road, proceeding for several more miles before reaching a second turning. This one was open, but the road beyond it was narrow as well as unmade, a strip of weedy grass growing down the centre. As he drove along it, the trees, hawthorns for the most part, closed in from either side, their thorny fingers whispering along his roof and side panels. Deep ditches ran down both verges, so if he veered a few inches either way the car would topple. If this was the main entrance to the Thornton farm, God knew what unkempt state the farm itself was in. Perhaps Mervin Thornton had been a 'gentleman farmer' in name only.

When Heck broke out into daylight, he found himself trundling over a bridge built entirely from timber, but treacherously narrow; it spanned a gully, whose steep, foliage-covered sides plunged down twenty feet to what, from the brief glimpses Heck had of it, looked like a small but fast-flowing river. It was maybe thirty yards from one end of the bridge to the other, and Heck drove slowly and carefully. The safety barriers were green with mildew and looked ready to collapse. By the violent shuddering under his wheels, the planking composing the main body of the bridge was in an equally flimsy state. When he finally made it to the other side, sweat coated his brow in a fine dew.

'Hate to see what the knackered one looks like,' he said to himself as he burrowed on through another tunnel of undergrowth, heavy tussocks of thorny weed scraping his undercarriage and snagging in his wheel arches. On the basis of what he was seeing here, it was perhaps less surprising that Mervin Thornton had managed to blow himself up 'like a bloody great balloon'. He clearly didn't have much of an eye for health and safety.

Then Heck was through the mini-jungle, the matted vegetation swinging apart like a pair of gates, and he found himself on a broad drive, approaching an extensive stone-built house set in the midst of neatly mown lawns. The house was whitewashed and comprised various wings and annexes, its exterior covered in climbing rose bushes, all now in full bloom. Its wooden front door was also painted white, and decked with black ironmongery. A tan Range Rover and blue Citroën estate were parked outside, neither of which Heck would have fancied testing out on that rickety bridge. He parked alongside them, shoved his laptop into the glove box, climbed out, and walked up the path. Before he could knock on the front door, it opened.

A tall, fair-haired man stood there in a green sweater and green canvas trousers. 'And you are?' he asked curtly.

Heck showed his warrant card. 'It's about Mervin Thornton.'

'I see.' The fair-haired man regarded Heck with some uncertainty, but suddenly seemed less hostile. 'In that case, you'd better come in.'

Freda Thornton was in her early sixties, with thick, somewhat unruly fair hair, only touched around its fringes with grey. She sat rigidly upright on her sofa, wearing a shabby brown cardigan and clutching a tissue in one hand.

She was smooth-skinned and strong-featured; handsome rather than pretty, with deep grey eyes, though at present they were moist and distant. Her cheek was pale, her lips clamped together. Her son, Charles Thornton, who had admitted Heck, was somewhere in his early thirties. He had inherited some of her looks: strong, even features – broad cheekbones, a square jaw, a straight, patrician nose. His eyes were also grey and his hair a dusty gold, cut in a strangely old-fashioned style: a short back and sides with a comb-over parting. He too sat on the sofa, while Heck was perched awkwardly on the armchair. There was a low coffee table between them, set with a bone china tea service. Heck sipped the weakest brew he'd ever tasted from one of the most delicate but expensive cups he'd ever handled.

A look of apparent bewilderment crossed Charles Thornton's face as he tried to recall the death of his father.

'It was a strange kind of accident,' he said. His voice was resonant, educated. 'I mean, if he'd died normally . . . the way people of that age tend to die. I don't know – cancer, a heart attack, perhaps it would have been easier to deal with. But he was so hale and hearty. And then something as bizarre as that . . .'

Heck nodded understandingly. This accident had been pretty grotesque even by the standards of those others he was investigating. Before setting out that morning, he'd perused several photographs of the corpse; Mervin Thornton's lower torso had distended horribly until his farm overalls had looked like a second skin around him, bulging in all the wrong places. His swollen face had turned a gruesome shade of purple-grey thanks to a million ruptured capillaries, while his bloodshot eyes had bulged from their bony sockets like golf balls ready to explode. Heck could only hope and pray that the undertakers had worked their usual magic before Mrs Thornton had visited the corpse, though by her glazed expression the entire experience had dealt her a savage blow.

'One thing I don't understand,' Thornton added, somewhat pre-empting Heck's next question, 'was why Father wasn't able to free himself from the valve before he was pumped full of gas. I mean, okay, there was extensive bruising on his body, which suggested that he'd had a heavy fall, but there

190

was no bruising to his skull or anything like that. Theoretically he should have been fully conscious.'

That knowledge alone ought to torment this family for the rest of their days, Heck thought.

'I mean . . . why didn't he just get up and stagger away?' Thornton peered at Heck as if expecting an answer.

Heck shrugged. 'It's baffling, I must admit. The shock of the puncture wound maybe? Compressed gas acts very quickly. It's possible that he only had to lie there for a few seconds, in a disoriented state.'

'That suggestion was made at the inquest,' Thornton said. 'And these medical men; you have to trust them.'

'Yes, of course.'

'How can we help you, Sergeant?' This was the first time Mrs Thornton had spoken. In fact, it was the first time she'd acknowledged that Heck was in the room – it was her son who'd made the tea – though Heck had no doubt that she was aware of him and had been following the conversation closely. Now, she stared at the detective with a piercing intensity.

'I was rather wondering that myself,' Thornton said. 'The coroner's verdict was accidental death.'

'Are you here to tell us something different?' Mrs Thornton asked.

It was difficult to read the expression on her face. Her wet eyes suddenly gleamed with curiosity – and maybe something else. Hope? Could it be that some revelation about her husband dying by another's man's hand rather than through some ridiculous stroke of misfortune would provide closure for her? Would that be something she could more easily comprehend? Strange if true, but you could never second-guess the workings of the human mind after life-changing events like these.

'I don't know,' Heck replied. 'And that's the honest truth.

191

It's not police-speak for something else. Perhaps you could tell me, though, who else was present on the farm that day?'

'Just Mother and me,' Thornton replied. 'Oh, and Tilly.'

'Tilly?'

'My younger sister. Before you ask, she's not here today. She's at college in Guildford.'

'There were no labourers on the farm?'

'Father didn't have many employees. He and I did most of the work ourselves.'

Heck glanced at Thornton's hands; they were large, cross-cut with old scars, the fingernails ragged and dirty. Despite his refined appearance, he clearly did his bit.

'We do have a livestock manager and a dairyman,' Thornton added. 'But neither were present at the time. It was a Sunday evening you see.'

Sunday evening, Heck thought. *Another moment chosen when no one would be around.* 'And there was nobody else on the property at all? No tradespeople, no visitors, no guests?'

'Nobody.'

'Do you ever have trouble with trespassers here? I mean people coming onto your land who shouldn't.'

Thornton mused. 'We've never really noticed if we have. I mean we're quite isolated. We don't get passing rough . . . children messing around, teenagers drinking. We just don't see people like that.'

'How about travellers, squatters?'

'Again, no. We've always borne in mind that we might have a problem with thieves. But there's only one way onto the farm by road.'

And that road itself would put most visitors off, Heck almost said aloud.

'And we have a security camera there,' Thornton added. 'Father had it installed on the off-chance.'

192

'A camera?'

'Yes. It's in a concealed position, so most people don't even know it's there.'

'Have you checked the footage from the day of the accident?'

Thornton nodded. 'I did, yes. More through routine than anything else. Nobody came to the house that day. At least not along the main drive.'

'You don't seem very happy, Sergeant?' Mrs Thornton asked, again in that curious, penetrating way. 'If there's something you're not telling us, that's hardly fair.' Her hand had knotted into a claw around its scrunched tissue.

'Mother,' Thornton said in a patient but weary tone. 'The sergeant won't want to *speculate* on something like this. He can only give us facts.'

'I assure you, Mrs Thornton,' Heck replied, 'the moment I uncover anything that contravenes the official version of these events, you'll be the first to know.' He glanced at her son. 'Is it possible I can have a look at the actual scene of the accident?'

Thornton regarded his mother for several long seconds, as if trying to both chide and reassure her at the same time. She returned his gaze, but said nothing else. Finally he turned to Heck. 'Of course, but there isn't much to see.' He got to his feet. 'I mean, we've closed up that particular shed. All the equipment that was used has been disposed of. Couldn't bear to have it on the property, if I'm honest.'

'I understand.'

'If you'll just hang on a sec.'

Heck waited in the living room alone with Mrs Thornton while her son disappeared into another part of the farmhouse. He sipped the lukewarm tea from its fragile cup and covertly watched her. She glanced at him once, but then looked away again – sharply, as though any kind of eye contact would lead to further conversation, which was something she wanted to avoid. Heck glanced further afield. The farm's living room was large, well-appointed and richly furnished. There was a deep rug in front of the huge fireplace; various horse brasses adorned the walls; the sideboard and other wooden fixtures were of dark, heavy oak. There was nothing in here to suggest the ramshackle, run-down hovel that Heck had first expected while crossing the decrepit bridge.

Various family photographs were gathered on the marble mantel. One depicted a man who simply had to be the late Mervin Thornton. It had been shot in a pub or the midst of a social event. He had short, white hair, white sideburns and a rather stern face. Heck wasn't sure how long ago the photo had been taken but, as the younger Thornton had said, for a chap in his mid-sixties, the older Thornton had looked to be in rude health. He was a far cry from the horrific, bloated travesty that he'd become on his death. Another photo portrayed Charles Thornton, but in his teenage years; he was standing alongside a small horse – a Shetland pony maybe – holding its bridle, while a little girl, no more than seven years old and with a pretty giggle on her pixie face, was seated in the saddle, wearing an overlarge riding hat.

'We can't drive over there, I'm afraid,' Thornton said, reappearing in a quilted doublet, a flat cap and a pair of boots. 'But it's only a five-minute walk.'

'No problem,' Heck replied. He nodded at the photo. 'Nice-looking little girl.'

'Tilly.'

'Ah, yeah.'

'That was taken on holiday in the Highlands of Scotland, a few years ago.'

'You say she's away at college?' Heck said. 'In the middle of summer?'

'Tilly's twenty-two now. There isn't a lot for her here. Certainly not under the present circumstances.'

Heck nodded; he didn't suppose the funereal atmosphere in this remote place would be conducive to any kind of emotional recovery.

'She doesn't see her future in farming, anyway,' Thornton added. 'Divides her time between here and there . . . increasingly there, even when university is in recess. Shall we get going?'

'Of course.'

Thornton led the way out through the front of the house and round to what Heck thought was its east side, where he noticed a number of additional outbuildings, barns, storehouses and such, but then veered away in the opposite direction, trudging along a stony track between enclosed paddocks, most of which were deep in lush grass.

'We used to run a stabling business at one time,' Thornton explained. 'Not to mention a stud. There was a riding school on site as well, and a dressage team. Even the local hunt made use of our facilities.'

'Must've been pretty lucrative,' Heck replied.

'It was, but it was a lot of work and responsibility. In the end, Father closed it all down. It wasn't like he needed the money.'

'I take it there was no acrimony involved?'

'You mean unsatisfied customers coming back here for revenge?' Thornton shook his head. 'I don't think so. It was over a decade ago . . . but I don't recall any unpleasantness.'

'Your father didn't have any other enemies?'

'No one springs to mind. His personal motto was "do well by people, and they'll do well by you". At least, that's what he always taught me.'

Heck considered this, glancing beyond the paddocks. Open land stretched to every horizon: meadows, pasture dotted with cattle, occasional other buildings. It occurred to him that a place like this could be quite vulnerable.

A small wooden structure loomed ahead. It was about the size of a small house, but severely dilapidated. Its timbers had warped and weathered. Its few windows were broken and half covered by planks.

'As I say, we don't use this particular barn anymore,' Thornton said. 'Father always kept his tractor here, so . . . well, we just don't.'

Two heavy doors were closed at the front, latched by a chain so old that it was little more than a length of rust. The ground in front of it was bare earth, but deeply rutted by old tyre tracks, which had baked hard in the summer sun.

'It was just out here, out front, where I found him.' Thornton stood back.

Heck surveyed the area. As he'd been told, there really was nothing to see. 'I don't suppose anyone took any fingerprints – the gas cylinder, the tubing, the valve?'

'No. Never entered anyone's head it might be a crime.'

Heck crouched to examine the solid ridges of earth. Various bootprints were visible alongside the tracks, but no treads could be distinguished, which was understandable; in the recent warm weather, the upper surface of this barren patch would have blown away as dust. In any case, all kinds of people would have been here for legitimate reasons since the accident. He stood up again, beating grime from his hands. 'Can I look inside?'

Thornton obliged, though it seemed to take him an effort of will to remove the chain and lug one of the heavy doors open. Beyond it lay hollow emptiness; the usual smells flooded out – rotted hay, age-old manure, a hint of petrol. There was nothing in there of obvious consequence.

'I hope my visit hasn't distressed your mother too much,'

Heck said as they made their way back. 'You understand I have to ask all these questions?'

'I wouldn't worry. Mother's been through an emotional mangle. She's not herself at all. Nothing can make things worse for her at present.'

They reached the main drive, and Heck halted by his car. 'I'll obviously let you know if I uncover anything. But the probability is this was just a tragic accident.'

'One part of me hopes it was,' Thornton replied. 'Then we'd at least know that nobody wished Father ill. But on the other hand . . . I can't stand thinking that something so terrible happened through Father's own clumsiness. I mean he knew what he was doing – he'd worked the land all his life. He could fix machinery. He could manage animals . . .'

He shook his head, perplexed.

Heck offered his condolences again and, as the tall young farmer walked towards the house, climbed into his Peugeot, spun it in a three-point turn, and headed back along the drive. There were clearly some similarities between this incident and the others, but again it was tenuous. Could you really fall so heavily on a metal nozzle that it would pierce your body, and lie there in such a state of stupefaction that you were unaware it was filling you with gas? But alternatively, how could someone deliberately do that to Mervin Thornton? How would the assailant have known in advance that the old farmer was planning to reinflate a tractor tyre that day – unless they'd been following him, observing him?

Heck jolted on through the dense shrubbery, half-oblivious to the rattles of twigs and leafage down the flanks of his car. He was still trying to puzzle it through when light fell across him, and aged timbers began rumbling and vibrating beneath his wheels. If Mervin Thornton's death was murder, it could only have happened as part of some premeditated plan, which categorised it firmly with those other deaths – as much as it was possible to actually say 'firmly' in these circumstances.

Then Heck's world tipped over.

Literally.

Several things flashed to his attention all at the same time: the figure of Charles Thornton in his rearview mirror, red-faced, waving his arms; the succession of deafening, splintering *cracks* that could only be a series of age-old wooden joints fracturing; followed by a truly nightmarish sensation as the car tilted sideways and slid. Heck's offside flank buffeted the safety barrier, which sent a nauseating judder through him as he fought the wheel. The barrier disintegrated, falling away like soggy paper, and with a cacophonous tearing and rending of mildewed wood the rest of the bridge went with it. Heck could do nothing but cling on as his vehicle plunged sideways and down amid beams and shattered planks, twisting in midair, caroming from the canyon's side with a crash of crumpling bodywork – and then he was upside down, still falling. His seatbelt snapped loose just as the Peugeot struck the water, and he was slammed down on top of his cranium, the blow sending a shockwave up his spine.

Agonised dizziness followed as he hung there, nauseated, body twisted, only vaguely aware of the darkness engulfing him, of a pond-like stench as icy black-green water poured through the rear offside window, which had smashed inwards. Only when it rose past his hairline, his eyes, and then inundated his mouth and nostrils with its vile taste of slime and weed, did he come gargling and choking to life, pulling himself around and upright – floundering and splashing as he discovered that he was already three-quarters submerged. The capsule of the interior tilted again as it sank; already there was scarcely a speck of light left, and the airspace was running out fast.

Chapter 18

At first, Heck could do nothing but blindly scrabble.

With deep, shuddering groans of metal, he both heard and felt his Peugeot as it slowly, steadily descended into the unseen depths. Fighting down panic, he battled across the flooded interior to the broken window. He sucked in a chestful of oxygen and ducked his head under, attempting to thrust himself out through the inrushing torrent, but not only was he pushing against an icy, inexorable tide, he slashed his clothing and raked his flesh on fragments as he tried to wriggle through a narrow aperture, the frame of which had buckled out of shape.

There were more creaks and groans, another thundering impact as something huge struck the car: a beam from the collapsing bridge. But none of that mattered, because Heck was almost out – *except that, no, he wasn't.*

At first he put his lack of progress down to the force of the current gushing past him, but now realised that he was actually jammed in the window frame, held between jagged, unyielding jaws. He kicked and struggled, bubbles fizzing between his gnashing teeth – to no avail. There was nothing to gain leverage against, nothing to purchase. More bubbles hissed in his ears, black/green shadows swam around him, what little light there was diminishing overhead. Slowly, a terrible pressure was building in his ears; his cheeks bulged they were so packed with air.

And then someone was alongside him – only a quarter visible in the sub-aqua gloom, but Heck glimpsed a square jaw and dusty yellow hair swirling. A pair of big calloused hands clasped his shoulders – but they didn't pull as he had expected; instead, they pushed him backwards. At first Heck tried to resist this, only to belatedly realise its purpose. Though it took a mighty effort of self-control, he relaxed and pivoted round into his former position, from where he felt his body slide smoothly back into the interior, which was now completely underwater. Once he was clear of the window frame, the figure outside was able to take the car door by its handle and, bracing his booted feet against the warped bodywork, yank on it hard. With a dull *clunk*, the door opened and Heck swam out. Together, he and his rescuer kicked hard for the surface.

Heck remembered hearing once that the average adult male has a lung capacity equivalent to that of a grey seal, which theoretically meant that, if you don't panic, you can hold your breath under water for up to forty minutes. Heck had probably been in the depths of the river one minute at most, but he knew that two or three seconds longer and his lungs would have exploded. When he burst into open air, Charles Thornton alongside him, the canyon walls soaring blackly above and the sagging, skeletal remnants of the bridge half blocking out the sun, it was the greatest relief in his life.

As he struggled towards the nearest embankment, his feet clouted the submerged hulk of his Peugeot – his lovely maroon 308, all fifteen grand's worth. But what the devil did that matter? He was alive.

Coughing and gasping, he grappled with waterside

foliage before he was able to pull himself up onto dry ground. Thornton, who'd managed to get up first, gave him another helping hand, hauling him by the collar of his shredded jacket. From here, it was a tough climb to the top of the embankment – more heavy vegetation and lots of steep, crumbling soil, but only when they'd made it up there, and were perched on flat ground between the overhanging trees, did Heck allow himself to flop. His head drooped onto his chest, his shoulders heaving as he wheezed for breath.

Eventually he glanced up at the young farmer, who was standing, gazing down into the canyon where the outline of Heck's Peugeot appeared to be moving in the current, jostling its way along the narrow channel, for the most part still submerged.

'Thanks . . .' Heck stammered, shuddering. 'Just . . . thanks.'

'I'd say no problem,' Thornton panted, 'but bloody hell, I thought you were a goner. What on earth were you thinking?'

Heck was slow to respond. 'Excuse me?'

'Surely it was obvious that bridge was dangerous?'

'Well – might've helped if it had been sealed off.'

'It is. This is the farm's north entrance. It's been closed off for years. That's why I ran after you when I saw which direction you were headed in.'

Heck got slowly, exhaustedly to his feet. 'What are you talking about?'

'You should have gone out the way you came in. Through the south entrance.'

'That was the one that was closed. There was a sign across it.'

Thornton, whose cheeks had coloured – presumably as he'd been contemplating the potential outcome if culpability

201

for this incident was proved against him – now paled. 'You must've got confused.'

'No I didn't.' Heck indicated the hanging remnants of the bridge. 'I definitely drove in this way. I was almost a goner that time too.'

'But there's a chain across the north entrance. And a warning sign.'

'Not anymore. They must both have been moved.'

They regarded other, their dripping faces dappled by afternoon sunlight. 'Dear God,' Thornton said, no longer pale but white. 'Are you serious?'

'How else could I have got in?'

'I'd better go and check.'

'I'll come with you.'

'Are you all right? I mean, you just nearly drowned.'

Heck rubbed at the top of his head, which felt bruised but was otherwise undamaged. 'I'll not pretend I'm not shaken. And I think I've just drunk half the River whatever it is.'

'The Tat.'

'Half the River Tat. But the outcome could have been worse, thanks to you.'

They made their way back to the farmhouse on foot, sodden. If Mrs Thornton thought it unusual, or unacceptable, that her son should enter the family home in this state, she made no demonstration about it – at least none that Heck heard while he was waiting outside. Thornton reappeared with car keys in hand. He and Heck climbed into the Range Rover. They headed along the drive in a different direction, following a long, curving route towards the farm's southern boundary. Clearly this was the way Heck was supposed to have entered. Within a few minutes they were driving through woodland, though much of this had been cut back from the road. When they crossed the bridge near the farm's south entrance, it was in far better condition than the other one; built solidly from concrete and stainless steel, and wide enough for two vehicles to pass side by side.

'Father had this one constructed about ten years ago,' Thornton explained. 'When it became obvious the original bridge was past its best, he brought in a surveyor and it was condemned. I'm sorry about that, Sergeant – we should have had it demolished some time ago.'

'No apology needed. It wasn't you who directed me across it . . . or your father.'

About a hundred yards further on, they reached the road. As Heck had said, a safety chain was blocking access. The warning sign hung in the middle of it. They climbed from the car together. Thornton stood scratching his head. 'I just don't understand this.'

The chain had not been secured in this position. By the looks of it, someone had simply woven it round a narrow tree trunk at one end, and had hooked it over a low bough at the other. Thornton made a move to pull it free.

'Be better if you didn't,' Heck said. 'We'll need Scenes of Crime to take a look.'

'I can't leave it here,' Thornton replied. 'I need to put it back over the north entrance; at least until I can find something else. We'll end up with another disaster.'

Heck thought about this. 'You're right . . . here.' He dug a pair of latex gloves from the ragged hole that remained of his jacket pocket and handed them over. 'If you can sort that out quickly and then put the chain indoors somewhere? And make sure no one else touches it.'

Thornton nodded. He removed the chain, threw it into the back seat of his Range Rover, and then drove them along the main road to the north exit, where he suspended it again across the entrance.

'What would someone gain by doing this?' he asked.

'What would someone gain by pumping compressed gas into your father?' Heck replied.

'You think this was another attempt to commit murder?'

'If it was, it very nearly succeeded.'

'But that's ridiculous. I mean . . .' Thornton's words petered out. He looked as tortured by that thought as he was amazed. 'I mean, who . . .?'

'We need to find out, Mr Thornton. And we need to do it quickly. You said you had a camera over the main entrance?'

'Yes. Yes, of course!' Thornton drove them back to the south entrance, and there pointed up into a tall fir tree on the other side of the road. The camera was indeed well concealed, because Heck still couldn't see it.

As they drove back towards the farmhouse, Thornton became deeply thoughtful. 'Does this definitely mean my father *was* murdered?'

'We can't say that for sure.'

'But he died by accident; or at least it appeared to be an accident. And if you'd died in that river that would have appeared to be an accident too.'

With a grimace, Heck extricated a long strand of river weed from under his T-shirt. 'Correct. But we have to keep an open mind. The chain business could easily have been someone messing around without realising how much danger they were causing.'

He didn't tell Thornton what he was really thinking: namely that if all the other possible victims on his list – Harold Lansing, the car thieves in Leatherhead, the delivery driver Gordon Meredith – had been the subject of foul play, their accidents had come about after they appeared to have been singled out and stalked. This incident was not quite the same: the chain had simply been moved to another location, and the perpetrator had fled. Any visitor to the farm who didn't already know that the north entrance was dangerous could have come along and crashed through the bridge. Leaving it so much to chance felt like a deviation from the pattern. Unless of course – and Heck didn't give voice to this theory either – unless he himself, as the main investigator, was the one who'd been singled out and stalked.

Back at the farmhouse Mrs Thornton, who listened to the story her son told her with silent astonishment, broke out of her grief-stricken reverie, becoming busy and efficient. She still spoke only in monosyllables, when she spoke at all, but showed Heck upstairs to a bathroom, where he was given access to the shower, and when he had finished found an old black and white tracksuit waiting for him, along with some clean underwear, some white sports socks, and a pair of white training shoes. When he came downstairs again Mrs Thornton had built up the fire, and pushed a mug of hot spearmint tea into his hands.

'Thanks very much,' he said.

She nodded curtly, and moved off down the corridor to the kitchen.

Heck watched her go, mildly puzzled. She'd asked questions before – desperate, it seemed, to discover whether or not her husband had been murdered, and yet now, when strong evidence had emerged that hostile forces *were* gathering here, she was content to say nothing. The only obvious conclusion was that the Thornton family were hard cases; traditional old rural English stock – they could take things on the chin, and didn't flip out when the worst came to the worst, choosing instead to bide their time and wait.

Heck wished he felt so steady. The shock of the crash was finally trickling through him, leaving him weak and sick. He attempted to deal with this the way he always did, by blocking it out and focusing on practicalities. He'd managed to salvage his keys, his wallet, his warrant card, and the slide-key to his hotel room, all of which had been in his jacket's inside pocket, but his mobile phone was kaput, and of course he'd now lost his car and his laptop – probably for good.

'Sergeant Heckenburg?' came Thornton's voice. 'Want to look at this?'

Heck wandered along the kitchen corridor, but diverted en route into a spare reception room, which Thornton had adapted into an office. He too had taken off his wet things, had climbed into a pair of shorts and a sweatshirt, and was swigging from a mug of mint tea. He was seated in front of a desktop computer, on the screen of which a black and white MPEG was running.

Heck leaned down to get a closer look. The MPEG was centred on the farm's south gate, and had been shot from the high vantage of the fir tree opposite. Thornton had paused the video, waiting for Heck to come in. He hit 'play' again.

The image jerked into motion – it was grainy and constantly pixellated, but otherwise it possessed better-than-usual clarity. An indistinct vehicle flashed past from left to right.

'That's him, I'm guessing,' Thornton said, 'on his way to the north gate.'

'Either on his way to collect the chain, because he already knows it's there,' Heck said. 'Or checking out your whole perimeter, in which case he's about to find the chain.'

'This was taken at two-forty this afternoon – not long before you got here,' Thornton replied, fast-forwarding for six minutes before the vehicle reappeared.

This time it was coming from the other direction. It pulled up alongside the south entrance, perfectly framed in mid-screen. It was an old van. No make or model was immediately distinguishable, but two furtive figures climbed from its driving cab. One was slightly shorter and chunkier than the other, but both were obscured in dark clothing and balaclava hoods.

'Okay, so we're not dealing with a bunch of daft kids,' Heck said, refusing to give voice to the sudden excitement he felt.

A duo of suspects in the Harold Lansing case; a duo of suspects here.

Clearly the two interlopers knew exactly what they were going to do, because they didn't hang around to scope out the territory. They went quickly to the back of the van, opened it, and lifted out the pile of chain and the wooden signpost, then lurched round to the other side and briefly were out of sight while they stretched the metal links across the entrance. Very soon afterwards they scampered back into view, jumped into the vehicle, and it wallowed away from the kerb.

Heck shouted and Thornton hit 'pause'.

The van froze with its number plate vaguely visible.

'Can you enlarge that registration number?' Heck asked.

Thornton's fingers rattled over the keyboard and the image was cut down to a quarter of its size before expanding to fill the screen. It worked – the registration mark was much larger, but still clear enough to be readable.

'Don't suppose you've got a paper and pen?' Heck said.

Thornton rummaged in a drawer, and handed him an empty notebook and a biro.

Quickly Heck jotted the VRM down – GD14 FED.

'I take it that'll help you catch them?' Thornton asked.

Heck nodded. 'That *has* helped me catch them.'

Mrs Thornton did her best to dry Heck's clothes for him, but they were still damp an hour and a half later, and they reeked of the riverbed. Instead, she packaged them in brown paper and told him he could hang on to the clothes he'd borrowed. Charles had plenty of tracksuits.

'I'll try and arrange for someone to come and get your

car out of the river,' Thornton said while Heck waited for a taxi. 'Not sure how we'll go about that, to be honest. Think we'll need a crane.'

It was now early evening, but it was still daylight outside. Even so, Heck was impatient to get back to Reigate. 'Thanks for everything you've done,' he replied. 'Obviously any expense you're put to, I'll cover it.'

'It isn't a problem.' Thornton stood by the fire with his hands in his shorts pockets. 'I'm just glad you're alive.'

'Me too.' Heck glanced from the farmhouse window and saw a vehicle approaching from the direction of the south entrance. He turned back to his hosts. 'Listen . . . I'd like to tell you more, but to be honest I don't know enough even to put two and two together at this stage. I'll freely admit this case – if it *is* a case – is as weird as they come.'

'The main question is are *we* in danger?' Thornton asked. 'Do we need to move into town maybe?'

'I'm sorry, but I can't answer that either.'

And it was true – Heck couldn't. Had someone set their stall out to murder Mervin Thornton? And if so, as part of some personal vendetta or as part of the series perpetrated by Gail's 'psycho pranksters'? If it was the former, were the rest of the Thorntons also in danger? He didn't know. If it was the latter, did that mean they were safe? He didn't know that either. Likewise, the incident with the derelict bridge – was that another blow against the Thornton family or, as he increasingly suspected, had that been aimed at him? There were way too many questions and not nearly enough answers.

'All I can say is this,' he added. 'Whoever these people are, on the very off-chance they're still interested in you, I don't think they're going to come knocking at your door with a gun. Their style is more complex, dare I say more sophisticated, than that. However, I do think it would make sense if you were to stay alert . . . at least until I'm able to get a full team onto this.'

Thornton nodded. 'If that's what you think.'

Heck assessed them carefully. Charles Thornton worked outdoors all day and was strong, handy, and quite clearly brave. From his manner and conversation, he was also intelligent and educated. He looked a little pressurised by the situation, as any person would be, but on the whole was cool and relaxed. Mrs Thornton was seated on the sofa, hands clasped tightly together; a sure sign of tension. She nodded at Heck as he spoke, without smiling, watching him in that intense way of hers. It was almost defiant; as if she understood that he was here to help, but had decided not to take advantage of it. She certainly wasn't the ghost he'd encountered when he'd first arrived. Again he put this down to her being part of that tough, postwar generation who were always at their best when danger threatened. Whatever it was, neither of the duo struck Heck as vulnerable, especially not when they were together.

A horn tooted outside.

'Listen, I've got to go,' Heck said. 'Now my mobile's out of order, I haven't even got a direct number I can leave with you. But I'm based at Reigate Hall Police Station. And I know where you are, so I can get in touch easily enough.'

The Thorntons nodded again and saw him to the front door.

It was now after seven in the evening and there was very little traffic on the roads, but the journey back to Reigate still wasn't quick enough for Heck. When he finally returned to the station, he paid the cabbie and dashed inside through the personnel door. The first friendly face he saw was Sally Bullock, who had briefcase in hand and was walking towards the exit. She looked startled to see his shabby old tracksuit and mussed hair, not to mention the small nick on his face caused by a tooth of glass when he'd attempted to vacate the sinking car.

'Is Will Royton in?' he asked, breathless.

'He's gone home now. What happened?'

'It's a long story. But I'm minus a car and a phone, so I'm going to need to borrow both for tomorrow.'

'You've had an RTA?'

'Nothing that simple. Is Gail Honeyford around?'

Sally shook her head. 'She hasn't been in all afternoon. She went to look into that dirigible accident over in Tilford.'

'She did?' Heck couldn't help his surprise.

'Aren't you working on that together?' Sally asked.

'Yeah, by the sounds of it.'

He headed into the CID office, pleased to know that Gail was at least partly onside, though secretly glad that she wasn't here at present, because a question-and-answer session was something he didn't need. There were no other detectives in the office, just an elderly woman working her way along the aisles with a vacuum cleaner. Heck slid behind his desk, grabbed up the phone, and called Reigate Comms, asking for the PNC. It took only seconds to get a response on the registration number he'd spotted by the Thornton farm entrance. It came back as a grey Bedford van reported stolen not two days ago from the Skelton Wood estate, which if he remembered rightly lay somewhere between Brixton and Herne Hill in south London.

Heck sat back and tapped his teeth with his pen. Then picked up the phone again and bashed in the number of the CID office at Brixton Police Station.

'CID at Brixton, DS Powers,' came a gruff but efficient female voice.

'Angie, it's Heck.'

There was brief silence, followed by a low chuckle. 'Well, well . . .'

'Glad I caught you.'

'You know me. I'm always here.' Angie Powers was a personable and athletic young black lady whom Heck had worked with on the Robbery Squad in Tower Hamlets. 'Long time no speak,' she said. 'How you doing?'

'Well, I've got a belly full of river water, a cut on my face that's probably already festering with tetanus or hepatitis, or something equally horrible . . .'

'Normal day in SCU.'

'Yeah. Aside from all that, I'm cool. Listen, Ange: Skelton Wood.'

'Uh-oh . . .'

'Things as bad there as ever?'

'If by that question do you mean does ninety per cent of the crime in Lambeth ward originate on the Skelton, is it a powder keg just waiting to blow, does every druggie scrote, gang-banger, and wannabe blagger between here and Wapping seek to emulate its residents, then the answer's yes.'

'And who's running it?'

'How do you mean?'

'I'm tailing a van that's done a job. Maybe more than one job – it was swiped on the Skelton two days ago. Does that sort of thing happen randomly down there, or does someone need paying off first?'

'Good question. To my knowledge, nothing moves on the Skelton without the say-so of the Snake Eye Crew.'

'Never heard of them.'

'New kids on the block. In some ways they're relatively small time. Still operating as low-profile racketeers. But there's a lot of them and their star's rising.'

'Are Trident on the case?'

'No interest for Trident. The Snake Eyes are multi-ethnic. They're controlled by a kid called Julius Manko. He's a nutter, not to put too fine a point on it. He'd kill you as soon as look at you. His preferred weapon is a razor-edged machete.'

'And this works, does it?' Heck asked. 'I mean he intimidates all the local tea leaves?'

'Most of the local tea leaves have joined his crew.' She mused on the question. 'It might be possible some idiot could come along who doesn't know the score, helps himself to a motor and by pure luck gets clean away. It's just about feasible. But if this van's been used in a couple of jobs . . . what're we talking about, robberies?'

'Something worse.'

'Okay, well, if we're talking serious people with serious intent, they'll either be connected to the Snake Eyes or they'll have bought their permission beforehand.' DS Powers paused. 'Heck . . . you're not thinking about going down there?'

'No choice, I'm afraid.'

'You'll need more than your gumshield.'

'I will have. I've got my wit, my charm . . .'

'I'm serious. Look, call into our office first. I can probably arrange you some support.'

'Much appreciated, Ange. But I'm not even asking questions at the mo. Just gonna try and blend in.'

'Good luck with that. Everyone on the Skelton's either a criminal or a victim. Which one are you going to be?'

'You know me, love – I walk a fine line between both.'

Chapter 19

The Skelton Wood estate comprised six square miles of the grottiest blocks of flats Heck had ever seen, and he'd seen quite a few. Even in the go-ahead twenty-first century, there were blighted corners of Britain's urban jungle which, in terms of employment, health and general social welfare, seemed to have been forgotten by time, and this was certainly one of them. The entire estate appeared to be made from grey, faceless concrete; not just the buildings, but the underpasses, the walkovers and the occasional rows of caged-off shopfronts. Graffiti ran wild, the usual obscenities intermingling with football slogans, snatches of street poetry, and incomprehensible, cryptic symbols, which almost certainly served as gang tags. There was much dereliction: some entire blocks were closed to access, their doors and windows covered by steel grilles; there were also rows of gutted houses, while stolen and fire-damaged vehicles were regularly dumped here and simply left unclaimed, rotting.

Even on a fine summer's morning Skelton Wood was a spiritless sprawl; drab, litter-strewn – the monolithic apartment houses didn't look any less dingy in bright sunlight, the rubbish-clogged wastelands between them still didn't resemble the restful green spaces they once were intended to be.

Heck had parked his black Mazda, which he'd taken from the CID pool at Reigate Hall, near Brockwell Park, about a mile away. He'd travelled the rest of the distance on foot. It wasn't eight o'clock in the morning and there were very few people about, but he wasn't taking any chances. He always brought 'scruffs' with him whenever he was working away from the Yard, and so today wore jeans with the knees torn out, a sweat-stained Saxon T-shirt, and an age-old Wrangler jacket thick with motorbike oil. He hadn't bothered shaving either, and had donned a pair of trainers that had once been white but now were coffee-coloured.

Late the previous night he'd changed his mind about liaising with Brixton, had called Angie Powers again, and had visited her office first thing that morning. He still hadn't wanted any assistance; this was to be an open-ended recce – infiltration by a single unit who wasn't well known on this manor – but before going out there he'd mugged Angie and her team for all the info he could. They'd assured him that deadbeats of every sort routinely gathered on the Skelton because the Snake Eyes were always recruiting; anyone could find work with them so long as their background checked out and they didn't mind getting their hands dirty.

In addition to this, they'd told him about 'the Roost'.

This was a dilapidated structure at the west end of what had once been an all-weather football pitch. The pitch had originally been constructed by a charitable organisation to give the local youth a focus and outlet that was not concerned with gang violence, but hooligan elements had met there to fight rather than play, an ongoing melee from which the Snake Eyes had eventually risen to prominence. It was still known locally as the 'Football Field', even though sport was no longer played there and it was covered with bricks and bottles, some of them dating from that original inaugural battle. The Snake Eyes had taken over the Roost, as they called it, for their official clubhouse, but although they'd now outgrown it, having tentacles all over the estate and even beyond, it still had a role to play in their operation. They held 'club nights' there – wild drunken revels which went on all night with music blasting across the estate; their soldiers hung out there during the day, gambling and taking drugs, but basically on call should muscle be required some-where; and the official Snake Eye tattoo was still given there. This sigil was always worn on the palm of the left hand: affiliates wore it without colour, except for the socket, which was done in reptilian green; regulars – trusted associates – wore it with the retina coloured blood-red, while so-called officers had the whole thing, including a diamond-shaped pupil done in blue. The gang's top men, of whom there was only a handful, wore the sigil on both palms.

They were a committed crew; that much was obvious. Heck didn't like to think what the hygiene conditions were like inside the Roost's tattoo parlour, or if the tattooists had the first idea what they were actually doing, or even whether they used clean needles or safe ink. But that was not his concern; at present, he had to find a way to contact them. That morning at Brixton he'd gone through a list of their known personnel and though he was familiar with a few faces, there was no one with whom he had any kind of understanding. But that couldn't be the whole story. Snake Eye numbers fluctuated, and local plod wouldn't necessarily know everyone existing on the gang's fringes. There was still a chance there'd be someone here he could work with.

He didn't walk the streets of the Skelton openly, but he didn't try to hide either. There could be no scurrying from lamppost to lamppost, or ducking into doorways; that would be guaranteed to attract attention. But on the whole he stayed

215

in the back alleys, side streets, and subways, and he kept his ears and eyes open. Even then he was taking a risk, though at least Brixton had provided him with a radio in the event that he really got into trouble. Angie Powers had told him about an excellent vantage point for spying on the Roost. It was the upper back room at number fifteen, Cooper's Row; a line of terraced properties long empty and under a demolition order which, thanks to the Met, would not be enacted for some considerable time yet. It stood about two hundred yards from the Football Field, but on raised ground. The actual houses on Cooper's Row were closed off by a fence of corrugated iron, but police surveillance teams had ensured there was a detachable panel in this fence to one side of the house.

Heck found everything as Angie had told him. He ascended to Cooper's Row by a flight of stone steps, at the top of which, rather menacingly, the Snake Eye symbol had been spray-painted onto a gatepost, but beyond that lay an ordinary cobbled street reminiscent of that old traditional London of full employment and working-class values, which might or might not have been real but which so many yearned to see again. The panel in the fence at number fifteen was exactly where Angie had said it would be. It was a little unnerving lifting it out of place, but Cooper's Row was overlooked on its other side by the wall of an abandoned warehouse in which there were no windows or apertures, so there was no one to see him enter. On the other side of the fence he replaced the panel as he'd been instructed, and entered the building through its front door, a key having been left under the loose paving stone in front of the step. Internally, there was nothing left but boards and bricks, and occasional patches of decayed plaster. It stank of stale urine, but there were no real nasties in there: no syringes or crack pipes, no used condoms, which suggested that its easy accessibility was a secret known only to the cops.

Heck ascended the stairs and entered the rear bedroom. As he'd been told, the main window in there contained only half a sheet of jagged glass, but gave a near-panoramic view of the Football Field and the Roost. He stood to one side and took a pair of brass-plated binoculars from under his jacket.

The Roost was a low, ramshackle structure made of wood and tarpaper; some parts of it were blackened as if attempts had been made to burn it, and it was covered top to bottom with gang tags. Though it was still early in the day for London's criminal elements, a couple of cars were parked on the open ground in front of it, and a few individuals were hanging around. Heck spotted a burly Jamaican-looking guy with dreads, and a white guy in a vest and shades, slouched on deckchairs, enjoying the sun and smoking joints. Another white guy stood close by; he wore a pink hooded running top and black shorts; his thin, bare legs were covered with tattoos. He was talking to a Chinese girl in a black minidress. It was certainly true about the Snake Eyes operating a non-racist agenda; in which case they clearly weren't dumb. Heck had often thought it crazy that so many inner-city gangs continued to fight each other on ethnic grounds, rather than pooling their resources and assembling an A-team from the best of the best.

With a metallic *click*, a gun was cocked behind him.

The streaked sweat down the middle of Heck's back froze.

'Okay, homeboy,' said a quiet voice. 'Just relax. The hands . . . spread 'em.'

Heck made to turn.

'*Don't look round! Hands!*'

Slowly, Heck lifted his hands.

'Nice.' Clearly, whoever was behind him had now seen the expensive pair of binoculars. 'Drop.'

Heck did so. The binoculars landed with a hefty *clunk*, which, in other circumstances, would have made him wince.

'I'll bet some once-proud owner's still crying about them, eh?' the voice said.

Heck made no reply, but his heart was going nineteen to the dozen. He didn't expect a bullet in the back – not if they weren't sure who he was. But if he got hauled down to the Roost, it could turn nasty very quickly. They liked to kneecap their rivals as well, Angie Powers had told him, not to mention 'pan-fry' their faces in bubbling chip fat, while Julius Manko reportedly collected the fingers and thumbs of those who fell foul of his favourite machete.

'Now you can turn round,' the voice said. 'Slowly . . . very fucking slowly. Keep those hands well in the air.'

Heck pivoted to face his captor, who was a youngish guy, only in his early twenties, but by the looks of his slick black hair, dark colouring, and handsome, aquiline features was of Mediterranean descent. He was wearing grey joggers and a blue anorak, which hung open on a naked chest and flat, washboard stomach. The gun he held was a shiny black Glock 26. This was in his right hand. With his left, he gestured for Heck to keep his own hands raised. As he did, Heck glimpsed the Snake Head mark on his captor's palm. There was no option but to act and act fast – but there was still four or five feet between them, and the Glock was trained directly on his forehead. And then something happened that was totally unexpected.

A third figure came quietly into the room behind the gunman.

Though she too wore old jeans and trainers, and a ragged, dirty sweat-top, there was no mistaking Gail Honeyford. The gunman saw the expression on Heck's face as it unavoidably altered. By instinct, he half swung round, but not quickly enough to prevent the karate chop she landed on the back of his neck. He gasped and staggered forward, straight into a right hook from Heck, which sent him tottering sideways, and a short, crisp left, which finished the job. He hit the floor out cold, his gun clattering into a corner. Heck scrambled after it, knocked the safety back on, and tucked it into the waistband of his jeans before throwing himself over the gang-banger's inert form and checking his vital signs. The guy was still breathing, so Heck rolled him over onto his front and cuffed his hands behind his back.

Only then did he glance up at Gail, who was watching with fascination. She wasn't a brand-new cop, but it was probable that down in leafy Surrey she didn't witness this kind of action every day. Heck moved past her to the bedroom door and glanced down the stair to ensure there were no more surprises in store. 'What the hell are you doing here?' he finally said.

'Well that's gratitude, I must say,' she replied. 'I got your message, didn't I? You know, the one you left on my desk telling me exactly where you'd be. Brixton filled in the details.'

Heck dragged the unconscious body into a corner. 'I'm surprised you even read it.'

'Well . . . when I heard the boss had loaned you a mobile and one of the CID cars, not to mention his prized pair of opera glasses, I thought that even you might be onto something.'

'Unusually open-minded of you.' He scooped the binoculars up to see that they weren't damaged and moved back to the window.

'Look, Heck . . .' She sounded awkward. 'I think I owe you an apology.'

He barely heard her as he peered towards the Roost. By the looks of it, none of the Snake Eyes hanging around down there had been alerted. Their spotter clearly hadn't had a chance to report that there were strangers on the patch.

'I've not been able to find anything in Harold Lansing's

private affairs to suggest he had enemies or was in any kind of trouble,' Gail said. 'Not only that, I went to the blimp crash site yesterday, and well . . . put it this way, it looks very likely that balloon ruptured because someone shot at it with a rifle.'

Heck looked round at her. 'Yeah?'

'There were at least three bullet holes in it.'

'You should've told me this straight away!'

'I tried to. I was with the Air Accident team from Aldershot for ages, but I tried to ring you afterwards – several times while I was on the way home. I couldn't get you.'

'Oh yeah – I lost my own mobile in a river.'

'The main thing, Heck, is that some crazy bastard hung Gus Donaldson upside down from that giant dirigible, let him float over the countryside long enough to catch the nation's attention, and then shot him down. At least that's what it seems like. And it's so bonkers that it kind of matches the other cases, don't you think?'

Heck was almost amused by her change of direction. 'You sure about all this, Gail?'

'No, I'm not sure.' She looked frustrated. 'I guess I just can't understand murder without purpose.'

'Course you can't; there's no such thing.'

She glanced up at him, confused.

'On the surface, these crimes may seem senseless,' Heck said. 'But they aren't to the perpetrators. Look at it from their point of view – try to imagine the joy of pure, unfettered immorality. The pleasure they derive from meticulous planning, from trawling for a suitable victim, the excitement on the day itself as they wait to see if the plan will come together, the sense of fulfilment when it does . . .'

'You almost make it sound sexual.'

'Hell, it's more than that. It doesn't just give them a buzz. It makes them feel mega-powerful, godlike. Especially when

220

they pull off a spectacular stunt like that one with the blimp. Especially when you consider that in normal life they're flyspecks beneath most other folks' notice.'

'Flyspecks or not, they clearly have access to high-powered firearms,' she said. 'So I've asked one of the lads back at the nick to compile a list of everyone in the county who holds a Firearms Certificate. Of course that's likely to be a lot because Surrey isn't exactly averse to gun clubs and field sports.'

'And even then it won't help us if the rifle's being held illegally.'

'I know, but it's a start. I've also sent a memo to the boss this morning. I think we should mobilise a full murder team on this.'

'What did he say?'

She shrugged, disappointed. 'He told me to see what we find in south London first. We're looking for a grey Bedford van, I understand?'

'That's right, though it may have been burned and dumped by now.' Heck gave her as brief an account as he could of the events leading up to the incident at Thornton Farm, and described the vehicle and the suspects he'd seen on the CCTV. 'Charles Thornton was going to email the file to me. I lost my laptop in the river, but it'll still be sitting on the server, so we can access it back at the nick.'

Gail looked surprised. 'Are you saying they were after *you*?'

'I don't know . . . genuinely. One side of me doesn't want to believe that, because that would mean they know who I am, and let's face it, almost no one at Reigate Hall nick knows who I am – so that much insight would be a bit of a worry. On the other hand, it might just be that whoever set old Mervin Thornton up for his own balloon accident noticed the damaged bridge and thought it too good an opportunity to miss.'

'You mean they came back and stage-managed another random accident?'

'Yeah. I just happened to be the first Joe who came along.'

'Or they're targeting the Thorntons?' she said.

'But that wouldn't explain Lansing or the driver who was killed on the A24. It doesn't explain the car thieves in Leatherhead.'

'Or alternatively, it means those two attacks on the Thorntons are completely unconnected to all the other deaths.'

'That's possible too,' Heck conceded. 'At present, almost anything is possible; which is why I *don't* think we can assemble a full Murder Squad just yet.'

'Okay. So what have the Snake Eye Crew got to do with all this?'

Heck wandered back to the window. 'Maybe nothing. Maybe everything. Angie Powers is a DS at Brixton. She and her mob know this lot better than anyone. They reckon if the van got lifted from round here, the Snake Eyes will either be responsible or will know who did it.'

'Who's the owner of the van?'

'Asian shopkeeper called Patil. No form whatsoever. He's totally out of the picture.'

There was a groan as the handcuffed gang-banger stirred.

'What do we do with this fella?' Gail said.

Heck assessed him glumly. 'Well . . . we could lock him up for criminal use of a firearm. But that's hardly going to help us maintain covert surveillance on his mates.'

'Nor is cutting him loose,' she said.

'But cutting him loose is exactly what you're going to do,' someone else butted in.

They spun to face the doorway – to find that yet another figure had appeared there. This one was older than the previous guy, burly and bearded, and wearing worn, fringed motorbike leathers. He had a pudgy, brutish face, and covered them both with a submachine gun.

'Good to know Brixton's obbo point is as secret as they said it was,' Heck muttered, raising his hands again.

On hearing this, the motorbike guy's expression changed; he looked puzzled.

'About time you showed up,' the guy in the cuffs said.

Heck now noticed the newcomer's weapon: it was a Heckler & Koch MP5; not the sort of gun that street hoodlums acquired easily. 'Who are you?' he asked.

'*I'm* asking the questions!' the newcomer retorted, his accent strong Liverpool. 'Who are *you*?'

'We're police officers.'

'Prove it.'

Slowly, cautiously, Heck reached into his Wrangler – the new guy kept his MP5 rigidly levelled – until Heck drew out his warrant card and tossed it over. The new guy caught it with one hand and examined it.

'Serial Crimes Unit,' Heck said.

The new guy glanced at Gail.

'DC Honeyford,' she told him. 'Surrey CID.'

He blew out a long breath, lowered his weapon and chucked Heck's warrant card back. 'DS Brogan – Flying Squad.'

Heck dropped his hands. 'Always enjoy meeting new colleagues.'

Brogan snorted. 'I'm not sure DC Bernetti will see it that way.'

They glanced at the handcuffed body in the corner. 'This lad's Flying Squad too?' Heck said. He scuttled over there, thumbing his handcuff keys from his pocket. 'He's got a Snake Eye tat.'

'Meaning you two haven't?' Brogan displayed his own left palm, which also bore the Snake Eye sigil, affiliate status. 'You might as well have come here naked.'

Gail helped Bernetti to his feet. He was bloodied around the mouth.

'You all right?' Heck said, handing him back his weapon.

'Yeah . . .'

'Sorry about that.'

The young cop rubbed at the side of his jaw. 'You've got a good right hand.' Gingerly, he felt at the other side. 'And a good left.'

'I thought you were someone else.'

'It would have helped us if we'd known you were on the plot,' Gail said to Brogan. 'I take it you didn't bother informing anyone at Brixton?'

'Yeah, we should've done that,' Brogan replied. 'Then they could've sent *more* people down who aren't wearing the official insignia.'

'What are you guys doing here anyway?' Bernetti asked.

'Investigating a couple of murders in Surrey,' Heck said. 'There's a possible Snake Eye connection.'

Bernetti looked baffled. 'Surrey?'

'We think it's part of something bigger,' Gail explained.

The Flying Squad men glanced at each other, and then Brogan strode to the door. 'You'd better come with us.'

'Why?' she asked.

'Because if you're following the same leads we are, it *is* bigger. A lot bigger.'

Chapter 20

Once they were well away from the Roost, Heck and Gail were ushered into the rear of an unmarked van. DS Brogan got in with them, while Bernetti climbed behind the wheel after first calling ahead. The engine rumbled to life, the vehicle juddering violently as it navigated its way through a network of trash-filled alleys.

'These come right off when we get home,' Brogan said, extending his palm again, but smearing the lurid tattoo with his thumb. 'But it's better to have a falsie than none at all.'

'And that works?' Gail said sceptically. 'Don't you have to be a known face in this neck of the woods?'

He shrugged. 'We don't move among them freely, if that's what you mean. We watch them from LUPs like Cooper's Row. This is just insurance, in case we run into one of them by accident. There are so many of them, they don't all know each other.'

'What've you got on them?' Heck asked.

'All sorts. But the boss'll fill you in.'

'Who's he?'

'DI Hunter.'

'Not Bob Hunter?' Heck said.

'Yeah.' Brogan glanced over at him, and a light of recollection came into his eyes. 'That's right. He used to work in your firm, didn't he? Got kicked out.' Brogan smiled to himself and shook his head, as if this situation was getting better and better.

'Is this bad?' Gail asked quietly.

'No,' Heck said. 'Bob's an okay bloke. He's not . . . well, he's not our biggest fan. SCU's, I mean. Relations could be better.'

Bob Hunter had been a detective inspector in the Serial Crimes Unit, and had made impressive contributions to several of their investigations. However, things had gone badly for him during the hunt for a pair of armed rapists known as the M1 Maniacs. During the course of that enquiry he'd overseen the commission of crucial errors, which had led to Gemma Piper downgrading him to duty officer. A former Flying Squad man, Hunter had been so angered by this that he'd sought a transfer and had finished up back with his old mob, where, being a cocky character inclined to corner-cutting and wideboy-ism, he'd found his spiritual home. Despite all this, he and Heck had always got on well enough, though Gemma Piper wasn't exactly Hunter's favourite person, and as Heck's presence might now mean Gemma had an interest in this case too Heck wasn't sure that Hunter would welcome him with open arms.

He was reacquainted with his former gaffer in a local Flying Squad safehouse; a three-bedroom flat over a transport café just off the East Dulwich Road. The place was accessible from a central yard, which could only be entered via an arched gateway and an unlit flight of narrow, musty stairs. It was a nondescript building from the outside, and the average punter wouldn't have cocked a snook at it, but at the top of those stairs it was a fully equipped command post, crammed with TV monitors, computer terminals, and desks covered with forms and coffee cups; its walls were papered with pages and pages of notes, homemade diagrams, and photographs, primarily mugshots.

Hunter was enthroned in the midst of this chaos in a swivel chair, various of his Flying Squad team busying themselves around him.

When Brogan came in, leading Heck and Gail, the DI leaped to his feet red-faced. 'What the hell, Heck? You been punching out my fucking officers?'

Hunter was a squat, bullish man with granite features and a shock of blond/grey hair. He looked every inch the hard-bitten, time-served detective that he was, but he'd put on weight since Heck had last seen him, particularly around the belly. In an old T-shirt and baggy khaki trousers, he looked unusually slobbish, though like the rest of his team he was armed, a Glock pistol tucked into a holster at his hip.

'Sorry guv,' Heck said with a helpless gesture. 'Blue on blue.'

'If memory serves, you bloody specialise in those.' Hunter switched his gaze to Gail. 'This the sweetie from Surrey?'

Heck sensed Gail's hackles rising, so quickly intervened. 'This is DC Honeyford, sir. She's working a murder case with me. She knows what she's doing and she's saved my arse twice already.'

Hunter continued to eye her as though unconvinced. Eventually he sniffed, and threw himself back into his chair. 'If you're working in Surrey, Heck, what're you doing in south London?'

'Seems we have a mutual interest in the Snake Eyes.'

'Well . . . so long as you haven't blown our close target recon. Kicking off with our lot only a stone's throw from the bastards' base.'

'I don't think anyone noticed, sir.'

'We'll know soon enough,' Hunter replied, which Heck read to mean that the Squad had someone on the inside.

Now Gail spoke up. 'Do you mind me asking what the Flying Squad's interest in the Snake Eyes is, sir?'

'Yes, I bloody do, DC Honeyford.' Hunter folded his arms. 'At least, until one of you jokers can tell me exactly what *your* interest is.'

Again Heck explained what they knew about the events in Surrey, leaving nothing out. As he did, other Flying Squad officers stopped what they were doing to listen. When Heck had finished, Hunter shrugged. 'Doesn't sound like a Snake Eyes MO to me.'

'Nor me,' Heck agreed. 'But the van's obviously important.'

Hunter pondered that. 'If the van got lifted round here, it's highly possible the Snake Eyes were responsible, or at least knew who was. Still don't see what they'd have to gain from causing a bunch of fatal accidents.'

'I did wonder if these murders might have an in-house purpose,' Heck said. 'Maybe they're a form of game for gang members to play? Perhaps an initiation for new boys?'

'Not something I've heard of,' Hunter replied. 'They do have to pass tests to become regulars, and that usually involves committing crime – but not staging RTAs or using toy aeroplanes to attack fishermen.'

'The biggest kick the Snake Eyes get is terrorising people,' Brogan said. 'It's all about rep. They don't hide what they do.'

'And they don't do it down in Surrey, either,' Hunter added. 'That wouldn't impress anyone. *This* is where it counts: the badlands, bandit country.'

Brogan had only come over to join them after making his MP5 safe and stowing it in an open steel cabinet. Heck noticed that several other carbines were already in there.

'You're obviously expecting to move on them soon?' he said.

'If we're lucky,' Hunter replied. He grabbed a pen and made a couple of quick alterations to a report before signing it off at the bottom. 'All right . . .' He spun back to face them. 'Here's *our* interest. And I really don't want this going back to Division, DC Honeyford, even down in Surrey, because these bastards are organised and they've got ears everywhere, maybe even inside the job.'

Gail made a zipping motion across her mouth.

'You heard of the 'Ndrangheta?' Hunter said.

Heck was surprised. 'Mafia splinter group, aren't they?'

'Sort of. Based in Calabria, southern Italy. Very secretive, ultra-violent. Also massive coke-traffickers. The Snake Eyes are trying to get in with them. The dealing they do here is low-level. Grass, crystal meth. Rubbish stuff, street-corner business. And they're quite happy for everyone to think that's the length and breadth of their ambition. But in reality they're sourcing better product to move into more lucrative markets. The 'Ndrangheta can provide, but it'll cost. To meet that cost, the Snake Eyes are blagging like there's no tomorrow. At the moment it's pubs.'

'Pubs?' Gail said.

'Mainly across south London. It's that pattern that first caught our attention. We're talking violent pub robberies, the masked assailants always barging into the premises late at night, just before closing . . . emptying the till at gunpoint, robbing any punters who still happen to be in there.'

'Can't believe it nets them very much,' she said.

'They're making gains, trust me. Two or three grand a pub, and they've done at least thirty that we know about already.'

'You mean there are some we *don't* know about?'

'Not every blag gets reported,' Heck explained.

'Correct,' Hunter said. 'Some of these dives have card schools in the back rooms, drug dens upstairs. Couple of knocking shops have been done too. They're getting turned over at a rate of knots. It's always the same crew – six strong, masked, gloved, heavily armed. They come and go in stolen motors which every few weeks or so we find torched.'

'Can you be sure it's the Snake Eyes?' Heck asked.

'The clever money says yes,' Hunter replied, presumably referring to his insider. 'The amount of indiscriminate shooting says the same. They must've let off five hundred rounds so far. It's a miracle we've only had one casualty – some brawny, suntanned bonehead of a barman, who'd started believing the publicity of his own tattoos. He had a go and they shot his fucking knees off. Won't be pumping much iron down the gym now.'

'Guv . . .' A junior Flying Squad officer stepped forward and handed Hunter a phone. 'It's Kenny.'

Hunter put the phone to his ear. 'Talk to me, Ken.' He listened intently. 'Okay . . . usual time? How many targets? All carrying? Okay . . . no, that's good . . . excellent. Is he indeed?' Hunter broke into a broad grin, which was something Heck hadn't seen very often, not even when they'd worked cheek-by-jowl. 'That's the best news I've had all day, mate. No, well done . . . you're a prince. Yeah, okay, speak to you later.' He cut the call and turned to Brogan. 'Danny, get the rest of the lads in. I want a quick briefing. And alert SCO-19.' Brogan nodded and moved away. Hunter turned back to Heck. 'Seems the job goes live tonight. The target is the Heart of Stone in Lewisham. What's more, Julius Manko himself is coming out to play. How much time you got?'

'As much as I need,' Heck said.

'That roving commission of yours again, eh? Well, it seems these goons are getting greedy. They hit their last pub last week and they're moving again already. Even though you're an AFO, Heck, you're not part of the team, so I can't take you across the pavement. But there's no reason why you can't observe. You up for that?'

'Absolutely.'

'Still don't think you're gonna get much out of this. The Snake Eyes are a tight crew. They won't grass each other up easily – or anyone else. And that's if they've actually got something to do with these murders, which I strongly doubt. You could be on a hiding to nothing.'

'That's been the name of this enquiry so far.' Heck glanced at Gail and winked.

She didn't look impressed.

Julius Manko looked every inch the street-gang sleazeball that he reputedly was.

Heck perused several photos of him. A couple were official mugshots; others had been taken from covert positions while he'd gone about his everyday business. He possibly was Polynesian by origin; he had a natural tan with an oval face and large jaw. His hair was jet black and shaved into a 'Mohican' strip, the scalp to either side covered with tribal tattoos. He was somewhere in his mid to late twenties, broad-cheeked and bull-necked. An old but very nasty scar connected the left corner of his left eye to the left corner of his mouth. One of the surveillance pics had caught him coming out of the Roost wearing only ripped jeans and a thin vest, which exposed a strong, muscular physique also covered in tattoos.

'Looks like a handful,' Heck commented.

Bob Hunter, who was seated in the front passenger seat, chuckled. 'Don't knock it. Today's a red-letter day. Manko's got fifteen levels of fall guys underneath him. It's a rare event when he comes out and does the dirty himself.'

'You sure that intel's good?' Gail asked. She and Heck were in the back seat.

231

Hunter snickered. 'I would say so. It took the lad we've got inside six months to earn their trust.'

'You've been tracking the Snake Eyes so long?' Heck said.

'Nah.' Hunter adjusted his shades as Brogan, who was driving, steered them into Peckham Rye and glaring midday sunshine. 'But the Organised Crime Division have. He's officially working for them. They had to pull him down from Durham to make sure they had someone who wasn't likely to get clocked. His cover story was that he'd just come out of the Scrubs, where he'd served three for battering two bobbies senseless. That's the kind of nutcase Julius Manko likes to work with.'

'So tonight could be the culmination of a lot of blood, sweat and tears,' Heck said.

'Well our lad has been building up evidence like billy-o, but up till now he's never had enough to slot Manko himself.' They passed from Peckham High Street into Queen's Road, heading in the direction of New Cross. 'This is strictly off the record,' Hunter added. 'But we've even let them do a couple of pubs because Manko wasn't playing.'

Heck glanced sidelong at Gail, who looked amazed by such an admission. Despite the two murder arrests she'd made, high-level operations of this sort, and all the machinations they involved, had so far eluded her, so hearing that the investigating unit had received prior information about expected robberies and had taken no action to intervene came as a big shock, much as it did, to an extent, to Heck – though in his case only because he knew how much shit would hit the fan if it got out. This was typical Bob Hunter of course. While Hunter had been in SCU Heck had never accepted that he was quite as slapdash as Gemma felt he was, but he'd often been concerned about Hunter's readiness to cut legal corners.

'How're things up at the Yard?' Hunter asked. 'Ship hasn't sunk without me, I see.'

Heck shrugged. 'We keep things turning over.'

'Yeah . . . got a result up in the Lake District, didn't you? That nutty bird.'

'That was a close one.'

'Good result though. And then Nottingham, wasn't it? The Lady Killer?'

'That wasn't just me.'

'Come off it,' Hunter chuckled. 'You got the collar. Nothing like teaching Counties how to do the job. What do you think, DC Honeyford?'

'I wouldn't know, sir,' she replied tartly.

'Bet her ladyship's over the moon with you,' Hunter said, addressing Heck again. 'She dragged you back into bed yet?'

'What's it got to do with you, Bob?' Heck replied.

'Which means she hasn't. You poor sod.'

'Why don't we just keep our minds on what we're doing, eh?'

Hunter turned in his seat and regarded Gail over the tops of his shades. 'It may surprise you, DC Honeyford, but Heck here used to give it to his super. Not when she was a super obviously. When they were both DCs at Bethnal Green. Soon as she started getting promoted she dropped him like a stone.' He glanced at Heck. 'Or was it the other way round? Can't remember. Think it was, wasn't it?'

'What does it matter?' Heck said.

Hunter turned back to the front. 'You're just like the rest of us now, pal . . . tired footsloggers who aren't getting any.' He chuckled again.

'I see pissant stuff still tickles you.'

'Just having a giggle, mate,' Hunter said. 'This is the calm before the storm. Might as well enjoy it.'

Chapter 21

The Heart of Stone pub stood at the junction of Ashby Road and Wickham Road. From Bob Hunter's perspective, the situation report on arrival was not ideal. Only a hundred yards north, Wickham Road connected with Lewisham Way, one of south-east London's main arteries. If the blaggers got away in that direction, it would be difficult forming last-second barricades to effect containment, even though Division had confirmed they'd have support units standing by. In the other direction, it connected with Brockley Road, which was another major thoroughfare, while Ashby Road itself provided a rat run through from Brockley Road to Breakspears Road, which also joined with Lewisham Way, creating in effect a network of escape routes. In truth, this was probably why the Snake Eyes had zoned in on it; apparently Manko's crew had scoped out numerous pubs south of the river, and only a relative handful met the criteria they'd set themselves.

That said, there were some benefits to be gained from this particular plot. The broad triangle of pavement between the pub front and the junction of the two roads was bollarded off, which wouldn't allow the blaggers to drive right up to its doors – that was a lot of pavement they had to cross, and in which they could be caught amid three separate assault teams. There were several multi-storey flats overlooking from the south, where SCO-19 could perch their snipers, and an excellent combined observation post and lying-up point, or LUP as it was known in the trade, directly across the road from the pub, on the junction's south-west corner: this was a three-storey building, the ground floor of which had previously sold electronics, though this shop was now closed, its window painted out, while the two apartments above it were untenanted.

After the area had been covertly swept for Snake Eye spotters – the Flying Squad even employed scanners to search for radio signals – the team assembled quickly and quietly. Two 'gunships' – armoured troop carriers filled with Flying Squad detectives and plain-clothes firearms officers from SCO-19, but disguised to look like everyday scruffy work vans – found good positions: the first parked in a cobbled alley on the right side of the pub, the second in an entry on the junction's north-west corner. Just after midday, Hunter and Brogan entered the pub, ostensibly as customers but in reality to take the landlord into a back room and tell him exactly what was happening. The raid was only expected to occur at eleven o'clock that night – up to now they'd all happened at around eleven – but unsurprisingly the landlord concluded that it was better if he and his staff vacated the premises from early evening onwards, to be replaced by male and female undercover officers. More problematic would be the customers. The Snake Eyes were almost certain to make a couple of drive-bys during the day, so every aspect of normality had to be maintained, which meant the pub must stay open and members of the public had to be allowed to come and go. Hunter sought the advice of a higher authority back at the Squad's HQ before deciding that punters would be admitted to the pub and served until ten p.m., from which point on all would be taken into protective custody and removed from the premises via plain-clothes vehicles parked at the rear; it would be explained to each and every one that they'd only be detained for a couple of hours. Any objecting, demanding they be released or allowed to make phone calls, would, if persuasion failed, be arrested on suspicion of conspiracy to rob. It was a high-risk strategy, but not as risky as the situation for those additional undercover cops, who, one by one, would replace them inside the Heart of Stone.

All day as these preps were underway Heck and Gail could do nothing but sit in the upper room of the OP, while around them inner London baked.

'Summertime in the city, eh?' Gail said, her brown hair hanging in damp ringlets over her forehead. There was no air conditioning in this empty building, and, though it had plenty of windows, for the moment they were to remain closed and those inside were under instruction not to approach them during daylight.

Heck swigged from a bottle of water, which he handed over to her. 'Bit of a culture shock after Surrey, I suppose.'

She took a gulp and wiped her mouth. 'Not to me. I lived round here for three years. Or near here. When I was a student. Took sociology at Goldsmiths.'

'Did you graduate?'

'With a first.'

He nodded. 'Well done.'

'At least you're not laughing at the fact it was sociology.'

'A degree's a degree.'

'I can't imagine Bob Hunter would see it that way.'

'Probably not.'

'Heck, do you trust him?'

Heck pondered that. 'Not entirely.'

'Oh . . . great.'

He shrugged. 'This is a complex operation, and I never had Bob down as a man for detail. But put it this way: they've done months of work on this firm, they've amassed a shedload of intel . . . we might as well stick around for the take-down.'

'So that's what this is? A spectator sport? I thought we were trying to trace a stolen vehicle?'

Heck took the bottle back and swigged from it again. 'The Snake Eyes are the key to that. And this is the best chance we've got to get close to them.'

'If there's any of them left to talk.' She nodded to the other side of the room, where two Squad guys were setting up cameras and laying out weapons. Aside from the Glocks and MP5s, there were pump-action shotguns, sledgehammers, hickory staves that looked more like pickaxe handles than police batons, and several heavy ballistics shields. 'What's Hunter trying to do, start a war?'

'I think you'll find it's the Snake Eyes who started the war,' Heck replied.

'Yeah. And as soon as that lot get zapped, another group will arise to take their place.'

'What are you crying about? That's why we've got jobs for life. Look, if you're bored, Gail, it's best to try and get some kip. Could be a long day.'

As if determined to practise what he preached, Heck folded his arms, rocked back on his fold-away stool until it was leaning on two legs and his head and shoulders resting against the wall, and closed his eyes. To Gail's amazement, within a very few minutes, he was snoring gently – though she supposed he *had* been up from very early that morning, roughly five a.m., in order to commence his recce on the Skelton.

Eventually she too began to nod off. But this didn't last long before Bob Hunter and three of his lackeys came banging back into the upper room, causing such a din that she almost jumped from her chair. The overweight DI wasn't wearing the heat well either. His T-shirt was plastered to his chest and back; fresh droplets ran down his beery red face.

'Rise and shine, boys and girls,' he said. 'Got some kit for you.' He tossed them a duffel bag each. 'That's everything I owe you in one fell swoop, Heck, including the M1 nutters. So no calling favours after this.'

They opened the bags and pulled out blue baseball caps with black and white banding, Squad radios with earpiece attachments, both tuned to a dedicated channel, a pair of night-vision goggles each, and two lightweight Kevlar undershirts.

'Just to be on the safe side,' Hunter said when he saw Gail glance at him. 'Your two guv'nors know what you're doing today, I take it?'

'It's all been okayed,' Heck said.

'Good, cos there're enough people here I'm responsible for.'

'Wouldn't want to add to the weight of your task, Bob.'

'Glad we understand each other, Heck. Anyway, all we've gotta do now is wait.'

'That's what we *were* doing,' Gail said, slumping back on her chair.

Hunter shrugged. 'Patience is a virtue, DC Honeyford. You want to join some specialist team, it's something you'll have to learn – and quickly, given that it's still eight hours to contact. Take my advice, try and get some kip.'

As the afternoon wore into evening, a heavy, stultifying silence descended on the OP. Those officers gathered there whiled away the long, tedious hours by playing cards, listening to iPods through earphones, or studying for exams. Hunter busied himself with one of his juniors, poring over a map of the immediate district which they'd spread between them on a low table, and taking occasional quiet reports from inside the pub. Heck continued to doze, though not especially comfortably. Gail barely slept at all.

At around seven that evening a Squad member came up by the back stairs, carrying a cardboard box containing ten newspaper-wrapped portions of fish and chips, and several fresh bottles of mineral water. Everyone ate and drank. When eight o'clock came and daylight was diminishing, the team began checking their weapons and body armour. By nine o'clock, dusk had fallen over the city and there was a general atmosphere of wind-down; fewer honking horns, fewer pedestrians around, streetlights winking to life one by one – at which point Hunter received a call from his insider. The job was still on; the Snake Eyes were saddling up. He passed this news to his subordinates, and sent word to put Division on stand-by. Medical facilities in the neighbourhood were also alerted.

Full darkness had fallen by now, and the team in the OP were allowed to approach the windows. For the first time that day, Heck surveyed the Heart of Stone. It was an innocuous, two-storey building of red brick, with frosted, ornately etched ground-floor windows. A typical London street-end boozer, no doubt with a U-shaped bar inside, polished woodwork, crimson upholstery, and glinting brasses. Apparently DS Brogan was acting landlord and DC Bernetti, having recovered from the brief beating he'd suffered earlier, one of his barmen.

Several times in the past, Heck had been involved in breaking up armed robberies; it was potentially one of the most dangerous jobs any law-officer could undertake, though these days in the UK, with Specialist Firearms Officers present in strength, the police usually had the edge both in terms of firepower and training. The hoods themselves seemed to know this, because it rarely finished up in a gun battle, though resistance did happen on occasion. This time, given the reputation of the Snake Eyes, that felt more likely than not.

Heck's eyes strayed up and down the adjoining streets, scanning for anything even vaguely suspicious: vehicles prowling slowly, blokes hanging around without clear reason; blokes more heavily dressed than seemed normal on a hot, muggy night like this. Of course he didn't expect to see anything *so* obvious. Even the blaggers were more professional in the twenty-first century.

'It's all about speed with this lot,' Hunter said quietly, as if reading Heck's thoughts. He adjusted his night-vision goggles and peered along Wickham Road, focusing on various entries and alleyways. 'They're in and out like lightning. That's why they come team-handed, so they can get the whole plot under control quickly. Still a bunch of cowboys though. They always put a clock on the job – two minutes and they're out. But they fire warning shots, they clobber people. Anyone gets in their way, it's goodnight.'

'Time they were put out of action,' Heck replied.

'That's the plan. We catch 'em at it tonight, especially with Manko in harness, we can nab the entire cartel. It'll be the goal of the season.'

Heck glanced at his watch. Half-ten had stolen up quickly; the show officially went live – as in the raid was deemed imminent – from quarter to eleven, though by now the pub ought to be occupied solely by undercover police. He crossed the room and sat down alongside Gail, who looked stiff and wary, hair still damp on her moon-pale brow. Theoretically it should be cooler now, especially as Hunter had allowed several window panels to be opened, but the room remained stifling; its atmosphere reeked of sweat.

'You all right?' Heck asked.

Her mouth crooked into a half-smile. 'It's ridiculous . . . I'm nervous as hell.'

'What's ridiculous about that?'

'Well, *I'm* not going to be in the firing line, am I?'

He shrugged. 'We want things to work out. It's only natural.'

'I don't need words of wisdom, Heck. I've told you – I'm not a rookie.'

'So you keep saying.'

'I know.' She sighed wearily. 'Look, I'm sorry, okay? All this is new to me. I'll not deny it; but don't keep mothering me. Makes me even more jumpy.'

'Whatever you say.'

'And stop being so bloody understanding as well. I prefer it when you're snappy.'

'You're a right headcase, you know.'

'Thanks.'

'That's partly a compliment. That's what Gemma always says about me.'

'Gemma Piper, is that?'

'Yeah. Head honcho back at SCU.'

'She must be a tough cookie to hold that job down.'

'They don't call her "the Lioness" for nothing.'

Gail regarded him curiously. 'This is the one who used to drag you into bed?'

'It was more of a two-way thing, to be honest.'

'Funny . . . didn't have you down as a ladies' man.'

'I'm not, but . . .' Heck smiled, 'she can be as demure and elegant as any woman out there, but there are times when the last thing you'd call Gemma Piper is a lady.'

'I think that's a case of too much information.'

He chuckled. 'I mean she can be a right tough nut – like you said.'

'Roger, received!' came Hunter's voice as he took a message through his earpiece. He glanced around at his team, little more now than featureless outlines in the gloom. 'All collaterals are definitely off the plot. Everyone stand by.'

Heck glanced at his watch. It was ten minutes to eleven. With a succession of clicks and snaps, magazines were slotted into place and safeties removed as the handful of Squad members in the upper room pulled on their caps and filed downstairs to their final assault position, which was just inside the front door to the electronics shop.

Hunter checked his Glock before sliding it back into his holster, though as OIC he'd be remaining here, supervising from a position of good vantage – unless of course it all went to hell.

And no less than five minutes later, it did.

'What the fuck . . .' Hunter said disbelievingly.

Heck and Gail had now joined him at the window with night goggles in hand. They were equally amazed by the sight of a large heavy goods vehicle – an artic, eight or nine tonnes at least – pulling up on the double yellow lines just to the right-hand side of the pub, completely blocking the alley in which the first gunship was installed.

'That's a delivery lorry,' Heck said. Even from up here, even over the throbbing of the HGV's massive diesel engine, he could hear the multiple clinks of crated beer. The artic's trailer was open at either side, and one of its green tarpaulin hangings inadequately fastened; it had rustled backwards en route, revealing stacks of gleaming bottles.

Hunter lowered his goggles. 'At this fucking hour?'

'What if it's the Snake Eyes?' Gail said.

The same thought occurred to Heck and Hunter. Had the gang hijacked a wagon and brought it here as their own Trojan horse? Down below, a couple of officers disguised as bar staff, one of them DC Bernetti, had emerged from the premises, and could only stand there bewildered as the artic's engine was switched off and the driver and his drayman clambered casually from its cab, pulling on heavy-duty gloves. The plain-clothes men engaged them in a swift conflab, though whatever was being said, the new arrivals were having none of it. The driver shook his head adamantly and strode inside the premises, his workmate and the undercover cops tagging behind. A split second later, Bernetti reappeared in the doorway. His voice came crackling over the air.

'*What are we going to do about this, guv? The driver says he's behind on his schedule, but that this is his last load and we have to take it off his hands. He absolutely won't take it back to the brewery.*'

'You sure he's kosher?' Hunter responded. 'The driver, I mean?'

'*What? Yeah . . . I think. He's an older fella. Nowty bugger too.*'

Fleetingly, Hunter looked frozen with indecision.

Bernetti's voice came through their earpieces again. '*They're asking for the bloody landlord now. I think they've clocked that we're not staff.*'

'Bob, we're out of time,' Heck advised. 'This crew always arrives at eleven. It's bang on that now. Call the job off and close the pub.'

'And lose the whole bloody thing?' Hunter retorted.

'Better that than it kicking off with civvies on the plot.'

'No!' Hunter shook his head. 'They know pubs don't close that early – they'll suss they've been grassed and our man inside'll be wearing his bollocks for earrings.'

From somewhere nearby, possibly at the far end of Wickham Road, there was a loud and prolonged screeching of tyres.

'Shit,' Gail said under her breath.

'Bob, you've got to act now,' Heck said. 'Lock the pub up.'

'Sod that – lock the driver up!' Hunter barked into his mouthpiece. 'And his mate. Get them out through the back door, pronto.'

'Bob, it's too late for that,' Heck warned.

But even as he spoke two vehicles came hurtling into view from opposing directions, a BMW 1181, and a Vauxhall Insignia, two high-performance cars, both no doubt stolen to order earlier that evening. They skidded to a halt one to either side of the triangular paving in front of the pub.

Hunter still looked glazed, as though he couldn't believe how quickly he'd lost control of the situation. This was a Flying Squad OIC's worst nightmare – civvies caught in a shoot-out. And it would be *his* fault; he should have asked the landlord if any tradesmen were expected to call later in the day, and he evidently hadn't.

Seeing Hunter's inertia, Heck grabbed the radio and shouted: 'All units, go! Hit 'em on the pavement! Don't let 'em enter!'

It was a quick reaction, but the blaggers were quicker still. Six of them, masked in balaclavas and bulked up in black flak jackets, had spilled from the cars, three from each, and were galloping towards the pub's main door. The Squad's response was hampered. Firstly by an unfamiliar voice giving them orders – which caused momentary hesitation, and secondly because the first gunship was still trapped in the side alley behind the artic.

Though it later transpired that the team had disembarked from the alley gunship swiftly and efficiently, there was insufficient room for them to sidle their way past the lorry, even on foot. In one fell swoop, this had reduced police numbers on the ground by a third. It also meant that the other two assault teams, one bursting out from the door to the electronics shop, the other leaping from the gunship in the north-west entry, were at a disadvantage as the attempted containment would be open on its east side. As Heck had hoped, the pub door slammed closed in the blaggers' faces before they reached it, and they found themselves with nowhere else to go.

Though this still left them with one deadly option.

The night was already filled with loudspeaker cries of 'Armed police!', 'Drop your weapons!' and 'Get on your knees!', but these were lost in a hail of echoing cracks and staccato blasts of light as gunfire was exchanged in every direction.

With a deafening *ptchuuung!*, a nine-millimetre soft-point ricocheted from the wall close to the window where Heck and Gail were standing. There was a protracted metallic rattle, accompanied by strobe-like bursts, as someone opened up down there with a submachine gun. It was one of the robbers, a lanky goon who was drilling rounds at the second gunship; he clearly wasn't used to handling such a weapon – it jerked all over the place, spraying lead across the entire junction, hitting no one in particular, though the officers who'd poured out of the second ship and had the longest distance to advance had now gone to ground, one behind a bollard, others diving and rolling or sheltering behind their shields, all returning fire. With a shrill squawk, the lanky guy dropped his weapon and fell onto his side, clutching his groin, from which blood was suddenly geysering.

The getaway driver in the BMW bottled it and hit the gas, swerving the motor around in a reckless U-turn, causing the team from the electronics shop to scatter, though they emptied their pistols into the vehicle as it passed them by, perforating its bodywork, sending it slewing sideways, black smoke boiling from under its crumpled bonnet, until it slammed into a kerb with such force that it tipped and rolled, demolishing a shop window.

The pub door was yanked open again, and a muzzle appeared. Two rapid shots followed, both from an MP5, dropping a second blagger in his tracks; he hit the deck like a sack of spuds, a fount of dark liquid pumping from what looked like a severed artery in his neck. In the OP they were forced to duck again as another stray shot hit its window dead centre; the pane shattered in front of them, a million shards cascading to Earth.

Everything seemed to be happening at a thousand miles an hour, and yet despite the intrusion of the delivery wagon the Squad were on top of things. Two of the robbers were now down, and a third and fourth, who'd apparently flung away their weapons as soon as the opposition appeared, had collapsed to their knees with hands raised and heads bowed, cowering in the midst of the crossfire. A fifth blagger, this one armed with a sawn-off, stumbled back towards the Vauxhall, ratcheting and discharging like a madman, only for a cherry-red dot to pinpoint his left shoulder. With a *BOOM* from overhead, a rooftop sniper spun him like a top. Somehow he stayed upright, but another sniper-round struck his right shoulder, spinning him back the other way. The pump flopped down to his side, his hand still locked around its pistol-grip, his finger discharging the weapon a final time – straight into his own right foot, which blew apart like a hunk of raw beef.

While all this was happening the front passenger window of the Insignia shattered outwards, and a Webley six-shooter was thrown clear of the vehicle, indicating that the second getaway driver had also had enough. This left only one of the blaggers in action, and armed officers were advancing on him from all sides, weapons levelled. But this last one had no intention of surrendering. He pegged off two more shots from his handgun – by its volume and recoil, Heck fancied it for a Smith & Wesson, the famed Magnum .44 – and veered away towards the artic's passenger door, reaching into his jacket with his free hand and drawing out a long, shiny blade.

'Manko!' Heck breathed.

Most of the team trapped behind the HGV had apparently

given up attempting to slide past it and had run back along the alley and circled the pub, as they were now appearing from its other side. Only one of them, a big, bearded guy, had thought to try and scramble underneath it. It was pure bad luck that as soon as he emerged and jumped to his feet he found himself nose to nose with the most dangerous member of the Snake Eye gang. Before the astonished cop could draw his Glock, Manko had struck with his machete, a vicious backhand blow across the throat.

The cop dropped to his knees, shuddering. His gargling squeal was heard way along the street. Manko kicked him backwards and clambered up into the cab through the passenger door. The HGV driver must have left his keys in the ignition, because the vast vehicle now thundered to life.

'Fucking shit!' Hunter bellowed. 'Contain that bloody HGV! That's Julius Manko for Christ's sake!'

But most of the officers on the plot were busy, either cuffing the suspects who'd surrendered or applying first aid to those who'd been shot. The closest man to the lorry could do no more than drag his wounded colleague out of the way of its massive wheels as it juddered forward, fumes pumping from its exhaust pipe, and barged its way across the junction.

'We need Wickham Road and Ashby Road blockaded at both ends!' Hunter howled into his radio as he dashed down the stairs. 'Now! Right now! Get me those ARVs . . .'

Heck and Gail leaned from the window. The HGV was already heading west along Ashby Road, gusts of sparks erupting as it rammed and shunted parked vehicles. A divisional patrol car got too close, was sideswiped out of the way, and went clattering into a lamppost. Around fifty yards ahead of the lorry there was a rapid accumulation of spinning blue beacons; multiple other police vehicles attempting to form a barricade. Heck and Gail watched, breathless. The artic might succeed in hammering its way through; but again it might not. If there were armed response vehicles up there, there'd be another exchange of fire and this time Manko was outgunned.

Perhaps thinking the same, the gang leader opted for avoidance, the HGV suddenly jackknifing left and plunging out of sight along a narrow ginnel, raking fresh showers of sparks from the concrete corner.

Heck snatched a torch and shone it down on Hunter's map, which was still spread on the planning table. 'Bloody labyrinth!' he said, pointing out a confusion of narrow, intersecting alleyways.

'He'll never get through that way,' Gail said.

'Unless he comes directly behind us!' Heck jabbed his finger onto a single unnamed thoroughfare that was accessible from the side street Manko had taken, was broader than many of those around it, and after running parallel for some distance with Wickham Road connected with Geoffrey Road, which connected in turn with Brockley Road.

Heck threw the map down and dashed across the room to the door, alongside which there were three tagged keys hanging from hooks. Each one belonged to an unmarked car waiting in the yard at the rear. Heck snatched the first one, which looked like the key to a Ford. He vacated the room, but instead of clumping down the staircase to the front he followed the passage to the rear, and descended the back stairs.

'Heck, what're you doing?' Gail demanded, stumbling after him.

'What do you think?'

'Are you seriously stealing a car from the Flying Squad?'

He reached the bottom and glanced up at her. 'We're pursuing a suspect. What's so off-kilter about that?'

'Heck – this job is none of our business.'

'We've just watched a police officer get his throat cut.

That's *totally* our business!' He hurried outside, indicating a Ford Escort in the corner of the yard, turning and tossing the key to her. 'Why don't you get her started?'

'Heck, I just don't think—'

'If it'll put you at ease, DC Honeyford, that's an order!' He ran out through the gate. Beyond it lay a maze of darkened back alleys. He worked his way through these as best he could, shouldering past dustbins packed with foul-smelling refuse, finally taking a cut-through to the unnamed road. He reached it just as the artic trundled past in a north-to-south direction. It couldn't travel fast as it had to force its way, with much grinding and crunching, past innumerable parked vehicles. Both its front headlight clusters were already shattered. The tarpaulins on the rear trailer hung loose, the straps dangling where their buckles had snapped. Several crates had fallen out, cans and bottles rolling on the road, many of them broken, beer foaming into the gutters.

Heck wasn't really thinking straight when he jumped aboard; he simply went for it. And it wasn't even difficult.

He gripped a tarpaulin, planted a foot on the steel runner. And then he was moving along, being carried on the flank of the juddering goliath. Dragging the material back even further, he was able to clamber inside the trailer, finding himself amid teetering stacks of beer. He stumbled to his feet – only for the lorry to swing round a tight corner, presumably out into Brockley Road, and then pick up speed, jolting against kerbstones, swaying from side to side as it raced to overtake other road users. There was a cacophony of blaring horns. The gritty plank floor bucked as the artic bounced over a speed ramp. Heck was flung down between falling crates and smashing bottles.

'Heck to DI Hunter!' he shouted into his radio, cupping his face against flying glass. 'Receiving, over?'

There was a distortion of static before Hunter replied. *'Receiving. Go ahead.'*

'Managed to get aboard the suspect vehicle, guv. It's an Aveco HGV. I've got a partial index. It starts Juliet-Alpha-eight-three, over.'

'Can you repeat that, DS Heckenburg?' Even over the air, with a welter of ambient noise behind him, Hunter sounded astounded. *'You are on board the suspect vehicle?'*

'That's affirmative, guv. But I'm stuck in the trailer.'

The artic collided with something. This was an especially heavy impact, and Heck was hurled sideways – all the way across the deck, his earpiece coming loose. More beer crates fell and broke open, bottles and cans spilling forth. Heck crawled on his elbows and knees towards the billowing tarpaulin and tried to peek past it. 'I can't say where we are for sure – oh, wait! Crofton Park! That's affirmative. We've just passed Crofton Park on the left. So we're heading south down Brockley Road. Fifty plus, over.'

Chapter 22

As a serving police officer of four years' experience, Gail Honeyford had never known anything like the last few hours. After that prolonged, nerve-racking wait in the OP, the situation had suddenly exploded. The gory shoot-out at the Heart of Stone hadn't been unexpected. But the actual sight of men dropping like ninepins, the agonised screams torn from irreparably shattered bodies, had made her flinch, and yet it had all happened too quickly for the true horror of it to register. The gunfire had sounded like a fireworks display, the stroboscopic muzzle-flashes had resembled a pyrotechnics show. Even now it didn't seem real to her – at least superficially, though deep down she already suspected she was hurting. You didn't watch people die at point-blank range, or at least you didn't stand agog, eyes bugging, while blokes blasted each other with firearms, without it damaging you in some way.

And now this.

She was racing along Brockley Road in a rackety old Escort, which had probably been around the clock at least twice, in pursuit of a juggernaut with a maniac at the wheel. The target vehicle was about fifty yards ahead, careering through red lights, sending other vehicles spinning in every direction. There were thudding impacts on all sides; bumpers slamming into tenement walls, fragments of glass and buckled bodywork catapulting outwards as side panels collapsed, as street signs were flattened and shop windows imploded. This was against all the rules in modern police work, of course: pursuing a suspect at high speed through a built-up area, though as far as Julius Manko was aware, *no one* was pursuing. She was in an unmarked car; she had no beacon, no siren. He was driving like a crazy man to get away from the scene of a vicious crime he'd committed and, as Heck said, that couldn't be allowed to happen.

Gail veered left to right as more and more beer bottles were discarded from the rear of the lorry, exploding like cluster bombs on the road surface ahead of her. And yet she was distracted by the frantic cross-talk on her radio. It sounded as if a DC Breedon had suffered a severe laceration to his windpipe, but was still breathing and *'where the fuck was that ambulance?'* Three of the robbers, meanwhile, were critical; one of them was almost certainly dead at the scene.

She heard Heck's voice too, as he struggled to give directions.

'Approaching Brockley Rise, still heading south,' he said, *'I think . . . can't be sure.'*

Gail clung to her wheel for grim death as, with a deafening scrunch of gears, the artic bore straight over a roundabout, mashing two 'keep left' signs and digging 'battlefront' trenches through the flowerbeds in the middle. It almost lost control as it swerved sharply left. Again her knuckles turned white as she copied the manoeuvre. Belatedly, it now struck her that she was in a better position than Heck was to provide directions.

'DC Honeyford to DI Hunter, receiving, over?' She tried to remember the call sign on the Escort's keyring. 'I've taken

Foxtrot-Alpha and I'm in pursuit of the target vehicle, which has just turned into . . .' She glanced sideways as a street sign flickered past. 'Stanstead Road.' Gail had a passable knowledge of south London's geographical layout, but the rest she'd have to guess. 'I think we're heading east. We've just passed St Dunstan's College, and are now on Catford Road . . . hang on, we're heading south again along Bromley Hill. Full index on the target . . . Juliet-Alpha-eight-three-Delta-Papa-Kilo, over.'

'*Received*,' Hunter replied, sounding strangely less-than-impressed. '*Just stay in contact with him. Do not – repeat, do not – attempt to impede the target or bring it to a halt. Air support en route, over.*'

'Wilco,' she replied.

Ahead of her the artic blistered along London Road, swerving sharply to avoid another HGV pulling out in front. The massive trailer swung hard into a metal crash barrier, almost tangling itself in the mangled scrap. There was a further blaring of horns, but the artic tore on, leaving a high-sided van to shunt the second lorry from behind, and a third vehicle, a Renault Clio, to screech sideways to avoid the pile-up, crossing the junction and hitting a telegraph pole which, with a torturous cracking of timbers, fell backwards into a garden, dragging down a mess of live cables writhing like fiery snakes. It was all Gail could do to skid through this labyrinth of destruction unscathed. The target was now far ahead, on Widmore Road. Even as she watched, it veered left again. She had to get her foot down just to keep sight of it, but she knew she couldn't let it go. She was the only officer in contact; apart from Heck of course.

As this occurred to her, there was a bleeping from her jeans pocket. She fished the phone out and glanced at its screen. It was not a number she recognised.

She slammed the device to her ear as she drove. 'Heck – is that you?'

'Yeah, it's me,' he shouted. 'Well done for staying on his arse.'

'You all right?'

'For the moment. But I'm getting a right pummelling in here. *Ouch!* This had better lead us to that bloody van, I'm telling you . . . not to mention those bloody pranksters!'

'Heck, if you just hang in there, the cavalry aren't far behind me!'

'They're gonna have to be bloody quick!'

'What do you mean?'

'Am I right in thinking this goon is circling back round towards central London?'

'We're currently on Chislehurst Road, heading east.'

'Shit!' Heck swore. 'That settles it. He *is* circling back, which doesn't make much sense unless he's heading for the Blackwall Tunnel.'

'Why would he be doing that?'

'The choppers'll be here in minutes. They'll put heat seekers on him. That means there's nowhere else for him to go. But the tunnel will screen him from that while he dumps this crate. All he has to do then is hijack another vehicle and he's as good as gone. I'm thinking aloud, Gail, but this is the best shot we've got – to reach the Blackwall Tunnel, he's got to hit the Southern Approach, going past the Old Dover Road. You've got to get ahead of him.'

Even in the midst of the most hair-raising pursuit of her career, she didn't like the sound of *this*. 'How do you mean?'

'You've got to prevent him getting there. Cut him off somehow.'

'Heck, I'm in a Ford Escort, not a tank – *oh shit!*' She swore as the steering wheel was almost jerked from her hands. Part of the artic's undercarriage – a huge piece of riveted piping – had come bouncing back towards her, crashing under her nearside wheel. It took everything she

254

had to keep the curve as she swung sharply through a four-road intersection.

'You okay?' Heck shouted.

'Yeah. Look, I think you're right. He's going up Prince Imperial Road. That's back towards the Thames, isn't it?'

'Eventually, yeah. But you've still got to get ahead of him.'

'I don't see how . . .'

'Listen, there's a short cut you can take. Go left, hitting White Horse Hill and up Mottingham Road, through Mottingham and Blackheath. Keep going along Winn Road, Baring Road, then up Burnt Ash and Prince of Wales. Floor it, and you'll get ahead of him at some point.'

'And then what?'

'I don't bloody know. You'll have to improvise. *Owww* . . .'

'What's up?'

'Getting thrown around like a shuttlecock in here. And it's filled with beer and broken glass. Cutting me to buggery!'

'Heck, how am I going to head him off?'

'Use the sat nav. There ought to be one. It's a Flying Squad car. I'm sure they're not still living in the 1970s.'

Gail glanced left. There was indeed a sat nav mounted on the dashboard. 'What good's that going to do?'

'See if there are any hold-ups between where you are now and where Manko's trying to get to. If you can shepherd him into some roadworks or a contraflow system, he's had it. If he's forced to slow down or stop, I can get out of here and try to get into the cab.'

'You'll do no such thing,' she shouted. 'He's armed and you're not.'

'Well if you're here, there'll be two of us.'

'Great. Two police funerals for the price of one!'

'That's the job, Gail. Get to it.'

Even as she sped through Chislehurst, Gail was fraught

255

with indecision. She'd had one order from DI Hunter, and one order only – to stay in contact with Manko but not to interfere with his flight. Heck, who was junior to Hunter, had now told her exactly the opposite. But Heck was *here*, embroiled in the actual fight, and Hunter was miles away. Through the window she could hear a whooping of distant sirens. She fancied (or perhaps hoped) she could also hear the *chudda-chudda-chudda* of a pursuing helicopter. But Heck was undoubtedly right. If Manko got to the Blackwall Tunnel, even at this time of night, there'd be any number of vehicles in there he could hijack. Then he could drive out again, probably with hostages, completely invisible to the eye in the sky.

Coming up on her left, she now saw the turn to White Horse Hill – a signpost pointed towards Mottingham.

With squeals of rubber, she veered in that direction. As the target vehicle vanished from sight she grappled one-handed with the sat nav. It came to life quickly. Still one-handed, with the south London streets flipping by outside in a near-blur, she tried to tap in the coordinates for the Blackwall Tunnel. A map sprang into view, the most direct route highlighted ahead of her – as Heck had said, through Mottingham and Blackheath. She was now flying along Mottingham Road, which became Mottingham Lane, then screeched into Baring Road, where she fiddled again with the sat nav, sending a request for notifications about hold-ups and detours. Her sweat-soaked hair prickled as she spied a flashing red cross to indicate a temporary road closure on the Southern Approach to the tunnel itself. A diversion was in place, shunting river-crossing traffic towards the Rotherhithe Tunnel, four miles west. If Manko got there first, he'd still be okay; the Rotherhithe would serve his purpose just as well. But this was a chance she couldn't afford to miss.

Thankfully the streets at this late hour remained relatively clear, though as Gail throttled along Burnt Ash Road even the handful of fellow road users had to swing out of her way. But she was almost there; the tunnel could only be minutes ahead of her. As she raced along Lee Road and Prince of Wales, she reasoned that she had to be in front of her prey by now; she was faster, she'd had less ground to cover. As she entered Westcombe Hill she glanced at the sat nav, and realised that she was running parallel to the southern end of the Southern Approach. She risked a glance right and, flickering between the buildings, saw an enormous wreck of an object, jolting and juddering but still travelling at frightful speed. Her heart missed a beat; partly with elation that she and Heck had been right, but also with fear because Manko was much further ahead than she'd expected. The diversion from the Southern Approach was now less than a mile ahead; it rerouted traffic onto Westcombe Hill at a point where the two roads nearly merged, through a virtual bottleneck, and yet still they were running almost side by side.

Had Manko noticed her yet? Would it be a game of chicken, a case of who blinked first?

'*Shit!*' This was insane. This wasn't responsible policing. But this guy had tried to kill a fellow officer, and God knows how many others. He wasn't getting away with it.

Gail rammed her foot to the floor, rocketing through the last few sets of lights. Her phone rang again.

'Where are you?' Heck stammered.

'Can't talk,' she said. 'Almost there, brace yourself.'

The two carriageways were drawing together. The buildings in between them – scrapyards and ramshackle huddles of Portakabins – were diminishing. Manko must now have seen signs that the road ahead was closed. Gail flicked another glance at the sat nav. Manko would be swinging over imminently. She looked at her speedo, wondering how much faster she dared go, and was stunned to see that she was already touching ninety. Ahead of her, the Southern Approach rose upwards as it passed above the shopping centres servicing the Millennium Village. It was covered with yellow visi-flashers. Midway up it, she spied a series of barriers made from cones, sawhorses and fluttering red and white tape. The crossover lane was fast approaching. She looked right again. The artic was there, towering over her, a wounded hulk on wheels, its tarpaulins billowing, its sagging frame dragging a monstrous trail of smoke and sparks. Even as she gazed up at it, it slid across the carriageway towards her. Would Manko risk a collision at this speed? Every molecule in Gail's body – every instinct, every thought she'd ever had for her family, her friends, her loved ones – was screaming at her to back off, to hit the brakes, hit the brakes, hit the brakes . . . she floored the pedal again.

And veered right.

Not just refusing to move for the swerving juggernaut, but challenging it.

Causing it to shift right again.

Directly ahead, the concrete divider hurtled right at them – a massive impregnable buttress, like a motorway stanchion. Even a diehard headcase like Julius Manko had no option. With shrieking tyres, he swerved back into his own lane, and then he was screaming away and above her.

Astonished that she was still alive, Gail hit the brakes, even though the road ahead was completely empty, and the Escort turned through a full 380-degree skid, sliding across another intersection and slamming to a halt in a gravel-filled lay-by, buffeting a wastebin, scattering a sea of litter.

Gasping for breath, she clambered out and looked up at the vast faceless underside of the flyover, listening to a deafening series of impacts as the broken-backed giant ploughed through the roadworks. Still panting, she ran back the way she'd come, jabbering incoherently into her radio.

Chapter 23

It seemed highly unlikely that Julius Manko had a licence to drive a heavy goods vehicle. Even if he did have, it seemed equally unlikely that he'd have the skill to navigate his way through the maze of roadworks on the Southern Approach to the Blackwall Tunnel at seventy miles an hour without finally losing control.

Somehow or other the diesel-powered leviathan remained upright, even though its air brakes were fully applied, even though it fishtailed as its wheels locked and it crashed sideways through one barricade after another, mowing down noticeboards and temporary lights, tangling its axles in tape, scattering cones and visi-flashers, flattening Portakabins, caroming from one concrete abutment to the next. It groaned and squealed as it spun in lazy circles, shedding bottles and cans like a dog shaking off fleas.

In its mangled guts, amid fountains of beer and avalanches of splintered glass and broken, lopsided crates, Heck was tossed around like a rag doll. At one point he was half ejected onto the blacktop, grasping wildly at shreds of tarpaulin, swinging from it like an ape before being flung back inside. The final tectonic jolt came when the artic slid over the central reservation and wrapped itself round a lighting tower built from heavy steel and fitted into an immense cement glove: axles buckled, couplings snapped and hoses split, spraying showers of coolant and hydraulic fluid.

Heck came to rest face down in a nest of froth-soaked rubble, his clothing shredded by broken glass, his hands and knees bleeding from multiple cuts. Several moments after the mechanical monstrosity had ground to a standstill, he lifted a dazed head and glanced sideways. Through clouds of steam and hanging tatters of tarpaulin, he glimpsed a lone figure limping away. It was Manko. He'd stripped off his fatigues and his balaclava helmet; his impressive tattoo-covered physique was covered only by a vest, but he was also wearing a shoulder holster with his pistol in it, and a large leather scabbard on his left hip, in which his machete was fastened. A bottle rolled away across the deck and the hoodlum spun round, drawing both his gun and his knife, scanning the trailer's devastated interior.

Heck lay where he was, holding his breath. Manko stood his ground, but clearly saw nothing more than darkness and wreckage. One whole side of his face was masked with blood and he was visibly shaking. At last he turned away and lumbered on, clearly intending to circle the vehicle – and that could only be to get even with whoever had been following him.

'Gail,' Heck said under his breath.

He shifted position, conscious to avoid making noise, though once again cans and bottles rolled, fragments of glass tinkled together – and yet none of that mattered because suddenly there came the distinctive *boom!* of a Smith & Wesson .44.

'*Gail!*' Heck said, louder this time.

Throwing caution to the wind, he scrambled to his feet and tottered across the trailer to its nearside, peeking out through the ragged curtains. Manko was standing in front of him, about five yards to the right. He was staring southwards down the Southern Approach, which was scattered with more wreckage than it seemed possible for any road surface to accommodate. He'd clearly recovered some of his composure, because he stood in swaggering posture, machete resting on his shoulder, peering along his Magnum's nine-inch barrel, regardless of the fast-approaching sirens, unconcerned that from somewhere in the sky came the reverberation of rotor blades.

Heck followed his gaze, and saw a figure scurrying for cover.

Boom! – Manko fired again, the massive recoil kicking his forearm upwards.

A street sign Gail had just ducked behind folded under the impact.

She scrambled away, diving and rolling across the tarmac.

Manko took aim a third time, this time very carefully, eyes squinted, steadying his arm – so focused that he didn't notice Heck alight from the trailer behind him, grab a shovel, and stealthily approach. The first time the gang-banger realised someone else was there was when the shovel was hurtling down at his gun hand. He twirled to face this new opponent, but it was too late – the steel blade struck the Magnum handgrip hard, slicing flesh and bone in the process. The gun went clattering to the ground, detonating one final time, a slug careening from the tarmac, missing Heck by inches.

Manko lurched backwards, braying with agony.

Fleetingly he was distracted from Heck by the sight of his bloodied right hand, from which a number of digits hung at impossible angles. Then his scream became a roar, and his face a picture of gore-patterned fury. He rounded on Heck, raising his glimmering blade and slashing down with it.

Heck parried with the shovel's handle, though the wooden shaft was sheared clean through. The second blow came equally fast, but Heck was able to weave backwards and evade it with ease – and he quickly realised why. Manko was right-handed; that hand now a useless knot of flesh and mangled bone. He couldn't even gain balance from it. The third swipe, a massive backhander, overreached itself. He tottered, and the toe of Heck's right training shoe impacted in his groin. Manko stumbled away, half-doubled with pain, his eyes rolling.

'Put the blade down, sonny,' Heck snarled. 'You're nicked.'

Manko bared his teeth before turning to run – only to find Gail, wet-faced with sweat as she slid to a halt in front of him. Somewhat ridiculously, she'd armed herself with a traffic cone – and yet it sufficed. Manko went straight at her, attempting to stab rather than hack or slash. Gail hefted the cone, trapping the weapon in its funnel-like interior. With a deft twist she broke Manko's grip on the hilt, and suddenly he was unarmed. The gang-banger turned again, but he caught a right hook from Heck on his cheekbone. It sent him staggering back against the artic – only for him to roll athletically backwards into the trailer's interior and scramble through it to the other side. Heck vaulted up in pursuit. Gail threw the cone down and hurried round the front of the vehicle to try and head him off. But Manko was already accelerating away, sprinting through those sections of road-works not yet demolished. He might have been hurt, he might have been bloodied – but he was clearly fit. Cackling, he threw a mocking glance over his shoulder. And thus didn't notice when he barged through another barrier of tape, struck an outer rim of breeze blocks, and found himself sprawling face down into an oblong cavity that seemed to cross the entirety of the road. Shouting unintelligibly, he plummeted four feet before splurging full length into a bed of wet cement.

Heck and Gail covered the last few yards at a walk, breathing slow and hard as their sweat cooled. When they came to the breeze-block rim, Heck lifted a visi-flasher, casting a dim yellow radiance into the shadowy pit. Manko had managed to roll over onto his back, but now lay twisted, half-submerged in the grey sludge, which had clumped in his hair and on his clothing, coating his cheeks and caking his limbs. He was a muscular lad, but now he might as well have been a worm in glue.

'Get . . . get me out of here, man!' he jabbered in his curious south London patois. 'Telling you, man – gemme the fuck out of here!'

Heck spotted a long metal pole propped against a tarpaper shed. He brought it over to the pit, where he braced one foot against the breeze-block rim and cautiously poked it downwards. Manko was so buried that he could barely reach up to grab it, but that didn't matter because Heck lowered it until its cylindrical tip was pressed against his breastbone – at which point he leaned forward, pressing his whole weight down, slowly but surely shoving the wriggling hoodlum deeper into the mire.

'What are you doing?' Gail said.

'Usually it's our lot who get buried in the foundations of bridges,' Heck said. 'Not today.'

'What the fuck you doing, man?' Manko shouted. 'Respect man, respect . . . yeah? Lemme out of here – cool it, yeah?'

'Heck!' Gail protested.

'Today Julius Manko is really going to learn the meaning of hardcore,' Heck replied. 'He's gonna be breathing it!'

'No!' She grabbed the pole, but Heck shook her off.

'Okay man, I'll talk, yeah!' Manko screamed. 'I'll fucking talk!'

'Oh, I know you will.' Heck leaned as hard on the pole as he could. With a gurgling *slurp*, Manko went several inches deeper into the cement, which drew an even shriller shriek from his constricting chest. 'But I'm not sure it'll be good enough, Wanko . . . you see I want the entire criminal history of you and your crew . . . and every toerag you know who isn't crew . . . every single crime you and your boys have ever committed. You feel me, *bro*?'

'Yo man, stop this crazy stuff! Hey lady, stop him, yeah – I'll tell you everything!'

'*Everything*? You gonna tell me *everything*, Manko, or just what it suits you and your boys in da hood – or is it da block? Sorry, I never know.'

'Yeah man, sure thing . . .'

'*Nah!*' Heck leaned on the pole all the harder. The half-sunken form was now almost completely submerged, heavy wet muck surging up over his throat and under his chin.

'*I said I'll tell you everything!*' Manko's voice was a falsetto shriek.

'About the murders?' Heck queried.

'Yeah man, about the murders.'

'I can't hear you, *bro*!'

'*About the murders!*' Manko howled. '*About the murders!*'

Directly overhead now, by about fifty feet, a Metropolitan Police helicopter hung motionless, its blades cutting the air in a steady monotone, its two searchlights creeping along the wreckage-strewn approach road. At any second the first beam would alight on Heck and Gail, and their hapless captive.

Almost reluctantly, Heck withdrew the pole. 'Telling you, Manko man – you don't know how lucky you are today. You really don't.'

Chapter 24

Julius Manko was only booked into Brixton Police Station after first being taken to University Hospital Lewisham. On arrival at the Custody Suite, he had stitches over his left eye, and his right hand was encased in plaster. But despite this, and despite having a very long chat with his solicitor first, and even though it was now nearly two in the morning, the gang leader was apparently eager to talk. There was stuff he needed to clear up, he said.

This amounted to a virtual laundry list of criminal activity, not to mention full details of all those Snake Eye members who'd participated.

Heck and Gail watched patiently through a two-way mirror while Bob Hunter and one of his sergeants led the interview. Various others occupied the observation room with them, including a detective chief superintendent from the Flying Squad, and two senior members of the CPS, the latter sallow-faced and rumpled as they'd been dragged out of bed. Manko, who looked distinctly less menacing in his paper Custody suit, was a trifle pallid too, but still talking animatedly.

Heck, who'd also called in at Lewisham A&E and whose

hands and forearms were covered in sticking plaster and antiseptic, listened carefully. He wasn't sure what kind of off-the-record discussion had taken place between Manko, his solicitor and the various legal bigwigs now assembled here at Brixton, but it seemed most likely the hoodlum had negotiated a 'some kind of reduced sentence' deal in return for turning Queen's Evidence. It wasn't as if the hoodlum would have had much choice; the pub robberies and the attempted murder of the detective at the Heart of Stone would have secured him a life sentence on their own. By the same token, while Manko was undoubtedly a player and it would be a real feather in the Flying Squad's cap to put him behind bars, in exchange for his cooperation they were getting the names and addresses of an awful lot of other active criminals, and by the looks of it would be clearing up a vast number of unsolved crimes.

And so it droned on, the prisoner laying endless charges against his fellow gang-bangers: robbery, burglary, car-jacking, arson, assaults on rival crews, possession of weapons, possession of drugs with intent to supply and so forth. Manko wouldn't have it that he himself had ordered or involved himself in any murders, but explained that certain members of his crew – and again he named them – had probably acted unilaterally.

'Christ's sake,' Gail groaned, glancing at her watch. 'Are *we* going to get a chance to talk to him, or what?'

'Probably not tonight,' Heck replied. 'To be honest, I'm wondering if there'll be any point.'

'Why?'

He nodded at the door, and they stepped out into the corridor.

'He didn't recognise me,' Heck said. 'I could see that in his face. When I got out of that lorry, picked up that shovel, and came at him, his expression was like "Whoa, who the fuck is this guy? What's this guy's problem?"'

Gail shrugged. 'Anyone would under those circumstances.'

'Not someone who'd tried to assassinate me the day before yesterday.'

'You mean the bridge at the farm?'

'If that trap was deliberately set for me, it's most likely because whoever's perpetrating the crimes in Surrey knows I'm onto them. Stands to reason, yeah?'

'Well . . .' She shrugged again. 'It was another staged accident, I'll admit that.' But she didn't look totally convinced. Gail had an irritating habit of starting to doubt their leads very quickly.

'The point is,' Heck said, 'that incident at the bridge couldn't have been anything to do with Manko. He's never once mentioned me by name. He doesn't know who I am, Gail. Not from Adam. And there's something else. All the time I've been back in London, I've kept SCU busy. Soon as I learned we were looking at the Snake Eyes, I asked them for some DNA work. I requested all the members of the crew we've already got on record, which is probably most of them, be cross-checked with the blood we found in Harold Lansing's tooth. While I was in A&E, I received this text from Eric Fisher – he's our main analyst.' Heck held up his phone.

DNA done. All neg.

Gail regarded the message with growing weariness and frustration. 'What about the murders Manko mentioned when we were arresting him?'

'He didn't say which murders, and by the sounds of it he's dobbing his mates in for quite a few. But not ours . . . sadly.' Heck yanked at his collar with a thickly plastered forefinger. 'Anyway, we were never totally sold on the idea that our murders were down to the Snake Eyes themselves.

Just that if the van was pinched on their manor, they might be connected to them.'

'So, after all this, we're not going to talk to them at all?'

'We'll see what opportunities there are with the rest of Manko's crew in the morning. It's a bit late now.'

Gail looked more than peeved. 'And in the meantime, the bloody Flying Squad get the lot and we get nothing?'

'Everything that's happened tonight has happened with the cooperation of the Flying Squad – and that doesn't come easy. It's only because of them that we've even got near Manko's mob. In return for that, the least we can do is let them reap the reward for the months of work they've put into this firm.'

'Heck, *we're* working important cases too.'

'Gail, get real.' Heck led her away from the door to the observation room. 'Manko's empowering himself while he's in there. Wheedling his way into the Squad's confidence by helping them clean up hundreds of outstanding crimes. He's their new best pal. We go in next, the guys who broke his fingers with a spade and tried to drown him in cement . . .'

'*We?*'

'All right, me: *I* go in there. He'll just clam up. There's no need for him to talk to me, because he's getting the deal he wants right now. But listen, by tomorrow everything's going to be different. Manko will have delivered his mates, and all bets will be off. No one in the Snake Eyes will know who to trust, so they'll *all* be ready to talk. That's when me and you go in.'

'Okay, okay.' She nodded, hearing this and perhaps, deep down, grateful that they were finally calling it a day. 'So – what do we do next?'

Heck gave it some thought. 'We've given our statements and arrest reports. Might as well have a drink.'

'Excuse me?'

268

'Don't worry, you've earned one.'

'I know I've bloody earned one. But it's two o'clock in the morning, and I haven't even got a pad to crash in tonight.'

'I've got a bed and brekkie off Clapham Common. There's easily room for two. Anyway, I'm only talking a quick nightcap. And the Squad have invited us, so it'd be rude not to go.'

Gail pondered this, clearly not appreciating the idea. 'Seems wrong . . . after all that carnage on the road.'

'*You* didn't cause it.'

'I know that, but—'

'You maintained a safe distance while you stayed in contact with the target vehicle, on the orders of a senior officer?'

'Yeah, course.'

'Manko only crashed because he tried to run you off the road?'

'Suppose so.'

'There you are.' He headed for the exit. 'Some professional standards arse-wipe asks questions, that's what you tell them. Bob'll certainly back you up.'

'How can you be sure?' she said, following.

'He's the bloody Sweeney. That's what they do.'

The quick nightcap turned into several.

The Squad gave them directions to a backstreet nightclub in Wandsworth where, despite their dirty and ragged state, their warrant cards were all they needed to gain admission through the back door. Beyond that, a burly black bouncer directed them up a rear staircase bathed in aqua-green light to a private bar overlooking a dance floor crammed with revellers and ablaze with stroboscopic disco lights, but insulated from the noise and heat by floor-to-ceiling two-way mirrors.

Various other members of the Flying Squad were already

in there, either lounging around tables or seated at the bar. Heck exchanged a few words with them, to muted laughter, then crossed the room to the crushed-velvet sofa where Gail was seated and handed her a bottle of lager. He slumped into the facing armchair and pulled gratefully at a bottle of his own.

'This place has got to be owned by a gangster of some sort,' Gail said.

'I'd imagine it is,' he replied.

'And don't tell me . . . he's grateful to the Squad for wiping out his competition tonight?'

Heck chuckled. 'Maybe – or maybe something similar sometime in the past. I think this is a regular haunt of theirs, to be honest.'

She glanced around at the slick, modernist décor, the low-key lamps, the plush carpets and wall-hangings. Belatedly, she seemed to become self-conscious about her less-than-glamorous state, trying to straighten and comb her hair with her fingers.

Heck was about to comment on this when he was called over to the bar by a couple of Squad members. He swapped some banter with them, and there was more ribald laughter. When he returned, he was carrying a tray with a bottle of champagne and two flutes perched on it.

Gail eyed this curiously. 'You didn't give the impression you knew these fellas before?'

'I don't know them,' Heck replied, sitting again. 'Well, I know Bob because he used to be SCU. A couple of the others by name and reputation, but that's all.'

'So what is it – you guys in the Met, you just party on down every chance you get?'

'I'm not in the Met.'

'No, of course. National Crime Group.'

'Don't pretend you're not impressed.'

270

She arched an eyebrow. 'With what exactly?'

'With all this. With what you've participated in tonight.'

'We were almost killed.'

'Yeah, but we hooked a big fish. Thanks to us, half the tearaways in south London are about to go down.'

She sipped her lager. 'I've caught murderers before.'

Heck relaxed into the upholstery. 'I knew there had to be a reason why you stayed on Manko's tail. It's the buzz, isn't it? The thrill of the chase?'

'I was more concerned for you, if you want the truth.'

'Yeah, I heard that.' He grinned. 'What was it you said? "You will do no such thing. He's armed and you're not." Did I detect a bit of partnerly concern there?'

She shrugged. 'You were a fellow officer in danger. Plus, we'd just seen him cut the throat of another fellow officer.'

'Yeah.' Heck twisted the champagne cork. 'That's why I wanted him too.'

'How is that guy . . . what was his name, Breedon?'

'Adam Breedon. He'll be okay apparently, but he'll have a nasty scar.'

Gail watched absently as he yanked the cork free. 'Why would he strike out so violently? Manko, I mean. Why would he slash a guy's throat, drive like a madman, knocking other road users out of his way? Any number of people could have died.'

'And it would have been worth it from his point of view.' Heck poured two generous measures of the foaming vintage. 'Look at what he stood to lose. I mean, he started out with nothing, a despised no-mark in a part of the city that doesn't care about its own let alone foreigners. By the sweat on his brow and the blood on his blade, he carved himself an empire. Zero to hero. And now it's all gone . . . just like that.'

'You almost sound like you admire him.'

'I don't admire him at all.' Heck pushed a brimming flute

271

across the tabletop towards her. 'I think he's a filthy lowlife who doesn't deserve the leniency he'll now be shown for handing over his so-called mates. It's bullying, narcissistic scrotes like Manko who've turned inner-city Britain into a hellhole. But he's the reason these guys over here –' Heck stuck a thumb in the direction of the Squad members seated at the bar, a couple of whom raised their glasses in response – 'probably the most difficult coppers in Britain to impress, think you and me are now the bee's knees. This bubbly's on them, by the way. And trust me, that doesn't happen often.'

They remained in the upstairs bar for another hour or so, finishing off the champagne and sinking another couple of lagers each. During all this time more and more members of the Flying Squad arrived, having finally been released from duty at the end of a long and tumultuous shift, the noise levels rising steadily. Bob Hunter didn't show, but that was hardly surprising – as OIC on the Snake Eye investigation he'd now be at the hub of what could be days of interviews and interrogations. But several other characters turned up who didn't look as if they were police officers at all: shady, slimy-looking guys in cheap suits and earrings, with scars on their necks and tattoos on their hands. One wore a grubby overcoat and a trilby, an image discomfortingly reminiscent of Jack 'the Hat' McVitie, the famous gangster executed by the Kray twins in 1967.

'I don't know if I'm overly fond of this place,' Gail said, eyeing this latest newcomer as he stood at the bar, chatting chummily with Squad members.

Heck threw down the last of his lager. 'We can get out of here, if you want. It's late.'

'Sounds like a plan.'

They said their goodbyes and headed down the stairs to

the cobbled backstreet at the rear of the club, where an open gate led to a private parking lot. Both their vehicles were now waiting there, but only Heck fished his keys out.

'You going to drive after all that booze?' Gail asked disapprovingly.

Heck gave this some thought, opened his car's boot, and took out his grab bag. He closed up again and shoved the keys back into his pocket. 'We can walk.'

They sauntered down Brixton Road side by side. It was now the 'graveyard hour', as Heck had used to think it when still a young constable patrolling a succession of lonely late-night beats: three o'clock in the morning to four o'clock, a time when, even in a metropolis like London, you met scarcely a soul – at least nobody who was out and about for legitimate purposes. The occasional car growled past; a couple of cats came up to them, wanting to make friends – aside from that, the streets were empty.

They spoke idly about the events of the day, Gail openly expressing amazement that she'd partaken in such a dangerous operation.

'Is that the way you always do it?' she wondered, as they turned into Acre Lane. 'Just pitch yourself in, regardless of personal safety?'

'Not always,' he said, unsure whether she sounded impressed or was simply drunk. 'I didn't want the bastard to get away, though. Not when he was the main objective. That said, I didn't think he'd get as far as he did. They ought to have boxed him in more effectively. Course, no one expected him to make his getaway in a bloody HGV.'

'And how does your gaffer feel about that kind of bobbying?'

'Told you it doesn't happen all the time.'

'That isn't answering the question.'

'Well . . . Gemma's a straight bat. So she bollocks me for

it. She won't even like it that we've been hobnobbing with the Sweeney. Reckons they're a right bunch of cowboys.'

'Perceptive woman. How long were you seeing her for?'

'Oh, a good while.' He sighed wistfully. 'Seems aeons ago now.'

'So what happened? Is it true she ditched you when she got promoted?'

'No.' Heck smiled to himself. It was amazing how often this subject came up; folk wondering if Gemma suddenly decided she couldn't rocket off into law enforcement super-stardom with an anchor like him still attached. But that wasn't how it had happened at all. 'Things went on. I got a tad concerned about some of the risks she was taking, and that pissed her off a bit . . . started the ball rolling, so to speak. She was still happy for us to stay an item, but, well, when she first got promoted she wanted to cool things a little. Stop sneaking off to the locker room together whenever we got a spare minute on shift, live in our own apartments – that sort of stuff.'

'You mean make it respectable?'

'Suppose so.'

'And lemme guess: you didn't like that?'

'Idiot that I am.' He shrugged. 'I got vexed because I felt she was moving away from me anyway. Took it all as a big slight, told her to sling her hook.'

'Oh, smart move . . .'

'There are things I've done in my life that I regret more, Gail. But not many.'

'And how does she feel about it?'

'I don't know. Let's face it, she's a super – it's not like I can just ask her.'

'Best to get on with your life, eh?'

'That's what I keep telling myself.'

She put her arm through his as they strolled, in what was

almost a consoling gesture. He certainly didn't assume there was anything else there, except perhaps that it was the middle of the night and maybe it afforded her a sense of security. She even leaned against him as they walked, her female curves melding into his body. Gail was a good-looking girl with a trim, pert figure that was strangely enhanced by her rough street garb, which, now that he thought about it – the jeans in particular – fitted her like a glove.

The bed and breakfast where he'd booked in overlooked Clapham Common from The Avenue. It was a pub called the Green Dragon, and his room was on its second floor. The pub was now closed and in darkness, but Heck had a key to the back door. They stumbled up an unlit stair one behind the other, Gail's hands gripping him by the hips. The room had its own en suite and was newly furnished and done in blue pastel shades, with walnut panelling around the bed's head-board. The one and a half sized bed was covered by a fresh, plump duvet, but Gail still stopped short at the sight of it.

'Okay,' she said from the doorway. 'So where do I sleep?'

'Don't worry.' He stripped off his Wrangler and kicked off his trainers as he headed to an armchair in a corner. 'I sleep just as well sitting. This'll do me.'

'You sure?' She sounded uncertain – perhaps wondering if she was being patronised again, though not convinced the alternative would be any better.

Heck set the alarm on his watch. 'We've got to get up early anyway so we can have a piece of Manko's mob before the Flying Squad start charging them.' Without further ado, he unbuttoned his jeans and, wearing only his T-shirt and a pair of boxers, settled down on the chair, closing his eyes. Gail moved to the light and switched it off before she too undressed. He tried to arrange himself comfortably as he listened to the gentle rustles of clothing, and then the soft creak of bedsprings.

275

A minute or so passed before her voice said from the darkness: 'Heck . . . what are you doing over there?'

'Sorry, am I snoring?' He tried to change position.

'No, you're not snoring. And you know damn well you're not. You got cut up today. You can't be comfortable.'

'This chair's fine.'

'This bed's better. And there's plenty of room.'

'You don't think we'd should try and get some sleep?' he said. 'We're up first thing.'

'You cheeky sod. Don't be so bloody presumptuous.'

'Anything you say.' He groped his way over there. A dim light penetrated the curtain from the street beyond, and when he got close this was sufficient to show her lying on top of the duvet, propped up on a single elbow. It glimmered delectably on her smooth, naked form.

Chapter 25

As so often was his way, unless he'd been drinking the night before, Vincent Budd was up with the dawn. It had been an excellent summer thus far, each morning arriving to the choral singing of myriad birds and in a haze of rose-tinged mist, before the sun itself peeked over Leith Hill and poked its golden fingers through the dense tracts of coppice enclosing Carpham village.

This morning in particular was finer than most, the heat rising steadily, a pearlescent sky glimmering through the thick green canopy. Vinnie unzipped his khaki coat and slung it over his shoulder as he trudged his secret woodland trails, moving from one snare to the next, bagging his game: four rabbits, two quail, and a partridge. Not a bad haul by any standards.

For a big man and an elderly man – okay, at sixty he perhaps wasn't old, but he was no longer an athlete, as his unsuccessful flight from the police five days ago had proved – he had good endurance. It wasn't uncommon for him to cover eight miles or more during his dawn rambles, and all of that along twisty, unmade tracks, clambering over culverts and fences, traversing heath and hedgerow. The confidence of a lifetime spent in the great outdoors enabled this. But he wasn't healthy. After he'd left the police station the other day he'd felt absolutely terrible – legs shaking, unable to get his breath for long periods. That was why this morning he was taking it easy. No running, climbing or jumping – just a nice, steady walk – and why he would now have to be extra careful as he crossed Lord Astbury's spread. This was a large shooting estate, 2,000 acres at least, comprising twenty-five drives and extensive woodland; a poacher's paradise had it not been for Tommy Slugton, the head keeper here, aka Old Sludger.

Sludger wasn't a young man either, but he was a former paratrooper who'd seen action in Northern Ireland and the Falklands, as he never ceased to tell people while in his cups down in the village pubs. He had an iron core of fitness, and a mean-as-sin attitude. He hadn't laid hands on Vinnie yet, but he had on most of the district's other poachers and, according to the stories, he'd given several of them a good kicking before marching them off to the cop shop. Sludger had proclaimed it a personal ambition to bring Vinnie to book. They'd exchanged words to this effect in various taprooms late on Saturday nights.

'Just you keep trying,' had been the keeper's parting shot the last time they'd encountered each other. 'Just keep trying, my lad, and one of these mornings I'll be waiting for you.'

Vinnie wasn't here on Lord Astbury's estate now because of that. He didn't believe in silly dares or challenges. Taking game was his profession, and personal pride didn't come into it. In fact, Old Sludger's threats might well have dissuaded him from ever coming here had the estate not lain across his normal route home. He certainly wasn't going to circum-navigate it, though as usual he took care to stick to the thickest belts of trees: Amberly Wood, Dunstan's Hollow, Woodhatch Bottom, Shawcross Spinney. It was down there, in a dense grove of birch and willow, when he was perhaps farthest from prying eyes, where Vinnie checked a few more of his traps – because yes, though he rarely made it his goal to specifically poach in these woods, they were on his regular round, so why not try his luck now and then? It wasn't as if it couldn't be rewarding – grouse and woodcock often strayed down here. All he needed to do was roll himself a few cones from twine and bark, smear their interiors with gluey resin, conceal them in the undergrowth, and lay trails of seeds up and into them. It was as easy as blinking. Using this simple, traditional method, he'd once trapped himself a brace of pheasant. Mind, it didn't look as if he'd been quite so fortunate on this occasion. The birds often sat still once they were caught, but today the undergrowth looked particularly motionless. Vinnie dumped his coat and game bag and rummaged through, just to check.

With a *clash* of steel, something like a guillotine snapped on his right wrist.

Vinnie's first response was numbing shock that such blinding pain was possible.

His second was dull realisation that he'd almost certainly broken his arm.

His third was utter disbelief, because he'd now attempted to drag his hand back out of the leafage, to find it held fast in what could only be described as a mantrap: two serrated steel blades bound in an iron frame, chained and padlocked to the bole of a tree some three or four feet away. Never in his career had Vinnie used an implement like this. Certainly not of this size – because this thing had to have been designed to catch something large, like a wolf or bear, of which there were precious few in Shawcross Spinney.

He gazed at it, goggle-eyed. His arm had been trapped just above the wrist joint, the razor-tipped teeth having sliced through the flesh and dug deep into the fractured bone. His hand had already gone cold – there was no sensation – and was slowly turning blue. Thick, hot blood welled out. Slowly, as Vinnie knelt there, the pain spread up past his shoulder and down through his torso. Vainly, he tried to grapple with the trap with his other hand; but he couldn't even find the release catch, let alone activate it. So feeble were his attempts to pry the brutal jaws apart that they might as well have locked.

'Sludger,' Vinnie said through a mouthful of froth.

He was going dizzy, his heart pounding again. Had Sludger done this? Had he found Vinnie's cones and put something else there instead? The question was answered for him by an amused but slightly muffled voice.

'Well, well Mr Budd . . . how clumsy of you.'

Vinnie looked dazedly up. Two figures advanced idly down the treed slope.

Had it been possible for his racing blood to run cold, it doubtless would have done. One of the figures was tall, one short. Both wore grey industrial overalls and, as he'd seen before, masks. The taller one bore the face of Oliver Hardy, the shorter one the beaming visage of Stan Laurel. It was Hardy who had spoken. Now he spoke again.

'What an unlikely accident. An experienced woodsman like you caught in one of your own traps.'

'I never . . .' Vinnie stuttered. 'I don't ever . . .'

'Amazing, truly. Though doubtless the anti-blood sports lobby would regard it as poetically just.'

'Please, I never spoke . . . I never said nothing . . .' Words briefly failed Vinnie. The pain in his arm was too much; the drumming of his heart was overwhelming him.

They stood there motionless, hands on hips.

'I told the coppers nothing,' he managed to add. 'Didn't tell 'em . . .'

'If only we could take your word for that, Mr Budd.'

Vinnie regarded them mouth agape, the breath wheezing from his lungs. The pain was easing slightly, but only because his entire arm was deadened to all sensation. Blood still dripped from his crooked wrist.

'I didn't report no names. Didn't see no faces.'

'Of course you didn't,' Hardy said. 'But that's because we don't take chances, not because you believe in keeping your mouth shut. It really is a foolish thing, though – to have any kind of dealings with the police. I mean really, Mr Budd. A man in your profession? Can you seriously afford to lose the little respect you've got left?'

Vinnie hung his head, his bush hat dropping to the ground. Fronds of thinning red hair, saturated with sweat, hung over his face. 'You've got to help me – gemme out of this.'

'Perhaps.' Hardy pondered. 'But first a few precautions.'

Vinnie could do nothing but kneel there, his heavy body slumped forward as Laurel crouched next to him and, with rubber-gloved hands, commenced a thorough search, feeling first through Vinnie's discarded coat and game bag and then moving to his trousers, burrowing into every pocket and pouch, yanking out hooks, nets, balls of twine, even taking the razor-edged hunting knife from its sheath, and then lifting the cuffs of his trousers to peek down the sides of his boots – at the end of which mission he glanced up, shook his head, and gave an eerie high-pitched chuckle.

'No mobile phone?' Hardy said. 'How unprofessional of you. What would happen if you'd suffered a real accident out here?'

Vinnie couldn't answer. He'd never felt as sick in his life, or as weak.

Hardy shook his head with disapproval, even when his smaller compatriot handed him the hunting knife. He examined it before adding: 'Even this wouldn't have been much good to you. That trap, which was imported all the way from Siberia, was designed to hold a thousand-pound bear. No human could break it open, and of course we've jammed the release, as you've doubtless realised.'

He handed the knife back to his accomplice, then hunkered down, gloved hands steepled in front of him. That terrible plastic smile, once a source of joy to millions, now made an image of evil that Vinnie knew would haunt him for the rest of his life.

'I'll tell you what I think, Mr Budd: you're a self-sufficient kind of chap, aren't you? And I reckon you'd go to any length to avoid being caught somewhere you shouldn't. Am I right? And even if some malicious old keeper had been very sneaky and *had* set this trap for you – which he didn't by the way, as I'm sure you know, though it's highly possible that's how it'll be explained – the last thing *you'd* want to do is admit he'd outwitted you. You'd do anything, wouldn't you, to get away from here without other folk knowing what's happened. Go on, admit it.'

'Please,' Vinnie burbled; his relentless heart was agony against his ribs. 'I beg you—'

'Oh no.' Hardy sounded disappointed. 'Such a big chap. Who by all accounts has been in and out of prison, who's drunk pubs full of young buckos under the table. "Please . . . I beg you"? It would be sad if it wasn't so pathetic. Anyway, not to worry, Mr Budd.' Hardy stood upright again. 'Because we're going to do exactly what you want. We're going to get you out of this trap. Not only that, we're going to ensure that our role is kept secret. That's right, Vinnie. It's going to look like it was all your own work. Your friends, if you had any, would be so impressed.'

Vinnie was almost too groggy to understand this – until Hardy leaned down and, rather gently, began handling his arm as though studying the extent of the damage.

He tut-tutted. 'That must hurt a lot. But don't worry. All

bad things come to an end. And yours, Mr Budd, is going to end just about . . . *there*.'

He prodded with his fingertip an inch above the point where the steel jaws had clamped shut. Vinnie still didn't know what he meant, nor did he notice that Laurel was now leaning over him from the other side. In fact he only grasped what was happening when, with a flash of steel, Laurel struck him with his own knife.

The first chop didn't sever clean through the mangled limb, but it made a neat incision, laying the flesh wide open. Vinnie tried to jerk back, combined squawks of horror and outrage lodged in his phlegm-filled throat. It took Hardy to wrap his arms round Vinnie from behind and hold him in position before the blade could be applied again – and again – and again.

The poacher's eyes widened in mortal horror, stunned whimpers issuing from his drooling mouth, as steel chewed steadily through flesh; as with a series of sickening *thuds*, meat and bone were systematically parted, jets of arterial blood raking the air, spattering all over the three of them. Even so, it was quicker than he might have expected. With a massive grunt from Laurel, and a vicious final slash, the last threads of tissue were sliced and his stump was freed.

Not that they were finished yet.

Vinnie's vision was dimming and his heart now beating in wild, irregular rhythms. Despite this, they hauled him to his feet, where he stood rocking back and forth.

With heartfelt congratulations for his strength and courage, they slapped his back and draped his coat over his shoulders. One of them took his remaining hand, spread out its fingers and placed the knife's blood-slick hilt between them. Had he the gumption or wherewithal, Vinnie might have used his weapon to lash out at them, but in truth he no longer knew where he was or what had happened. His ribcage felt as though it was shrinking, crushing the vital organs inside. There was a roaring in his ears. The world around him had turned black. He barely felt the pain of his dismembered arm.

A brief, lucid thought struck him – that it was only three miles to the nearest road. If he made it that far and some early riser saw him, they might still get him to a hospital on time. He took a slow, careful step, and another. There was further clapping from behind, more enthusiastic encouragement.

'Keep going. You're almost there. Well . . . maybe not.' Ribald chuckles followed.

Vinnie didn't hear them. All he knew was the ground rushing up to meet him, but he never felt it – not even when it struck him full in the face.

Chapter 26

Heck's watch alarm woke him just before six. He yawned and sat up, even though he'd actually only had a couple of hours' sleep. He'd pay for that later in the day, but at present there were things to do. He scratched his tousled head and glanced around. Milky daylight filtered into the room, spilling luxuriously onto Gail's fine contours as she lay face down alongside him. Her hair was spread in a wide arc across the pillow; only a crumpled sheet lay over the small of her back.

He leaned down and kissed her exposed neck – she stirred and muttered slightly – and then he lumbered into the bathroom, where he emptied his bladder copiously and stepped into the shower. The scorching spray did its bit to fully revive him, a sachet of shampoo taking care of his gritty, sweaty mane.

When he'd towelled himself down, pulled his shorts on, and returned to the bedroom, Gail was still asleep. But stronger daylight now poured through the curtains, and he saw something that halted him: three small, circular marks on her peachy right buttock. He sat alongside her and probed them with a gentle fingertip. They were indents in the flesh, as if tiny, circular sections of its upper layer had been removed, leaving only rugged pinpricks of scar tissue. When he checked further up her body, he saw another one – on the side of her right breast. He didn't need to examine that one closely to know it would be identical to the others. There were all sorts of innocent reasons why people picked up nicks and scars, but cigarette burns left their own unique signature. He touched the marks on her bottom again. This time the muscle clenched slightly. He realised she was awake, and saw her looking over her shoulder, watching him sulkily from under her messy locks.

'Stand up for me,' he said.

With unusual acquiescence, she slid from the bed and stood with her back turned. There was another small burn on her lower spine, previously masked by the bedsheet.

'Turn round, eh?'

She did so. Another mark showed just above the line of her pubic hair.

'And before you ask,' she said, 'no . . . I don't actually like it rough. But he had his needs, and I was with him.'

Heck took her by the wrists and drew her towards him. Again, she obliged. His hands alighted at the sides of her breasts and roved down her slender torso. Just left of her sternum there was another noticeable indent. A lack of surface blemish didn't disguise it.

'Was it one of his needs to break your ribs?' he wondered.

'That wasn't intentional,' she replied, lips quivering. 'I don't think.'

He took her right hand in his, thumbing at a distortion among the carpals; this was only slight – he wouldn't have spotted it if he hadn't been looking. 'Was it intentional when he dislocated your wrist?'

'That was a difficult arrest.'

He glanced up at her. 'Is that what you told Will Royton? When you presumably had to sit in the office for four weeks, answering the phone.'

Her eyes glimmered with tears. 'You're not surprised by any of this, are you?'

'I've been in this job for nearly two decades, Gail. I've seen it a hundred times before.'

'I bet you've never got this close to it, though. Caressing it, the way you are now. I bet you've never kissed it the way you did last night.'

He stood up and smoothed out the coverlet for her. 'Sit down. I'll make you a brew.'

'Oh yeah – because I'm a soft little woman, and that's all it takes.'

'Well if *you* don't need a brew, *I* do.' He crossed the room and flipped the kettle on.

Gail sat on the bed, naked, hugging herself. Her eyes weren't exactly brimming, but they remained moist. 'I should've known you'd notice when the sun came up. Bloke like you, eyes like a bloody hawk. Last night was a bad idea for all sorts of reasons.'

'Milk?' he asked. 'Sugar?'

'I don't want any sodding tea!'

Heck continued to stir. This was something else he'd seen before: victims lashing out in times of stress, particularly in relation to what they perceived to be their own inadequacy; they had to disprove suspicion that they might be weak.

I'm not going to be bossed around or made to feel like an office junior.

It perhaps seemed odd that, the previous night, she'd sought to conceal the evidence, turning the light off before she undressed, and yet this morning had appeared resigned to the inevitable revelation of it – but psychologically it was all entirely consistent. Intimacy such as they'd enjoyed last night often broke a barrier between the twosome involved. It was almost as if, once you'd made love to a person, there was no real point keeping secrets from them. Not that this ever made things better for you, particularly if you'd only got it on with the other party out of a brief desire for close companionship.

'You know,' he said, 'anyone can get trapped in an abusive relationship. A woman, a man. A civvie, a cop. There's nothing to be embarrassed about.'

'I'm not embarrassed.'

He handed her a cuppa. Even though she'd said she didn't want one, she accepted it. He also handed her a neatly folded grey-and-white chequered handkerchief, which he'd taken from his jeans pocket. She dabbed at her eyes.

'Okay, not embarrassed,' he said. 'How about bewildered?'

'Bewildered?'

He sat in the facing armchair. 'You're a very competent detective, Gail. Better than that in fact. You did something last night that only two or three other officers I know in all the police forces of England and Wales could have matched. And if *you* didn't know how good you were before, you do this morning. So now more than ever, you're wondering, "How the hell did I ever let these things happen to me?"'

She sipped her tea absently. 'It's not that, it's just . . . you think you love someone . . .'

'Or you think you *need* them. Or both.'

She regarded him cautiously, as if maybe – who knew? – he was someone she really could trust with this ultra-personal information. But then, slowly, her expression twisted into a frown. 'Is this what they teach them in battered wives counselling? Don't tell me you've majored in that as well?'

'I just told you I've seen it all before. That's why I'm not surprised.'

'You might not be surprised, but I can tell you're disappointed.'

'Why would I be?'

'I can look after myself, Heck.'

'You've already proved that. You kicked the bastard out.'

'But not far enough, eh?' She got up and headed for the bathroom. 'That's what you're thinking. You've seen the way he follows me around like a shadow.'

'What's really bugging you, Gail?'

She stared back at him. 'Excuse me?'

'What's the real beef? I mean, I've just said I don't think you're any the less an exceptional officer because of this – so what is it?'

'What do you think it is?'

'Let me guess. You're worried that if you take any further action against this clown, he'll play his trump card. Make it public knowledge about the kind of relationship you two had.'

'Wouldn't you in his situation?'

'You think he'll want it known that he's a bully and a sadist.'

'Oh, for Christ's sake, he won't care. He's the alpha male of alpha males – he defines himself by how much he can control me.'

'And as long as you tolerate the way he's behaving now, you're letting him.'

'What would you have me do?'

'I dunno. Fill his car with bent gear. Load his hard drive with illegal porn . . .'

'Grow up!' She stormed into the bathroom and turned the shower on.

He followed her in. 'Gail?'

She pulled a bunch of towels down from the rack. 'I'm wriggling free, Heck. It'll be over in due course.'

'That isn't how it looks to me.'

'Why's it giving you such a problem? Look, surely you can see that if this stuff leaks out, my reputation in Surrey will be worth shit.'

'Ask for a transfer.'

'Yeah, because it's that simple.'

'Apply to SCU.'

She glanced around at him. 'Some chance. I've got less than a year in divisional CID.'

'My word counts for a lot.'

'Really?'

'Well, no. It probably doesn't, actually.'

'That's one thing I'll say for you, Heck. You're disarmingly bloody honest.'

'Look, it's your call, Gail. This arsehole is going to keep on tormenting you. It may be from a distance, but he's enjoying it now as much as ever. You can either put up with it, or you can shake him off.'

'You know, I was wrong about you. One thing you clearly haven't majored in is counselling brutalised spouses. Because that's got to be the biggest load of bullshit I've ever heard.' She stepped into the shower and slammed its door behind her.

Before Heck could reply, his phone began bleeping in the bedroom.

'DS Heckenburg,' he said, grabbing it up.

'Heck, it's Brogan.'

'Morning.'

'My guv'nor says there's something you might be interested in.'

'Yeah?'

'We've been nicking the rest of the Snake Eyes since five this morning. Turning over every drum on the Skelton. There are lock-ups, squats, you name it. There's all sorts of stuff here relating to crimes they've committed. If you want to have a gander, now's the time, because an awful lot of stuff's getting bagged and tagged.'

'Be there in twenty.'

He was clambering into a fresh set of casuals when Gail re-emerged wrapped in a bath towel.

'Time to hit the road,' he said.

She glanced at the digital clock on the TV, which only read 6.45. 'Already?'

He assessed her as he pulled his trainers on, briefly taken by how she looked with her hair hanging in sparkly-wet ringlets. In truth, her bodily scars were inconsequential; they could have happened to her under any normal circumstances and nobody would bat an eyelid. The psychology of the problem was more the issue here, but ultimately it wasn't for him to offer advice where it wasn't wanted. Not that he was much good at that kind of thing anyway.

He explained about the call he'd just had. She thought about this as she sat on the armchair and dried her hair. 'Suppose you'd better get down there then. I'm going back to Reigate.'

Heck was in the process of chucking his dirty stuff into his grab bag, but now he looked up. 'Since when?'

'Since I made the decision five minutes ago. We've got about nine thousand pages of paperwork to catch up with. Not to mention a progress report for Will Royton. If nothing else, he'll need to know about Manko . . . so he can make some kind of garbled explanation when the internal enquiries start flying.'

'We've still got to find out where that grey van came from.'

'I'm sure that doesn't take both of us.'

Heck straightened up. 'This is a wind-up, yeah?' She looked puzzled, as if she didn't even understand the term. 'Gail, not long ago you asked why all this was giving me such a problem. I'll tell you: because personal issues are one thing, but personal issues affecting your ability to do the job are another. That actually *would* lessen you in my eyes.'

'It's nothing to do with any of that.'

'Course it damn well is.' Again, he hadn't intended to raise his voice, but time was running out fast. 'If you can't stand being with me because I now know what you consider to be your dirty little secrets, fine. No problem. We'll never so much as shake hands again. But don't you dare think I'm letting you take time off work for it. So get bloody dressed and get your stuff together. I'm going back to the Skelton right now. I'll expect you there in fifteen minutes. No later.'

Chapter 27

The Skelton Wood didn't feel so menacing with a massive security presence on it.

When Heck arrived, the air crackled with radio static and there were police vehicles everywhere: not just local patrols, but PSUs – heavy troop carriers loaded with tactical support units. Quite a few buildings were sealed off with crime-scene tape; even certain roads were closed – he'd had to flash his warrant card just to be passed through. ARVs were stationed on various corners with clutches of firearms officers gathered near them, though most of these were now drinking coffee and eating bacon butties. Fire crews were also present, reeling in their hoses after dousing the blackened shells of shops or the twisted relics of cars. It seemed there had been disturbances here during the early hours, but they hadn't lasted long. As was so often the case, even in a desperate neighbourhood like this, not everyone was as supportive of the local criminal gang as its members might have liked to imagine.

The mopping-up work was now being undertaken by the Flying Squad and divisional uniforms, who were moving among the lock-ups, garages and basements, wheeling out scowling individuals in plastic cuffs. One or two of these had tried to resist and were suitably bloodied – after all, police officers had been shot at and one had suffered a severe throat wound; it was never going to go easy for them. However, some of the handier Snake Eyes had come quietly and even had the decency to look scared. The top tier of their organisation had vanished overnight. Not only that, the leaders they had trusted were now serving up the lesser soldiers. The entire Snake Eye world had shattered in the space of a few hours. No one knew what awaited them next.

Heck parked his borrowed Mazda alongside a row of police carriers being loaded with boxes and evidence bags. Even at a quick glance, these contained masses of incriminating paraphernalia: knives and guns, sacks of pills, sachets of weed and powder, wads of cash, wallets, iPhones, iPads, and other expensive gadgets.

'DS Heckenburg?' a voice said. Heck looked round. DC Bernetti was approaching. Like most of the other Sweeney guys on the plot, he was still armed, his Glock visible on his hip. 'Bob's got someone you might want to speak to.'

'Where is he?'

'Thirteen, Talbot Court.'

Heck shrugged.

'Through there.' Bernetti pointed across the Football Field to its north side, where a black passage led between two conjoined apartment houses. 'Second floor.'

As Heck headed over there another car roared into place alongside his own. It was a yellow Fiat Punto. Gail got quickly out and fell into step alongside him. Heck couldn't resist a smile, but neither said anything as they walked across the field and down the passage, which was strewn with bricks and bottles from last night's battle. At the end, a flight of concrete steps took them up to a gantry overlooking a row of back gardens that were little more now than rubbish tips. A uniform was on guard duty here.

'Looking for Bob Hunter,' Heck said, showing his ID.

The uniform stuck a thumb over his shoulder, and three doors along they found number thirteen, which was standing open. DS Brogan was just inside. As before, he had an MP5 carbine slung over his shoulder. He nodded into the darkened interior.

The first thing Heck and Gail noticed on entering was the smell: damp bedclothes, unwashed bodies, stale urine. When they pushed through into the living room they found it poorly furnished and littered with beer cans and dirty underwear. Instead of a carpet, lino covered the floor, brown and peeling at its edges. Bob Hunter was present, along with two other Flying Squad officers. A fourth person was also there, someone Heck didn't know. He was seated in a low, slouch-backed armchair, wore a tatty grey sweater and blue tracksuit bottoms and slippers. He was no more than thirty, but scarecrow-thin, his face looking thinner still thanks to the overlarge glasses perched on his hawk-like nose and his immense featherduster of brown/grey hair. A roll-up, so shrivelled and twisted that it was difficult to imagine it contained any tobacco at all, was stuck behind his ear.

He stared to his front, paying attention to nobody, though his demeanour wasn't that of a tough guy – it was more as if he was lost in a world of his own. However, any questions Heck might have had about the guy's dazed state were answered when, across the room, he spied a table covered with bottles, dirty spoons, and syringes.

'Meet Billy Peerson,' Hunter said, not bothering with a preamble. 'Despite resembling a wandering mental patient, this is the Snake Eye Crew's chief accountant.'

Heck regarded the guy in the armchair with astonishment. 'This fella is?'

Hunter nodded and rubbed at the back of his neck. He was white-faced from lack of sleep, but still looked fully awake. 'He was once a high flyer in the City. But it seems his habits got the better of him. He fell from grace . . . all the way down to Skelton Wood. But he can still crunch a few numbers when he wants to. Isn't that right, Billy?'

Peerson said nothing, but continued to gaze into the near distance.

'This is Detective Sergeant Heckenburg,' Hunter said. 'He's investigating a series of murders down in Surrey.'

Peerson seemed to flinch – his right cheek twitched, and he glanced up.

'Yeah, that's right,' Hunter said in an ominous tone. '*A series of murders*. This gets better and better, doesn't it?' He glanced at Heck. 'Billy here is quite nervous about getting charged with money laundering, handling stolen goods, possessing drugs, aiding and abetting a series of armed robberies, and so forth. So, again despite appearances, he's actually very happy to talk to us. And it's all going down on paper soon . . . isn't it, Billy?'

'Had nothing to do with any murders,' Peerson said in a dull, vaguely uncertain voice, which even now carried a hint of the grammar-school education he'd so casually thrown away. 'Not in Surrey. Surrey's not our patch. We never had anything going in Surrey.'

'Perhaps you'll let DS Heckenburg be the judge of that,' Hunter answered. 'Tell him what you told me about the vehicle log. Like I said, your cooperation will not go un-rewarded.'

'Erm . . .' Peerson sniffed and, when snot came bubbling out, wiped his nose on his sleeve. 'The crew had different ways to, erm, to generate cash. Quick cash.'

'You don't say,' Heck replied.

'One was stealing vehicles to order,' Hunter put in.

Heck nodded. 'That could be interesting.'

Peerson sniffed again and dug through his matted locks to scratch at his scalp, which unleashed a shower of dandruff. 'Some other firm needed a motor for a job, the crew would provide one at short notice. For an upfront fee.'

'They stole them from around here?' Heck asked.

Peerson shrugged. 'Where else? Someone's car goes walkies here, no one complains. Everyone knows the crew'll be involved.'

'Not anymore,' Brogan chuckled.

'True, true,' Hunter said wistfully. 'But I'm sure Billy'll get used to the new world order pretty soon.'

Peerson looked puzzled by this exchange. He glanced from one to the other. 'It's a good place to get a motor. Nothing'd come back to you, you see. They'd report it eventually – few days later perhaps. Say some Glaswegian geezers lifted it.'

'And as book-keeper, did you maintain a record of these transactions?' Heck asked.

Peerson threw an arm towards a sideboard. Its cupboards had been opened and paperwork strewed the floor, but a pile of leather-bound ledgers had been laid out along the top, presumably by Hunter and his team.

'If you want a look, Heck, get to it,' the DI said. 'I've got to book this lot in soon.'

Heck strode over there and leafed through several pages, most of which were filled with scrawled biro, in many cases incomprehensibly, though pound signs were littered throughout, often with telephone numbers attached.

'I'm looking for a grey Bedford van, Billy,' Heck said, handing a couple of the ledgers to Gail. 'Perhaps you can give me a hand. Registration G-D-1-4-F-E-D.'

Peerson brushed another hand through his unmanageable hair. 'Reckon . . . yeah, reckon I remember that.'

'Well come on, help the man out,' Hunter urged him, taking him by the sleeve and tugging him to his feet.

Peerson trudged across the room as though half asleep. 'It was recently. We usually charge ten grand for vehicle supply.'

'Only ten, eh?' Hunter snickered. 'Me and you are in the wrong job, Heck.'

'Maybe less this time.' Peerson worked his way through the pile of remaining ledgers, and selected one. 'They lifted it outside that Asian corner shop on Morgan Avenue.'

'Yeah, and he *did* report it, as it happens,' Heck said. 'Straight away.'

Peerson shrugged as he flicked pages. 'Pakis, you know.' He paused to take the roll-up from behind his ear, filched a lighter from his pocket and tried to strike a flame. 'Law unto their fucking selves since they got militant. They'd have known about it soon.'

'You're going to know about it, son, if you don't get a move on,' Brogan advised him. 'These are law-abiding people your mates have been terrorising.'

Peerson didn't respond until he managed to light his cig, at which point he continued glancing through the ledgers, puffing foul smoke. 'This one,' he finally said, tapping a page. He coughed as he read down its figures. 'Grey Bedford van . . . knew I remembered. Yeah, there was no fee this time.'

Heck looked down at the page and saw the letters 'F/R' scribbled alongside the registration mark. 'FR?' he said.

Peerson nodded. 'Favour returned. We must've owed someone.'

Heck read on. 'And the buyer was "Jack Smith".' He glanced at Hunter, who shrugged, then at Gail, who shook her head. 'What's his real name, Billy?'

Peerson pushed the ledger into Heck's grasp and shuffled

back towards his armchair. 'We don't ask – so long as their money's good.'

'And what was the favour?'

'Above my pay grade.' Peerson coughed again. 'I just keep books.'

'Sorry, pal,' Hunter said to Heck. 'Looks like I brought you here for nothing.'

'No you didn't.' Heck glanced down at the page, noting the date of the transaction – 22/7. 'We'll get Billy here to look at some photos.'

'Don't need to,' Peerson said, relaxing back into his chair, blowing more vile smoke. 'He's still in London – I saw him last night.'

'When and where?' Gail asked.

'About seven o'clock. He's stopping at the Lambeth Royal.' Peerson closed his eyes as he inhaled. 'Was walking over to it from the kebab shop across the road.'

'The Lambeth Royal?' she said.

'Cheap hotel,' Brogan explained. 'Right shithole. Prozzies, druggies, the lot.'

'You sure it was this Jack Smith?' Heck asked.

'Sure.'

'What does he look like, this fella?'

Peerson blew smoke from his nostrils, which seemed to relax him even more. His eyelids fluttered.

'Don't go to sleep on us, Billy! I said what does he look like?'

'Erm . . . short, stocky. Anorak on. Jeans.'

'Was he alone?' Gail asked.

Peerson gestured vaguely. 'On his own, yeah. Had two kebabs though. Rolled up in paper, you know.'

Hunter looked at Heck. 'This mean anything to you?'

'Rings true,' Heck said quietly. 'There were two of them on the CCTV. One was short and stocky. I'm just wondering why they're hanging around here? I mean, they're staying in a flop, so they're obviously not locals. But if they've been doing jobs in Surrey, why aren't they stopping down there?'

'Maybe *they're* not Surrey lads either?' Hunter suggested.

Heck was perplexed. Whenever they turned a corner in this case, there seemed to be another one just beyond it. 'Okay,' he said, indicating to Gail that it was time to leave. 'Thanks for your help, Billy. Hope it gets you a couple of years off your twenty-stretch.'

Peerson's cheek twitched again; he threw a querying glance at Hunter.

'Ignore him,' Hunter said. 'You deliver and we'll sort you out.'

'I've a special interest in that ledger, Bob,' Heck added as he walked to the door.

'Yeah . . . I'll make a note of it.'

'Jack Smith?' Gail said, when they'd exited onto the gantry. 'You sure you believe that junkhead? He was stoned out of his mind.'

'Not necessarily when he filled that ledger in.' Heck looked lost in thought. 'The Snake Eyes provided our perps with that van on 22 July. That's two days before I hit the river up at Thornton Farm.'

'The timings are right at least.'

He strode off along the gantry. 'Next stop the Lambeth Royal.'

'Think it's as great a place as it sounds?' she asked.

'All I'd say is have you still got your body armour from last night?'

'Yeah, it's in the car.'

'Good. Put it on.'

Chapter 28

The Lambeth Royal stood down a side street off Stockwell Road and was a rather soulless building, though that perhaps hadn't always been the case. It was Victorian in origin, about four storeys high and, in terms of its architecture, resembled a large, rambling townhouse, though its redbrick façade was encrusted with soot and its gutters filled with weeds and bird's nests. It was accessible via a short drive, which was potholed and strewn with litter. As they trudged up this, Gail glimpsed a face grinning from the matted undergrowth to one side. It belonged to a goblin seated on a stool. It was cut from marble or some other white stone, but was now grey with grime and crumbly with moss.

'Salubrious or what?' she said quietly.

'Yeah,' Heck replied. 'And check that out.'

Left of the house, an offshoot of the drive led under a car port, its corrugated plastic roof bowed beneath layers of autumn leaves. In the shadowed space below, they could make out two vehicles; one a beaten-up Volvo with a rusty engine grille, the other a grey Bedford van. The latter's registration plate read: GD14 FED.

They approached the front door, which stood open on a

porch filled with the trampled rags of innumerable give-away newspapers. A fanlight over the top had once sported handsome stained glass but was now broken and dusty. Beyond this they entered a cavernous foyer, where more decayed fragments served as remnants of a grander past: a chandelier minus bulbs and hung with cobwebs as thick and black as rotted drapery; wood-panelled walls that were dented and scratched; an ornate brass handrail running up the main stairway, now green with age. On the right, enclosed in a cubbyhole, there was a small counter, on the other side of which a desk clerk in his mid-twenties reclined on an over-stuffed leather armchair. He was a lean, emaciated sort with a nose ring and a goatee beard, wearing a Nirvana T-shirt and a woolly hat pulled down over a mop of stringy, shoulder-length hair. His spiked leather wristbands only served to enhance the thinness of his pipe-cleaner arms. He was reading a music magazine, which he only lowered slowly on realising they were there. Eventually he stood up.

'Can I help?' His accent betrayed Staffordshire origins.

Gail displayed her warrant card. 'You've got a Jack Smith staying here, I understand?'

The desk clerk seemed unimpressed. 'Have I?'

She put her ID away and produced a folded twenty. 'I'm sure it won't be difficult for you to check.'

The clerk sniffed indifferently. 'Gonna cost you more than that.'

Heck lunged across the counter, grabbing him by the collar. 'More than it'll cost you for a new top set?' For a second they were nose to nose – so close that Heck could see scarlet inflammation and yellow pus gathered around the nose-piercing. 'It's very simple, pal . . . we've had a trying few days, and are in no mood to get fucked in the arse by some sociology student street-guy wannabe. Understand?'

'Erm . . .' The desk clerk still tried to affect indifference, but he wasn't fooling anyone. 'Yeah, sure, but I gotta check the register, know what I mean?'

'I'm sure you don't, actually,' Heck said. 'I'm sure you'll have no problem remembering someone who's checked in here for several days. I'm damn sure it would be an event in your life if someone wanted to stay here longer than a single afternoon. Am I right?'

The clerk still tried to pretend this was nothing to him, but the Adam's apple was quivering in the middle of his throat. 'Listen . . . we don't want any trouble here.'

'You don't know the meaning of trouble, son. Not yet. How many of them are there?'

'Only seen two. They booked room fourteen. That's a twin.'

'When did they check in?'

'I'll need to look at the register for *that*.'

Heck released the clerk and he tottered backwards. He glanced once, regretfully, at the twenty-pound note as it disappeared into Gail's pocket, and filched something from a side drawer that looked like a school exercise book. He flicked through it quickly. 'July 22. Didn't give a checkout date.'

Heck turned to Gail, and she nodded. They moved to the foot of the staircase.

'But they're not in now,' the clerk added.

Heck glanced back, irritably.

The clerk shrugged. 'Saw 'em go out first thing. Didn't say when they'd be back.'

'They weren't doing a runner by any chance?' Gail asked.

'Didn't have bags with 'em.'

Heck glanced past him. On the other side of the cubbyhole lay a small back office. 'We'll wait in there with you,' he said.

For the first time the desk clerk looked disgruntled, but

he still lifted a hatch in the counter. 'This'll do our rep a world of good.'

'You don't tell anyone, neither will we,' Gail replied as they made their way through.

The back office was actually little more than a tea-making area. It had a table with a kettle and a couple of dirty mugs on it, another armchair, a small portable television, and a free-standing heater, though this was currently switched off. Its walls were dingy and peeling, its carpet impacted with crumbs. Heck positioned himself to one side of the entrance, so that he could view whoever came to the counter, and settled there to wait.

Gail perched on the edge of the armchair. 'How long are we giving this?'

'As long as it takes, I think – don't you?'

She nodded resignedly.

'Don't worry,' he said. 'It'll probably be an education.'

And he wasn't far wrong on that. The next arrivals at the counter were a couple. The girl, who was black and buxom, but no more than eighteen, wore flip-flops, indecently short cut-offs, and a bikini top; despite her dusky skin, needle tracks were visible on both her arms. The guy was white and somewhere in his late sixties, wearing a black shirt and a white clerical collar under his pale grey jacket. His severe, unsmiling manner was more than a little ominous.

As the odd twosome headed upstairs together, the desk clerk stuck his head back into the office. 'By the looks of that, isn't just her pussy that's going to get pounded, eh?'

The cops remained blank-faced.

'Don't worry,' the clerk added. 'He isn't a real vicar. That's just his kink.'

'Well that's a load off,' Gail said.

The wait dragged on, and a few minutes later another couple came in. The woman was grossly overweight, bare-legged and wearing clattery high heels and a short, billowy summer dress. She had styled blonde locks and a pretty face – though it was less so under a pancake of thickly applied make-up. On her arm there was a bone-thin Indian man, who nodded politely while she signed the register. No sooner had they vanished up the stairs than a third person entered, nodding at the clerk but saying nothing as he followed them. This third character was short, bearded, bespectacled, and wore a beige tracksuit with white piping.

'That's her husband,' the clerk said matter-of-factly, when this man too had vanished upstairs. 'She's not a full-time tom, but he pimps her out two or three times a week. Always comes and watches while she gets stuck in.'

'Each to their own,' Heck remarked.

'That's one way to look at it,' Gail said.

The clerk shrugged. 'All got to make a living, haven't we?'

'You *would* call it that!' she muttered. 'You little toerag.'

He smirked. 'Get off my back, darling. I'm helping these women.'

'Helping? You're exploiting them just as much as any of their johns.'

'And what exactly are you lot doing?' The clerk looked amused. 'These girls are up shit creek. Their lives are a mess, but I don't see *you* lifting a finger.'

She stared daggers at him.

'There's nothing, is there?' he said. 'There's nothing anyone can do, so don't give me crap for putting a roof over their heads.'

'Slimy bastard!'

'Chill out, Gail,' Heck interrupted. 'This isn't what we're here for.'

'In other words I'm right and you're wrong,' the clerk laughed.

'Hey!' Heck stabbed a finger at him. 'It's the building we

305

need, not you. You can spend the rest of the day in the bin out back.'

The clerk smirked again and wandered out to his desk.

Gail gazed sullenly at Heck. 'We should do him for managing a brothel.'

'Good luck with that. In the trade, this is called a private hotel.'

She averted her eyes, cheeks flushed. 'Taking us to some sweet places, this investigation.'

'Relax,' he said. 'We're almost done.'

'Yeah . . . God knows what kind of weirdos we're gonna be meeting in a few minutes.'

'They might not be as weird as all that, actually.'

It took a second for the import of this to sink in. She glanced up at him. 'Do you want to run that by me again?'

Heck frowned as if he wasn't sure about this himself, which in truth he wasn't. When he spoke now, it was quietly, confidentially. 'While we were digging out those Snake Eye goons, I got to thinking . . . and this is only a theory . . .'

'Which is all we ever seem to have.'

'Most crims who do well have a kind of animal cunning. We know the ones we're after are a step ahead of that. But suppose this lot are *several* steps ahead?'

'I don't get you.'

He looked thoughtful. 'Julius Manko and his crew were happy to stay low-profile – small-time dealers, committing street-punk crimes like blagging boozers. But in reality they were building a distribution network with the 'Ndrangheta.'

'So?'

'Suppose our killers are bluffing too? Suppose, just suppose this crazy game they're playing is actually a smokescreen?'

'But I thought they were getting off on it, really enjoying themselves?'

'Okay, suppose it's a partial smokescreen?'

Before she could respond, there came a hissed warning from the front desk.

Heck flattened himself against the wall on the right. Gail moved to the wall on the left. They couldn't see who was there, but now heard the desk clerk speaking.

'Everything all right, mate?'

There was a grunted reply, and the rattle of a key as it was handed over. A pair of feet thudded away up the staircase.

'That our Mr Smith and his mate?' Heck asked, appearing at the clerk's shoulder.

'One of 'em,' the clerk said. 'The one who does all the talking.'

'Where's the other?' Gail asked.

'Dunno. Haven't seen him yet.'

Heck pondered, and then lifted the hatch and sidled out.

'Hey mate, listen.' The clerk suddenly looked twitchy. 'If there's any damage up there, you're gonna have to pay.'

'What, you mean like if we wreck the place? You sure you'll be able to tell?'

'Ha ha, very funny. But it's not coming out of my wages, okay?'

Heck was now at the bottom of the stairs, listening, but he also kept one eye on the front door, acutely aware that at any moment the second of the two suspects could come sauntering in. Common sense bade him wait until the second target was on the plot, but another voice advised that it would be easier to tackle one than two, and that this was a chance he couldn't miss.

There was only dimness at the top of the stairs, but he fancied he could hear noises: the squeaking of age-old bedframes, occasional cries of pleasure – whether real or simulated, it was difficult to tell.

Gail had now emerged from behind the counter as well, but he rounded on her quickly. 'Best if you stay down here.'

'What – why?'

'To cover my back. It'll be just my luck if the second one turns up while I'm in mid-arrest.'

She looked uncertain. 'What if the first one's a handful?'

Heck turned to the clerk. 'Big fella, is he?'

The clerk shrugged. 'Five-six. Out of shape.'

'I'll take five-six and out of shape.'

'Heck, wait!' Gail protested. 'What if he's armed?'

'I'll think of something. I always do.'

While Gail moved reluctantly back behind the counter, Heck headed upstairs.

The treads creaked; the walls on either side were damp and scabby; the air was rank with odious smells: smoke, sweat, rotten cabbage. When he reached the first floor a single passage ran from one side of the building to the other, laid with mouldering carpet and littered here and there with crack phials and used condoms. Occasional dust-enshrouded bulbs created the dullest illumination. For some reason, unless it had all been his imagination, the squeaking beds and ecstatic voices had fallen silent.

Heck ventured forward, following the numbers on the doors – five, six, seven, eight, but glancing over his shoulder as the top of the stairs diminished behind him, acutely conscious of the space beyond it, which was an unlit recess. It was too easy to imagine someone concealed there, watching him. Turning a corner, he entered another dingy passage, now conscious of a curious sound – a low rumble, like distant thunder except that it was ongoing.

A figure crossed the passage ahead of him; flickering through his vision from left to right, and then was gone.

Heck froze. For a crazy second it had been like one of those ghost stories, where some hapless investigator is confronted by a phantom shape walking out of one wall and disappearing through another; until he shuffled forward a few feet and realised that two doors were open and facing each other. A faint pall of daylight lay between them, and he now recognised the dull thunder as the sound of water pouring into a metal tub.

The figure crossed back, now in the opposite direction. It was too dim to make out any detail, but Heck saw a stocky, bullish shape with a paunch, dressed only in underwear.

He ventured forward again, and was about five feet away when he spotted that the door on the right was number fourteen. As he did, the figure re-emerged, now naked except for several neck chains and a towel round its waist. It was halfway across the corridor when it suddenly halted and turned.

It was a toss-up which one of them was the most astonished.

Mark Heckenburg or Alan Devlin.

Both their mouths dropped open. Both stammered an incoherent exclamation.

Devlin even had to fit his partially steamed-up glasses onto his nose, as if he didn't trust the evidence of his own faltering vision. 'You fucker . . .' he stuttered, before swivelling and fleeing along the corridor.

Heck charged in pursuit. Devlin glanced once over his shoulder as he ran, bare feet slapping the aged carpet, his glasses flying off in the process. At first Heck wondered if there might be another room Devlin had access to, but now he saw a fire-escape door at the far end. Devlin went straight for it, buffeting its panel of grimy frosted glass with his shoulder. With a shattering *crack*, it sagged outwards, but it was clearly filled with safety wiring and so remained in place. Frantic, Devlin dropped his towel, standing naked and hairy as he wrestled with the push-bar, which, from his inability to budge it, was jammed. He struggled desperately before spinning round and dropping to a half-crouch, his eyes narrowed. Several feet away, Heck slowed to a wary prowl.

'You stupid bastard,' he said. 'How many years have you avoided jail for? And now you're going to make up for it in one go.'

Devlin darted forward, going first to the left – Heck jumped to block his path – and then dodging right. Heck stuck his foot out, catching him across the shins.

Devlin fell full length, barking his knees and elbows on the floor, shouting in pain. As he tried to get up Heck grappled with him from behind, having to bend him forward to draw both wrists behind his back and cuff them together.

A nearby door opened. The housewife-whore with the styled blonde hair, which now looked distinctly tousled, stuck her head out. 'Oooh,' she said in a tone reminiscent of umpteen *Carry On* movies. The door opened wider, and her bearded, bespectacled husband also stepped out, his tracksuit pants round his knees.

'What's going on here?' he asked with interest.

'Police,' Heck replied. 'Get back in there and shut the door. Lock it if you can.'

Devlin gargled with pain as Heck levered him upright by his chained wrists, contorting them into an X-shape in the small of his back.

'Is this for real?' the husband asked, his interest bordering on fascination.

'*I said get out of my fucking sight!*' Heck roared at him.

The beard and his wife disappeared, the door banging shut, a bolt thudding home.

'At one time they'd have cleared out of this place like a swarm of rats at the first sign of cops,' Heck said into Devlin's ear as he frog-marched him back along the corridor, stopping only to scoop up his glasses. A couple of other doors opened as they passed, but immediately closed again when Heck glared at them. 'Shows how much moral authority we have these days, eh?'

'What do you fucking expect?' Devlin retorted, grimacing with pain. 'Fitting people up, brutalising prisoners.'

'On which subject . . .' Heck said, reaching the door to number fourteen, which still stood ajar, and kicking it wide open. 'Me and you are going to have a little chat.'

They entered the room, which unsurprisingly was a hovel: more stained carpet, two iron-framed beds covered by dingy sheets, a window along whose ledge lay several years' worth of dead, desiccated flies. He'd no sooner shoved Devlin onto the nearest bed than the phone bleeped in his pocket.

'Heck,' he said.

'The second one's here,' came Gail's urgent voice. 'He's on his way up now.'

Heck just had time to cut the call and jump back as the door to the bedroom swung open. Devlin tried to shout a warning, but Heck pitched forward at full velocity, hitting the door with both hands. It slammed backwards, hitting whoever was in the process of entering with incredible force. Wayne Devlin was flung sideways against the jamb – the door had clearly struck his head, because his eyes were rolling like pinballs. He rebounded, only to catch a stinger from Heck right in his teeth, which dropped him senseless and gory-mouthed to his knees.

Gail appeared, panting. She drew her cuffs and assisted Heck as he threw the second hoodlum over onto his front and twisted his arms behind his back. Meanwhile, the older Devlin lay naked on the bed like some fantasy film orc; his leathery brown body with its flabby gut, cheap jewellery and tattoos, unashamedly displayed, his penis a crinkle-cup stub in a nest of grey, thinning pubes. When Gail glanced up at him, he fixed her with a lewd, wet-mouthed grin.

311

'I presume someone's going to tell me what's going on here?' she said.

Heck beat the grime from his hands as he stood up. 'I'll tell you.' He regarded the older prisoner with a colder, harder expression than Gail had seen from him at any time in the enquiry so far. 'Seems we've been led down another blind alley – and we've picked up two dog turds en route.'

Chapter 29

'Right, Alan,' Gail said, 'here's the way things are. Thanks to information received from a member of the Snake Eye Crew, we've now identified you as the same person who, on 22 July this year, acquired a stolen vehicle from the Snake Eyes. The vehicle in question was a grey Bedford van, registration GD14 FED.'

Devlin said nothing, merely glowered across the interview-room table. At least he was now dressed, albeit in the obligatory paper suit, while a duty solicitor was perched alongside him, scribbling notes. The only personal item Devlin was still in possession of was his pair of bottle-lensed glasses; the rest was bagged and stored away in one of the Brixton Custody Suite's numerous property lockers.

'At the time,' Gail added, 'you were masquerading under the alias Jack Smith. Later that day, you used this same alias to check into a south London hotel, the Lambeth Royal, where you rented room number fourteen – which is where you and your son, Wayne, were arrested earlier today. Outside the hotel was the same grey Bedford van, which we've now impounded for forensic analysis, though it didn't take an FSI to identify the stockpile of offensive weapons we found in there.'

'Not looking too good so far, is it, pal?' Heck remarked.

'Depends where it's headed, doesn't it?' Devlin said.

'We're getting to that,' Gail continued. 'Thanks to CCTV footage taken at the south entrance to Thornton Farm, Woldingham, Surrey, on 24 July, we saw the same Bedford van, which by this time had been in your possession for two days. We also saw the driver of the van and an accomplice in possession of a warning sign, which they were in the process of deliberately moving, thus allowing the free passage of traffic over a bridge so dangerous that it had officially been condemned. As a direct result, a couple of hours later that day, Detective Sergeant Heckenburg crashed his car into the River Tat and very nearly drowned.' She paused. 'Do you deny any of this?'

Devlin smirked. 'You're saying that because that van was at the hotel where I happened to be staying, that means I'm responsible for an attempted murder in a place I've never been to, God knows how many miles away from where I was stopping?'

'Answering questions with other questions won't help you, Alan,' she replied. 'Unless you're denying that this person we saw was you.'

'I don't have to deny anything. You prove it was me, or we're all wasting our time.'

'There were two men on the CCTV footage, Alan. One of them was short and thickset, like you. The other one was tall and rangy, like your son, Wayne.'

'So what?'

'Alan – you should be aware that attempting to murder a police officer is an extraordinarily serious offence.'

Devlin chuckled. 'What are you talking about, attempting to murder? Unless you've got our faces on film, you're pissing in the wind.'

'You know that's bollocks,' Heck interjected.

Devlin jabbed a finger at him. '*You've* had it in for me

ever since the trial up in Nottingham. You tried to kill Jimmy Hood instead of arresting him. And after he got sent down, you threatened all sorts.'

'Is this the reason you set your trap for DS Heckenburg?' Gail asked.

'I didn't set any trap.'

Heck sighed. 'Alan . . . why bother with this charade? We've got statements, we've got video evidence. We can put you in front of an ID parade if we need to. The forensics lads are going through the van as we speak. You know we've got more than enough to charge you already.'

'Do it then.' Devlin sounded scornful, but his cheeks had coloured. 'You won't, will you? Because you don't know it was us. Not for sure. You haven't got any faces, you haven't got nothing.'

'How do you *know* we haven't got any faces?' Heck asked him.

Devlin stuttered before replying. 'You . . . you told me.'

Heck frowned. 'All we told you was that we'd got two guys on film. So how do you know that we either have or haven't got their faces?'

Gail leaned forward. 'Look, Alan – no one actually died. So you're not going to go away forever. You can make it even easier for yourself if you come clean.'

Devlin sat back, unconsciously putting distance between himself and his interrogators. 'I *assumed* you haven't got their faces. Otherwise you wouldn't be asking these dumb questions.' He tried to sound confident, but it was obvious bravado. 'I know how this stuff works.'

'Do you also know that on the day in question I was present at Thornton Farm investigating a series of other similar murders?' Heck asked. 'Which were all committed after first being disguised as unlikely accidents?'

'Eh?' This time Devlin looked genuinely baffled.

'Believe it or not, you aren't the first bloke to have this idea,' Heck said. 'Oh . . . unless you're the same bloke?'

'What are you wittering on about?'

'We know you live in Nottingham, Alan,' Gail said. 'But we've no idea why you're down in Brixton. It's not the sort of place people would normally pick for a holiday. How about Leatherhead? You ever been there? Say around 29 January this year?'

'I don't even know where Leatherhead is.'

'Okay, what about Dorking? We're looking into an unexplained death there too.'

Devlin's cheeks had now turned beetroot-red. 'You're not fitting me up, if that's what you think the game is. I've kept my nose clean all these years . . .'

'Until 16 July this year,' Heck said. 'When your old mate, Jimmy Hood, was sent to prison for the rest of his life, with the judge expressing regret that he couldn't actually hang the bastard.'

Devlin pointed again, finger quivering. 'That judge was out of fucking order!'

'And with the kind of irrational thinking that is always your sort's undoing, you decided to get even; isn't that right, Alan?'

'This is garbage.' Devlin turned to his solicitor. 'They haven't got anything on me. Tell them we've had enough.'

The solicitor made no verbal reply, but his sceptical expression implied that he held a different view.

'Let's cut to the chase, Alan,' Heck said. 'You tried to kill me on the bridge at Thornton Farm. We know that for a fact. All that matters now is why. You removed that safety chain and warning notice, either because you've been setting up bizarre fatal accidents all over Surrey or because you knew I was shortly to arrive and you wanted to get even with me for putting Jimmy Hood away.'

316

'I've never even been to Surrey until four days ago,' Devlin snapped.

'So you at least admit you were in Surrey at the time of the bridge incident?' Gail said.

Devlin glanced from one to the other, breathing hard. Spittle slathered his lips; the hue was visibly draining from his cheeks. 'Jimbo was sick,' he finally said. 'You have to understand that. Sick in the head.'

'And you're not?' Heck replied.

Devlin shot him a look, but now it was devoid of malice. Suddenly, he seemed tired. 'I felt it was unjust what had happened to him. *Really* unjust.'

'If you're expecting to find sympathy for a rapist and murderer of old ladies, you're in the wrong place,' Heck said.

'So it's okay he now has to spend the rest of his life in a hole, like a rat – supposedly for his own protection? Even that doesn't stop the screws giving him hell.'

'What's this, Alan?' Gail wondered. 'An attempt to create extenuating circumstances?'

'You tried to kill him, Heckenburg. You're just as guilty of attempted murder as me.'

'So is that an admission?' Gail persisted.

Devlin glanced round at her. 'I'll hold my hand up – but only to that thing with the bridge. I didn't have anything to do with any other murders. And our Wayne had nothing to do with any of it.'

'But he was with you at Thornton Farm. The security camera caught two of you.'

'He was just doing what I told him.' Devlin removed the glasses from his sweat-slick nose and rubbed their lenses with his thumbs. 'He comes over like an 'ardcase, but truth is he's thick.'

'You know why that doesn't work for me, Alan?' Heck said. 'Because your Wayne played his part well enough back in Nottingham, when the two of you tried to divert us to Matlock so Jimmy Hood could escape.'

'Listen to me.' Devlin rapped on the table. 'Our Wayne's as thick as *that*. He can't see the consequences of his actions. He doesn't ask questions, he just plays a role, does what he's told.'

'Still sounds to me like he was aiding and abetting attempted murder at Thornton Farm bridge?' Heck said.

'Hardly. When we got to the farm's north entrance, I was the one who went up the road. I was the one who checked the bridge out. He stayed with the van, so he didn't know nothing about the river. When I got back, I told him your car would go into a ditch. That you'd probably get roughed up a bit, but nothing worse.'

'You'd better hope Wayne's version of events matches that,' Heck said. 'We'll be speaking to him shortly. Course, if you can join all the dots for us right now, that interview might not take very long.'

'First I need a guarantee you won't be charging him with attempted murder, not even with aiding and abetting.'

Heck shook his head. 'No guarantees, Alan. Like I say, we've already got you bang to rights. This is just for clarity.'

'You'll ruin that lad's life.'

'He's already halfway to doing that himself.'

'Just as long as you know he had absolutely nothing to do with these other accident-murder things, and neither did I.'

Gail mused. 'We can only make a decision on that when we know exactly what happened at Thornton Farm.'

'Okay . . .' Devlin half smirked again. 'But I'm telling you, you won't like it.'

'I didn't when I got dumped in the river,' Heck said.

'No, this is worse. You think I'm a bastard, you should look to some of your own.'

'Explain,' Gail said.

'You probably won't believe this.'

'Try us.'

Devlin looked at Heck again. 'It was in all the papers about Jimbo – you must've seen that? Me badmouthing you and all them Nottingham coppers.'

'So?'

'That's how he found out about me.'

'Who found out?'

'One of your mob.'

Gail looked puzzled. 'Another police officer?'

Devlin nodded. 'He got in touch by phone, said he'd been reading the papers and thought I had a case. But he reckoned it was all done and dusted for Jimbo.' He glanced at Heck. 'Said there was nothing to be done legally, but if I wanted to get back at you in other ways he knew where you were; said you were a bit off your normal patch down in Surrey and didn't know your way around. It wouldn't be a bad time for us to come and bushwhack you. "Bushwhack". That was his word, not mine.'

Heck listened intently. Gail on the other hand looked astonished and not a little doubtful. 'Some bloke you don't know rang you up with information like that – right out of the blue, encouraging you to ambush a police officer? And you just bought it?'

Devlin shrugged. 'Not at first. I asked him why he was doing this. He said you were a bent bastard, Heckenburg, and needed taking out. Said you were always being investigated but no one on the force could touch you, you were that cute.'

'What was this copper's name?' Heck asked.

'He wouldn't give me his name. But I'm not fucking stupid. I rang him back on the same number a bit later that night. Someone else answered, and said they were on a DS Pavey's phone. That ring a bell? Detective Sergeant Pavey?'

Gail and Heck regarded Devlin in stiff silence.

He shrugged. 'You don't believe me . . . you've got my phone in your lock-up. Feel free to access its records. I don't mind. You'll see I've been in contact with this fella.'

'How did you feel about all this?' Heck finally asked.

'Manna from heaven, wasn't it? I only knew you as a name. You could be working anywhere in the country, no one was going to tell me. And then this comes along. Normally I wouldn't have acted on it, but I'd only just been to visit Jimbo, and he's having a nightmare. Can't eat, can't sleep, can't stop crying. I had to put things right for him, any way I could.'

'So you took Pavey up on his offer?' Heck said. 'Is that what you're telling us?'

'He hadn't made an offer as such. But I came down here the next day, got hold of a knocker I could do a job in—'

'How did you know to approach the Snake Eyes?' Gail interrupted. She still sounded sceptical. It had taken her a tad longer than Heck to get used to the idea that a fellow police officer was implicated in this.

Devlin regarded her with something like pity. 'Everyone knows everyone else in this game.'

'What're you saying, Alan?' Heck said. 'That you're *still* an active gangster?'

'Let's just say I still know plenty firm in Nottingham.'

'Oh, I'm sure.'

'You don't break off those kinds of relationships, Heckenburg. They're lifelong.'

'And how did this relationship work out for you?' Heck asked.

'I went to see some faces . . . told 'em who you were, where you were, that I wanted to square things up for Jimmy.'

'And they sent you to the Snake Eyes?' Gail said.

Devlin shrugged. 'Why not? The target was in Surrey, the Snake Eyes were south London-based. Well within strike range. Seems the Snake Eyes owed our lot for some deal they've had going with them. Don't ask me what, because even if I knew, my life wouldn't be worth living if I grassed it up. In return, the Snake Eyes found me a billet and a motor to do the job in. But that's the only involvement they had. The rest was down to me.'

Heck pondered this; oddly enough, it rang true. 'And how did you know about Thornton Farm?' he asked.

Devlin adjusted the glasses on his sweaty face. 'You'll have to ask your mate Pavey. It was the morning of 24 July. He knew we were down here by then – keeping tabs on us, I suppose. He called us again; said you were up in East Anglia, but stopping somewhere called Thornton Farm on the way back. He even gave us the address. Said it was well isolated, ideal for what we had in mind. But we had to scoot to get there ahead of you.'

Gail now looked incredulous at what she was hearing. 'How did DS Pavey know about that dangerous bridge?'

'He didn't.' Devlin glanced at Heck again, eyes gleaming with a touch of his old belligerence. 'That was all me. We were just going to lie in wait. Run you off some lonely road. Give you a kicking. But when we checked the place out and I saw there were two bridges . . . well, seemed perfect. No one would ever know it was deliberate. Not even you.'

Heck returned the penetrating gaze without speaking.

There was a long, thoughtful silence.

'One thing we need to be clear about, Alan,' Gail finally said. 'When you moved the danger sign, leaving that dangerous bridge open to the public, was it your precise intention to kill Sergeant Heckenburg?'

'Not kill him as such. Just fuck him up.'

'It was a river. You surely realised there was an extremely good chance he would die.'

'What was it you said to me once, Sergeant Heckenburg?' Devlin chuckled. '"Accidents happen"?'

'What about DS Pavey?' Gail asked. 'You say he didn't know about the dangerous bridge. But did he at least know that you planned to seriously injure Sergeant Heckenburg?'

'Well, I can't answer for him. But I wouldn't say he brought me all the way from Nottingham to give lover boy here a tickling. Would you?'

It was early evening when Gail emerged from the personnel door at the rear of Brixton Police Station. Heck was waiting, arms folded, leaning against his Mazda.

'Done?' he said, as she approached.

She nodded. 'Charged him with attempted murder and, bearing in mind that motor of yours, criminal damage to the tune of fifteen grand.'

Heck smiled. 'That was a nice touch. What about the lad?'

'Conspiracy to commit grievous bodily harm.'

'He's only young, but given his record he should get a couple of years at least.'

'Then you'll have to watch your back all over again.'

'Occupational hazard. In the meantime, DC Honeyford, your busy shift is about to get a hell of a lot busier.'

She nodded glumly.

'What's your theory?' he asked her.

She shrugged. 'Ron must have overheard me and Will Royton discussing your proposed trip to Thornton Farm. He was in the canteen at the time. I should've realised. Bastard's always earwigging. Even when there's nothing in it for him.'

'You know what you've got to do?'

'Yep.'

'I can do it for you – if you want?'

She gave him a sharp look. 'No. This one's on me.'

They drove back to Surrey, one behind the other, taking

322

the A3 down to the M25, and the A25 to Reigate. Their cars came to rest side by side in the station car park. They got out and locked the doors.

Gail looked strained and nervous as she took in the night air, but as before, her street garb of jeans, sweat-top and trainers suited her. Young though she was, despite her slight tendency to neurosis, it was now plain to Heck that she was right at home in the macho world of CID. She didn't just look like a plain-clothes cop, she sounded like one. She had the guts, the attitude and the nous. She might not be as tough as Gemma, but she was on her way. Though first there was a certain monkey she needed to get off her back.

'These are great collars, you know,' Heck said. 'They'll put your name in lights for this lot.'

'Yeah, sure.' She took a deep breath. 'At the end of today it'll probably be a good idea if I put in for a transfer.'

'Nah . . . what little I know of Will Royton, I don't think you'll have a problem.'

They crossed the green together on foot, approaching the Ploughman's Rest side by side but several yards apart, like gunfighters advancing on a saloon. Heck almost expected someone to burst out and challenge them. When they entered the downstairs bar it was crowded with drinkers, which created a warm, jovial atmosphere. Ron Pavey was in the midst of it, slumped against the bar counter, holding court among his usual clutch of junior detectives. He didn't initially notice Heck, who leaned on the door jamb to watch. Pavey only spotted Gail as she wove her way through the throng towards him, not recognising her at first as she wasn't her usual preened self. When he did, he made a double take. Then he grinned broadly, pushing out his arms to create an alley through his noisy posse.

'Well, well, look what the cat dragged in,' he said. 'Don't tell me you've been doing some real police work at last?'

'Ron Pavey,' she replied, taking the pint from his hand and passing it to one of his cronies, and then snapping a cuff on his wrist, 'you're being arrested on suspicion of conspiracy to murder Detective Sergeant Mark Heckenburg.'

'What?' he laughed, his eyebrows arching, though his cheeks had reddened.

She twisted his arm into a painful gooseneck. He gasped as she forcibly turned him round. There were mutters of surprise and consternation. A bottle went over as the space around him widened. Other conversations fell silent.

'You don't have to say anything unless you wish to, though it may harm your defence if you fail to mention something you may later rely on in court!'

'What the fuck . . . you stupid bitch!' he shouted.

She snapped the other bracelet into place. 'Anything you do say will be given in evidence.'

'*Fucking idiotic airhead bitch!*' He wrestled violently. '*What's this fucking game about?*'

'A little help here, please,' Gail said, struggling to hold on to him.

There was brief inertia around her before two or three of the other detectives, though half-dazed with surprise, laid hold of the prisoner.

'We'll walk him to the nick,' Gail said. 'No point calling for transport when we're this close.'

Pavey continued to struggle and swear while she and her assistants wheeled him across the thunderstruck barroom. As they passed each other in the doorway, Heck grinned into his face and said: 'Well, well . . . look what the cat dragged *out*.'

Chapter 30

'Heck? It's Eric.'

'Hi, mate,' Heck said, having to cup his other hand to his ear to shut out the uproar in the Custody Suite. Several officers from Street Thefts had now arrived, a couple of senior rank, and were in loud, angry dispute with Gail Honeyford, Sergeant Maxwell, who was the Reigate Hall Custody Officer, and Will Royton, whom Maxwell had called in as soon as he'd clapped eyes on his latest prisoner.

'Sounds like it's all kicking off there?' Eric Fisher said.

'You have no idea,' Heck replied, stepping into an empty interview room and closing the door. 'Anyone ever talks to you again about sleepy Surrey and its quiet country lanes, don't you believe it.'

'Listen mate, have you got five minutes?'

'The paperwork mountain has just grown exponentially, but I've always got five minutes for you, Eric. Better make it no more than that though – this isn't my phone, the battery's running low and I haven't got a charger for it.'

'Okay. Listen, you wanted me to chase up these weird accidents, and see if there were links between the names involved, yeah?'

Heck pulled up a chair. 'That's true.'

'At first it was an absolute non-starter. Most of these people don't even live in the same part of the country. None of them have got any kind of form, let alone criminal records I could cross-reference, or anything like that. The ones down as APs have no connection whatsoever to each other or to any of the people accused of injuring them.'

'Okay. Well, you tried . . .'

'Hang on, that's not the finish. I was ready to knock off, but kept telling myself "one more push". I got to thinking about doing searches on surnames in general, rather than specific individuals. I mean, it was still a long shot. But guess what?'

'You didn't come up with something?'

'Yes I did. The Thornton family.'

'Okay . . .?'

'Seems there's a younger sister, Tilly.'

'I haven't met her,' Heck said, 'but I've heard about her. She's away at uni.'

'Yeah, well back in 2007 she was at public school in Gatcombe, which is just outside Reigate. In the April of that year, she was at a house party there. Apparently it was going on all night. A neighbour complained and got fobbed off with a mouthful. He called local plod, and the party was broken up. Quite a few of the kids got arrested for being drunk and disorderly. Tilly Thornton was one of them. Thanks to having a clean record, she got off with a juvenile caution, but I don't suppose her family were very happy.'

'Okay,' Heck said again, trying to keep his voice steady. 'Now tell me who the complaining neighbour was. I know you're dying to.'

'Heck, it was Harold Lansing. He moved out to the country later, but at the time he was a townie. His house was in Gatcombe.'

'Eric – contrary to what they say about you, you are a prince among men.'

'I take it you're happy?'

'I'm happier.'

'Well here's some further info to complete the job.'

'Go on.'

'Maybe a coincidence.'

'Just tell me!'

'Tillly Thornton's a student at the University of Surrey. Guildford Hall of Humanities.'

'I know.'

Fisher paused. 'So was Dean Torbert. Remember him? The spoilt brat in the Porsche?'

'Was he indeed?' Heck had to conceal tremors of excitement as he slipped out of the interview room and sneaked past the heated debate still raging in the Custody Suite.

Gail was standing her corner despite Pavey's colleagues from Street Thefts alternately pleading with her to drop the whole thing, insisting it was all some ridiculous misunderstanding, or making ill-concealed threats about what might happen if it proceeded. Such height of feeling was only to be expected. You didn't arrest a fellow copper without it causing an eruption. But Will Royton, having seen and heard at least some of the evidence, was standing foursquare beside his own detective, and now it sounded as if the local internal enquiries mob were en route.

Heck sidled unnoticed into the outer passage before asking Fisher: 'Did Torbert and Tilly actually know each other?'

'That, I can't tell you. Surrey Uni's a big operation.'

'Like you say, it could be a coincidence.'

'Another one?' Fisher said.

Heck pondered it again. 'You got an address for Tilly?'

'I'll text it to you when I can dig it up.'

'Good work, mate. Guildford's only fifteen minutes' drive away.'

Fisher sounded surprised. 'You're off to see her *now*?'

'Without going into the details, I don't particularly want to hang around *here*.'

It wasn't just that Heck hoped to avoid the fireworks going off by the dozen in the Custody area. That other thought had now come back to haunt him – the one that had briefly struck during the battle with the Snake Eyes; that sometimes criminals were even cleverer than you thought, that sometimes they played games within games.

Harold Lansing was connected to the Thorntons. So, possibly, was Dean Torbert. All of a sudden these deaths looked less like a random series and more like a conspiracy.

Heck needed to know more, and he needed to know it *now*.

Guildford was another of those places that had never once been on Heck's radar all the time he'd served in the National Crime Group. It was a bustling shopping centre and a seat of local government, but also of rich historic interest and famously one of the most expensive places to buy property in England. By the sound of it, Guildford Hall of Humanities was an old and venerable institution which provided a wide variety of studies. According to further info provided by Eric Fisher, Tilly Thornton, whose only image Heck could call to mind was that of a cherubic toddler seated on a Shetland pony, was shortly to commence her final year in a degree course combining European History and Religious Studies.

The college's various residential blocks were congregated around the main campus. Heck, whose attention was divided between the road signs and a scruffy old map spread across his steering wheel, was looking for a specific hall of residence, which was named after one of the college's co-founders. He finally located it just off the High Street, at the north end of a pleasant square filled with shrubs and fountains. It was a tall, functional building, part of a terrace, but elegant in that traditional not-too-decorative Edwardian style. He ascended a low flight of steps. At the top, a brass plaque was set into the bricks to one side of the front door. Alongside the university's famous stag icon, engraved black lettering read:

Darleen Anderson House
Guildford Hall
University of Surrey

The door, which was covered in shiny black lacquer, was closed and locked; an illuminated keypad was fixed to its left-hand jamb.

Heck gazed up the building, which stood to a height of three storeys. Light only shone from two or three of its windows; unsurprising given that it was now the official summer holidays. He pressed the doorbell, opened his wallet, and held his warrant card to the camera over the lintel. It was several seconds before the intercom crackled and a stern female voice said: 'Hello?'

'Yeah, hi,' he said. 'I'm a police officer. Detective Sergeant Heckenburg. I could do with speaking to one of your girls please. Her name's Tilly Thornton. I believe she's on the premises.'

There was a protracted silence.

'It's rather late,' the voice finally replied.

Yeah for me too, he was about to respond, but checked himself. 'Look, I'm sorry, but this won't take long. It's concerning her recent bereavement.'

Another silence followed, broken by a dull *clunk* as a lock was disengaged and the front door creaked open. Heck walked through, and found himself in a wide hallway with a black-and-white tiled floor and towering rubber plants ranged down either side.

Here he was confronted by a tall, broad-shouldered woman in a heavy purple dressing gown. She had a vaguely mannish aspect, but her shiny brown hair, of which there was an awful lot, was stacked high like a disorderly Madame Pompadour wig, and fixed in place by a series of thick wooden pins. Doubtless this formidable lady was the bursar or concierge. She'd emerged from an apartment on the left, and dried her hands on a dishrag while regarding him with apparent deep suspicion.

'Who did you say you were again?' Her voice was deep and powerful.

It now occurred to Heck, rather belatedly, that he was still in casuals: trainers and jeans, a leather jacket over his old sweater. He displayed his warrant card a second time. 'DS Heckenburg.'

She scrutinised it closely. 'And it's concerning Tilly's father's death?'

'That's correct.'

'You'd better go up,' she said. 'You'll find her on the third floor, room thirty-five.'

'Thanks. Erm, you're . . .?'

'Dr Allacott.'

Heck nodded and smiled, and headed past her along the hall, but then stopped and turned back. She was still watching him.

'Do you mind me asking, Dr Allacott – what kind of girl is Tilly? I mean since the accident?'

The woman's hard frown softened a little. 'You mean how's she handling it? There isn't more bad news, I hope?'

'No, but . . . well, I don't want to put her under any undue pressure.'

Dr Allacott gave it some thought. 'She came back here about a week after the funeral. I haven't seen a great deal of her, you understand, but enough to, well . . .' She seemed vaguely embarrassed. 'She hasn't been quite the way I'd have expected.'

'Can you explain that?'

She folded the dishrag and stuffed it into her capacious dressing-gown pocket. 'You need to understand, I thought it was probably a good idea her coming here after the funeral, even though we're out of term-time. She shares her digs with another girl, Zara Jolley, who's a rather zany character. I thought Zara might cheer her up. Only . . .'

'Only?'

'Only she didn't seem to need it. Tilly must still be in shock. I mean, she's not exactly running around clicking her heels, but she's not in mourning either. If you get my drift.'

Heck did. 'How did Tilly get on with her father?'

'Perfectly well, as far as I know. At least, she was always happy to accept his generosity. I mean, his cheques paid for her residence here. I think he used to send her spending money too. Most of the girls who stay during the holidays do so because they have jobs locally. Tilly never has. She's never needed one. She's not alone in that, of course.'

'No. Well, thanks, Dr Allacott.'

'Room thirty-five,' she reminded him, as he proceeded along the passage.

Heck ascended the building via an old fashioned cage-lift, which rattled and wheezed and took an unexpectedly long time to reach its destination. The first floor lay quiet and in darkness, but on the second several doors stood open, lamplight spilling out of them. Voices and faint music could be heard. A girl of about nineteen, also wearing a dressing gown, was standing by an open window, smoking what looked like a joint. Another girl strode past her, wearing only a vest and knickers. With good security downstairs, the residents were probably justified in feeling safe enough to leave doors open and wander around in their scanties.

When Heck left the lift on the third floor he padded down a carpeted corridor, passing several more doors standing ajar. More music came to his ears, along with chatting voices and occasional laughter. Number thirty-five was not locked, but as soon as he tapped on it a cheerful voice responded: 'Come in!'

Heck entered a surprisingly small room. It was snug, but cluttered. A right-angled sofa had been shoehorned into a corner, facing a low table on which sat a television, a satellite box, and a DVD player, not to mention various items of clothing and several unwashed plates. The rest of the tight space had been given over to study: two desks were jammed side by side against the main wall. Both had computers and Anglepoise lamps and were littered with books, pens, and messy paperwork. Two noticeboards were fixed to the wall, one over each workstation; these too were plastered with documents, though not all of the educational variety. Some were posters for rock concerts, others were group photographs taken in bars or at street demos.

On the left, a short, dim corridor led off to what presumably were the bedrooms; Heck entered just as a vague figure disappeared through a door at the end of it. 'Not be a sec!' called the voice that had admitted him.

He loitered there, feeling awkward – though not as much as he did two minutes later when the figure, who was a girl of about twenty, reappeared in the corridor and sauntered back towards him, naked except for a bath towel, which she held in front of herself as she tried to straighten it. She was of mixed race and incredibly pretty, freckle-faced and with a delectable mass of frizzy hair.

When she spotted him, she froze in mid-stride. 'Oh my God!' She clasped the towel to her body.

'Whoa, I'm sorry,' Heck said, averting his eyes. 'I'm here to see Tilly. But I thought . . . I thought Dr Allacott would have told you I was coming up.'

'She probably did,' the girl said, giggling. 'She'll have sent a text, but I had these on.' He risked a glance at her as she yanked out a tiny pair of earphones. 'Heard you knocking, but didn't hear that little car-crash sound my phone makes. Hell, I'm really sorry – I thought you were one of the girls.'

'First time that's ever been said to me.'

'Oh God, what must you think of me? Look, just hang on, yeah – I'll not be a mo. I'm Zara, by the way. Who are you?'

'Mark. Mark Heckenburg.'

'You're a friend of Tilly's, you say?'

He produced his warrant card. 'I'm a police officer.'

Her mouth dropped into a perfect, red-lipped 'Oh!'

'It's to do with Tilly's dad.'

'Ahhh, I see. Look hang on . . . let me get dressed.'

She turned and scuttled prettily back down the corridor, exposing her pert posterior as she did. Heck remained where he was, vaguely amused by the incident, but still sizing up the apartment, which appeared to possess that usual 'student flat' aura of burgeoning intellect and abject slovenliness. On the desk to the right, the stationery lay in complete disarray, but there were also books by Kafka, Proust, and Dostoyevsky. On the other, which he took to be Tilly Thornton's – mainly because several of the photos pinned to the noticeboard had been taken at Thornton Farm, and featured Charles and Freda Thornton, and the late Mervin – there were volumes concerned either with history or religion. The top one lay open on an image so bizarre that Heck couldn't help but pick it up. It was the reprint of a woodcut dating from several centuries ago, in which a painfully thin man wearing a frock coat and cravat, knee breeches, stockings, buckled

333

shoes and a periwig strode along a cobbled street. In one hand he wielded a heavy club, and with the other held a skull mask to his face. An odious creature, something partway between a rat and a deformed human foetus, peeked from his pocket. In the background, everyday common-folk hurried away along alleys.

Heck scanned the block of adjoining text:

The dreaded Mohocks . . . a criminal organisation of the eighteenth century, whose activities went unpunished thanks to their semi-aristocratic status. The Mohocks were a self-styled gang of young men, rakes and dandies for the most part, who terrorised the inner districts of London between the years 1700 and 1714. Inspired by ghoulish tales from the New World concerning the murderous hit-and-run raids of the Mohawk Indians, the Mohocks commenced a reign of fear in the metropolis derived entirely from their own sadistic sense of humour. They neither robbed nor raped, but committed acts of purposeless brutality seemingly for its own sake, treating each and every outrage as a huge practical joke.

This was the Age of Reason. Religious beliefs had dwindled in Britain, and with them – in certain quarters at least – any notion of right and wrong. Hailing from a social class who often stood aloof from the law, the Mohocks followed the examples set by other heinous but untouchable bands in that era, such as the Muns, the Hawkubites, the Scourers, and the even-more-notorious Hellfire Clubs, by revelling in acts of evil simply because they were allowed to.

Their victims were often drawn from the lower orders, particularly from among beggars and other vagrants, as these unfortunate folk had no judicial or political voice. Their fate might be sealed with elaborate and ingenious cruelty, and yet would cause barely a ripple in wider London society.

In one instance, an old woman was held upside down in the barrel where she had been washing clothes until she drowned. In another, a ploughboy was dragged over his own plough blade after the harness straps were mysteriously unbuckled. Fireworks were once used to stampede cattle down a busy backstreet, trampling a number of persons to death, including children.

The Mohocks made no attempt to disguise their involvement in these atrocities, and on several occasions repaired to the nearest tavern afterwards, to toast each other and congratulate themselves on their inventiveness. Anyone brave enough to try and apprehend these scoundrels would be beaten or shot . . .

The book had a library stamp on its inside leaf. Its title was printed in gold: *Chaos And Immorality: The Roots of Social Breakdown.*

Heck checked several other books on the desk. *Do As Thou Wilt* discussed 'the psychology of self-indulgence'. *Crocodile Smiles* focused on 'history's most alluring anti-heroes'. The last and largest, which bore on its cover an impressive cartoon portrait of Batman's nemesis, the Joker, was entitled *To Them It's Just Fun*, and purported to be 'a study of thrill-killers throughout the ages'. When Heck flicked through it, he saw chapters dedicated to leading exponents of the art, Caligula, Tamerlane, and Vlad the Impaler, intellectual advocates such as Torquemada and the Marquis de Sade, and finally its lesser lights, Jack the Ripper, the Zodiac Killer, and others. At the end, there was another chapter on gangs and cults. Several of these latter pages had been bookmarked; when Heck glanced at them, he saw that passages on the Mohocks and the Hawkubites had been underlined in pencil. When the author described the Duke of Wharton, the founder of the Hellfire Clubs in England, as 'a deviant to his bones, who lived only to shock and dismay the rest of society', it had been trebly underlined.

'Tilly went home yesterday,' came a voice from his rear.

Heck turned sharply and placed the book back on the desk.

If Zara Jolley thought it odd that he'd been glancing through her flatmate's textbooks, she didn't say so. She'd said that she was off to get dressed, but in fact she'd only put on a silky ankle-length kimono, which showed plenty of bare, shapely leg as she walked back towards him.

'I see,' Heck replied, slightly distracted by this. 'Sorry – Dr Allacott didn't seem to know that.'

'Tilly goes home quite a bit; she doesn't bother telling her anymore.' Zara cocked her head to one side as she fastened various hairbands in place. 'It's that gorgeous brother of hers, Charles. He always seems to need help on the farm now that their dad isn't there. Called her the night before last and asked her to pop back. She went yesterday. Said she'd be gone a couple of days.'

'Okay.' Heck nodded. 'Just out of interest . . .' He indicated the books on Tilly's desk. 'All this stuff . . . seems a bit strong?'

'That's for her thesis. It's due in by Christmas, so she wanted a head start.'

'Seems an odd choice of thesis for someone doing religious studies.'

'Gimme a break!' Zara giggled. 'Tilly doesn't believe any of that Holy Joe crap. Tilly hasn't got a religious bone in her body. Quite the opposite. I think she only picked that course for a joke, thought it would be really funny to get a degree in religion – some kind of amazing irony. I mean she's like that, she's an arch piss-taker.'

'She is?'

'She once gave her name on an official college survey as Mya Nus. Get it: "my anus"?'

'Erm, yeah,' Heck said.

'You don't know Tilly at all, do you?' Zara cocked her head the other way, a consciously cute gesture. 'Then again – perhaps you do?'

'What time did she leave?'

'Mid-morning yesterday. Something urgent had come up, she said.'

'Okay, thanks.' Heck moved to the door.

'Can't tempt you into staying for a cuppa?'

'No time, I'm afraid.'

Zara smiled saucily. 'You really looking for Tilly to talk about her dad?'

'Sorry?'

'You seem very keen to find her.'

'This could be quite important.'

'It always is.' She smiled again, indulgently, and in a voice that implied he had her full permission, added: 'Go on then. I'll let her have you all to herself . . . this time.'

'Shit, Heck,' Eric Fisher groaned. 'I'm at home now.'

'I wish I was,' Heck replied, as he headed out of Guildford along the A3. 'You don't have to stop whatever it is you're doing. I just want to pick your brains.'

'The few remaining. Go on.'

'I've got to make it quick, because this phone's almost dead. The Thornton kids – Charles and Tilly.'

'Yeah?'

'You didn't get any other curios on them?'

'Well . . .' Briefly, Fisher's stentorian breathing was the only sound. 'The arrest report concerning Tilly Thornton. Apparently she gave Surrey quite a bit of grief.'

'How do you mean?'

'Gobby. "You know who I am?" All that sort of stuff. Seemed to have the idea her old man was some kind of country squire.'

'They can't have been short of a few bob.' Heck sped one-handed down the ramp onto the M25. 'I've seen the size of that farm. They used to run a horse stud and a dressage stable. Kicked it into touch because they didn't need the money.'

'Oh yeah, I think he was worth a bit, old man Thornton.'

'How much of it do the two kids stand to gain now he's popped his clogs?'

'Nothing at the moment. His wife Freda's still alive. Unless he made a special will, she's the sole beneficiary.'

Heck considered this as he drove. 'I've met Mrs Thornton. She's an odd fish.'

'Odd how?'

'Part of the time I was with her, I got the feeling . . . I dunno, not so much that she was keeping stuff from me, but that she was struggling with something inside, and yet saying nothing. A bit weird when you think I was there to find out who'd killed her husband.'

'After what happened to *him*, who wouldn't have gone a bit weird?'

'Yeah. I'm just wondering if it's a weirdness that's been imposed on her.' Heck recalled the now-curious moment at Thornton Farm when Mrs Thornton, having initially shown interest in his enquiry, was gently admonished by her son, after which she lapsed into troubled silence. 'Is she being manipulated maybe? You know, controlled?'

'You mean by her kids?'

'Up to now I've been working on the basis these accidental deaths are like practical jokes; a bit of a giggle that some nutcase is having with us.'

'And that ties in with the Thornton kids, how?'

Heck described the textbooks he'd seen in Tilly Thornton's apartment. 'She seems inordinately interested in this eighteenth-century gang, the Mohocks. A bunch of practical jokers who literally knocked 'em dead. Played fatal pranks on people, just for a lark.'

'So she's studying evil as part of a religious course.' Fisher sounded unimpressed. 'Doesn't that go with the territory?'

'Okay. But then there's the Harold Lansing and Mervin Thornton link. Both are on the list of victims and both were known to Tilly. Then we've got Dean Torbert, who *might* have been known to her. Like you said, that's all quite a coincidence.'

'Oh – on the subject of coincidences, there's been another strange accidental death down in Surrey today. Only heard it on the wire about ten minutes ago.'

'Specifically where?'

'Place called Shawcross Spinney, private hunting estate.'

'Please tell me it's as simple as some plummy-voiced prat shooting his own foot off?'

'If it was that straightforward I wouldn't bother you with it, pal. But it was that poacher you locked up five days ago.'

'Vinnie Budd?' Heck almost lost control of the car. 'How did it happen?'

'Seems he caught his hand in one of his own traps, and tried to hack it off with a knife.'

'What? Tried to hack his own hand off? No one'd do that, would they!'

'Depends on his mental state, doesn't it? If he was ill, or something . . . anyway, ended up butchering himself in the process. The local big nob's gamekeepers found him around midday. Well dead by that time. Cause was given as heart failure caused by rapid blood loss.'

Heck gave no immediate response. Fleetingly, all he could

think about was Tilly Thornton being called back to her family farm yesterday.

Something urgent had come up.

'So what do you think?' Fisher asked.

'I still need more, Eric. A lot more.'

'There's not much more you can do at this time of night. Or me.'

'No, I suppose not.'

'So what's what's-her-name doing?'

Heck got his foot down, accelerating along the motorway from 80 to 100. 'Gail's busy. But I'm going to need to speak to her pronto, so you'd better clear the line.'

'Suits me,' Fisher said, yawning. 'Speak to you tomorrow.'

When Fisher had rung off Heck checked his messages, but found nothing from Gail. He hadn't really expected anything. She was doubtless still up to her neck in in-house controversy. He called her anyway, but found that he had to leave a voicemail.

'Gail, this is Heck,' he said. 'A lot of stuff's happened in the last couple of hours. I know it's late, but I very much want to have a chat with Charles Thornton, so I'm on my way over there again now. Call me as soon as you can.'

Chapter 31

Even though it was now several hours since she'd first arrested Pavey, Gail's legs were still shaking. She went tiredly back into the CID office, cup of coffee in hand, and slumped at her desk, barely noticing what time it was.

'You need to think about this very carefully,' Will Royton had warned her in his private office, after he'd first arrived back at the nick – not because he was such a dinosaur that he couldn't tolerate the sight of a fellow copper under arrest, but because he knew there were many others in the job who were, and he wanted to lay it on the line for her before they proceeded to involve the IPCC. 'He's already shouting back there that this is vindictiveness on your part. That you're his ex, that you couldn't take it when he broke up with you and that you've been looking for any way you can to stick it to him.'

Hot-faced, Gail had denied this, but at the same time had explained as best she could about her actual relationship with Ron Pavey. Royton had turned pale as he'd listened to the full gory details, but at least had done her the courtesy of not interrupting. She still wasn't sure whether his apparent immediate acceptance of this story should be a relief to her or a slight.

'In a way, that makes it even worse,' he'd replied. 'If all that stuff comes out, and it will – Pavey will make damn sure it does, if for no other reason than to ruin your standing in this department – they'll think it even more likely that you're a woman scorned. They're also going to question your moral fibre. They're going to say that you put up with this so-called abuse for months and months without raising a complaint. They'll say that you're disingenuous and dishonest, or at best that you lack strength and character. They'll say that it was only later on – when you got this new fella in your life, another seasoned DS with a streetwise reputation – that you felt sufficiently empowered to launch a revenge attack.'

Gail had wanted so much to take issue with that. To respond with outrage, insisting that Heck wasn't her 'new fella', yet only twenty-four hours ago, very ill-advisedly it now seemed, she'd been in bed with him. It had been nothing – a quickie, a bit of stress-relieving nookie – but it seemed there was always a price to pay for such lapses of personal dignity.

'Either way, Gail, Pavey's defence will have a field day,' Royton had added. 'They'll put you through the eye of a needle.'

'Sir, I'm a police officer. That means I'm a professional witness. I can take it.'

'Okay, fair enough. But there's something else too. Mark Heckenburg will already realise this, but I want to make sure *you* do as well. You know how difficult it is to prove conspiracy to commit murder. And that's on a good day. Unless Pavey cracks, which is highly unlikely, your entire case against him is going to hinge on the word of a toerag called Alan Devlin. Do you think he's going to stand up to this level of scrutiny?'

She couldn't give any kind of honest answer to that.

'I mean what if he doesn't?' Royton had asked. 'Then the wheels are really going to come off. If Pavey walks, how bad is it going to look? It won't just be a matter of getting ostracised by a few pig-headed idiots who've never joined the twenty-first century. There'll be no future for you on this division, maybe not in this force, maybe not in the job . . . if nothing else, you can forget that long line of promotion boards that I know you were hoping for.'

'Sir, if we turned a blind eye to every crime we were confronted with, just because it looked like it might go belly-up in court, we'd have no credibility as coppers. Not to the general public, and not to ourselves. And you know that.'

He'd nodded soberly. 'I do. Of course I do. But I just want to be sure that you understand what you're getting into, Gail. This is a potential world of crap. It really is. But for what it's worth, I have no doubt that Ron Pavey is a controlling shithouse who has no interests other than his own. I've never liked him. You send him to jail, and you'll be doing us all a favour. But the odds are against it.'

Gail now sat alone in the otherwise empty CID office, feeling more drained – both physically and emotionally – than she could ever remember. Beyond the windows, as always on late shifts, the opaque blackness of night seemed to fit against the panes like something tangible and solid, blotting out the world beyond. At least her part in the investigation was largely done. CPS advisers would be arriving shortly, to assess the case. Professional Standards were already interviewing Pavey. On the subject of which, they'd also mentioned something about wanting to speak to Heck.

She glanced around distractedly, wondering exactly where he might be. It seemed unlikely he'd have signed off and hit the sack without coming back to the nick first and seeing what was happening. She surveyed her desk, wondering if he'd perhaps left her a written note – and her eyes alighted on a neat but large stack of freshly printed paperwork filling her in-tray. The sight of it would have been depressing at the best of times, but now it might as well have been a pile of boulders she somehow had to shift. She picked idly at the top sheet, wondering what it was. Her interest was briefly – but only *briefly* – kindled when she recognised it as a complete listing, including names, addresses, dates of birth, occupations and so forth, of the county's licensed firearms owners. She'd requested this herself of course, but ultimately it lowered her spirits even more, because while this was the work she was supposed to be engaged in at present, she'd become so distracted by other events that she'd almost completely lost track, not to mention her enthusiasm. Okay, so somebody had shot down the blimp that had killed Gus Donaldson; seriously – could that really have anything to do with Harold Lansing's death? Heck had crashed his own car into a river after being mischievously led onto a flimsy bridge; but that had had nothing to do with Lansing, and surely proved how easily these curious incidents could fall into a false pattern.

She sipped her coffee, which was lukewarm and basically *yuk*, as she flipped through a few more sheets, her eyes focusing on little more than a mass of meaningless text.

Until she saw the name 'Thornton'.

She replaced her coffee on the desk and looked more closely at it.

Mervin Thornton, of Thornton Farm, Woldingham, had applied . . .

Wasn't that the same address where Heck had suffered his accident?

Gail sat stiffly upright. All sense of torpor fell slowly away from her.

Thornton Farm.

But hold on – wasn't Mervin Thornton also a casualty?

Wasn't he the one who'd managed to blow himself up like a football, pumping himself full of compressed gas?

Her neck hairs still tingled as she examined the document. Not only had Mervin Thornton held a firearms licence, but he'd been a regular at various gun clubs – and was the owner of a Remington 597 Long Rifle.

Of course, if Thornton was already dead it kind of discounted him from the enquiry, except that there was nothing to physically prevent the transfer of this rifle into someone else's possession.

Didn't Mervin Thornton have two grown-up children?

And weren't she and Heck looking for *two* killers?

But where the hell was Heck now?

With sudden urgency Gail dug her mobile from her pocket and found a single message waiting. She played it back and, with an air of near-inevitability, listened to the voice of her partner as he told her how things were moving on apace and that he was on his way, right now, to the Thornton farm. She bashed in his number.

There was no response. She tried again, but still there was no response.

Heck shoved the lifeless mobile into the glove box, climbed from the Mazda, and locked its door behind him.

The farmhouse stood in darkness, which was hardly surprising given that it was now somewhere between two and three in the morning, though there was a faint ambient glow from beyond its steeply tilted roof, indicating that lights were still on in various of the outbuildings. But the initial thing that caught his attention was his Peugeot, sitting some twenty yards to his right, battered, crumpled, and reeking of mud and algae.

He approached the vehicle glumly. It was a write-off for sure. But in managing to drag it from the river,

Charles Thornton had been as good as his word. Heck felt a brief pang of uncertainty, not to mention guilt, as he wondered if *this* was the reason why the head of the Thornton clan had been so keen for his sister to pop back home and help.

Heck turned to the house, wondering if he should leave this latest question-and-answer session until the morning – and was surprised to see the front door open and a ghostly figure standing there. It was Freda Thornton, wearing a floor-length white nightgown and a white woollen shawl, the two ends of which she clasped to her breast. She regarded him with her usual cold but lifeless intensity.

'Hello, Mrs Thornton,' Heck said, approaching. 'Really sorry I've disturbed you. Truth is I only dropped by on the off-chance you folks might still be up. Bit naughty of me, I suppose. Should've realised you wouldn't be. Thing is, I was looking to enquire about my vehicle, which I can see your son has very kindly recovered. Also, I need to take a statement from Charles about the incident at the old bridge. The person responsible has been arrested, you see, and is in the process of being prosecuted.'

The way her mouth crooked into an abrupt, V-shaped smile was more than a little disconcerting, not least because it was the first display of any emotion he'd seen from the woman, but secondly because there was no apparent reason for it.

'You can speak to Charles if you wish,' she said in a distant tone, which didn't at all seem to match her curious grin.

'I won't be disturbing him?'

'It's no trouble at all.'

Something about her easy compliance at two o'clock in the morning made Heck wary. 'Well . . . I don't think he'll want to be giving me a statement at this hour.'

She ignored that, pointing to the corner of the house. 'He and Tilly are round the back. You'll find them in the main barn.'

'Oh – well, I suppose that's different. I mean, if they're actually up and about. Unless they're doing something important, of course?'

'It's nothing important.' She continued to smile.

Okay, she'd been weird before. But this was *really* weird. Hardcore play-acting if ever he'd seen it.

'Is someone in there with you?' Heck asked, trying to look over her shoulder.

'I don't know what you mean,' she replied, *still* smiling.

'Are you okay?'

Only now did her smile falter. 'Of course I'm okay. Why shouldn't I be?'

'Mrs Thornton – is there anything you perhaps want to tell me? I mean while there's just me and you.'

She maintained her forced smile, but her eyes widened at this – as though alarmed. 'I thought you came here to see Charles?'

'Well . . . technically I did.'

'Then technically you'll find him in the barn, Sergeant. Now please go. It's most rude of you to have called at this hour!' She stepped back and banged the door closed – a little unnecessarily, Heck thought.

He remained on the step for a few seconds, wondering why he felt as if he was under surveillance. Slowly, cautiously, he moved towards the corner of the house, glancing up at its blank, black windows as he did. He was uncomfortably conscious that he had neither a radio nor a working telephone with him. The only thing he did have, when he rummaged in his jeans pocket, was his grey-and-white chequered handkerchief; the one he'd offered to Gail in the London bed and breakfast. It seemed a ridiculous thing to do, but he wadded it into a ball and, just before turning the corner, dropped it alongside the path.

As he'd seen the first time he'd visited here, the farmhouse was a large, ungainly structure, which appeared to have been built and rebuilt over several centuries, as a direct result of which it now comprised numerous wings and annexes. He turned one corner after another, crossing various small yards, before spying an open doorway from which lamplight issued. This wasn't connected to the main house, but gave entry to a very large freestanding structure built from timber, breeze blocks, and corrugated metal.

'Your basic main barn,' he said under his breath.

When he entered, he saw flattened straw on the ground and bare electric bulbs dangling overhead, but it wasn't the vast, church-like space he'd expected. The barn's interior appeared to have been compartmentalised by wooden-slatted dividing walls. This first area was being used as a garage. On the far side of it there was another door, this one large enough to admit two cars side by side, though at present a heavy steel shutter had been pulled down on it. There was only one vehicle inside.

Heck approached it in near-reverential silence.

It was a Land Rover, metallic green in colour.

As he circled round it, memories were stirred of the iron bridge over the River Mole, and the wooded lane near Harold Lansing's house. He peered through its tinted windows. Of course, there was nothing on view that was even vaguely incriminating.

Then he heard a voice somewhere else in the barn. At first he wasn't sure which direction it was coming from; this big, echoing structure, subdivided with God knew how many partition walls, was likely to possess some odd acoustics. Even so, there was something about the voice that wasn't quite right. It was high-pitched and quavering. It said: 'I've brought you some hardboiled eggs and some nuts.'

A deeper voice responded with something unintelligible,

and a chuckle. Heck thought the latter voice might belong to Charles Thornton.

After that, there was silence.

On the other side of the garage, another narrow doorway stood open. Heck glanced through it and down a long, straw-filled corridor again lit by hanging electric bulbs. Along the timber-slatted walls hung a variety of farming tools and other accoutrements: hoes, forks, ravels of rubber tubing and so forth, though midway along there was a row of eight hooks, from each one of which was suspended what looked like a set of grey overalls.

Heck walked slowly down there and stopped in front of them. Two of them were spattered with dried reddish-brown fluid. It might be wood-stain, though on the other hand . . . He was determined not to jump to conclusions about what he was viewing here. He couldn't afford to. Nothing he'd seen thus far would lack for a reasonable explanation. What did a green Land Rover and some dirty overalls prove except that he was out in the country? When he fancied something rustled on the other side of the wall on which the garments hung, he peeked through the gap between the slats, but saw nothing except another dim-lit passage, and beyond the slats on the far side of that an area of total darkness. This place was like a rabbit warren.

'Why don't you do something to help me?' came the voice of Charles Thornton. At least, it had sounded like Charles. As before, it wasn't possible to trace the direction.

A tittering laugh followed.

Heck pivoted in a full circle, feeling confused and disoriented. He wondered if maybe Charles and Tilly were outside, and he'd heard them through an open window. He moved on to the end of the passage, only to find that it turned ninety degrees into another passage that was almost identical, though in this case there were two doors on the left, spaced about fifteen yards apart. He moved to the first and glanced through into what looked like another spacious vehicle bay, though this was occupied by some immense, mud-caked farming contraption, on the other side of which he could just about distinguish another wide doorway with a steel shutter.

'I have nothing to say,' came the distant voice of Charles Thornton.

The remaining stretch of passage seemed even dimmer than it had before, but it was only as Heck proceeded down this that he realised why: elsewhere in the barn, possibly in the corridor he'd just come through, the electric bulbs had been switched off. He halted in his tracks. Or had they gone off of their own volition? Were they on a timer?

'You can lead a horse to water, but a pencil must be lead.'

There was another titter of laughter.

Heck had heard that particular phrase somewhere before, but he didn't attempt to recollect it because something else had now distracted him. About five or six yards ahead on the right, suspended among the shovels, spades, and saws, was the bright green frame of what looked like a bicycle. When he stood directly in front of it, the crimson logo on its central shaft revealed that it was a Boardman's racing bike. Hooked over one of its handlebars was a blue racing helmet, complete with silver flashes.

'I'm not as dumb as you look,' the voice added, much closer.

Heck spun round, and gazed through the second left-hand door into yet another chamber. This was also lit dimly, but sufficiently for him to discern a breeze-block pillar hung with what looked like items of folded garden furniture – and a toy aeroplane.

He strode dazedly towards it.

There was no mistake. It was a large radio-controlled

350

model, an Art-Tech recreation of an original Sopwith Camel, with a wingspan of about three and a half feet, painted blue and yellow. Its left tail fin had broken off, while its upper left wing hung at a crazy angle, having been reattached with strips of sticky tape. He didn't need to examine it closely to see that it had also suffered water damage, and that its interior was clogged with mud and the green/brown stems of river weed. Underneath it there was a leather satchel from which hung two long scrolls of silky textured photographic paper. When Heck took one by the corner and shook it out, he saw a large, circular image – clearly taken with a telescopic lens, to create a long-range distortion – of the road outside Harold Lansing's house.

Movement stirred in the corner of his vision.

Heck turned to face the doorway through which he'd entered. A shape had just ghosted past it. But now something else distracted him: to his left there was yet another short passage, this opening into a much wider space that was mostly veiled in shadow, though a single bulb burned at its far end, casting a restricted pool of light over another huge, double-sized entrance, on which two heavy wooden doors had been closed. What looked like a shiny new chain was woven between their handles, but it wasn't this that struck Heck as much as the two flattish, flesh-coloured objects hanging one at either end of it.

Hair prickling, body greased with sweat, he strode forward, passing into this next and largest chamber. Long before he reached the two objects, he knew what they would be. But when he finally padded up to them, his worst suspicions were confirmed.

Masks.

Cheap plastic masks with threaded elastic, of a sort you could purchase at Blackpool or Rhyl or Margate, or on any decrepit pier or tatty fairground. Yet they still bore the distinctive genial features of those much-loved comics, Stan Laurel and Oliver Hardy.

There was an echoing *clunk* from somewhere to Heck's rear.

He glanced behind. Nothing stirred in the chamber save the grass seeds and grains of dust that his own entrance had swirled into the air; and yet the place, though it was already dim, now seemed dimmer still. Another of the lights elsewhere in the barn had been switched off. A second *clunk* followed, and the bulb in the adjoining chamber vanished. Suddenly all areas save the tiny island of light around the wooden double doors were cloaked in blackness.

Heck's neck hairs bristled, but still he spied nothing.

The doors at his back were chained, and the chains were held in place by a heavy padlock. If that wasn't enough, at the base of either door vertical bolts had been rammed point-down several inches into special boreholes in the concrete floor and locked in place. He pushed against the doors anyway, wondering if he could exert enough force to create a narrow gap between them and slide out that way – and almost jumped out of his skin at a thunderous metallic clattering and the grating mechanical growl of a diesel-powered engine hammering to life.

A bank of headlights struck him from the far side of the chamber.

He staggered back, shielding his face against the initial blinding glare, though his vision quickly attuned and he found himself staring in disbelief at a colossal hunk of farm machinery as it manoeuvred its way out of the darkness. What Heck knew about agriculture he could have written on the back of a speeding ticket, but he didn't have to be an expert to recognise that a combine harvester – fifteen tonnes of heavy, juddering metal, grinding, clanking gears and spinning, gleaming blades – was revving towards him.

At first he was frozen with indecision. The steel giant's grain platform was about twelve yards across, ideal for cutting broad swathes through phalanxes of ripened wheat, but it didn't fill the barn from one side to the other. It was about twenty yards away when Heck attempted to dart round it, and yet the leviathan shifted direction with a speed and agility born of modern hydraulics, pivoting nimbly towards him. Beyond the wall of flashing steel and shimmering light he caught brief glimpses of the driver: a slim, short-haired young man installed behind the Perspex screen of the cab, leaning forward eagerly, shifting levers with practised ease.

Heck could do nothing but retreat as it slowly but surely backed him into a corner. Here the mechanical brute halted, the sheer width of its platform preventing further progress and leaving him in a tiny triangular space. But its engine continued to run and the cutter-bar to spin its array of blades and scythes less than a couple of feet away, blasting grit and straw all over him. With a driver this skilled, the machine could easily be brought round until it was flush against the wall, or maybe only a deft adjustment would be required to scoop him onto its platform, where he would be threshed and shredded until the marrow came out of his bones.

Heck retreated until the slatted barn wall struck him in the back. He glanced up at the cab again, to see that the driver had now climbed out and was peering down. What Heck had first taken for a young man was actually a young woman, almost certainly Tilly Thornton. She was clad in grubby grey overalls, but was of a slim, wiry build, had very short fair hair and plain features – it wouldn't have been difficult, in the midst of a road accident, for some panicky lorry driver to mistake her for a male cyclist.

Before Heck could shout up at her to turn the machine off, the air caught in his throat as a thin, strong ligature was tightened across it. Two hands had emerged from between the wooden slats, one to either side of him, and had slipped a loop of cord over his head, though he only needed to claw at the loop, which had already tightened like a garrotte, to find that it was made of flat, sharp-edged nylon. It was a cable tie, and its clip was already being shoved against the nape of his neck, the band cutting into the flesh of his throat and the windpipe underneath.

Heck wrestled with the ligature, only to be yanked backwards, striking the timber wall with massive force. The tie was quickly secured on the other side, the planking pressing against the rear of his skull. He couldn't even turn his head to glimpse his assailant through the gaps, but it was plain who had snared him.

'Put your hands out,' Charles Thornton's voice instructed. 'One to either side . . . just like Jesus on the cross. Do as I say, or I'll choke you to death.'

Heck had no choice. He could just about breathe – any further pressure on his throat, and he would strangle. He lifted his arms out wide, and one after another they were seized, cable ties were slipped round his wrists and they were tightened, binding him securely. A fourth tie was looped over his head, pulled into place across his brow and constricted to the point where he thought it was going to crush his skull. A fifth was then applied to his legs, binding his ankles together; this latter felt less secure than the others – it couldn't fit snugly round *both* limbs, but Heck knew it would take a massive struggle to get free of it. He stood there, breathing hard, his head, neck, shoulders, and basically his entire body immobilised. He'd never felt more vulnerable. As if sensing this, Tilly Thornton gave another of her trademark high-pitched titters, clambered back inside the cab, and began manipulating the controls.

Heck tried again to struggle but, as he'd already surmised, it was futile.

354

With fresh clouds of exhaust from its rear, the harvester laboriously shifted its position – was it going to come at him from the side, as he'd feared? If so, there was no way to avoid it. Its wall of glinting blades cast a hypnotic spell as they rotated ever faster.

Chapter 32

'Well, well,' came a cheerful voice.

Heck could only look to his front, so he didn't see Charles Thornton until the combine harvester had chugged backwards for ten yards or more, and shut itself down.

As Tilly Thornton climbed out again, lithe and wiry as a monkey, her older brother wandered casually into view. He too wore grey farming overalls, the top three press studs of which were open, exposing a broad, bare chest, its thick, curling hair damp with sweat. Heck had the odd, brief notion that Thornton was naked underneath, a vaguely repugnant idea. He didn't know what Charles and Tilly had been doing in here while they were waiting for him to turn up, and now decided that he didn't want to know.

Thornton was armed. A rifle hung over his shoulder by its strap: a Remington 597, from what Heck could see. A man-stopper in any sense of the term.

'"You can lead a horse to water, but a pencil must be lead"?' Thornton said, addressing the quote to Heck as if it was a question. '"If you had a face like mine, you'd punch me right in the nose"? No?' He seemed disappointed. 'You didn't recognise any of those gags? Some of the best lines from the kings of slapstick comedy.'

'Sorry,' Heck said, eyeing his captors warily. The nylon tie across his forehead was agonising, especially as stinging sweat was dribbling down from it into his eyes.

'I suppose if I'd said "that's another nice mess you've got me into", that would have been too much of a giveaway?'

Heck tried to shrug.

Thornton shook his head. 'What a crying shame. How many other people could get a laugh by putting a human body through a sawmill? Or sucking some poor klutz down a pipe into the waste disposal system? How about dropping a pile of bricks through a chimney onto someone's head?'

'Before my time, that's all,' Heck said.

'Oh no . . . inspiration is timeless, Sergeant. But you already know that, don't you?'

'Well, yeah, I suppose. Yours goes all the way back to the eighteenth century, doesn't it?'

Thornton glanced at his sister. 'So he *did* get nosy.' He turned back to Heck. 'Meet Tilly, by the way.'

'Hi Tilly,' Heck said.

'Hi,' she said with mock-enthusiasm. Such ridicule didn't suit her. As he'd already observed, she was plain-looking with hard, lean features. The little girl from the Shetland pony photograph was vaguely recognisable, but all traces of pixie cuteness had gone. 'So you thought you'd check out my homework?' she said. 'I should never have left it lying around like that, but I'm such a messy person. I'm surprised you had the time, though, before Zara fucked your brains out.'

'She didn't do that.' Heck tried to feign disappointment. 'Was she supposed to?'

'She wasn't supposed to do anything. But she can't help herself.'

'Well . . . she *did* show me her bare bottom.'

Tilly hooted with laughter. 'I knew it. She is *such* a slapper. Don't be flattered though, Sergeant, seriously. You'd have been the eighth or ninth this month.'

'Suppose it was Zara who phoned ahead?' Heck said. 'Told you I was coming, eh?'

'No.' Tilly looked po-faced. 'She might've done if she'd thought you and me were an item; wanting all the sexy details, that kind of thing. She'd probably have rubbed one out while I was telling her. That's happened before now.'

'Nice . . .'

'But with you just being a copper and all . . .'

'So how did you know I was coming?'

'You can thank Iron Knickers Allacott for that. She sent me a text.'

If Heck had been able to, he'd have kicked himself. He should have realised the text sent by the Guildford concierge would have acted as a warning that he was en route.

'Good job for us she's so efficient, eh?' Tilly added. 'She's all bark and no bite, though. She lets us have blokes on the premises all the time. She can hardly object, you see. When her own boyfriend turns up and fucks her, she howls the place down—'

'This is all very interesting but it's hardly relevant,' Thornton interrupted, smiling broadly, though his smile didn't reach his eyes, which were fixed on Heck like a pair of gibbous moons. 'Find Sergeant Heckenburg's keys and move his car. Put it in one of the outhouses, so it isn't visible from the front. We can dispose of it properly later.'

Tilly hastened to obey, rifling Heck's pockets until she located his keys.

'And bring the stuff we talked about,' Thornton said.

The girl hurried off, leaving the barn through a side exit that had previously been concealed in shadow.

'You think dumping my car will save you?' Heck said. 'You seriously think I won't be missed? The rest of the team know exactly where I am. When I don't return, they'll come straight here, looking for me.'

'Sergeant Heckenburg – in the short time I've known you, there's been at least one attempt on your life. It seems you make enemies easily and widely. We may fall under suspicion for a time, but they won't be able to prove anything.'

'You won't have a chance to conceal the evidence, Thornton. They're on the way now. The whole shooting party.'

'Dearie me.' Thornton looked disappointed. 'If they were, would you really have just told me that they'll come here if you're missed? That was a poor effort, Sergeant. Nought out of ten. That said, I'm intrigued that you got here in the first place. You joined a lot of dots where there basically weren't any. Is that what you do, make lucky guesses?'

'Sometimes luck comes into it. For you too, I reckon.'

'Well of course. I mean, not every spectacular accident we've attempted to stage in the last few months has paid off. But that means it's all the more satisfying when it does.'

'You're round the bloody bend, pal.'

'Oh, I wouldn't say so.' Thornton sounded offended. 'I just enjoy myself. Course, not everyone gets it. I was thrown out of college, you know – Brasenose at Oxford – for being a practical joker. The old drawing pin on the chair routine, the old bucket over the vice-principal's door.' He sighed. 'My luck *really* ran out that day. No sense of humour, these upper-class toadies. Every one of them pointed the finger. I think they'd expected it to be water. When it turned out to be paint, they were a little freaked.'

'I'm talking about the incident at the bridge,' Heck said.

'Ah yes . . .' Thornton's expression lightened. 'Well, our luck was definitely in that day. Imagine how disconcerted I was when you turned up here, asking questions about Father, saying it might have been murder. And then all of a sudden someone attempts to kill you while you're with us – by setting up a ridiculous accident, no less! Coincidences *do* happen, you see. I must say, I thought that would put me in the clear. The way I dived into the river and heroically saved you. I wouldn't have done that in normal circumstances, you understand. But here was a chance I couldn't pass up. And then, Sergeant . . . *then* . . .'

He stepped out of sight, only to return half a second later with something in hand. Heck gazed in disbelief at his own laptop.

'I only found this when we went through the wreck of your car the day before yesterday,' Thornton said triumphantly. 'It was in the glove compartment, which is near enough airtight. Can you believe that? I mean water got in, obviously. But only a little bit. We managed to get it working again, and accessed all your recent reports.' Thornton shook his head. 'Never heard of encrypted files? How about security passwords? Slack work, Sergeant. Loose lips sink ships, and all that. Or at least they sank poor Vincent Budd.'

Heck could barely conceal his loathing. 'You chopped that poor bastard's hand off, didn't you?'

'Hmm. Bit risky, that. If the coroner buys that as death by misadventure, I think we'll need a new coroner, frankly.'

'I wonder what other murders-for-gain you've fitted into this pattern of yours?' Heck said. 'Your father's maybe?'

Thornton regarded him with interest. 'You know for a fact my father was murdered?'

'There may have been one unlikely coincidence on this farm, but I'm damn sure there weren't two.'

'Well, you're right of course. And your instincts were right when we chatted about it the other day. Father really should have been able to extricate himself from that valve before he got turned into a real-life windbag.'

'You held him down, I'm guessing?' Heck said.

'We knelt on him. Took both of us, because he put up quite a fight. Hence the bruising all over his body.'

'Must've felt good?'

'You don't know the half of it.'

'Just tell me one thing, Thornton: was that what all this was about? Killing your father and inheriting Thornton Farm?'

'I haven't inherited Thornton Farm.'

'No, but your mother's obviously suffered some kind of breakdown. I can't believe she'll stand in your way for long.'

Thornton regarded him carefully. 'There's something you need to know, Sergeant Heckenburg. My father was a complete domestic tyrant. I'm sure you've encountered those characters before?'

'Once or twice.'

'He was a violent pig, who would demand absolute obedience and would leather the living hide off you for the slightest infraction. But you know the worst thing about him?'

'I'm sure you're about to tell me.'

'It was the mental oppression he created. He had absolutely no sense of humour. He never smiled. Never found anything amusing.'

'A practical joker like you must have gone down a storm.'

Thornton shrugged. 'I'm no psychologist, you understand, but maybe Father was the origin of that? In a house where there is no natural laughter, you try to make your own. But we did love our little jests, my sister and I. Always have. Superglue on the cow's udders, cold tea in the whisky decanter – Father didn't drink whisky but he gave it to all his guests.' Thornton grinned at the thought. 'What else? Oh yes: salt

361

in the sugar bowl, sugar in the salt shaker, urine in the farm labourers' kettle . . .'

'You guys were an absolute scream.'

'The best one was the easiest. Locking the toilet door from the inside and climbing out through the window, so no one could go all day. That was Tilly's forte, she being so skinny and all.'

'Every one a winner, eh?'

Thornton shrugged again. '*We* thought it was funny. Course, with Father never laughing at anything, it made no difference whether he did or didn't. Apart from one year, I suppose, when he caught us sprinkling the barbecue coals with gunpowder. It wasn't even very dangerous, just some stuff we'd drained out of a few fireworks. It wouldn't have done any more than make a bit of smoke. But Father was *so* unimpressed. Not only did he give us both a whipping, he took away our entire video collection of slapstick classics – Laurel and Hardy, Buster Keaton, The Three Stooges, Norman Wisdom. I mean we'd only ever been able to watch that stuff in the attic, on the spare television – he couldn't stand to have it downstairs. But now he went a whole lot further. He burned it all on a bonfire. Made Tilly and me watch. Hundreds of pounds' worth of wonderful movies, bought over several years with our own hard-earned pocket money, off to the Film Vault Invisible.'

'And for that he was earmarked for destruction?' Heck said.

'Well that wasn't the only thing, but it didn't help his cause. You see, Sergeant, even when he wasn't dishing out the punishment, Father would subjugate us merely with his presence. He was that kind of dour, downbeat chap. We all lived in his shadow, under his thumb . . . though I suppose Mother was the real victim. And the main beneficiary.'

'Beneficiary?'

362

'She was a mouse, you see.' Thornton gave another of those soulless, pointless chuckles that his family seemed to specialise in. 'Barely there at the best of times. She obeyed without question. Father didn't just make all the important decisions in their lives, he made *all* the decisions. When he suddenly departed the scene after so many decades, well, she was hapless. Didn't know what to do with herself.'

'So now she takes her orders from you and Tilly?'

'More or less.' Thornton pondered this. 'Despite the shock-horror of it, I think she was quite happy to go along with the accident story. She could never stand the thought that *we* might have been the cause. Of course, *you* offered a brief glimmer of hope – if you'd named us as the culprits that would have taken the terrible responsibility away from her.'

'And the fact that *she* hadn't named you already was down to what – family loyalty?'

'Maybe. If so, we couldn't trust to that indefinitely. You see, Sergeant . . . you can be crafty with people, you can be clever, you can try to make them see things your way . . .'

'Assuming your mother was sane, I'd imagine that was fairly difficult.'

'She knew what a dull, brutish oaf Father was. As I say, she'd taken the brunt of it. But some people aren't . . . well, they're just not as ready to act the way others will.'

'Or as ready to get measured for a straitjacket.'

Thornton smiled again, but thinly, tolerantly. 'In the end, the best way to govern someone's actions is with force – or the threat of force.'

'Terrorise them, you mean?' Heck said. 'To the point where they're almost on the verge of collapse.'

'It's easier than you may think.'

'Especially when they know what you're capable of, eh?'

Thornton shrugged grandly. 'You can't beat making a good example of someone – or several someones.' His sister now re-entered through the side door, dragging a canvas holdall. 'Everything all right?' he asked.

'Fine. Mother's in bed.'

'No one else around?'

'I drove up to the road and back. It's all quiet.'

'You got the stuff?'

'It's all here.' She toed at the holdall.

'Excellent.'

Heck eyed the bag uneasily, but made an effort to focus on Tilly. Suddenly it seemed vital to keep them talking. 'Your brother's just been telling me about your plans. How you fabricated a series of accidental deaths to conceal the murder of your father, and had a few giggles along the way.'

'He got there in the end,' Thornton said. 'Even though most of it was guesswork.'

'Very little guesswork actually,' Heck retorted. 'The flaw in your plan was the murder of Harold Lansing. The fact that you made two attempts on his life indicated he was no random target. That he too was someone you *wanted* to eliminate. He was also the only other person on the list with any real connection to your family. The other deaths, though, were clever. A real double bluff. Even if a bright spark like me actually twigged they were deliberate acts, he'd go looking for some crazy trickster múrdering indiscriminately rather than someone looking to get rich quick. As grieving relatives of one of several victims, you and your sister could have hidden in plain sight.'

'Whether you guessed or not, you're remarkably close,' Thornton said. He glanced sidelong at Tilly. 'But I've often thought my father's policy was the best one. Give orders and leave *nothing* open for discussion.'

The girl cast her eyes down.

Heck fixed on her, sensing a possible weakness. 'So it was *your* idea to put Lansing on the list?'

She glanced back up. 'Harold Lansing was a complete shitarse!'

'That's not the impression I've had.'

'I don't care what impression you've had. I got arrested because of him.'

'You got off lightly, love.'

'Lightly?' She seemed genuinely astonished.

'You got a slapped wrist,' Heck said. 'They didn't even take your DNA. If they had done, we might've ended this bloody madness days ago.'

'I was grounded all summer, you bastard! I missed two weeks in Magaluf with my friends, which I'd been looking forward to since the previous January.'

'What . . . so you burned Lansing alive?'

'It was better than he deserved.'

'How about Dean Torbert? Was it better than *he* deserved?'

Tilly shrugged, as if she'd never given the other fatality in the accident a moment's concern. 'It was only the fate that loser would have brought on himself eventually.' Then she grinned. 'Masterclass in timing though, that one . . .'

'I *did* wonder how you pulled it off,' Heck admitted.

'It wasn't at all difficult.' Her grin curved into a crescent; it was like a jack-o-lantern as she enthusiastically recalled her and her brother's cleverness. 'Torbert studied political science, believe it or not. Couldn't have cared less about it, of course. Didn't turn up for lectures, missed his tutorials. But he liked his car, and he loved to show off. He was only a casual acquaintance, but when I intimated to him that we ran an illegal road-racing club he was very eager to join. I told him that all new members had to pass a test: a speed trial along a certain stretch of road we knew. One that was very private and very quiet.'

'Especially at seven in the morning, eh?' Heck said.

'Bang on, Sergeant. And each day he was there on the

dot. We told him he had to get from A to B in the shortest time possible. Of course we didn't tell him what the pass mark was, but said he had five chances – on five consecutive days—'

'Let me guess,' Heck interrupted. 'That was the five days Lansing's housekeeper and gardener were away on holiday?'

She grinned all the more. 'Very useful to us that old Mr Beetham, the gardener, kept his own personal schedule on a wall in one of his potting sheds. We were still at the planning stage, but we didn't have to poke around very hard to find it. Five days marked "Cornwall" gave us the perfect window of opportunity. But if the Beethams *hadn't* been coming home after that, we didn't think we'd be able to pull the deception off much longer, even if it was no dice. The weather, you see. Can't trust the weather forecast past five days in this country. Fine thing if it had started raining, and our mirror-photo still showed a nice sunny morning, eh? Unnecessary caution, as it turned out. We struck lucky on the fourth morning.'

'I'd say you were unlucky it took you that long,' Heck said, 'given how OCD Lansing was about leaving the house at seven each day.'

'Well of course; but we only knew that Lansing had survived his fishing accident, not that he'd been off work. We'd no idea the fourth day of the trial was Lansing's first day back in. So actually we hit the spot first time.'

'You must be proud.'

'Why not, it was a staggering result – a work of genius!'

'It was folly,' Thornton cut in. 'Totally unnecessary. I said so then and I say it again now. Apart from Father, all the victims should have been chosen at random. They should have been completely untraceable to us, and if we missed them, well no loss – there were always more fish in the sea. But alas . . .' Almost casually, he fidgeted with the rifle, knocking off its safety catch. His eyes briefly glazed. 'I gave in. I mean, what's a man to do, Sergeant? I should have put my foot down, but women can be so persuasive. We've always been close, my sister and I. Some would say too close, though I'd take issue with that. When you're under the knuckle all day, you seek comfort anywhere you can. Anyway, the point is that targeting Harold Lansing *was* undisciplined of us – but it was entirely my fault.'

'It'll be even more your fault if my body turns up riddled with .22 calibre slugs,' Heck said. 'You think they'll explain that away as an accident?'

That comment seemed to bring Thornton to the present. He restored the safety catch. 'Not at all, Sergeant. You've actually proved to me that the brightest thing about you chaps isn't your buttons. It's clearly the case that almost anything we do to you will be queried. However, we may still manage to mystify and confuse your people.'

He glanced at Tilly, who smiled excitedly and knelt down beside the holdall, from out of which she extracted a large metal funnel, some two feet in length and tapering from its wider end, which was about fourteen inches in diameter, to its narrow end, which was about five inches. Heck didn't know what this signified, but new chills ran through his body. He tested his wrists against the nylon ties, but there was no movement there. The planking to which they were fastened was equally unyielding.

'You really don't think someone's going to trace you at some point?' Heck said. 'You did these jobs in your own vehicle, for Christ's sake! That was one of the biggest clues we had. It'll be on film somewhere, along with its number plate.'

'Fake plates, Sergeant Heckenburg, fake plates,' Thornton replied. 'We're not completely stupid.'

Tilly stood up, tilting the funnel first one way and then

the other, but it was her brother who now stepped close to Heck, smiling – before delivering a crushing, two-handed blow with the butt of the rifle to the upper surface of his left foot.

Heck couldn't help it. He shouted out in agony, and in that same second Tilly shoved the narrow end of the funnel into his mouth, ramming it in several inches, squashing his tongue, wedging his jaws so wide apart that their hinges ached. Heck gagged and choked, tasting rust-flavoured saliva. He was still able to breathe, though the air rasped horribly in the funnel's interior. Barely able to move, there was nothing he could do to dislodge the thing, but perhaps to be on the safe side Tilly vanished again, only to reappear at his shoulder with a roll of duct tape, and wind strips of the stuff round the funnel and then round the slats to either side of Heck's head. She fastened it securely in place, angling it slightly upwards.

'I've often heard it said that police officers are big drinkers,' Thornton remarked, laying his rifle in the straw. He broke off to chuckle at the sight of Heck's eyes bulging. 'Oh, don't worry, Sergeant . . . if that were true, there'd be no mystery or confusion if they were to find you full to bursting with alcohol. So I'm hardly going to reach into Tilly's magic holdall and produce five crates of beer and six bottles of whisky. I love my old-time comedians, but I'm no Tommy Cooper.'

Tilly tittered again, but Thornton snapped his fingers and she scuttled back to the holdall, rooting inside and lifting something else out. When she brought this to her brother, Heck wasn't quite sure what he was initially seeing. It was a glass cylinder – it looked like an old jam jar with a removable lid. But there was something he couldn't at first identify inside it; a shapeless jumble of pinkish-grey digits, roughly the size of a child's hand. It was only when it twitched that a bolt of horror went through him.

'Allow me to introduce *Sicarius hahni*,' Thornton said, turning the jar slightly, to reveal air holes punched in its lid. 'Better known as the South African sand spider. We acquired a number of these exotic specimens a short time ago, and achieved one of our most spectacular results to date. Sadly, we weren't able to retrieve all the others before they perished in the winter cold. This one was inert for quite some time afterwards, but as you can see, with a bit of tender, loving care . . .'

The spider was now spread wide inside the jar, quivering.

Heck struggled wildly. The timber wall groaned and shuddered, but he was still immobile. He halted, sweating, eyes riveted on the jar. He then tried to clamp his teeth on the funnel, but didn't make an indent; tried to spit it out but it wouldn't budge.

Nightmare images of the murdered car thieves swam before his inner eye: tortured features; puffy, bloated flesh.

Tilly stood nearby with hands jammed into her overalls' front pockets. Her eyes and mouth widened with near-sexual excitement as Charles placed the jar against the rim of the funnel and slowly began to unscrew its lid.

'This is where the mystery and confusion come in,' he said in explanatory mode. 'You see, this little chap lives in the Kalahari Desert and has almost no contact with humans; which is a good thing, as a single bite will not just cause deep and widespread necrosis of the flesh, but also excessive blood-clotting. The ultimate outcome is cardiac arrest, but that won't occur with any kind of – what's the phrase, ah yes – merciful speed. Oh, and in case you were wondering, there's no known anti-venom.' Thornton chuckled. 'Just imagine, Sergeant, what they're going to think when they cut you open. They won't believe their eyes, and of course if you've already digested this little chap, they'll be even more baffled.'

With a gentle *plop*, the lid came free.

There was a *clink* of glass as the rim of the jar touched the rim of the funnel.

Heck could barely move, though his lungs were working with tremendous exertion. He couldn't see much because the upper part of the funnel screened the jar from him, but he could tell from the expression on Thornton's face, which was slowly lengthening and tightening as if he, like his sister, was approaching an orgasm, that he was carefully tilting it to the horizontal. There was a repeated tapping sound: Thornton's finger on the base of the jar.

Again Heck began struggling, fighting with every part of his body, and though there was some slippage of the cable tie round his ankles, from his waist up he was still held rigid. At any second he expected to hear the soft rumble of multiple legs in the funnel's interior – but before anything else could happen there came a shrill and frenzied jangling sound, so loud and unexpected that it drew a half-scream from Tilly.

Thornton jumped backwards. '*Damn and fucking blast!*' Froth spurted from his mouth. '*Goddamn blasting bloody hell fire!*'

With sharp jerks of his elbow, he screwed the jar's lid back into place. Despite the sweat stinging his eyes, Heck saw that the creature was still in its prison. He sagged in his bonds. That alone was such a relief that he could barely rationalise what had just happened. The alarm jangled again, this time protractedly. Heck glanced weakly up and spied a circular bell on a high beam, now being hammered by a clapper. An insulated cable snaked away from it along the bottom of an adjacent beam and vanished through a hole. Dully, he realised what this was: an extension of the farm-house front doorbell.

'Sodding, bloody, fucking hell!' Thornton snarled, rounding red-faced on his sister as if this was somehow her fault. His fury was so massive that she cowered away from him. 'Who the Goddamned bloody hell is calling at this fucking hour?'

She shook her head mutely.

'Go and see!' he bellowed. 'And make sure you get to the front door before that silly old bitch. Whoever they are, whatever they want, get rid of them! You understand?'

Tilly turned and scampered away.

'And go through the rear of the house!' he called after her.

She glanced back, white-cheeked.

'Just answer the door as if nothing's happening. Pretend you were in bed.'

She nodded and scuttled on, vanishing through the exit.

Thornton turned a glowering expression back to Heck. 'This is no more than a postponement, I assure you. You're still going to pay for your interference in our affairs.'

Chapter 33

Gail was uncomfortable ringing the farmhouse bell a third time; there was something annoyingly belligerent about people who hung on your doorbell – it put your back up before you'd even met them – but now at last she could hear movement inside the house. A series of chains and bolts were removed, and the door opened.

A girl in her early twenties stood there. Her short, fair hair was tousled and damp; her scanty nightwear revealed a spry, boyish figure.

'Can I help you?' she asked. Surprisingly for the hour, she looked neither groggy nor dazed.

'Hi.' Gail flashed her warrant card. 'Look, I'm so sorry about this. Detective Constable Honeyford, Surrey CID. I know it's terribly late, but I'm supposed to be meeting Detective Sergeant Heckenburg here?'

The girl looked confused. 'Detective Sergeant Heckenburg?'

'You know who I'm talking about? He was here a couple of days ago. The incident with the old bridge?'

'Oh yeah.' The girl still seemed vague. 'I think so.'

'You ought to.' Gail indicated the heaped sodden wreckage

on the drive. 'That's his Peugeot over there. I see you managed to drag it out of the river.'

'Oh yeah . . . *him*, yeah.'

Gail regarded the girl steadily, wondering why she wasn't buying this performance. The girl's nightwear consisted of a thin vest and a small pair of knickers, both of which were damp with sweat. That in itself wasn't necessarily suspicious. Some people preferred a hot bed, but somehow Gail wasn't convinced. Heck had definitely said he was coming here. It would be unlike him to change that plan without informing her.

'Do you mind me asking who I'm talking to?' Gail said.

The girl's face creased into a frown. 'I'm Tilly Thornton. This is my mother's farm, but in actual fact I do mind . . . at three o'clock in the morning. As you can see, Detective Heckenburg isn't here. He hasn't been here for several days.'

'Obviously there's been some kind of misunderstanding on my part.'

'An inexcusable one, if you don't mind my saying.' The girl folded her muscular arms. 'I'm going to have to ask you to leave. My father's only recently died, and my mother hasn't recovered from the shock of it yet. This is quite an intrusion.'

'As I say, I'm very sorry.' Gail still didn't step away. 'Just out of interest, is Charles Thornton on the farm at the moment?'

Tilly Thornton's expression hardened even more. 'Charles is in bed as well.'

'You see, he was one person Sergeant Heckenburg was definitely hoping to speak to.'

'That's as may be . . .'

'Would it be too much trouble to wake him up, and ask if there are any messages?'

'Yes it would. Of course it would.'

'Even if I was to tell you that this is really quite important?'

'This is ridiculous, that's what this is. Now I really wish you would leave. I've asked you once politely. Do I have to insist?'

She hasn't enquired what the problem is, Gail told herself. *Not once.*

'No, I'll go,' Gail said. 'As I say, I'm sorry for disturbing you.'

'You keep saying that, but you aren't actually leaving.'

Any normal person would be alarmed if the police called at their front door at three o'clock in the morning. At the very least, they'd want to know what it was all about. Yet Tilly Thornton has no apparent interest.

'I'll call again tomorrow,' Gail replied, pivoting away – but stopping when Tilly Thornton was halfway to closing the door. Tilly stopped too. They continued to eyeball each other.

She's very eager for this interview to end. Or she's very tired. And yet . . .

'Pardon me for saying this,' Gail said, 'but considering it's the early hours of the morning, you don't seem very sleepy.'

'You really are the limit! You come here at this hour—'

'Sorry Miss Thornton, but I have a job to do.'

'Why should I care about that?'

And still she doesn't enquire why I'm here.

'As I say, I'll speak to you tomorrow.' Gail turned and crossed the drive to her Punto, hearing the door thump closed. She glanced back at the farmhouse's windows to see if the chintz hangings might twitch. If they did, it was unnoticeable.

She climbed into her car and sat there, worried. Heck had the air of a disorganised cop, of an opportunist who made things up as he went along. But she was now aware this was a smokescreen; he was a clear-headed investigator who knew when to prioritise. If he'd said he was coming here in the small hours before dawn, there had to be a reason for it. It didn't add up that they'd neither seen nor heard from him. Not that there was much she could do at present. What was it that stupid girl had said – that she'd pushed things to the limit? That was true as well.

Gail switched the engine on. Her headlamps sprang to life, creating a tunnel of light along the side of the farmhouse. She peered down it absently, still wondering . . . wanting to drive away but some instinct preventing her.

'Well?' Thornton asked as his sister came back in, wearing slippers, knickers, and a vest.

'Another cop,' she said dismissively. 'A girl this time.'

Heck felt a brief surge of hope, though it was quickly dashed.

'I put her right,' Tilly added.

'What do you mean you put her right?' Thornton asked.

'She said she was supposed to meet Heckenburg here. I told her we hadn't seen him for days.'

Thornton pondered this uneasily; he didn't look as confident about it as his sister did. 'The main thing is she's gone now?'

Tilly nodded. 'I watched through the window. She sat in her car for a bit, but then drove off.'

Thornton still seemed unhappy, but glanced slyly at Heck. 'You may feel you have the upper hand here, Sergeant, but you haven't, I assure you.' He unscrewed the lid from the jar again.

As before, Heck set up a frantic struggling, though this time he put most effort into his legs. He'd already felt the cable tie loosen down there. It could never grip two separate limbs as tightly as one. With more strenuous efforts he might manage to yank his left foot clear, even if it was still throbbing from the blow it had taken. The problem now was time, because the jar was already open. Thornton flipped the lid away with his thumb. He took hold of the funnel, tilted it upwards and lifted the jar towards it.

'When they find you, Sergeant – *if* they find you – they'll link your death to those two car thieves'. But why should that worry us? Why should we want to hurt you? We're the ones who saved your life the first time and, as far as your colleague knows you didn't even arrive here tonight. You must have been attacked en route. Almost certainly by the same killer who's been staging disastrous accidents for his own demented pleasure.'

Heck caught another fleeting glimpse of the spider. It was spread out again, tautly, but now on the bottom of its glass prison, perhaps sensing that to leave such confinement would be the death of it. Impatiently, Thornton tapped the glass on the metal – once, twice, three times. The spider suddenly flirted forward, but clung to the jar's rim, a tangle of ungainly legs. Thornton shook the jar violently and shouted, only to be drowned out by a sudden, rising roar.

Heck recognised the roar for what it was before either of his captors did.

The engine of a fast-approaching car.

With a deafening *BOOM!*, the double doors exploded inwards. Broken chain and splintered woodwork flew in all directions as Gail's Punto came careering through. Its radiator grille had collapsed on impact, and now its front near side collided with the combine harvester's grain platform, the report like a hand grenade detonating.

More by instinct than logic, Tilly ducked, overbalanced, and staggered away at a crouch, though as she did she was able to scoop up the rifle. Her brother, initially too frozen to react, staring disbelievingly as the two smashed and tangled vehicles came to a rest together. His fixation lasted only a second, but it was all the time Heck needed. With a final, massive effort, he lugged his left foot loose from the cable tie, and swung it up in a straight-leg kick. He'd been aiming for Thornton's crotch, but his target jumped backwards. Instead, Heck struck the jar. The agony of such contact went through the damaged bones and cartilage in his foot like a pair of scissors, but the jar somersaulted up into the air, and its hideous occupant came pinwheeling out, landing with legs spread on Thornton's exposed chest, before scurrying down beneath the unbuttoned collar of his overalls.

The farmer reacted with frantic, desperate cries, slapping at his upper body and down around his crotch. A shrill squeal burst from his lips as the monster's fangs struck home. Now that Heck's legs were free, he wriggled and writhed energetically, though it didn't give him much extra leverage. He dragged with all his strength on the planking to which his arms were still bound – futilely, until help came from an unexpected source.

Tilly Thornton had backed away across the barn, her face etched with shock, but still with rifle in hand. Clearly she was torn: about whether to turn and run, or whether to aid her stricken brother.

'Kill them!' Charles howled in an unrecognisable castrato. 'Kill them . . .'

He sank to his knees, still clawing at himself, his features turning as grey as his overalls. In a kneejerk response, Tilly cocked the rifle and pegged off a round.

The powerful hollow-point slug struck the planking to the left of Heck's position and shattered it. Instantly, he was able to tear his left hand free, shucking off the cable tie. The right hand followed; he pulled the funnel from his mouth and flung it narrow end first at Thornton, catching him full in the face, smashing the bridge of his nose. Thornton rocked back on his knees, odious froth bubbling from his gaping mouth.

Tilly continued to retreat, rifle levelled, her attention divided between Heck, who'd ripped down a length of broken timber, jammed it behind the slat to which his neck was fastened, and begun crowbarring the structure apart, and Gail Honeyford, who'd now leaped from the Punto and, though sheltering on its far side, was shouting warnings.

'Put that bloody weapon down! There are police everywhere!'

Tilly winged a couple of shots at the Punto. Gail ducked as the remains of her windscreen were taken out. Heck at last loosened the final piece of planking, and threw off the nylon noose. He dropped to a crouch, but Tilly had started running – across the far end of the barn and out through the exit door again.

Gail vaulted over the crumpled bonnet of her car. 'You okay?' she said as Heck limped towards her.

'Yeah . . . yeah,' he stammered. 'How'd you know I was in here?'

'Saw your hankie lying outside. Spotted it just before I headed home.'

There was a gargled choking, and Charles Thornton twisted and jerked on the floor. His battered rictus of a face was now slathered with yellow/green goo, his mouth rimmed with blood. He jerked again as the hidden fangs savaged his flesh.

Only now did Gail seem to notice him. 'What's the matter with him?'

'He's getting intimate with a new friend.' Gail made to kneel down, but Heck stopped her. 'I wouldn't get too close. Apparently there's no anti-venom.'

'Anti-venom?'

Somewhere outside, an engine thundered to life.

'Never mind that.' Heck lumbered to the exit.

Gail hurried after him. 'Heck, if this girl's armed . . .'

'She's a murdering bitch, and she's going down.'

Outside, the summer night almost seemed cool after the fetid atmosphere in the barn. The vehicle they'd heard rev to life was a tractor. The light inside its cab showed Tilly Thornton hunched over the controls as it pulled slowly but steadily away across open pasture. It was already sixty or so yards ahead.

'Murdering cow!' Heck said again. 'She isn't getting away.'

Despite his injured foot, he ran in pursuit, sliding and tripping on the tussocky grass.

'Heck!' Gail shouted, following. 'Who are these people? Why've they done all this?'

'Because they could, Gail. Because they could – or so they thought.'

The rifle cracked, and a slug zipped between them. They dived and rolled for cover. The rifle cracked a second time. Another shot whistled past, this one so close to Heck's scalp that it almost parted his hair.

'Jesus!' Gail said. 'Is there more than one of them?'

'No, it's just her.' Heck got up and hobbled on. 'She'll have jammed the accelerator down. Used a shovel, or something. Come on, Gail – we've got the advantage.'

'Heck, she's got a rifle!'

'Yeah, but she's also lit up like a Christmas tree. We're not.'

The lights in the tractor's cab did give them a slight edge. They pursued it for maybe a hundred yards, slowly closing in before a third shot rang out, though this one was a speculator, the bullet going well wide. They were now close enough to see Tilly's wiry form as she clung to the open door of the cab, facing backwards. As they watched, she clambered up until she was on top of its roof, the rifle slung over her shoulder as if she was a commando. Once perched there, she began messing with some kind of appliance, rotating it to face them. It was almost too late when Heck realised what this was.

An ultra-strong floodlight blasted its beam towards them. He shouted at Gail that they should split up. But even as they ran zigzagging in opposite directions, further shots were fired, kicking up divots at their feet. Momentarily, the light turned entirely in Heck's direction. Another three shots rang out. He dived again, rolled again. Soil sprayed his face as a chunk of earth was torn smoking from its roots right in front of him. He heard the crazed laughter of the markswoman, though it slowly faded as the self-propelled vehicle drew further and further away, from thirty yards, to forty, to fifty.

The 597 Long Rifle had a maximum range of about two miles, Heck recalled from his firearms training. And it was anyone's guess how much ammo Tilly had.

He risked looking up. Far to his left, the spotlight spilled over undulating sward. Briefly, Gail was caught in its glare, half crouched. She attempted to dart away, and another shot sang out. Gail went down. Heck's breath caught in his throat, only for the policewoman to leap back to her feet and dash off in the other direction. The spotlight attempted to follow, but seemed unable to locate her. Exhausted, Heck pushed himself to another effort, straightening up and clumping on. The eye of the spotlight roved back towards him. It was searing bright, and rendered almost everything around it charcoal-black, though he could just about distinguish the tractor's awkward upright shape, jolting from side to side over increasingly rugged ground. Other objects slid into view alongside it: knotty pillars; heavy leafage.

Trees.

Though his left foot was agony – hurting so much that he grunted with every step, Heck increased his speed, closing the gap. If Tilly hadn't noticed she was heading into a wood because she was too busy watching her back, the tractor could easily collide with something. The spotlight flooded over him again. There was an instant muzzle-flash; Heck felt the bullet whip past his ear. As before, he tried to zigzag away – only for his right foot to plunge past its ankle into the depths of a rabbit hole.

He tried to drag it out again, but it was caught fast – he was held rigid in the light's full glare. Tilly Thornton had missed her targets when they were jumping about, but she couldn't be too bad a shot – she'd bagged the blimp from several hundred yards. He hunkered down, trying to crumple into a ball, but was still exposed. The hypnotic eye of the spotlight was fixed on him. Seconds passed in seeming slow-time as he sensed her taking careful aim.

'Shit,' he whispered.

The fatal shot was fired.

Yet the round didn't strike him. In fact, from the angle of the muzzle-flash, it looked as if the rifle was trained downwards. More shots followed – in rapid succession, all aimed down. Heck flinched each time, but could see no rhyme or reason to the fusillade, which continued unrelenting as though a spasmodic finger was locked on the trigger.

At last the magazine was spent.

Slowly, warily, Heck extricated his foot from the hole.

The lights of the tractor were still receding, more and more trees swimming into view to blot them out, but something told Heck there was no longer any need to rush. He advanced the last thirty yards at a walk, wafting through a pungent cloud of cordite.

'Heck?' came Gail's voice from the darkness to his left.

'It's okay,' he replied. 'The coast's clear.'

They could still hear the engine, a distant but dwindling rumble as the tractor trundled on across the farmland to who knew what destination.

'Oh my God,' Gail said when she finally joined him.

They gazed up at a lifeless, moonlit form dangling by its neck from a V-shaped crux in the lower boughs of a sycamore. It swayed in the strengthening summer breeze, the branch creaking. The empty rifle fell from the now nerveless trigger finger, dropping harmlessly to the ground.

'Oh my God,' Gail muttered again.

'Yep,' Heck agreed. 'He works in mysterious ways.'

Chapter 34

Freda Thornton was put into the back of a police car, apparently not knowing who she was or where she was, and in custody under the Mental Health Act. It was now well past dawn, but the various other police cars parked all over the Thornton farm continued to swirl their lazy, liquid-blue patterns through every nook and cranny and byre and outhouse. The dew-laden morning air was alive with radio static. Plain clothes were on site as well as uniform, not to mention crime-scene examiners, who'd arrived team-handed and were already cordoning off significantly large areas, both indoors and out, with rolls of fluorescent tape.

Detective Superintendent Gemma Piper stood alongside Detective Chief Inspector Will Royton as the bodies of Tilly and Charles Thornton, the latter of whom no longer looked human, were zipped into PVC bags and loaded into temporary caskets so the undertaker could remove them from the scene.

An ambulance waited on the drive in front of the main house. Heck sat on its rear step, a foil blanket draped across his shoulders, his leg propped up while a pretty young paramedic bandaged his left foot, which had swollen to about twice its normal size. She patiently explained for the third or fourth time that she didn't think a bandage would be sufficient.

'If this is just bruising, it's very extensive,' she advised him. 'You really should get along to A&E and have it X-rayed.'

'And then have to hobble around with a pot on my leg for the next six weeks,' he replied. 'No thanks. Even if it's broken, I can still put my weight on it. I've just chased a tractor half way from here to Sevenoaks. I'll be fine.'

She tut-tutted as she pinned the wrappings in place, and moved away. Heck pulled a sock back over it, only to groan when he realised that he wouldn't be able to fit it into his training shoe. He stood up tentatively. Now she mentioned it, the foot wasn't half hurting. It was possible the adrenalin of battle had subdued his earlier awareness of it. Gingerly, he took a step. *It's just about tolerable*, he thought. He took another step and grimaced with agony.

'You all right?' came a voice.

Gemma strolled along the drive towards him, hands in her overcoat pockets.

'Think I'll be limping for a couple of days,' he murmured.

She eyed him warily. 'I still find it amazing that all this carnage was acted out as cover for murder-for-money.'

He shrugged. 'I don't think it exactly came difficult to them. I mean, they turned Harold Lansing into a cheese toastie because Tilly Thornton missed a holiday. In all probability, they'd have kept adding people to the list who they had grievances against, real or imagined. More and more innocent bystanders would have got swept up. On which subject, Gordon Meredith is still in jail for something he didn't do.'

'I know,' Gemma said. 'I've been onto Joe Wullerton, and he's contacting the Home Office first thing. Should be grounds for a quick appeal, which most likely won't be opposed. *Should* be.' She sighed. 'I just hope you've got your paperwork straight, Heck, because CPS will have trouble believing this one – even from you.'

He took another careful step. 'You know me, ma'am. I always have my paper straight.'

'Yeah . . . eventually. After I've knocked it back about six times.' She glanced around at the house, its whitewashed walls tinged with gold in the rising sun. Bird twitters filled its shaggy eaves. 'Isn't the sort of place that routinely produces psychopaths, is it?'

'Takes all sorts.'

'Dunno – well-bred family. Moneyed. Educated. No history of abuse . . .'

'I'm not so sure about *that*.'

'Is a strict father an abusive father these days?'

Heck shrugged again. 'You want my take on this: goblins.'

Gemma arched an eyebrow. 'Excuse me?'

'You've never read Tolkien, or watched the Peter Jackson movies?'

'Yeah. What's that got to do with anything?'

'Goblins.' He gave it a little more thought. 'It's like humans are descended from earlier races. The good guys are descended from elves, the bad guys are descended from goblins.'

'I don't remember that in the movies.'

'It's something like that anyway.'

'You're trying to say that some people are just born bad?'

Heck nodded. 'It's particularly appropriate in this case. I mean, they got their kicks creating fatal accidents. That's kind of a goblin thing to do, isn't it? Or is that gremlins?'

'Heck, I thought you said you were okay?'

'I *am* okay.'

'When we get back to the Yard, I'm having you looked at.'

'Your prerogative, ma'am.'

'How's DC Honeyford anyway?'

'Why don't you ask her?'

'I'm asking *you*. I hear you and she worked pretty well together?'

'Nah . . . she doesn't like me much.'

'Well, that's easily explained. Will Royton tells me she's an excellent detective with great instincts and an admirable work ethic. But that she's also hot-headed, lacks discipline, goes at cases like a bull at a gate, is overly confident and has a dog's breakfast for a private life.'

Heck frowned as he sat himself back on the ambulance's rear step. 'I knew she reminded me of someone.'

'Exactly.'

'Excuse me, Gemma!' Will Royton called from the farmhouse doorway. 'Got my Chief Con on the phone. Any chance you can have a word?'

'Don't go anywhere,' Gemma told Heck, as she walked up the path. 'I'm driving you to hospital myself later on. Gonna make sure you get that foot X-rayed.'

'Ma'am, I don't—'

'And don't bloody argue. It's happening.'

As she vanished into the house, Gail came round the other side of the ambulance. She too was wrapped in a foil blanket. 'So you and me are alike, eh?' She sipped tea from a paper cup. 'I wasn't eavesdropping, but I couldn't help overhearing.'

'Eavesdrop away,' Heck replied. 'We're going to have to live in each other's pockets for the next few days to make sense of all this.'

'The spider's dead, by the way.'

'My heart bleeds.'

'Thornton squished it in his death throes.'

'He bought it surprisingly quickly.'

'Apparently it bit him sixteen times. It's a miracle he didn't go sooner.'

Heck pondered on that, and shuddered. 'Thanks for getting here when you did.'

She sat down on the step alongside him. 'I was only following your lead.'

'*You're* the one who called for an inventory of rifle owners.'

'Basic detective work.'

'Was it basic detective work that got you to the Blackwall Tunnel ahead of Julius Manko?'

'*You* mentioned the Tunnel first. I'd never have thought of it.'

'Yeah, but *you* got there.'

She stood up. 'Heck – stop this, will you!'

'Stop what?'

She turned her back on him. 'I don't need all this. Everything's scatty enough in my mind as it is.'

'Ahhh . . . what you mean is you don't need any help?'

She threw the cup aside. 'I don't need help I don't deserve.'

'You know, Gail.' Heck got painfully back to his feet. 'Your trouble is you're so busy telling people you can do this job on your own that you don't actually know you can. After all this, you'll have nothing to prove to anyone. So why don't you just chill out and enjoy the moment?'

She glanced at him, pale faced but with bright dots of pink on either cheek. 'You think I'm too inexperienced to apply for the Serial Crimes Unit?'

'Well, Gemma's impressed by you, I can sense that. But the answer's probably yes. I also think it'll look like you're running away. You've got some business you need to sort out down here first.'

'Yeah.'

'But you top and tail that bastard, Pavey, and you show his mates that you don't give a crap what they think; that you're a Surrey Police detective and you're going to keep on doing that job to the best of your ability regardless of any

387

shit they try and pull behind your back – and you do all that to your own satisfaction. No one else's. Yours. You do all that, then you give me a call and I'll give you a heads-up the first vacancy we get. But I'll tell you now, SCU is no easy ride. There'll be zero chance of promotion and when Gemma's on the warpath there isn't a beating you won't take.'

'If you can hack it, so can I,' Gail said.

Heck smiled. A few days ago he'd have scoffed at that, but she didn't need to say it twice now. The spell broke as Gemma came briskly back out of the farmhouse, car keys in hand. 'You ready?' she asked.

'Yes, ma'am,' Heck said.

Gemma deigned to notice Gail. 'Well done, DC Honeyford.'

'Thank you, ma'am.'

'Seems you both had a couple of close shaves this morning.'

'All in a day's work, ma'am.'

Gemma eyed her dubiously. 'Really? Well, there's no rest for the wicked. Your DCI would like a chat inside.'

Gail nodded and headed into the farmhouse. Gemma strode to her Mercedes, Heck limping after her. She offered to help him climb in, but he declined.

When they were seated alongside each other, she said: 'I've just had it explained to me in no uncertain terms that two respected members of the country set have died today. So when this story breaks, they're going to come at us from every angle.'

Heck shrugged. This was only to have been expected.

She glanced at him. 'So regardless of whether or not you've got a pot on your leg, I want to know for sure that your head's in the right place?'

'You've got it, ma'am.'

'You and me had a big fall-out last year, Heck, for which we were both partly at fault. I don't want that again. If you're staying in SCU, I want us all on the same side, I want

388

no one harbouring any grudges; I want you to be a good little soldier.'

He nodded.

'And no more talk about goblins or gremlins?'

'Promise.'

She arched an eyebrow again.

'I promise,' he said.

'Okay.' She put the Merc in gear. 'Let's do it.'

Can't wait for the next Heck
instalment?

Read on for an exclusive glimpse
of the next book in the series,

The Burning
Man

Chapter 1

Barrie and Les saw customer care as an essential part of their role as porno merchants.

Some might laugh at that notion, given pornography's normal place in the world. It was all very well people pretending it was near enough respectable now, but the reality was that even if you used porn, you tended not to talk about it; that you weren't generally interested in building a rapport with the providers – you just wanted to acquire your goods and go (said goods then to reside in a secret compartment in your home where hopefully no one would ever find them). No, one wouldn't normally have thought this a business where the friendly touch would pay dividends, but Barrie and Les, who'd jointly and successfully managed their street-corner sex shop for twelve years, didn't see it that way at all.

Certainly Barrie didn't, and he was the thinker of the twosome.

In Barrie's opinion, it was all about improving the customer's experience so that he would happily return. *Happily . . .* that was the key. Yes, it was about providing quality material, but at the same time doing it with a smile and a quip or two, and being helpful with it – if someone requested information or advice, you actually tried to assist, you didn't just stand there with that bored, bovine expression so common among service industry staff throughout the UK.

This way they'd more likely buy from *Sadie's Dungeon* again – it wasn't difficult to understand. And it worked.

Even in 2015, there was something apparently disquieting about the act of buying smut. Barrie and Les had seen every kind of person in here, from scruffy, drunken louts to well-dressed businessmen, and yet all had ventured through the front door in similar fashion: rigid around the shoulders, licks of sweat gleaming on their brows, eyes darting left and right as though fearful they were about to encounter their father-in-law – and always apparently eager to engage in an ice-breaking natter with the unexpectedly palsy guys behind the counter, though this was usually while their merchandise was being bagged; it was almost as if they were so relieved the experience was over that they suddenly felt free to gabble, to let all that pent-up tension pour out of them.

It was probably also a relief to them that *Sadie's Dungeon* was so neat and tidy. The old cliché about sex shops being seedy backstreet establishments with grubby windows and broken neon signs, populated by the dirty raincoat brigade and trading solely in well-thumbed mags and second-hand video tapes covered in suspiciously sticky fingerprints, was a thing of the past. *Sadie's Dungeon* was a clean, modern boutique. Okay, its main window was blacked-out and it still announced its presence at the end of Buckeye Lane with garish, luminous lettering, but behind the dangling ribbons in the doorway, it was spacious, clean and very well-lit. There was no tacky carpet here to make you feel physically sick, no thumping rock music or lurid light show to create an air of intimidation. Perhaps more to the point, Barrie and Les were local lads, born and raised right here in Bradburn. It wasn't a small borough as Lancashire towns went – more a sprawling post-industrial wasteland – but even for those punters who didn't know them, at least their native accents, along with their friendly demeanour, evoked an air of familiarity. Alright, it was possible to overegg that pudding. It didn't exactly instil what you'd call a family atmosphere in *Sadie's Dungeon*, but it meant there was something a little more welcoming about it, a little more wholesome.

'Fucking shit!' Les snarled from his stool behind the till. 'Bastard!'

'What's up?' Barrie said, only half hearing.

'Fucking takings are crap again.'

'Yeah . . .?' Barrie was distracted by the adjustments he was making to the Christmas display.

It was early December, and though it might seem incongruous for a sex shop to stick holly over its autographed porn-star wall-posters, and even stand a large Christmas tree in one of its corners (hung with miniature sex toys instead of ornaments), Barrie held a different view. As far as he could see, hardly anyone believed in God anymore, but that didn't stop the entire population of the town getting embarrassingly pissed on Christmas Eve, unwrapping a pile of prezzies on Christmas morning, and stuffing themselves to the gills with turkey and plum duff at Christmas teatime. How was this any more hypocritical? Besides, Barrie thought this particular display one of the better ones he'd constructed. It was located right at the front of the shop, at the top end of the central aisle so that it would strike the punters as soon as they walked in. It consisted of a life-size cardboard cut-out muscle man, laughing and naked, with a fake white beard glued on, and a metal peg pushed through at his groin, over the top of which a Santa hat had been draped to create the impression it was concealing an upright member. At his feet, a large red bag trimmed with white fur spilled out a heap of newly-imported American DVDs, all at special holiday prices. Above the muscle man's head hung a bunch of mistletoe, and over the top of that a row of flashing fairy-light letters read:

CHECK OUT SANTA'S SACK

Of course, Les had a point. Even the rapid approach of Christmas was no real consolation when the shop's takings were consistently poorer than they'd used to be. When *Sadie's Dungeon* had first opened, sales had initially been great, but ever since then – thanks mainly to the internet, and despite the lads' conscientious customer care routine – business had declined.

'We're not beaten yet,' Barrie replied, determinedly relaxed about it. 'The new rules will level the playing-field a little. Let's just see how it all pans out.'

He was referring to recent legislation aimed at internet porn producers, which abolished the depiction online of certain 'extreme' sexual activities, and thus pulled them into line with those BBFC prohibitions already in force where DVDs were concerned, so though porn fans the country over were outraged that their private recreation was yet again being meddled with by government, it was actually a positive where the shop-counter trade was concerned.

Or so Barrie said. And though Les wasn't entirely sure the benefits from this would feed through any time soon, he tended to listen to Barrie, who was undoubtedly the brains behind *Sadie's Dungeon*, and in Les's eyes a very smart cookie. He was also a grafter, getting stuck in wherever needed. Even now, though it was past seven o'clock, Barrie wasn't finished. All across the shop, the product was marked and racked in easy-to-find sections: *Bangin' Babes*, *Horny Housewives*, *Glamour Grans*, *Tearaway Teens* – Barrie sidled from one to the next, fastidiously checking that everything was as it should be after the usual day's fingering and fondling by the customers, and swiftly rearranging stuff where it wasn't.

'Sonja, we're almost done!' Les shouted down the corridor behind the counter.

''Kay . . . getting dressed,' came a female voice.

Which was when the bell rang as the shop's outer door was opened. The icy December breeze set the ribbons fluttering as a bulky shape backed in, lugging something heavy behind him.

'Sorry, sir . . . we're closing,' Les called.

The customer halted but didn't turn around; he bent down slightly as if what he was dragging was cumbersome as well as heavy. They now noticed that under his massive, silvery coat, he wore steel-shod boots and baggy, shapeless trousers made from some thick, dark material.

'Sir, we're closed,' Barrie said, approaching along the right-hand aisle.

Where Les was short, stocky and shaven-headed, Barrie was six-three and, though rangy of build with a mop of dark hair and good looks, his background was not the best – he knew how to use his height, how to impose himself. 'Hey, excuse me . . . *hey mate!*'

The figure continued to back into the shop, the door jammed open behind him, letting in a steady waft of wintry air. When he straightened up, they saw that he was wearing a motorcycle helmet.

'Shit!' Les yanked open a drawer and snatched out a homemade cosh, a chunk of iron cable with cloth wrapped around it.

Barrie might have reacted violently too, except that as the figure pivoted around, the sight froze him where he stood. He wasn't sure what fixated him more, the extended, gold-tinted welder's visor riveted to the front of the intruder's helmet, completely concealing the features beneath, or the charred-black steel muzzle now pointing at him, the rubber pipe attachment to which snaked back around the guy's body to a wheeled tank at his rear.

Les shouted hoarsely as he lifted the counter hatch, but it was too late.

A gloved finger depressed a trigger, and a fireball exploded outward, immersing Barrie head to foot. As he tottered backward, screeching and burning, it abruptly shut off, swirling oil-black smoke filling the void. The intruder advanced, a second discharge following, the gushing jet of flame expanding across the shop in a ballooning cloud, sweeping sideways as he slowly turned, engulfing everything in its path: the muscle guy with the peg penis; the orderly rows of DVDs, the shelves lined with books and magazines, the displays of skimpy undies. Les flung his cosh, missing by a mile, and then ran across the back of the shop, stumbling for the exit. But the intruder followed, weapon levelled, squirting out a fresh torrent of fire, dousing him thoroughly as he hung helplessly on to the escape bar.

The Christmas tree, already a glowing skeleton, collapsed in the corner. The suspended ceiling crashed downward, its warping tiles exposing hissing pipework and sparking electrics. But the intruder held his ground, a featureless rock-like horror, hulking, gold-faced, armoured against the debris raining down from above, insulated against the heat and flames. Slowly, systematically, he swivelled, pumping out further jets of blazing fuel, bathing everything he saw until the inferno raged wall to wall, until the room was a crematorium, the screaming howl of which drowned out even those shrieks of the two shop-managers as they tottered and wilted and sagged in the heart of it, a pair of melting human candles . . .

Chapter 2

The quarter of Peckham where Fairfax House stood was not the most salubrious. To be fair, this whole district of South London had once been renowned for its desolate tower blocks, maze-like alleys and soaring crime rates. That wasn't the whole story these days. It was, as so many internet articles liked to boast, 'looking to the future', and its various regeneration projects were 'well under way'. But there were still some pockets here which time had left behind.

Like the Fairfax estate, the centrepiece of which was Fairfax House.

A twelve-storey residential block, a literal edifice of urban decay, it stood amid a confusion of glass-strewn lots and shadowy underpasses. Much was once made in the popular press of the menacing gangs that liked to prowl this neighbourhood, or the lone figures who would loiter on its corners after dark, looking either to mug you or sell you some weed, or maybe both, but the sadder reality was the sense of hopelessness here. Nobody lived here, or even visited here, if they could avoid it. Several entire apartment houses were now hollow ruins, boarded up, vandalised and awaiting demolition.

At least Fairfax House had been spared that indignity.

Darkness had now fallen, and various lights showed from its grotty façade, indicating the presence of a few occupants. There were several cars parked on the litter-strewn cul-de-sac out front, and even a small sandpit and a set of swings on the grass nearby, fenced off by the residents to keep it free from condoms and crack phials. Even so, this wasn't the sort of place one might have expected to find John Sagan.

A high-earning criminal, or so the story went, Sagan would certainly value his anonymity. Unaffiliated to any gang or syndicate, he was the archetypical loner. He wasn't married as far as the Local Intelligence Unit knew; he didn't even have a girlfriend, or boyfriend for that matter. In looks – at least, from the photographic evidence provided to the surveillance teams – he was a bespectacled, mousy-looking man who worked by day as an office admin assistant, and as such seemed to lead a conventional nine-'til-five existence. This, presumably, was the main reason he'd flown beneath the police radar for as long as he had. But even so, it was a hell of a place he'd found to bury himself in. It wouldn't appeal to the average man in the street. But then, contrary to appearances, there was nothing average about John Sagan. At least, not according to the detailed statement Heck had recently taken from a certain Penny Flint, a local streetwalker of his acquaintance.

Heck, as his colleagues knew him – real title Detective Sergeant Mark Heckenburg – was currently ensconced in Fairfax House himself, though in his case lolling on a damp, badly-sprung sofa on the lower section of a split-level corridor on the third floor. Immediately facing him was the tarnished metal door to a lift that had malfunctioned so long ago even the *Out of Order* notice had fallen off. On his right stood a pair of fire-doors, complete with glass panels so grimy you could barely see through them; on the other side of those was the building's main stairwell. It was a cold, dank position, only partly lit because most of the bulbs on this level were out. No doubt, the ghastly hunk of furniture Heck was slouched upon would be flea-infested – who knew who'd thrown it out, or why – but it was December now, the barometer hovering just above zero, and most likely every bug in London was frozen to immobility.

Heck certainly was, or near to that.

He'd been here the best part of the afternoon, with only a patched-up jumper, a pair of scruffy jeans, a raggedy old combat jacket and a woolly hat to protect him against the cold. He didn't even have fingers in his gloves, or socks inside his rotted, toeless trainers. Of course, just in case all that failed to create the impression he was a hopeless wino, he hadn't shaved for a week or combed his hair in several days, and the half-full bottle of water tinted purple to look like Meths hanging from his pocket wasn't so wrapped in greasy newspaper that it wouldn't be spotted.

The guise had worked thus far. Several of the gaunt individuals who inhabited the building had been and gone during the course of the day, and hadn't given him a second glance. But of John Sagan there'd been no sign. Heck knew that because, from where he was slumped, he had a good vantage along the passage, and number 36, the door to Sagan's flat, which stood on the right-hand side, hadn't opened once since he'd come on duty that lunchtime. The team knew he was in there – officers on the previous shift had made casual walk-bys, and had heard him moving around. But he was yet to emerge.

Heck knew he would recognise the guy, having studied the photographs carefully beforehand. Purely in terms of looks, Sagan really was the everyday Joe: somewhere in his mid-forties, about five-eight, of medium build, with a pudgy face and thinning, close-cropped fair hair. He usually wore a pair of round-lensed, gold-rimmed spectacles, but otherwise had no distinguishing features; no tattoos, no scars. And yet, ironically, it was his workaday clothing that was most likely to make him stand out. In his efforts to look the part-time clerk he actually was, Sagan favoured suits, shirts, ties and leather shoes, and if it was cold or raining outside, an overcoat. But that wasn't the regular costume in this neck of the woods. Far from it.

And yet this was only one of many contradictions in the curious character that was John Sagan.

For example, who would have guessed that his real profession was torturer-for-hire? Who would have known from his outward appearance that he was a vicious sadist who loaned his talents to the underworld's highest bidders, and performed his unspeakable skill all over the country?

Heck wouldn't have believed it himself – especially as the Serial Crimes Unit had never heard about John Sagan before – had the intel not come from Penny Flint, who was one of his more trustworthy informants. She'd even told Heck that Sagan had a specially adapted caravan called the 'Punishment Room', which he took with him on every job. Apparently, this was a mobile torture chamber, kitted on the inside with all kinds of specialist devices, ranging from clamps, manacles and cat o'nine tails, to pliers, drills, surgical saws, electrodes, knives, needles and, exclusively for use on male victims, a pair of nutcrackers. To make things worse, and apparently to increase the sense of horror for those taken inside there, its whole interior was spattered with dried bloodstains, which Sagan purposely never cleaned off.

Penny Flint knew all this because, having offended some underworld bigwig, she herself had recently survived a session in the Punishment Room – if you could call it surviving; when Heck had gone to see her in her Brixton flat, she'd been on crutches and looked to have aged thirty years. She'd advised him that there were even medical manuals on shelves in the Punishment Room to aid Sagan in his quest to apply the maximum torment, while its central fixture was a horizontal

X-shaped cross, on which the victims would be secured with belts and straps. Video feeds of each session played live on a screen positioned on the ceiling overhead, so the victim could watch in close detail as they were brutalised.

As he waited there and watched, and took another swig of 'Meths', Heck recollected the initial reaction back at the Serial Crimes Unit, or SCU as it was commonly known in police circles, when he'd first broken the story . . .

'Why haven't we heard about this guy before?' DC Shawna McCluskey wanted to know.

Shawna had grown increasingly cynical and pugnacious the longer she'd served in SCU. These days she never took anything at face value, but it was a fair question. Heck had asked the same of Penny Flint when he'd been to see her. The primary explanation – that Sagan was an arch-pro and that those he was actually paid to kill were disposed of without trace – was viable enough. But the secondary explanation – that he'd mostly tended to punish gangland figures who'd betrayed or defied their bosses, and so those who were merely tortured and then released would be unwilling to blab – was less so. Contrary to popular belief, the much-mythologised code of silence didn't extend widely across the underworld. But then, Heck supposed that Penny Flint had been the proof of that. From what she'd told Heck, she'd had no idea who Sagan initially was and had merely thought him another customer. She'd gone off with him voluntarily to perform a sex service, or so she'd expected. When they'd arrived at what she assumed was his caravan sitting on a nondescript back-street in Lewisham, she'd had no idea what was inside it or what would happen to her when she got in there.

Perhaps if he'd simply beaten her up, Penny would have accepted it as justified punishment for a foolish transgression, but Sagan was nothing if not a conscientious torturer. In her case, once he'd got her tied up and helpless, it had been specifically sexual – the idea being, not just to hurt her in a deep and lasting way, but to deprive her of an income afterwards. And that was too much to tolerate.

'Why is Flint tipping us the wink now?' Detective Superintendent Gemma Piper, head of SCU, asked. 'She must've known about this guy for ages.'

'In this case I think it's personal, ma'am,' Heck replied.

'That won't cut it, Heck . . . we need specifics.'

'Well . . . she wasn't very forthcoming on the details, but she's got a kid now. A baby . . . less than one year old.'

'Bloody great!' DC Gary Quinnell chipped in. A burly Welshman and a regular attender at Chapel, he was well known for tempering his sometimes brutal brand of law-enforcement with Christian sentiment. 'God knows what kind of life that little mite's going to have.'

'The first thing it's going to get acquainted with is the Food Bank,' Heck replied. 'By the looks of Penny, she won't be working the streets any time soon. Unless she can find some johns who like getting it on with cripples.'

Gemma shrugged. 'So she's got a child and suddenly she's lost her job. Perfect timing. But how does grassing on John Sagan help with that?'

'It doesn't, ma'am. But Penny isn't the sort to go down without a fight. She told me that if she isn't good for the game anymore, she'll make sure this bastard's put out of business too.'

'So it's purely about revenge?' Gemma still sounded sceptical.

'Penny's an emotional girl, ma'am. I wouldn't like to get on the wrong side of her.'

It hadn't been a lot to go on, but it had been a start. Heck had touched other snouts for info regarding Sagan, but none had been prepared to talk. At least, not as much as Penny Flint. She'd given them the suspect's description, his home address, his place of work and so forth. In fact, just about the only thing she hadn't been able to deliver was the

Punishment Room, which he supposedly kept in a lock-up somewhere else in South London, though its actual location was his best-kept secret. They'd searched hard. But no avenue had led to his ownership of any kind of vehicle other than a battered old Nissan Primera, which he'd owned since 2005 and which was parked outside Fairfax House at this very moment. Of course, it didn't help that Penny Flint had no VRM for the Punishment Room. It had been late at night when Sagan had taken her to it, and not knowing what was about to happen, she hadn't been paying attention to detail.

This was no minor problem, of course. Despite the medical evidence proving Penny had been severely assaulted, without the Punishment Room there was nothing to physically link this act to John Sagan. It would be her word against his, and on that basis no prosecution would ever proceed.

'We need that caravan,' Gemma said. 'We could raid his flat, but what would be the point? If this guy's as careful as Flint says, every incriminating thing in his life is stored in this so-called Punishment Room.'

With regard to Sagan himself, it was highly suspicious how clean he seemed to be. No criminal record was one thing, but his employment, financial and educational histories were also unblemished. The guy appeared to have led a completely uneventful life, which was almost never the case with someone involved in violent crime.

'What we've got here is a real Jekyll and Hyde character,' Heck declared. 'Openly a picture of respectability, deep down – very deep down – a career degenerate.'

'Inspired comparisons with cool horror stories don't make a case,' Gemma replied. 'We still need that caravan.'

Short of putting out public appeals, which was obviously a no-no, they did everything in their power to locate the Punishment Room, but still came up with nothing. However, when Heck went to visit Penny Flint a second time, now in company with Gemma, it was the prostitute herself who made a suggestion.

'Why don't I just piss the local mob off again?' she said. 'They'll send him to teach me another lesson, and then you can nab him.'

'What are you talking about?' Heck asked.

'Christ's sake, Heck, this is easy. After he finished with me last time . . . I was half dead, but still conscious enough to listen to his threats. "If I need to see you again, it won't end so well," he said. And he really meant it, I'll tell you.'

'Who paid him to do that to you?' Gemma wondered.

'Don't be soft,' Penny snorted. 'I'm not telling you that.'

'Okay . . . no names, but what did you do to annoy them?'

'Gimme a fucking break, Miss Piper . . .'

'Hey!' Gemma's voice adopted that familiar whip-crack tone. 'We're not here at your disposal, Miss Flint. Our job is to enforce the law, not pay off private scores. And we can't do that flying blind. At present we don't even know who you are, never mind John Sagan. So the least you can do is enlighten us a little.'

Penny glanced at Heck. 'You gave me your word I'd be immune from prosecution if I helped you out with this . . .?'

Heck shrugged. 'Unless you've done something very serious, we're only interested in Sagan.'

'Okay, well . . .' She hesitated, briefly. 'Doing a bit of delivering, wasn't I?'

'Delivering what?' Gemma asked. 'Drugs? Drugs money?'

'Bit of both. You know the scene.'

'And let me guess, you were skimming?'

'What else?' Penny's cheeks reddened. 'Hey . . . you're looking at me like I'm some kind of criminal.'

Neither of the two cops commented, though both wanted to. Even so, she detected the irony.

'Don't get smarmy on me, Heck. Look at the state I'm in.

406

'I'm past forty. Even before that bastard Sagan tore my arse and pussy inside-out, how much shelf-life did I really have left? Anyway . . . I thought I'd been careful. Thought no one'd notice, but they did. And . . . well, you know the rest.'

'And you're seriously saying this firm would trust you with that job again?' Heck said.

'Yeah.' She seemed surprised he'd ask such a question. 'Sagan's a scary guy. They're sure I'll have learned my lesson.'

'And what you're proposing is to commit exactly the same offence all over again?' Gemma said. 'Even though you know what the outcome will be?'

'The difference is this time you lot'll be sitting on Sagan, won't you? You can jump on him as soon as he gets his Punishment Room out.'

They were impressed by her courage – in fact they were quietly startled by it. Heck wondered if her desire for revenge was getting the better of her common sense, to which she merely shrugged.

'Heck . . . we both want the guy gone. The only way we can make that happen legally is for you to catch him in the act with his Punishment Room. This is the quickest and most obvious way to make that happen.'

'Miss Flint,' Gemma said. 'This time you may have pushed things too far. He could just shoot you through the head.'

'Nah. The firm I'm talking about like to make a show. Besides . . . Punishment Room, gun? Why will it matter? Like I say, you lot'll jump on him.'

It had sounded simple initially, but of course there were complicating issues. The fact that, by her own admission, Penny Flint had been stealing from an underworld bigwig would make her an unreliable witness in a court's eyes. It would also allow the defence to accuse the police of conspiracy for 'encouraging' her to do this again. But then, if the team could write up their interest in Sagan as an anonymous tip-off, and go solely on any evidence they found inside the Punishment Room, they might be able to keep Penny Flint out of it altogether. Despite that, the risks of using a female civilian as bait would be extraordinary. Since the operation had gone live four days ago, Gemma had assigned a round-the-clock armed guard to her flat – all covertly of course, which had added an extra dimension of difficulty.

The same applied to the stake-out at Sagan's flat.

Thus far, in addition to slumping on this ratty old couch in his state of feigned inebriation, Heck had kept watch from behind a window in the empty low-rise on the other side of the cul-de-sac, and had sat for another eight hours in the back of a shabby old van parked right alongside Sagan's Primera. Other detectives in the surveillance team had spent hours 'fixing' a supposedly broken-down lorry on the same street, while another one – Gary Quinnell of all people, all six-foot-three of him – had donned a hi-viz council-worker jacket in order to sweep gutters and pick litter. The common factors had always been the same: damp, cold, the soul-destroying greyness of this place, and then the smell – that eerie whiff of decay that always seemed to wreathe run-down buildings. The word 'discomfort' didn't cover it; nor 'boredom'. Even their awareness that at any minute they could be called into action – an awareness that was more acute than normal given that every officer here was armed – had gradually faded into the background as the minutes had become hours and, ultimately, days.

Heck shifted position, but in sluggish, slovenly fashion in case someone was watching. He hitched the Glock under his right armpit. It wasn't a familiar sensation. Though every detective in SCU was required to be firearms-certified, and they were tested and assessed regularly in this capacity, he for one had rarely carried one on duty. In these days of specialist firearms teams, the gunplay tended to be left to the real experts – the heavily armed ex-military lads, who basically lived for it and would turn up at every incident looking like the SAS. But this was an unusual, open-ended operation, which no one was even sure would bring a result. Gemma had opted for pistols purely for self-defence purposes, thanks to Sagan's deadly reputation – though again there was no certainty that reputation had been well-earned.

And this lack of certainty was the real problem. There was no way Gemma would commit so many SCU resources to this obbo indefinitely. She was on the plot herself today, having arrived early afternoon, and was now waiting in an unmarked command car somewhere close by. That wasn't necessarily a good sign – it might be that she'd finally put herself at Ground Zero to get a feel for what was going on, maybe with a view to cancelling the whole show. On the other hand, it could also mean that Sagan's non-appearance today – all the previous days of the obbo he'd gone to work as usual – might mean something was afoot. They knew he only worked at his official job part-time, so perhaps to maintain the impression of normality he would only indulge in his extra-curricular activities on one of his days off.

Heck chewed his lip as he thought this through.

Penny Flint reckoned she'd dipped again into her employers' funds some four days ago. The retribution could come at any time, but if Sagan was a genuine pro he wouldn't respond with a kneejerk reaction. He'd strike when the time most suited him – not that they'd want him to leave it too long. That could be inviting the bird to fly.

'*Sorry to break radio silence, ma'am,*' the voice of DC Charlie Finnegan crackled in Heck's left ear. '*But two blokes have just gone in through the front door of Fairfax House, male IC1s, well-dressed . . . too well-dressed if you know what I mean. Can't help thinking I recognise one of them, but I'm not sure where from, over.*'

There was a brief lull, and then Gemma's voice responded: *'Be advised all units inside . . . we may have intruders on the plot. Could be nothing, but stay alert. Charlie, did these two arrive in a vehicle, over?'*

'Negative, ma'am . . . not that I saw. They approached from Parkinson Drive, which lies adjacent to Fairfax House on the southeast side. I'm making my way around there now, over.'

'Roger that . . . PNC every vehicle parked, and make it snappy. Heck, you in position?'

'Affirmative, ma'am,' Heck replied quietly – he could hear a resounding clump of feet and the low murmur of voices ascending the stairwell on the other side of the fire-doors. He checked his cap to ensure it concealed his earpiece. 'Sounds like I'm about to get company.'

'Received, Heck . . . all units stand by, over.'

The airwaves fell silent, and Heck slumped back onto his sofa, eyelids fluttering as though he was in a drunken daze. The footfalls grew louder, and then the fire-doors swung open and two shadowy forms perambulated into view. In the dim light and with his vision partly obscured, Heck wasn't initially able to distinguish them, though from their low Cockney voices he could tell they were both males, probably in their thirties or forties.

'Q&A session first, alright?' one said to the other. 'Don't let on we know anything . . .'

For a fleeting half-second the twosome were more clearly visible: shirts, sports jackets, ties hanging loose at the collar. And faces, one pale and neatly bearded – he was the taller and younger of the two; the other older and grouchier, with pock-marks and jowls.

To Heck they were unmistakable.

He held his position until they'd passed him, ascended the three steps to the dingy corridor and trundled off along it. Then he sat upright to watch their receding backs. Once they

410

were out of earshot, he scrabbled the radio from his jacket pocket. 'Heckenburg to DSU Piper . . . ma'am, I know these two. They're ours. DS Reg Cowling and DC Ben Bishop from Organised Crime.'

In the brief silence, he could imagine Gemma gazing around at whoever else was in the command car with her, mystified. 'What the hell are they doing here?' she'd be asking. 'How the devil did *they* get onto this?' He could also picture the blank expressions that would greet these questions.

'They're heading down Sagan's corridor,' Heck added. 'There'll be other villains living in this building, but if it's not him they're here for, ma'am, I'm a sodding Dutchman . . .'

'Can you intercept, over?'

'Negative, ma'am . . . they're virtually at his door.'

'Understood . . . Heck, hold your position. All we can do now is hope.'

Heck stood up, but slammed himself flat against the wall beside the steps, crooking his neck to peer along the passage. He understood her thinking. If he went running down there and tried to grab the two cops, there was every possibility Sagan would open the door and catch all three of them. If he kept out of the way, however, it was just vaguely possible the duo had some routine business to conduct with the guy and might be on their way out again in a minute, with no one any the wiser about the obbo. That latter option was a long shot, of course. Like SCU, the Organised Crime Division was part of the National Crime Group. They didn't deal with routine matters. There was one other possibility too, which was even more depressing. Suppose Cowling and Bishop were up to no good themselves? Could it be they were here to see Sagan for reasons unconnected with police-work? If so, that would be a whole new level of complexity.

Heck squinted as he gazed down the gloomy passage. The twosome had halted alongside number 36. They didn't knock immediately, but appeared to be conferring quietly. He supposed he could try to signal to them, alert them to an additional police presence, but the idea was now really growing on him that these two might have nefarious motives.

There was a loud thudding as a fist rapped on the apartment door. Heck held his breath. At first there was no audible response, then what sounded like a muffled voice replied.

'Yeah, police officers, sir,' Cowling said. 'Could you open up? We need to have a chat.'

Heck breathed a sigh of relief at that at least. They weren't in cahoots with Sagan after all. But now he felt uneasy for other reasons. Given the severity of Sagan's suspected offences, this was a very open and front-on approach – it seemed odd the two detectives had come here without any kind of support. Did they know something SCU didn't, or did they simply know nothing? Had ambition to feel a good collar overridden the necessity of performing some due diligence?

The muffled voice intoned again. It sounded as if it had said 'one minute'.

His sixth sense buzzing, Heck stepped out into the open. But before he could shout a warning, two thundering shotgun blasts demolished the door from the inside, the ear-jarring din echoing down the passage. Cowling and Bishop were blown back like rag dolls. The impacts as their broken bodies and the two payloads of shot struck the facing wall shook the entire building.

'This is Heck inside Fairfax House!' Heck shouted into his radio as he drew his Glock. 'Shots fired . . . immediate armed support requested on the third floor! We also have two officers down with severe gunshot wounds. We need an advance trauma team and rapid evac! Get the Air Ambulance if you can, over!'

A gabble of electronic voices burst in response, but it was Gemma's that cut through the dirge. *'Heck, this is DSU Piper*

. . . you are to wait for support, I repeat you are to wait for support! Can you acknowledge, over?'

'Affirmative, ma'am,' Heck replied, but he'd already removed his woolly hat and replaced it with a hi-viz, chequer-banded baseball cap. Climbing the three steps, he advanced warily along the corridor, weapon cocked but dressed down as per the manual. 'Both shots fired through the door from inside number 36. Sounded like a shotgun from here. Both Cowling and Bishop are down . . . by the looks of it, they've incurred serious injuries.'

'What's your exact position, over?' Gemma asked.

'Approx thirty yards along the corridor . . . but I'm going to have difficulty reaching the casualties. They're both still in the line of fire, over.'

'Negative, Heck! You're to get no closer until you have full firearms support . . . am I clear?'

'Affirmative, ma'am.' More by instinct than design, he continued to advance, but ultra-slowly, his right shoulder skating the right-hand wall. At twenty yards, he halted again. Neither of the shotgunned officers was moving; both still slumped on their backsides against the left-hand wall. The plasterwork behind them was peppered with shot and fragments of wood, but also spattered with trickling blood.

Heck's teeth locked together. In these circs, hanging back felt like a non-option. These were fellow coppers pumping out their last. He pressed cautiously on. And then heard a sound of breaking glass from inside the flat.

'Crap!' He dashed forward, only for a door to open behind him. He spun around, gun levelled. The thin-faced Chinese woman who peeked out gaped in horror. 'Police officer!' he hissed. 'Go back inside! Stay there!' The door slammed and Heck resumed his advance, radio back to his lips. 'This is Heck . . . suspect's making a break for it through a window. It's three floors down, so I don't know how he's going to

413

manage it. But his flat's on the building's northeast side, which looks down onto Charlton Court . . . we've got to get some cover down there, over.'

Even as he said it, Heck knew this would be easier said than done. The surveillance team on Fairfax House was no more than eight-strong at any time. Even with Gemma on the plot, that only made it nine – so they were spread widely and thinly. On top of that, though armed and wearing vests, they were geared for close target reconnaissance, not a gun-battle. No doubt, Trojan units would be en route, but how long it would take them in the mid-evening London traffic was anyone's guess. Heck slid to another halt as a dark shape appeared at the farthest end of the corridor, about twenty yards past number 36. By its size and breadth, and by the luminous council-worker doublet pulled over its donkey jacket, he recognised it as Gary Quinnell, whose lying-up position Heck had briefly forgotten was on one of the floors above. The burly Welshman had also drawn his firearm, and was in the process of pulling on the regulation baseball cap.

They acknowledged each other with a nod, then Heck lowered his weapon and proceeded, stopping again about five yards from the shattered doorway. 'Armed police!' he shouted. 'John Sagan . . . we are armed police officers! There's no point in resisting any further! Stop this bloody nonsense, and throw your weapon out!'

There was no reply. No further glass crashed or tinkled.

They were now a couple of yards to either side of the front door. From this close range, it was plain that Reg Cowling was dead. His face had been blown away; in fact, his head had almost detached, and hung lopsided from strands of glistening crimson muscle. However, Bishop, while wounded in the face, which was riddled with gashes and splinters, and the right shoulder, which resembled raw beef-steak through the rents in his smouldering sports jacket, was

414

vaguely conscious. He was ashen-cheeked, but his eyes, which by some miracle had both survived, were visible beneath fluttering, blood-dabbled lashes.

'Bastard went for head-shots,' Heck said tightly. 'Expected them to be wearing body-armour.'

Penny Flint had told them John Sagan was a professional killer. Here was the proof.

'This is Heck,' he said into his radio. 'Update on the casualties … both in a collapsed state and suffering extensive gunshot injuries. DS Cowling appears to be dead, DC Bishop is conscious and breathing . . . how long for, I can't say. We still can't reach them.'

Gemma's response broke continually and was delivered in a breathless voice, which indicated she was running. Before he could make sense of it, it was blotted out by another explosion of glass from inside the flat.

'He's going for it!' Quinnell warned. 'Must have decided the coast's clear!'

'I repeat, we are armed police officers!' Heck shouted. 'Throw your weapon out!'

The answer came in a third shuddering *BOOM!*, and what remained of the front door was blasted outward. Again, DC Bishop got lucky. The shot was directed above him, so though he was bombarded by wreckage, and gasped in agony, he was spared further pellet-wounds.

A loud *clunk/clack* from inside signified that a fourth shell had been ratcheted into place.

'Pump-action!' Heck said.

More glass detonated as it was struck from its frame. The detectives locked eyes across the open doorway, both their brows beaded with sweat.

'We can't just let him run,' Heck said.

Quinnell didn't argue the point.

Heck swallowed the apple-sized lump of phlegm in his

throat, and then wheeled partly around into the doorway, only his left arm, left shoulder and the left side of his head visible as he tried to pinpoint the target. Quinnell did the same from the other side.

But the immediate area, which was an actual living room, was bare of life. There was no sign of the guy. None at all.

They were vaguely aware of plain, simple furnishings as they scanned the place, of bookshelves that were empty, of bland pictures on the walls. But there were also doors to other areas, one on the left and one on the right. On the far side of the room stood three tall sash-windows. The left one had been smashed outwards.

'Doors first,' Heck said, running right, but finding only an empty bathroom. 'Clear!' he yelled, spinning back.

Quinnell had gone left. He reappeared from the bedroom. 'Clear.'

Heck darted for the broken window, which had had to be broken because by the looks of it, Sagan had only been able to lift the lower panel several inches. He flattened himself against the wall alongside it, and risked a quick glance. Some twenty feet below, a fair-headed figure in dark clothing – what looked like a heavy overcoat – and with the shotgun hung over its shoulder by a strap, was scampering away across the top of five flat-roofed garages standing in a terraced row. It was instantly apparent how he'd got down there. Some five yards to the left of the window, about six feet above it, there was a horizontal steel grating – the platform section of an old-fashioned fire-escape. The fire-escape stair dropped steeply down on the far side of that. There was no possibility of reaching either the stair or the platform by jumping. But the killer had prepared for this in advance by connecting a knotted rope to the underside of the grating, and looping it over a hook alongside his window, where it would hang down the apartment house wall unobtrusively.

All he'd had to do when the time came was get a firm grip, unhook it so that it swung away from the window, thus preventing anyone in pursuit using the same method, and slither down to the garage roofs.

Heck gazed dully at the hanging rope, swaying in the winter breeze a good five feet away. He was vaguely aware of Quinnell appearing alongside him.

'Bastard!' the Welshman said, spying the dwindling form of Sagan as he reached the far end of the garage roofs.

About sixty yards to the right of these, a uniformed police car swung over the grass into Charlton Court from the cul-de-sac at the front of the building. Unfortunately, this was only a divisional patrol – almost certainly it was responding to the call that had just gone out, and would have got here before anyone else because it was in the vicinity. But it wouldn't be armed, which rendered it next to useless. Besides, Sagan had now jumped from the left side of the garage roofs onto Bellfield Lane, which led away at a much lower level. As well as the rugged, rubbish-strewn slope slanting down to this, there was a high mesh fence along its edge, which formed an impassable barrier for vehicles. Sagan was a rapidly diminishing shape as he raced away along the lower road, intermittently vanishing as he ran through the patches of darkness between the streetlights. Still there was no sign of a Trojan unit.

'Check the casualty,' Heck said.

Quinnell nodded, and went quickly back across the flat.

Heck holstered his Glock and put his radio to his mouth. 'This is DS Heckenburg . . . urgent message. Suspect, John Sagan, is at large and on foot . . . male IC1, mid-forties, fair-haired, wearing glasses and a dark, possibly black over-coat. Currently escaping northeast along Bellfield Lane. Warning, Sagan is armed with a pump shotgun and more than willing to use it. For the cerebrally challenged, that means he's armed and dangerous. I repeat . . . John Sagan is armed and very dangerous!' He bit his lip, and then added: 'In pursuit.'

'Hey . . . *whoa!*' Gary Quinnell shouted, as Heck climbed up into the casement.

The hanging rope was only five feet away. Heck knew there was a good chance he'd make it, but he also knew that if he stopped to think about the chasm below – he wouldn't go any further. So he didn't think, just launched himself out, diving full-length – and dropping like a stone, maybe ten feet, before managing to catch hold of the rope. Even then, several feet of cold, greasy hemp slid through his fingers before he brought himself to a halt, ripping both his gloves and the flesh of the palms underneath.

Doing his best to ignore the blistering pain, he clambered down, alighting on the garage roof nearest the building. 'Suspect heading northeast along Bellfield Lane!' he shouted down to the two uniforms who'd spilled out onto Charlton Court from their patrol car, faces aghast at what they'd just seen. 'Spread the word!'

Without waiting for a response, Heck ran due north along the flimsy roofs, feet drumming on damp planks covered only in tarpaper, jabbering into his radio again, giving instructions as best he could. At the far end, he skidded to a stop, dropped onto all fours, turned and swung his body over the parapet. He hung full-length, and then dropped the last five feet, before careering downhill through grass and clutter onto the road.

'Bellfield Lane heading northeast,' he shouted, hammering along the tarmac. 'Any units in that direction to respond, over?' But the airwaves were now jammed with cross-cutting messages. 'Shit . . . come on, someone!'

As he ran, the vast concrete shape of a railway gantry loomed towards him. Above it, stroboscopic lights sped back and forth as trains hurtled between East Dulwich and Peckham Rye. Conversely, the shadows beneath the structure were oil-black, barely penetrated by the streetlights. The passage itself had been narrowed by corrugated fences thrown up left and right. In normal times this would be a muggers' paradise, but Heck was openly armed, and besides the night was now alive with sirens – it was just a pity none were in the immediate vicinity.

Beyond the railway overpass, a sheer brick wall stood on the right, but on the left there was more wire fencing, and behind that another slope angling down to a glass-littered car park. The fence was quivering, as though something heavy had just passed over it or under it. More to the point, its second section was loose in the frame, disconnected along the bottom, giving easy access to the other side. Heck swerved towards it, only to find that his quarry, nicely camouflaged in his all-black garb, had secreted himself flat at the foot of the waiting slope, deep in the shadow of the overpass. The first Heck knew of this was the muzzle-flash, and then the hail of shot that swept the wire mesh.

He threw himself onto the pavement, rolling away fast and landing in the gutter – where he remained, flat on his back, gun trained two-handed on the wall of fencing.

Until he heard feet clattering away again.

He scrambled up to his knees. A dark shape was haring off across the car park below, at the far side of which a concrete ramp led down onto yet another housing estate, this one comprising rows of near-identical maisonettes. Heck slid under the fence and gave chase, stumbling down the slope until he reached the level tarmac, all the time trying to get through on his radio.

'Is no one fucking listening to me?' he shouted. 'For what it's worth . . . still in pursuit, suspect still on foot, still armed, opening fire at every opportunity. Heading west onto the

Hawkwood estate. Listen . . . this is a built-up area with lots of civvies. Not many around at present, but someone's got to get over here fast. Over and fucking out!'

At the foot of the ramp, he vaulted a railing and ran along a boulevard faced on two sides by front doors and ground-level windows. Sagan was still in sight at the far end – a minuscule figure, which abruptly wheeled around, levelled the shotgun at its waist and fired twice. Heck was out of lethal range – Sagan was using buckshot rather than solid slugs – but instinct still sent him scrambling for cover behind a bench. Quickly, he knelt back up – Sagan remained visible, but it went against all the rules to open fire in a residential zone like this. You didn't even need to be a poor shot; ricochets could go anywhere.

To make matters worse, several doors had opened as curious householders peeked out.

Sagan darted left along a side-street. Heck vaulted the bench and gave chase again, shouting at the onlookers as he did. 'Police! Lock your doors . . . stay away from the windows!'

He rounded the corner and descended a flight of steps into a covered area. Sagan was again visible, framed in the exit on the other side of it. He let off two more rounds. Heck dived sideways, smashing through a decayed wooden hoarding and entangling himself in heaps of musty, second-hand furniture. Fighting his way out through a rear door, he sprinted along an alley, hoping to head the bastard off – only to emerge into another car park. Again, Sagan was waiting, shotgun levelled.

Heck ran low, scuttling behind a row of parked vehicles. Sagan blasted each one of them twice, bodywork buckling, safety glass flying, before turning, ascending a flight of steps and dashing down a passage between high, faceless walls. Heck slid over the bonnet of the nearest wreck and charged up the steps. He entered the passage, which was about fifty yards long; at the far end of it, Sagan was rapidly reloading. Before Heck could point his pistol and shout, the bastard fired, worked the slide, fired, worked the slide again; ear-shattering detonations in the narrow space. This time, as Heck pitched himself down, he pegged off three quick shots of his own, which caromed along the passage, missing their target but sending him ducking out of sight.

Heck retreated around his corner, wheezing, sucking in lungfuls of icy air. He risked a glance back. The passage still looked empty, but Sagan could be lying in wait, and once Heck was halfway along he'd be a sitting duck. Instead, he ran back down the steps, along the front of a row of caged-off shops, and around the base of a tower block. He'd expected to find open space on the other side, but instead there was the shell of an industrial building – a former soap-making factory by the scabby signs hanging loose on its outer wall.

Swearing, Heck panted the new directions into the radio as he set off running again. At the end of the factory wall there was a net fence and on the other side of that a deep canyon through which another railway passed. The London Overground, Heck realised, though at present it was a good twenty feet below him. He glanced right. The nearest way across it was an arched steel walkover about fifty yards off. A figure was already traipsing over this, slowly and tiredly.

Sagan. The killer and torturer was an arch-pro. But he was also in early middle-age. His energy reserves were finally flagging.

Heck scrambled in that direction, taking a short cut along a narrow defile between the factory's north wall and the railway fence. Initially he had to get through barbed wire, and then found himself negotiating thick, leafless scrub entwined with wastepaper and rubbish. Inevitably, cans and bottles clattered around his feet, causing such a racket that the figure on the bridge stopped and looked around – and began to run again. By the time Heck got to the bridge, there was no sign of him. Now exhausted himself, Heck lumbered up the steel staircase and over the top. A train thundered past below; a chaos of light and sound, illuminating the footway clear to its far end. There was a possibility Sagan could reappear over there – while Heck was hemmed between neck-high barriers of riveted steel. But that didn't happen. Heck made it to the other side, descended the stair to half way and halted, hot breath pluming from his body. Open waste-ground lay ahead, on the far side of which stood a cluster of dingy buildings: workshops, offices and garages, with an old Ford van parked at the front. Sagan was almost over there, moving at a fast but weary trudge – about sixty yards distant.

Heck raised his pistol and took aim, but he wasn't a good enough marksman to ensure a clean shot from this distance. Especially not at night. He continued down, and inadvertently kicked a beer bottle standing on the bottom step. It cartwheeled forward and smashed.

Sagan twirled around.

Heck ran down the last couple of steps and veered sideways. Sagan held his ground tensely – and then he strode back, shooting from the waist, like a character out of a western, working the slide again and again, pumping fire and shot. Heck scuttled and crawled, but found no more cover than bits of rubbish and sprigs of weed.

At which point a third party intervened.

'Drop it!' came a fierce female voice. *'Do it now, or I'll shoot you, you bastard . . . I swear!'*

Heck glanced up, to see a short, shapely figure in jeans, trainers, a leather jacket and a chequer-banded police cap circling around from behind the van, her Glock trained with both hands on the back of John Sagan's head. The gunman froze, the shotgun clasped in his right hand, his left held out to the side.

'I mean it, you dickless wonder!' the female cop shouted in a ringing northern accent. 'Drop that weapon now, or I'll drop *you*!'

Heck's mouth crooked into a smile as he rose to his feet. It was Shawna McCluskey. Someone had heard his frantic transmissions after all. And if anyone had, he ought to have realised it would be his old mate Shawna, who'd started off with him all those years ago in the Greater Manchester Police. Sagan remained rigid. From this distance, his face was unreadable. Dots of yellow streetlight glinting from the lenses of his glasses briefly gave him a non-human aura. His right hand opened and the shotgun clattered to the floor.

'Keep those mitts where I can see 'em!' Shawna shouted, encroaching from behind. 'You alright, Heck?'

'Never better,' he shouted, dusting himself down.

'Kick the weapon back towards me,' Shawna said, addressing Sagan again. 'Backheel it . . . *don't* turn around. And keep your hands spread, where I can see them . . . in case you didn't realise it, you fucking lowlife, you're under arrest!'

Sagan did exactly as she instructed, the shotgun bouncing past her and vanishing beneath the van. Now Heck could see him more clearly: his black overcoat, a black roll-neck sweater, black leather gloves, black trousers and shoes, his pale face, the thinning fair hair on top, and those gold-rimmed glasses. Yet still the killer was inscrutable, his face a waxen mask.

'DC McCluskey, on a lorry park off Camberwell Grove,' Shawna said into her radio. 'One in custody . . . repeat, one in custody.'

But only now, as she angled around her captive, did Heck

see the possible danger. Her Glock was trained squarely on Sagan's body, but side-on the target width had reduced, and Sagan's left hand was suddenly only inches from the muzzle of her weapon – and it was with this hand that he lunged, slapping the gun aside, and in the same motion, spinning and slamming his other hand, now balled into a fist and yet glittering as if encased in steel – a knuckleduster, Heck realised with horror – straight into Shawna's face.

She dropped like a puppet with its strings cut.

'*Shawna!*' Heck bellowed.

But he was still forty yards away. He raised his pistol, but again had to hesitate – Sagan had dropped to a crouch alongside the policewoman's crumpled form, merging them both into one. Heck ran forward again, shouting as the killer flipped off Shawna's hat, and smashed his reinforced fist several times more into her head and face. Then he snatched up her Glock and fired once into her chest, before leaping to his feet and bolting back towards the parked van.

Heck slid to a halt and fired. The van's nearside front window imploded as Sagan scarpered around it, returning fire over his shoulder, and proving uncannily accurate. Nine-millimetre shells ricocheted from the ground just in front of Heck. He fired again, but Sagan was now on the other side of the vehicle and shielded from view. A split-second later, a door slammed somewhere along the frontage of the building. Heck scrambled forward, but kept low. If the bastard was now indoors, he might have any number of concealed vantage points from which to aim.

'DC McCluskey down with head injuries and a possible gunshot wound,' he shouted into his radio, skidding to one knee alongside her, still scanning the grimy windows over-head.

The van provided partial protection, but it all depended on whether Sagan's desire to slot his pursuers was more of